CANDLELIGHT Ecstasy

"W-WHY . . . DID YOU . . . DO THAT?"
SHE ASKED BETWEEN BREATHS.

"For a reasonably intelligent woman, that's a pretty stupid question. Why do you think?"

"You're . . . attracted to me?"

He shook his head hopelessly, but there was a trace of humor in his eyes. "You're just now figuring that out?"

"I've been trying to figure you out since I met you," she said defensively. "Even now you're yelling at me!"

"Yelling? This isn't yelling. I'm just amazed that a beauty queen has to be physically assaulted before she realizes a certain man has been crazy about her for months!"

"But you've always been so disdainful. Right now you're telling me how stupid I am. And with all those things you said in your column about me . . ."

He made an exasperated sigh. "Didn't you listen to what I said before, about wanting to reject you before you rejected me?"

"You're rejecting me?"

"No!" he practically bellowed. "Don't be so obtuse!"

CANDLELIGHT ECSTASY SUPREMES

PRIVATE SCREENINGS

Lori Herter

A CANDLELIGHT ECSTASY SUPREME

Published by
Dell Publishing Co., Inc.
1 Dag Hammarskjold Plaza
New York, New York 10017

Dell ® TM 681510, Dell Publishing Co., Inc.

Candlelight Ecstasy Supreme is a trademark of Dell
Publishing Co., Inc.

Candlelight Ecstasy Romance®, 1,203,540, is a registered
trademark of Dell Publishing Co., Inc.

ISBN: 0-440-17111-3

Printed in the United States of America
First printing—May 1984

To Our Readers:

Candlelight Ecstasy is delighted to announce the start of a brand-new series—Ecstasy Supremes! Now you can enjoy a romance series unlike all the others—longer and more exciting, filled with more passion, adventure, and intrigue—the stories you've been waiting for.

In months to come we look forward to presenting books by many of your favorite authors and the very finest work from new authors of romantic fiction as well. As always, we are striving to present the unique, absorbing love stories that you enjoy most—the very best love has to offer.

Breathtaking and unforgettable, Ecstasy Supremes will follow in the great romantic tradition you've come to expect *only* from Candlelight Ecstasy.

Your suggestions and comments are always welcome. Please let us hear from you.

Sincerely,

The Editors
Candlelight Romances
1 Dag Hammarskjold Plaza
New York, New York 10017

CHAPTER ONE

Dale Chastain glanced up at camera two, which was focusing on her alert and very pretty face. A TelePrompTer carried, in large letters printed on a continuous roll of paper, the opening sentences of tonight's movie review for the five o'clock news. She had written and submitted it that morning.

Steven Froebisher and Andrea Miles, the co-anchors, were quietly talking with the floor director while all waited for the commercial break to end. Dale was on edge, as she always was just before she went on the air. She took out a small mirror kept on a shelf behind the long, curved desk where they all sat. She checked her makeup, her smoothly coiffed auburn hair, and adjusted the ruffled tie of the beige blouse she wore beneath a chestnut brown suit. A tiny microphone on a cord was pinned to her lapel.

The floor director was indicating they had ten seconds to go when suddenly a loud bang shattered the air-conditioned atmosphere of the studio. Dale jumped, as did the anchorpeople. Suddenly a small shower of smoky dust and tiny glass fragments floated down onto Dale's desk and over one arm and shoulder of her suit jacket.

"What's that?" Dale gasped, her usually subdued southern

accent suddenly reappearing in full force. Unconsciously she clasped her small hand to her chest as her heart began to pound.

"A light exploded above you," the floor director said, smiling nervously.

"Are you trying to start the Civil War again?" Steve quipped while Andrea murmured something about Dale's suit being ruined.

From out of nowhere an assistant appeared with a whisk broom to brush Dale off and clean up her desk. A makeup woman also came to her aid. As they meticulously fussed over her, the ten seconds flew by. All at once Steve was reading a report about plans for the State Street St. Patrick's Day parade to take place the following day. Dale barely heard him talking about pouring green dye into the Chicago River again this year.

The assistant with the whisk broom suddenly moved off, but the makeup woman continued to deftly brush bits of glass from Dale's hair. Her heart rate was still elevated and her head was still in a whirl from the commotion. She had been working in television for three years and nothing like this had happened before, at least not just before she was going to be introduced.

Keep your head! Be professional! she admonished herself.

She had pulled out a plum three months ago when a network-affiliated Chicago station offered her the position of entertainment critic on its nightly news. But she knew she was still on trial—a southerner in the North, a former beauty contest winner who continually had to prove she had brains. She knew her strong point was her effervescent personality; it had better not go flat now!

But she had better not appear giddy either. If only her pulse would slow down. She had always hated sudden loud noises.

All at once she heard Steve introducing her. What movie was she talking about? In alarm her eyes flew to the large printed roll above the camera. *Steamy Nights.* Thank heaven for the Tele-PrompTer! All she had to do was read. No, Steve was asking her a question; there must be time to kill. *Calm down! Smile! Concentrate!*

"Isn't a movie like *Steamy Nights* a little risqué for a small-town girl like you, Dale?" Steve's rare smile softened the authoritative look of his graying hair and staunch features.

Dale's brain and mouth seemed to work automatically. Resurrecting just the right amount of southern accent for the moment, she said, "Savannah is *not* a small town!" Her lively blue eyes were full of friendly comeuppance. "And I *am* over twenty-one! I don't think I would take my grandmother to see this film, however," she added, breaking into a soft chuckle while those around her, both on and off camera, laughed.

Turning her head directly to camera two now, she began reading from the TelePrompTer that was situated just above the TV camera, so that she looked as though she were gazing directly into the camera's lens.

"*Steamy Nights* is an unusual bedroom farce starring English actor John Trevor as a handsome young naturalist writing a wildlife book about the Florida Everglades—and, naturally, he leads his own wild life along the way. Somehow one gorgeous woman after another distracts him from his work, and he spends more time in his cozy rustic lodge than he does in the swamps. . . ."

About a mile from the TV studio, a man was sitting in his Lake Shore Drive condominium watching Dale Chastain on the large color television in his den. Beside him on the couch lay a late edition of the *Chicago Herald*. It was opened to the entertainment section, to Sloane Avery's column. The column contained the scathing review of *Steamy Nights* he had typed into his computer terminal earlier that day. On the coffee table in front of him was a large submarine sandwich he had picked up at a delicatessen on his way home from work and a glass of Chablis. Defrosting in his kitchen was a Sara Lee chocolate cake.

The mouthwatering cake was far from his mind now. He was listening to Dale give her nightly review, an odd quirk on his lips, his gray eyes intent. As he let himself be lulled a bit by her soft voice and charming accent, he studied her guileless features—the

11

straight little nose, the delicate arched brows, the sparkling eyes whose bright blue always seemed to radiate from the screen directly to him, the small square shoulders, the featherlike hands she sometimes used when she talked, as though she were sitting in someone's living room and not in front of a TV camera. It always amazed him how unaffected and natural she appeared. Over a year ago he had allowed himself to be subjected to one brief TV interview, and he had been stiff as a board.

"So though this film might be a little too much for my elderly grandmother," Dale was summarizing after a short clip from the movie had been shown, "I found *Steamy Nights* to be a breezy comedy, nicely tied together with a moral at the end. It may be a little short on plot, but John Trevor's performance as the bookish naturalist besieged by women is deftly handled. *Steamy Nights* is a delightful way to relax after a hard day's work."

Sloane Avery was shaking his head. *She doesn't know a damn thing about movies, but she chatters on about them so prettily, nobody cares,* he thought. He watched her turn her head quickly as one of the anchorpeople spoke to her. She seemed a little nervous tonight. He wondered if the station was clamping down on her. They would be fools to let *her* go. She was the best thing on the air, even if she couldn't tell a bad picture from a tolerable one.

"John Trevor is up to his ears in a scandal right now, isn't he?" Andrea Miles was saying. "Any late word on how the filming of *Ivanhoe* is going in England?"

"The producers and director are having a difficult time," Dale said. "Not only is there the . . . the situation between John Trevor and his co-star, Velvet Hunt, but they've been plagued by a lot of rain there in the Lake District where they're filming. That in turn has led to equipment failures. But they have so much invested already with the sets and costumes and top-rank actors that they apparently feel they'll pump in as much money as it takes to finish it."

"They're already way over budget, aren't they?" Steve Froebisher asked.

"Yes," Dale responded with a smile, "but with all the commotion over the film, it's bound to be a big box-office draw even if it isn't that good. For example, I bet you'll go just to see Velvet, won't you?" she asked him innocently, her lips twitching slightly.

Apparently caught off guard, Froebisher grinned awkwardly. "I'd better not answer that. My wife may be watching. We'll be back with more news after this. . . ."

Sloane chuckled and reached for his wineglass. She was back in good form. Anyone else who dared to embarrass a seasoned, stuffy newsman like Froebisher probably wouldn't get away with it, but he usually seemed willing to take it from her. And Andrea Miles was blond, attractive, and intelligent, but she came across like a cold fish. Dale made them seem human. Her few minutes on the air every night made a good balance for them. Froebisher, Miles, and the station manager no doubt knew it too.

He put down his glass and reached for his half-eaten sandwich. As he took a large bite and chewed, he wondered: Does she know her own worth? On the air she was all charm and spunk, but the few times he had seen her in person he had thought she seemed a trifle diffident.

But then, how could he judge? He had never actually spoken to her. He had only observed her from the other side of a small screening theater when she was talking to others.

Sometime he ought to go up and say hello. He had thought she might have wanted to meet him and would come over to introduce herself, but so far she hadn't. Maybe she didn't know the tall, heavily built guy in the wrinkled suit was Sloane Avery, Chicago's feared and respected movie critic. Or, if someone *had* pointed him out to her, maybe she had decided she'd rather not shake hands with a man whose fingers were always in a bag of sticky caramel corn.

He sighed and put the sandwich down. When was he going to get serious about going on a diet? Thirty pounds wasn't such a monumental amount to lose, but he could never get past ten. There was always a chocolate cake on some restaurant menu, or

13

he'd pass by an Auntie Kay's Candy Store near the newspaper office and come home with a two-pound box.

She was such a frail thing, no more than a wisp, and so damned neat! She always looked like she just stepped off the runway she had walked down in the Miss America Pageant. That was another chore he needed to do: Get himself some new clothes. He loathed shopping. Well, nobody expected a newspaperman to be elegantly groomed anyway. At least he fit the part.

He looked glumly at the remainder of the submarine sandwich. He was tired of it. After roughly rewrapping it in the waxed paper it had come in, he went into the kitchen and put it into the refrigerator. He might want it for breakfast. As he headed back to the other room, the Sara Lee cake beckoned to him from the counter. He paused only a moment, then opened the drawer where he kept his cake knife.

When Dale got home that evening to her Near North Side apartment, she put a frozen chicken and broccoli crêpe dinner in the oven, changed into slacks, and sat down to look at the evening *Herald*. After glancing at the front page headlines, she turned to the entertainment section. As she read Sloane Avery's column, her heart slowly sank.

She had expected he would pan *Steamy Nights;* she had been reading his column for years and knew there were very few films he liked. He especially despised movies that were lightly entertaining, apparently feeling a film wasn't worth making unless it had some meaningful message or revealed some enlightening truth. She differed with him on that. Spending time watching a comedy or adventure film with little intellectual value did not bother her. If it was enjoyable, she felt it was worthwhile as a vehicle of escape from real-world problems. She considered *Steamy Nights* such a movie.

But now, after reading Avery's column, she realized that the film did have some flaws that she had failed to notice. And, as always, he had stated his objections so cleverly and succinctly it depressed her. She always tried for wit in her reviews but usually wound up with phrases that were only mildly amusing. Avery's writing reeked of urbane, cynical intelligence.

Most of what Dale had learned, in fact, about the qualities that made a film good, average, or poor had come not from her college classes in filmmaking, not from the books she had read on the history of movies, but from religiously reading Sloane Avery's column. It was disheartening to think she still had quite a way to go before she was as perceptive and cogent as he.

She would improve, she assured herself as she put the paper aside. After tonight she at least could consider herself a trooper as far as maintaining poise on camera. She didn't know how she had managed to carry things off as well as she had after the light exploded, but she felt she had every right to consider herself an experienced professional in broadcasting now.

She had come a long way since the night she was crowned Miss Savannah seven years ago, a naive nineteen-year-old. A few weeks later she was Miss Georgia, then she was in Atlantic City for the pageant. After that had come a year of public appearances which had taught her how to think on her feet and do it with a smile.

After studying broadcasting and journalism at college and taking any classes pertaining to the movie industry she could find, she graduated and soon landed a job as weather girl at a local TV station in Atlanta. The fact that she had been Miss Georgia and first runner-up in the Miss America Pageant was probably why she had been able to beat her competitors for the job, and she was well aware of it. But that was all right. If she was pretty and looked good in a bathing suit, why should she be ashamed of it? It was only a starting point. Everyone would soon realize she had a mind, too, she had told herself.

She had to chuckle. It was three years later now and she was still fighting that battle. It hadn't been easy to convince a rival TV station in Atlanta that she could fill the position of movie critic for their nightly news, but she had managed it. Later it had taken a year of sending audition tapes to stations in larger cities before she had finally gotten an offer worth moving away from home for—WNBS-TV in Chicago. She had even studied with a speech expert for a time to lose some of her southern drawl in order to make herself more acceptable to the big city markets. Now, if she could manage to hang on to this job, she could consider herself a genuine success in the television industry.

She had lasted three months, and so far her fan mail was favorable. There had been a couple of newspaper articles about her, and Chicagoans were beginning to recognize her on the street. But the powers that be at WNBS were playing it close to the vest and had given her few clues as to what her status was in their eyes. So Dale had nothing to do but keep flashing her smile and doing her best. She loved working in television and adored movies and plays. She had carved out the perfect career for herself and she intended to stay in it.

The next afternoon Dale was stepping out of a small back elevator onto the seventh floor of an old building on State Street. She found her way to the small private theater she had already been to several times. A preview of a new war movie was to be shown, and she had been invited by the Hollywood production company's press agent to see it.

On entering the room she found the usual group of reporters. She spotted Alan Thornton, the movie critic from rival TV station WAAB, a young man with whom she had become somewhat friendly, to her surprise. He was standing next to Sloane Avery, and the two seemed to be enjoying a casual conversation.

It was Alan who had pointed Sloane out to her the first time she had come to a private screening after starting her job. At first she had looked across the room at him in awe. Upon studying him more closely while he was engaged in conversation, she remembered she had found herself surprised at his appearance. In his newspaper column he sounded hard-boiled and sardonic; in real life he looked like a big teddy bear, a little rumpled and almost cuddly. His face was too round to be handsome, although he had a pleasant appearance. He was tall and his body was large in a nonthreatening, soft sort of way.

16

He looked the same now, standing next to Alan, unbuttoning his big overcoat. She wondered if she should go up to them and say hello, knowing Alan, who was always very congenial, would make the introduction. Having admired Sloane Avery for so long, she was still nervous about meeting him even though he looked quite approachable.

No, she'd better not; she could already feel her heart rate accelerating at the idea of actually talking to him. Another time . . .

"Dale?"

She glanced at Alan, realizing he was calling to her. "Hello!" she answered. Oh, no, it was actually going to happen! Inhaling deeply for courage, she walked toward them.

Alan looked dapper with his clipped blond hair and trim suit. He had recently gotten married and his brand-new wedding ring glimmered brightly as he gestured toward the other man. "Have you met Sloane Avery yet?"

"No," she replied, her smile eager and nervous. She looked up at Avery, but he kept his eyes on Alan.

"This is Dale Chastain from WNBS-TV," Alan said.

"And Savannah, Georgia. I . . . happened to catch your review last night. How do you do?" Sloane said, sounding aloof and slightly condescending.

Out of habit Dale extended her hand, but Sloane appeared not to notice. He kept his in his pocket while his other hand clutched a small white bag that looked as if it had come from some confectionery store. She caught a faint whiff of caramel.

"Fine, thank you. How are you?" Dale responded with conditioned politeness as she quickly withdrew her hand.

"Fine."

There was an awkward silence for a moment. Even Alan seemed inhibited by the suddenly strained atmosphere. "I've been reading your column for a long time," Dale said at last.

"Really," Sloane replied in a dry tone.

"When I worked in Atlanta I subscribed to the major New York, Chicago, and Los Angeles newspapers so I could read

17

other movie critics' reviews. I always have admired your column the most."

He seemed slightly disconcerted, but said thank you in a tone that held little warmth. He was looking across the room now. His gray eyes seemed to take in everything but her. She had the distinct impression he wished to be elsewhere.

Clearly, he was not impressed with meeting her. Maybe it was because, next to him, she was a lightweight as movie critics go. He was the best. She supposed he had a right to look down on her.

Alan, apparently seeing someone else he wanted to speak to, quietly excused himself. She was left alone with Sloane, who now looked acutely bored and ill at ease.

"I particularly admired last night's column," she said, groping for conversation.

For the first time he looked directly at her, but his eyes quickly flicked away. "Why? In your review you completely disagreed with my assessment of the film."

"Yes, I did like *Steamy Nights* better than you did, but your criticisms were well taken. I guess I didn't think the flaws ruined the film quite as much as you did."

"There was nothing to ruin," he said. "The script was inane, the acting amateurish, the plot nonexistent. How could it *be* any worse?"

"John Trevor's performance was pretty good," she said, disagreeing shyly.

"Well, Trevor has such baby-blue eyes, I suppose women are blind to the fact he can't act," Sloane said.

Dale was startled. His statement struck a reactive chord in her on two levels. The remark about blue eyes annoyed her a little. She had blue eyes herself and didn't like the implication that that alone could enable a person to easily conceal his or her deficiencies.

But that was a minor point. His other inference, that women were not sensible enough to look for anything more in a man than a handsome face, unsettled her deeply.

From his columns she had always had the impression that Sloane Avery was unusually enlightened in his attitudes about women. He had forcefully decried a recent trend in movies of portraying women as helpless victims or witless targets of male brutality. In criticizing a film he would sometimes say the script or the director or even an actress had created "a poor image of a woman." He had used that phrase more than once, and she had thought it indicated a sensitive respect for the feminine gender. He had often written that he wished to see more film roles portraying women who were vital, intelligent, and complicated.

Now here was this same man standing in front of her, making a remark that implied she had been too stupid to look past John Trevor's eyes. Could she have misunderstood him?

"John Trevor has blue eyes?" she said with waspish innocence.

"Blue as yours," he said coolly.

She had no reply to that. What a conversation this was becoming! She lowered her eyes to the floor momentarily, and when she raised them she found he was staring at her. Her gaze unconsciously rose to his mussed dark brown hair, which was falling raggedly over his broad forehead. It was windy outside, but she had the feeling his hair was probably always a little unkempt. It went with the rest of him.

Suddenly he seemed annoyed and said, "Everyone else has found a seat. They're going to start the film." He turned away abruptly and walked down the center aisle. He chose a row and moved in a few seats. Dale was behind him, but walked past the row he had chosen.

"*This* is the best place to sit," he said. Irritation was still in his voice.

"What?" She sounded equally annoyed as she turned her head.

"Here." His long forefinger pointed to the seat next to him.

Sighing, she moved back to his row and sat where he indicated. "What's so special about this spot?"

He sat down next to her. "There's a theory that the ideal place to sit is twice as far back as the screen is wide."

"And that's right here?"

"According to my calculations," he replied. He opened up the bag he was carrying and she could see it was filled with caramel corn. "Like some?" He held the open bag toward her.

"No, thanks."

He popped a piece into his mouth. "It's also best not to see a movie on an empty stomach," he said while chewing.

"Why?"

"A low blood sugar level can affect your nerves and emotions; it can negatively alter your perception of the movie."

"Really?" she said with interest, though a part of her suspected he was putting her on.

"Absolutely."

As she wondered if she would have to listen to him chomping popcorn throughout the film, she reached into her purse for her notepad and pencil.

"What's that for?" he asked.

"To take notes. Don't you?"

He shook his head. "Anything important I manage to remember."

She took the putdown in silence. The lights were turned off and the film started.

The movie was a bore in her opinion, but since war movies were her least favorite type of film, she gave it the benefit of the doubt. She was too lenient, she had often told herself. If she didn't like something, she ought not to refrain from saying so in outspoken terms, like Sloane Avery. But she still hadn't overcome her wish not to offend anyone, either those who had worked hard to make the film, or people who had enjoyed watching it. She had been raised with the southern habit of cordial hospitality toward strangers. Insulting someone's taste went against her grain. She always felt compelled to ladle out her criticism gently and with a teaspoon.

After two and a half hours of battle strategies and exploding bombs, the film finally ended. The lights came up and she put away her notebook and pencil.

Sloane Avery stretched in his seat. "I suppose you'll give this one a glowing review."

"Why do you say that?" she asked, turning to look at him.

"I've never heard you give a bad review," he said. "But I suppose it would be unwise for Miss America to be bad-mouthing some producer or director."

Her brows came together. "What do you mean by *that?*"

"You probably want to be in Hollywood working with them someday."

"I have no aspirations to be an actress," she told him irritably. "And I wasn't Miss America. I was . . ."

"First runner-up. Sorry, I forgot. If you had won, you probably would have made it to Chicago even sooner. Or maybe L.A." He stood up and brushed bits of caramel corn from his lapels.

"There's no reason to assume that," she said testily, rising from her own seat. She picked up her heavy wool coat from the seat next to her. Sloane took it from her and held it for her to put on.

He said nothing as she slipped her arms into the sleeves. As he eased the coat over her lacy white blouse she felt his hands rest on her shoulders for a fraction of a second. It was nothing; he probably wasn't even aware of it. But it gave her an odd, disconcerted feeling.

He had turned out to be such a strange man. She couldn't make him out. One moment he was insulting her intelligence, the next he was almost polite. He got annoyed over nothing, never cracked a smile, and he didn't seem to have a very high opinion of her.

Why did he make her sit next to him? He could easily have avoided her. If he wanted to talk, why couldn't he say something nice?

He was putting on his topcoat, but followed her as she moved to the aisle. "Was it hard for you to accept not winning?" he asked.

"No, I never expected to win. I was surprised I made the ten

21

finalists. I entered the contest hoping to get one of the scholarships for talent. I did finish college with the money I won—after my year as Miss Georgia was finished, of course."

She heard him chuckle in his throat, but she didn't see what was funny. "So what did you think of the film?" she asked, deliberately changing the subject. "Are you going to give it one of your usual low ratings?"

Again he seemed irritated. "I make it a rule never to discuss a movie with another critic before my review is printed."

Well, pardon me! she thought. Was he worried she'd steal his ideas? At least he acknowledged she was a fellow critic. "Sorry, I guess I haven't learned all the rules yet."

"You have a lot to learn," he said dourly as they reached the elevator door. "But don't worry. You're cute enough; no one will notice."

They entered the elevator along with a few others and rode down in perfect silence. On the way she looked down at the pointed toes of her high leather boots, contemplating how hard she would have to kick to make a dent in his shin.

It was windy when they got outside, and Dale put her long wool scarf over her head. She paused on the sidewalk to say good-bye—her breeding dictated that she still be polite. "I'm glad to have met you, Mr. Avery."

He seemed a little taken by surprise, as though he hadn't expected they would be parting company already. There was a trace of confusion in his gray eyes as he looked down at her. The cold wind was whipping his hair about and now in the daylight she thought she saw a vulnerability in his face, in the thin lines about his eyes. Every time she looked at him he seemed to strike her differently.

"I'm sure we'll be seeing each other again," he said curtly. "What do you do now?"

The question surprised her. "I go home and change for the five o'clock news."

"Yes, of course. Do you have far to go?"

"No."

He hesitated. "Good." Almost imperceptibly he nodded his head once. "Good-bye." He turned and walked away.

Good grief! she thought as she continued toward the el station to take the rapid transit home. *Doesn't he have any social grace at all?* She respected his work; how could she not? But in looks and personality she found little to praise.

The weather had grown colder in the waning afternoon. She tightened the belt on her camel coat. Now disillusioned with her former hero, she found herself rather depressed. Well, she thought, she could just go on reading and learning from his column. If she avoided him in person, maybe she could recapture the admiration for him she had so long enjoyed which had just been shattered. She felt a strange sense of loss.

A few blocks away Sloane Avery was hardly aware he was passing an Auntie Kay's. *How can she be so beautiful?* he was thinking irritably. *She looks even better close up than she does on TV.* It was damned disconcerting! He didn't know how to behave around her. There he was, trying to look cool, toughing it out, and no doubt coming across like a boor.

Why had he said some of those things to her? Something in him had wanted to belittle her so he could feel she was within his reach. He had hit all her weak points trying to make himself look superior. She probably hated him.

She did say she liked his column though. Well, she ought to. He was superior in that. And that, he thought in discouragement as he walked through the imposing front door of the Chicago Herald Building, was about all he had going for him.

Things would definitely have to change. He was only thirty-six, after all. He must have something left to offer besides his ability to fill a newspaper column. What had he been doing the last dozen years? Working in his cluttered office or sitting in some stuffy theater; sleeping in his messy condominium or seeing some woman he wasn't really interested in.

He had reached his career goal years ago, soon after graduating from his university, where he had gained experience as editor of the college newspaper. He had been hired by the *Herald* then and shortly afterward replaced their retiring movie critic. It had all been extraordinarily easy for him. Now, after all these years, he was entrenched in a rut. He needed a new objective to strive for.

Was he aiming too high? he asked himself. Now, why should he think that? She was only first runner-up.

CHAPTER TWO

"Sit down, Dale," George Ellis, WNBS-TV's news director said in his usual curt manner. A former TV newsman, he was graying and handsome in an austere, stone-faced way.

Dale obediently took a seat in one of the metal chairs opposite his desk in the small glass-partitioned office. She was used to his cold, hurried personality by now, but she still didn't feel comfortable with it. She didn't know why he had expressly called her in to see him this morning, and she was uneasy. She still had no idea where she stood with him or with the station manager. For all she knew, he might be about to fire her.

"I have two things to discuss with you," he began without preamble. "We thought your movie reviews might be enhanced if we worked out a little rating system for you to use like the newspaper critics have—you know, Sloane Avery gives a movie two and a half stars or whatever. That idea appeal to you?"

"Sure!" Dale answered eagerly. Apparently she wasn't being fired.

"The station manager and I were toying with possibilities. Since you're from Georgia we thought peanuts or peaches might be kind of clever."

"Peanuts?"

He sighed impatiently. "Yeah—if you didn't like a movie you'd give it one peanut; if you liked it, maybe you'd rate it four or five peanuts."

"Oh, of course," she said, trying to keep her voice enthused. Somehow peanuts didn't turn her on, even if she did admire Jimmy Carter. "It might not appeal to all those Republicans in DuPage County though," she said.

To her surprise George Ellis actually smiled. "Well, we had pretty much settled on using peaches anyway. Obviously it's more appropriate."

Obviously? Oh. Sure. *She* was the Georgia peach. It figured they'd come up with something like that for a beauty contest winner. Well, she couldn't think of any better suggestion, and since she was so new at the station it was prudent not to argue. "That . . . sounds nice," she said, swallowing her dignity a little.

"Great. Now, we've also been thinking of adding some occasional variety to your spot. For example, when a movie star is passing through Chicago, we'd try to get them to appear on the five o'clock broadcast so you could interview them on the air. Think you can handle that?"

"I'm sure I can!" Dale's eyes perceptibly brightened. Clearly he was broadening her responsibilities. He must have confidence in her.

"We're also considering sending you to England to do some on-the-spot coverage of the filming of *Ivanhoe*. You like to travel?"

"I love to!" Dale could hardly believe it. All her life she had wanted to visit England. Some of her ancestors were English.

"We'll let you know more in a few days. That'll be all for now," he said in a dismissive way.

Dale wet her lips. "I . . . assume then that you've been happy with my movie reviews?" she asked.

"Your reviews have been adequate."

"Oh." She didn't know how to take that. Coming from him it might be a compliment.

"Your personality, however, has been like a shot in the arm

for the news broadcasts," he went on. "Our ratings have slowly but steadily increased in the last three months. We're attributing that mainly to your presence on the news team."

He spoke in such a deadpan, matter-of-fact tone that it took a second for the import of his words to sink in. She smiled only slightly, not wanting to show her feelings. "Thank you. I'm happy to hear that."

He gave a short nod and picked up his phone. It was clearly a cue for her to leave, and she did.

She walked back to her desk with a broad smile on her face. Her euphoria diminished when she saw Gary Murdock approaching. Murdock was a cameraman on one of the station's on-location coverage crews. In his early twenties, he was tall, lanky, and impressed with his own looks and self-advertised sexual prowess. His conceit hadn't been so apparent to her when Dale first met him a day or two after she started at WNBS. He had come up and introduced himself in a pleasant enough manner. His blond hair and darker eyebrows and moustache gave his neatly chiseled features a distinctive look, and she had thought he had fine eyes. When he casually invited her out to dinner one evening after the five o'clock news, Dale hadn't hesitated. But she had regretted it ever since.

"Hello, sugar. Nice threads you've got on today." His low voice always seemed to have a subtle, suspended threat in it, as though warning a woman she was in immediate danger of his irresistible masculinity. He was looking over her form-fitting royal blue jumpsuit with an admiring eye.

Dale sighed in irritation. She hated being called "sugar."

"Hello." Leafing through papers on her desk, she purposely did not look at him.

"Still trying to avoid me?"

"You guessed it." She didn't usually speak so bluntly to people, but she had given up trying to get rid of him in a gentler manner.

"You're making a mistake."

"I don't think so."

27

"You know, you've gotten awfully high-hat lately. I'm not good enough for you, is that it? A member of the news team can't associate with a lowly cameraman? Listen, *Miss* Chastain, I'm not going to be just a cameraman forever. I'm going places. You wait!" He had been shaking his finger at her and ended by pushing it lightly against the tip of her small nose.

Dale backed away. "I'm sure you are. But I wouldn't be interested even if you owned the station."

"So, I guess we're still hung up on our original problem, then—your fear of sex."

Dale glanced around. Her desk was in a large open room, and she hoped no one had heard him. "I'm not afraid of anything. I just don't care for a cheap, meaningless entanglement with a man whose only aim is to score!"

"How do you know that? You never even gave me a chance!" His tone was growing argumentative and ugly now. Week by week he was getting harder to handle.

"I didn't need to. Those two endless hours over dinner with you were enough to show me that your main quest in life is easy sex. I'm sorry if I didn't fall all over you. Why don't you go salve your ego with some other female? There are plenty of willing ones around these days."

"Listen, there's nothing wrong with my ego," he said, pointing his thumb to his chest. "I don't have to have the approval of some chick who thinks she's high class to know my worth. I don't need this garbage. I'm not going to waste any more time with you!"

"Good!"

He glared at her and pointed his finger again. "You had your chance. Someday you'll regret it, sugar."

Dale heaved a long sigh as he stalked off. She hoped this would be the end of his taunting advances. She didn't know why he singled her out so much. Perhaps she was the only woman who had rejected him lately and he had taken it as a challenge. His continuing failure to entice her with his usual sensual but shallow charm had made him resentful and then bitter.

28

But that was *his* problem, Dale told herself. She had tried to be tactful and nice in the beginning. When he had continually refused to believe she actually didn't want him, she was forced to become tough and a little rude. If he was unhappy, he had asked for it!

Dale glanced at her watch and then began to quickly put her desk in order. If she didn't hurry, she might be late for her appointment. A few minutes later Andrea Miles passed by as Dale was putting on her coat.

"Hi, Dale. Leaving to see a movie?"

"No, I have a doctor's appointment," Dale answered with a smile.

"Nothing wrong, I hope."

"Oh, no. I'm overdue for a yearly check-up, and I thought it would be good to find a local doctor anyway. If I get a bad case of the flu or something, my doctor back in Savannah wouldn't be much help."

Andrea laughed. "That's true! See you later."

Dale's face grew pale as she lay back on the examining table. Unconsciously her hand clutched the edge of the large paper jacket the nurse had given her to put on. "A lump?"

"You haven't noticed it?" the middle-aged doctor who was bending over her asked.

"No."

"See for yourself," he said and guided her hand to the outside of her left breast. "Do you give yourself monthly breast exams?"

"N-no," Dale said. A sense of panic coursed through her as her fingers felt the hard lump beneath the soft surface of her skin.

The doctor shook his head. "You should. Every woman should. Now we don't have any way of telling how long this has been there. You say the last time you saw a doctor was a year and a half ago?"

"Yes."

"He didn't find anything unusual?"

"No."

"All right." He motioned with his hand. "You can sit up now."

Dale did, wrapping the white paper jacket around her, hugging herself with her arms. The room suddenly seemed cold.

The doctor handed her a card. "I'm going to refer you to Dr. Whittaker. He's a good surgeon."

"S-surgeon?" She felt a little faint.

"What he'll do is check you and then perhaps order a mammogram, or he may try aspirating the lump with a needle. He may want to do a biopsy, which is a minor operation."

"I see." Her voice was small and tremorous.

"Now, there's no need to worry too much. Eighty percent of all breast lumps are benign. But you should see Dr. Whittaker as soon as possible."

Forty minutes later Dale quietly entered the small darkened theater. She was late for the private screening she was scheduled to see and the movie had just started. As she took the nearest seat in the last row, she saw Sloane Avery turn and glance at her. He was in his usual spot. As he turned she could see his white bag of popcorn.

She hadn't wanted to be late, but she was glad it turned out that way. Being as upset as she was, it now became an easy way to avoid Sloane. Over the last few weeks since she met him, he had always come up to her whenever they found themselves at the same screening, which was typically the case. Usually she wound up sitting with him. He apparently found it amusing to annoy her and spar with her. She didn't know why. He continued to be disdainful about her abilities as a critic. Maybe it bothered him that she had a job on TV and, of course, had more visibility than he. Still, she didn't sense that he was actually jealous. She couldn't figure him out at all.

At least it had worked out so she didn't have to deal with him today. She took a Kleenex out of her purse and blew her nose. On the way over in the cab, she hadn't been able to keep herself from crying. It was all such a shock—to start the day thinking she was perfectly healthy and then find out that she had something potentially very serious. And now of all times! Everything was going so well in her career. She didn't want to cope with this. Just the idea of having to see a surgeon shook her equilibrium to the core.

She put trembling fingers over her mouth, trying to calm herself. She had to concentrate on the movie. Tomorrow night she'd be reviewing it on the air. Focusing her mind on the film, she tried to forget for the moment the unsettling news of the last hour.

By the time the movie drew to a close, she thought she had managed to absorb enough to form an opinion of it in spite of her distracted state of mind. As the final credits were rolling up the screen, Dale rose from her seat to go. She was the first one out of the theater. As she waited impatiently by the elevator, she heard a masculine voice approaching from behind. She closed her eyes.

"You were late," Sloane Avery said, drawing up beside her in front of the closed elevator door.

"I . . . had another appointment that lasted longer than I expected."

"You missed some good popcorn," he said, holding up his crumpled empty bag. "The place where I buy it started selling a new cheese-flavored kind."

"Oh." When was the elevator going to come? Any moment she expected him to make one of his typical derisive remarks about her reviews. She was in no mood to cope with it now.

He spoke again. "Of course you might not like the cheese as well as the caramel, but I imagine it's less caloric."

She breathed a sigh when the light above the elevator came on. "Probably," she said as the door opened. They walked in and two other reporters hurried in after them before the doors closed. They rode down in silence. She had noticed that Avery didn't tend to speak to her much when others were nearby—another of his peculiarities. She was glad of it now.

They reached the first floor and soon were outside on the street. She rushed away without saying anything further to him.

"Well, that was a brilliant conversation," Sloane muttered to himself. He turned to walk back to his office after watching Dale hurry away. "Couldn't you have found a better topic than popcorn? Not everyone lives to eat junk food like you!" he berated himself.

She had hardly even noticed him today. Or maybe she was showing disinterest in order to avoid him. He still had a hard time being pleasant to her. He always felt more secure when he was picking on her. But, obviously, that didn't help make her like him! Today he had resolved to be more amiable, and then she had come late and ruined his plans. When the movie was over he was so nervous about approaching her in the short time left, he couldn't think of anything to say.

The wind picked up as he turned onto Michigan Avenue, heading toward the Herald Building near the river. He wondered why she had rushed out. She didn't usually do that. And her eyes had looked a little red. Maybe she had a cold and didn't feel well.

In any case he'd better get his act together. He was losing ground quickly. And he'd better do more than just play at dieting. He'd only shed two pounds—the equivalent of one box of Auntie Kay's. Things like substituting cheese popcorn for caramel weren't doing the trick. The time had come for serious measures.

Three days later Dale saw Dr. Whittaker. He turned out to be a slight, gray-haired man of about forty-five with a serious but likable personality.

"Okay, Dale," he said, after finishing his examination. "You have a fairly large lump, but I suspect it's benign. I'd like to set up a mammogram for you. If that doesn't show anything ominous, then I'd like to see you again in about a month to check if there's any change. We'll discuss then what to do next."

Dale relaxed and smiled a little. That didn't sound too bad. She'd had visions of being shipped off to an operating room. "All right," she said.

"My secretary will make the appointments for you. By the

way, I often see you on the ten o'clock news and enjoy your movie reviews."

"Thanks."

"In fact, my ten-year-old son will be envious that I've met you. He's begun watching the five o'clock news and has quite a crush on you!" Dr. Whittaker said with a grin. "Can I bring him your autograph?"

Dale hung up the phone on her desk at WNBS and let out a long sigh of relief. Dr. Whittaker's secretary had told her the mammogram she had had two days ago was negative. Dale hoped this meant she had nothing more to worry about. Of course her lump was still there. Every time she took a shower she purposely felt for it, hoping it might have disappeared. But if it didn't go away, she supposed she would get used to its presence if she knew for certain it was benign.

A half hour later, as she was finishing writing that evening's review, George Ellis called her into his office.

"Well, something good has come out of the delay in the filming of *Ivanhoe*," he told her.

"Really?" She couldn't imagine what. Three days ago the news had been received that *Ivanhoe*'s British director had gotten rather seriously injured in a car accident on the rain-slicked streets of Windermere. Three broken ribs and a concussion were going to keep him laid up for at least six weeks, thus delaying most work on the film for that amount of time. It had also meant that Dale's trip to England would be delayed, though she had been too worried about her health lately to care much.

"As you know, Velvet Hunt's current movie is having its premiere here next week, since it's about the Chicago fire. The delay on *Ivanhoe* has left her free to come here and promote it. We're talking with her publicist about getting her on the five o'clock news for an interview with you. It looks pretty certain."

"That's fine," Dale said. "How much air time will I have?"

"Maybe two minutes. By the way, make sure to bring up

something about her affair with John Trevor. It'd be great if we could get her reaction."

"Oh. Well, I'll try," Dale agreed reluctantly.

As they discussed further details of the impending interview, Dale couldn't help but be doubly thankful for the good news she had just heard from her doctor's office. Her mind could be free to concentrate on her job again.

The newsroom was abuzz all afternoon. But when Velvet Hunt at last arrived about a quarter of five, a near hush fell over the room. Typewriters paused their clicking and chatter stopped.

She stood there, only twenty-two, blond and radiant in a white wool dress, accompanied by an entourage comprised of her secretary, her publicist, and an "aide," whose function was not clear. The station manager and George Ellis hurried to greet her and introduce her to the staff and news team. Gary Murdock did not hesitate to push himself forward to meet the gorgeous film star. She smiled at him obliviously.

When it was Dale's turn to be introduced, Dale grinned, said "I'm very happy to meet you," and extended her hand. The actress, whose beautiful smile seemed to have gotten fixed on her face, murmured something pleasant and meaningless in return. Dale noticed the young woman's handshake was surprisingly limp.

Several minutes were taken to explain the logistics of the newscast to Velvet Hunt. As she went in for makeup she softly requested a glass of ice water so she could take a pill. Dale noticed three of her male co-workers, including Gary Murdock, stumble over one another to get it for her.

Dale couldn't quite see any longer what all the fuss was about. Velvet Hunt was unquestionably beautiful, but rather simpering and, Dale suspected, a little dim. There was a vacant look in the actress's much-touted violet eyes. Except in outward appearance, she seemed quite different from the vibrant creature that came across on film.

Not quite a half hour later, while the live newscast was on,

Dale and Velvet took their places at one side of the long, curved news desk. In a few minutes the cameras would be focusing on them as the interview was about to start. Dale whispered quietly to Velvet, asking if she was comfortable and if she wanted coffee or water. Curiously the actress now seemed much more in tune with what was going on. When responding to Dale's solicitous inquiries, her smile seemed genuine, and she appeared ready for whatever was to happen. Dale assumed it must be the cameras that had motivated Velvet to come to life.

Finally it was time for the interview. Steve Froebisher introduced them, noting that the movie star had just flown in from England.

"We're honored you could join us, Miss Hunt," Dale said with a grin when the cameras were on them. Velvet nodded and smiled. "I'll be seeing a preview of your new movie, *The Great Fire,* tomorrow, and of course the grand premiere will be on Friday at a downtown theater. You'll be there, won't you, to greet your fans?"

"Yes, I'm looking forward to it," Velvet said in the honeyed, clear voice she was famous for.

"And all of this, unfortunately, was made possible due to the latest delay on the movie you're currently working on, *Ivanhoe,*" Dale said.

"Yes, Ian Michaels, our director, had the most awful accident. But I spoke to him yesterday and he's doing well."

"*Ivanhoe* has been plagued by many difficulties, hasn't it?" Dale asked.

"Well, it's rained almost every day we've been shooting." Her violet eyes flashed a childlike astonishment. "And we've had equipment breakdowns, illnesses . . ."

"And personal problems on the set?" Dale prodded. Anyone who kept up with the news would know she was referring to the stormy consequences of Velvet's affair with her married co-star. Dale felt a little squeamish about mentioning it, but George Ellis had told her to bring it up. Dale had done so in the most oblique way she could find.

The actress's eyes clouded momentarily and she stumbled over her words. "Oh, there are always problems . . . especially on location."

"Of course," Dale said smoothly, hoping to put Velvet at ease again. *Well, I tried, George,* she thought silently. "How have you prepared for your role of Rowena? I suppose you read *Ivanhoe*?" Dale thought it was an easy question, but the actress seemed addled again.

"No, I haven't had time. I've been working so much. And they've made some changes in the story line."

"So it really wouldn't have helped to have read the original by Sir Walter Scott," Dale said, coming to her rescue. Dale was beginning to perspire a bit.

"No, it wouldn't have," Velvet said, smiling more securely now.

"Well, let's get back to *The Great Fire.* You shot some scenes for that here in Chicago about six months ago, didn't you? Near the Water Tower?"

"Yes!" Velvet said, brightening. "Because the Water Tower was the only building to survive the Chicago fire in . . . uhm . . . ."

"Eighteen seventy-one," Dale said, smiling.

"Yes."

"You play the role of a stage singer in the film, I understand. Is this the first role in which you perform vocally?"

"Yes. I took singing lessons for six weeks. I probably could have used a few more," Velvet said with a charming laugh.

Dale chuckled. "Well, we'll all have to see the film and decide for ourselves. Thank you for being here!"

"My pleasure." Velvet turned on her most radiant smile for the camera.

Dale relaxed as they broke for a commercial. She had grown tense. The interview had been more difficult than she had anticipated. She thanked Velvet again briefly as both got up from the desk. The actress now appeared slightly distracted and perhaps upset. But she smiled at Dale once more before moving off the set to join her entourage. As Dale passed by them on her way to her desk, she heard Velvet's secretary tell her that a car was waiting to take her to meet Sloane Avery for dinner.

Sloane Avery? Dale thought with astonishment as she reached her desk. *Velvet Hunt is having dinner with Sloane Avery?* Dale had to chuckle. What on earth would *that* be like? She envisioned them eating at some special place with circus decor and popcorn on the floor. Afterward they'd go to his place, where he'd offer her an after-dinner drink and a box of Cracker Jacks.

Dale left the TV studio laughing to herself. But all the while she was wondering why a beautiful, voluptuous actress was seeing a sloppy and irritating movie critic? Was Velvet angling for better movie reviews than she usually got?

But then Dale remembered something she had forgotten. She had been very surprised six months ago, when Velvet's last movie had been released, that Sloane had been almost a minority of one among the nation's top critics in giving her performance a good review. Since his cinematic standards were so high that he was rarely pleased, Dale had wondered at the time how he could have liked a performance even she had not been impressed with. In fact, there seemed to be a general consensus among critics and fans alike that Velvet's popularity stemmed from her very photogenic physical beauty much more than from her talents as an actress.

So, Sloane Avery was seeing Velvet Hunt tonight! *My, my,* Dale thought. The old maxim said that everyone had his price. Was that true of the renowned award-winning critic whose work she had admired all these years? She had already been disappointed with his looks and personality. Was she to be disillusioned with his integrity as well?

The next day Dale was in a peckish mood when she entered the back elevator to go up to the seventh-floor screening theater. She had just come from a brief discussion with George Ellis about her interview yesterday.

"You'll never make a hard-hitting reporter, Dale," he had said in his abrupt way. She knew he was referring to her questioning of Velvet Hunt about her affair with John Trevor. "But then, it doesn't go along with your sweetheart image, so it's probably just as well," he had added. "I should have had Andrea interview her. The audience would have expected her to be tough, and we might have gotten a more newsworthy interview."

That was what being nice got you! Dale thought as she opened the door and walked into the small theater. As soon as she did, she found herself accosted by Sloane Avery's hard stare from across the room. As he walked toward her, she noticed he had no bag of popcorn today.

"I saw your interview yesterday," he said. His face was stern and his gray eyes unwavering as he looked down at her. He didn't usually look her in the eye like that.

"What did you think of it?" she asked.

"Not much."

"Well, I'm sorry," she said, and turned to walk away.

He caught her arm. "Did you set out to embarrass Velvet Hunt?"

"No, not really."

"You certainly did a good job of it—making it look as though she didn't prepare for her role, making her look stupid."

"Actors are always asked how they studied for a part. I didn't make her look stupid. She did that all by herself!" Dale said, becoming quite irritated. She thought she had done her best to help the actress save face.

"You didn't have to make that reference to her problems with John Trevor!" Avery was glaring at her now, genuinely angry.

Dale's eyes lowered for a brief moment. "That wasn't my idea. The news director wanted me to bring it up."

"You didn't want to?"

"No."

"Don't you have enough personal integrity to stand by your own convictions?"

Dale's eyes flared. "Is Velvet Hunt a friend of yours or something?"

"Yes!"

Dale was quiet. She hadn't expected such a forthright answer. Finally she said, "I agree the interview didn't go well. I had expected an experienced actress to be able to field questions better than she did. I'm sorry if you or she were offended." Dale turned then, walked past Alan Thornton and a small group of other critics, and took a seat toward the back of the theater.

After shrugging off her coat, Dale sat and stewed over the two extremes of criticism she had gotten about her handling of Velvet Hunt. Her news director thought she was too soft, and Sloane Avery thought she had been deliberately mean. Now she had to sit through two and a half hours of watching Velvet Hunt on screen. She wished she could go home!

As she got out her notepad and pencil, she sensed someone approach. She looked up to see Sloane Avery taking off his big overcoat. He threw it over a chair and silently took the seat next to Dale.

Good grief! Dale thought, her shoulders drooping slightly. *Why on earth is he sitting here?* It wasn't even his favorite spot. She edged away from him slightly. The seats were close together and his broad shoulders and large body always took up so much room that he seemed to encroach on her space.

"Comfortable?" he asked, his eyes narrowing on her.

"Yes." She hid her irritation, silently chiding herself for not having enough *integrity* to tell him the truth.

They sat without speaking for a while, waiting for the other reporters to take their seats. Alan's group seemed to be engaged in a vigorous discussion, thus delaying the movie's start. Dale sensed a tenseness in the big man next to her, as though he were uneasy with the silence between them. He was sitting too still. Somehow it kept *her* from relaxing. Perhaps he felt bad about their argument a little while ago. Her sense of fairness dictated that she try to make conversation to put him at ease.

"No popcorn today?" she said lightly.

He turned his head and stared at her for a fleeting moment. His gray eyes were suddenly defensive. "No!" he said with offended sharpness. His tone implied it was none of her damn business. As he stared straight ahead again, Dale glanced helplessly at the ceiling. Why had he bothered sitting next to her?

That does it! she said to herself. She was sick of trying to be nice to people and getting nothing in return. Northerners were cold and self-centered. She wished she were back in Savannah!

Finally all the reporters sat down and someone turned off the light, a signal for the projectionist to run *The Great Fire.* Dale forced herself to concentrate. But as soon as she saw Velvet Hunt appear, a blond vision in a low-cut, scanty, old-fashioned corset, Dale found herself feeling slightly ill. She remembered the dimly insecure, vaguely troubled woman she had interviewed. But on screen Velvet was scintillating and very sexy in a naive, soft way. Every man's dream baby. Did that include the man sitting next to her? Dale wondered just what kind of *friend* Velvet was to Sloane Avery.

The Great Fire, which for its first two hours had more to do with the theatrical world of old Chicago than the massive conflagration that once devastated the city, was R-rated. Dale soon realized this was because of the movie's rather explicit love scenes rather than its language or violence. In fact this was the first picture in which Dale had seen Velvet Hunt semi-nude. It was also the first time she had sat through such a sexy movie next to Sloane Avery.

In the few weeks since they had first met, they had sat together —not by Dale's wish—through several films, and she had always found herself oddly uneasy when the love scenes had come on. She usually wished she could feel free to get up and move a few seats away from him. It seemed she became more acutely aware of his large male frame so close to hers. Sometimes she even felt she could sense his body heat. She didn't know why, but it unnerved her. And this had been during movies where the actors had been clothed!

Now, in the last third of this movie, she was uncomfortably watching a full-blown sex scene in which Velvet and her male co-star were apparently naked. He was fondling her large breasts, though the scene had been filmed at such an angle that her nipples were covered either by the sheets or by the actor's hands. It was a terribly erotic scene, with long, writhing kisses and lots of urgent, labored breathing.

Watching the extended foreplay, Dale's heart began to pound more rapidly. Under the sensual spell of the film, she grew unaccountably nervous. Even her hands were trembling. At last the actor moved over Velvet for the final screen consummation. As he came down on top of her, the actress's pink nipples and voluptuous breasts were briefly, but fully exposed. It came as a shock, and Dale almost gasped aloud.

She didn't know what was wrong with her. She had viewed scenes equally explicit before. But she had been alone then. Why did Avery's proximity bother her so? Was it because in the back of her mind Dale kept wondering if he had already seen this much of Velvet's stunning body personally? But what if he had? Why should that affect Dale? Why should she be so embarrassed, or whatever it was she was feeling? She didn't even like him.

Another thought occurred to her. Perhaps she was misreading herself. Maybe she was growing so stressed during this picture because a great deal of the focus in the love scene was on Velvet's beautiful bosom. Perhaps the fact that Dale had a lump in her own breast, and she was mentally dealing with all the possible consequences of that, made her upset. That must be it, she decided. There was certainly no reason why Sloane Avery's presence should bother her in the least.

But even that self-revelation didn't do anything to calm her. On screen Velvet and her co-star were deep in the throes of climactic consummation, the scene cleverly enhanced by brief cuts to scenes of the raging fire that was at the same moment beginning to destroy the city. Dale's breathing was growing a little shallow and her mind seemed to be in a spin. She wished she had a prescription for tranquilizers by the time the scene was over.

A half hour later the movie finally ended with a dramatic rescue of Velvet by her co-star near the Water Tower as the rest of Chicago went down in flames. Dale's fingers were still slightly shaky as she put away her pencil and notepad. She hadn't taken any notes this time. Rising from her chair and almost dropping her purse in the process, she picked up her coat. Glancing at Sloane, who had also risen, she murmured a rigidly polite goodbye. He immediately looked the other way. Dale sensed he was pretending not to have heard.

She quickly left and he did not follow her out this time. Though she wasn't entirely sure what to make of his behavior, she assumed he was still angry. Grateful to be away from him, she didn't really care whether he was annoyed about Velvet or the popcorn.

Dale hurried back to the station and quickly wrote out her review for that night's news. Since she had interviewed Velvet Hunt yesterday, the news director wanted Dale to review her picture tonight. Dale's earlier discomfiture faded as she typed out the review. Her nervous energy seemed to flow out through her busy fingers, showing up on the paper in her machine in unusually energetic phrases. Each sentence was curiously laced with just a touch of venom.

"*The Great Fire* is a film starring Velvet Hunt," Dale read from the TelePrompTer on the air several hours later. "It takes place in Chicago in 1871, the year of our city's historic conflagration. The title rather misrepresents the movie, since we see much more of Velvet than we do of the fire. She plays a stage singer who falls in love with the son of a wealthy society family. The story is very predictable, one we've all seen many times. If the writers thought throwing in a fire and Miss Hunt's off-key singing would make the story fresh and new, they were sadly mistaken. Miss Hunt's high-school-level acting ability only makes the plot seem more mundane. The sets, costumes, and photography are all nicely done, but unfortunately it's not enough to save this picture. The movie is R-rated, with long stretches of gratuitous sex and quite a bit of nudity. If you want to see this film to gaze at Miss Hunt's lovely body, go ahead. She *is* beautiful, but that's about the only thing that would make this picture worth your time."

Dale paused for a fraction of a second and smiled into the camera. "Starting today, I will be rating each movie I review." She laughed a bit as she glanced at the TV monitor and saw a row of five yellow peaches suddenly appear, flashing sporadically on and off below her chin like Christmas-tree lights across the screen. The graphics department had created the effect. "The scale will be one peach to five peaches, five being the highest rating. These are Georgia peaches, of course. Tonight I give *The Great Fire*"—she paused as, by design, the peaches zipped off the screen until only two were left—"yes, two fat peaches! Hardly equal to the movie's overpriced admission fee. And now back to you, Steve." She turned toward the anchorman.

"It sounds like you've really given it the pits!" Steven Froebisher said with a chuckle.

A few miles away Sloane Avery was watching his TV at that moment and scowling. "It sure does!" he muttered. He was glad Velvet would be at the grand opening of her film and wouldn't have heard Dale's scathing review. "The empty-headed little . . ." He stopped himself from finishing, knowing he was angry. He shouldn't begrudge Dale her opinion. In fact, he was amazed she had finally found fault with a movie. He didn't know she was capable of forming such a strong judgment!

Come on, now, he chided himself. Maybe she was in a bad mood today, too, as he was. It had been a miserable day. After being up late comforting Velvet last night, he hadn't gotten enough sleep. And trying to go all day without his usual snacks had made him grouchy. It had been stupid to react so defensively that afternoon when Dale had asked about his not having any popcorn. There was no use clinging to pride. If he lost the weight he intended to, she'd figure out he was dieting anyway.

And, he thought with a sigh, he supposed he couldn't really blame Dale for the way she had interviewed Velvet. She was only doing her job. He wondered if Dale assumed he was still angry when the movie was over. Her good-bye had sounded cold, and he had ignored her. Stupid! He had gotten so worked up watching that bedroom scene with Dale sitting next to him, it had taken away his presence of mind.

But that was beside the point at the moment. The point was that Dale, for some reason or another, had just given a very poor review. Velvet got little enough praise for her talent. Sometimes it seemed he was the only one who saw it. And it was a bad time in the film star's life for her to be subjected to needlessly harmful criticism. Perhaps it had been wrong of him to get so personally involved with an actress. But he had, and now he felt compelled to defend her when and where he could.

It seemed he would have to give Dale a little set-down. She was popular enough that it wouldn't hurt her. She ought to learn to review movies more thoughtfully and carefully. It was her job after all.

Besides, an open challenge would make her notice him a little more. It might also make her hate him. So what else was new? Anyone who looked like him needed to be daring with an almost Miss America.

CHAPTER THREE

It was late afternoon of the next day. Dale had picked up the evening *Herald* and was reading Sloane Avery's column at her desk. She had been anxious to see how he reviewed *The Great Fire*. It was a surprise to find he had found much in the movie to praise, particularly Velvet Hunt's performance. Well, she might have expected that. She was halfway through the column when her mouth fell open as she read:

> It has become popular among critics to show an intellectual disdain for actors and actresses who are extraordinarily beautiful. A pretty face can't have much mental capacity behind it, the thinking goes. A victim of this false rule of thumb has been Velvet Hunt. It has long been my opinion that Miss Hunt is one of the most gifted young women to grace the screen in years. Yet because she is so sensually beautiful, her true acting talent is largely overlooked.
>
> To be fair, shouldn't we apply the same sort of criteria to the critics who put these labels on our movie stars? For a few months now, many of us have been listening to the reviews of a very attractive former Miss America contestant turned movie critic on WNBS-TV. Shouldn't the lovely face

of this young woman lead us to assume that she hasn't the mental wherewithal to give a movie an in-depth review? No, you say? That's not fair?

Unfortunately, in this case, the above-mentioned critic may have proved the theory. Having grown accustomed to her wistfully trite, nebulous little reviews every evening, I admit to being slightly astonished at her outspoken opinions last night. It was painfully amusing to hear her accuse Velvet Hunt of the very thing for which she should be indicted: letting her beauty cover the fact that her capability is inadequate for her job.

But I'll keep on watching anyway. She *is* awfully cute.

In shock, Dale let the newspaper slip from her hands to sink down onto her desk. The nerve of the man!

"Dale? Oh, I see you've read it too."

She turned in her seat to find George Ellis standing next to her, holding a copy of the *Herald*'s entertainment section in his hand. Her spirits sank. Of all the people she might have hoped wouldn't see the article, her stone-faced news director topped the list. "Yes, I just finished it," she said in a troubled voice.

"Don't look so worried. This has possibilities."

"What do you mean? He's practically said I was brainless. He called my reviews"—she picked up the paper again—" 'trite and nebulous'! I don't understand. He's the one with the stature and reputation. Why does he need to humiliate me?"

"I don't know, Dale. What we've got to do is decide how to respond to this," George Ellis said in his authoritative monotone.

"Respond! Wouldn't it be wise to just ignore it?"

"I don't think so. Why look like you're going to just sit there and take it? If you handle it right, you might come out ahead."

While Dale looked doubtful, George pulled over a chair from the next desk. He sat down near the corner of Dale's desk, facing her. "Look," he said, "a while back, before you came to Chicago, a news commentator from one of our rival stations got into a friendly feud with Mike Royko. Royko made some humorous snipes in his column and the newscaster responded with witty comments on the air. Chicago loved it! And the extra publicity didn't hurt either of them. Maybe we can do the same thing here. In fact, this is potentially even better since you're a woman and . . . Is Sloane Avery married?"

"I don't know," Dale said with a shrug. "By the way he dresses, I wouldn't think so."

"How does he dress?"

"His suits are always rumpled and they all look like they're about ten years old. No wife would let her husband leave the house like that."

George nodded, looking just perceptibly amused. "You've met him then?"

"Several times, at movie previews. Somehow I always wind up sitting next to him," she grumbled.

A faint smile came and went over the thin line that was George Ellis's mouth. "He seems to watch you regularly, judging by those last two sentences he wrote. He even says you're cute. You don't suppose that he's . . . interested in you or something."

Dale chuckled derisively. "No. He just seems to get some sort of kick out of needling me. I didn't think he'd carry it over to his newspaper column though!"

"Well, he did. Now you've got to figure out what you're going to tell him and the public in response. I'll have Steve ask you about it on the air after your review tonight, so it will appear unplanned. You can reply then with one or two well-chosen sentences. Keep it clever and cute though. We don't want America's sweetheart turning into a bitch." Ellis eyed her a moment. "I guess in your case that's fairly unlikely."

"What should I say?" Dale asked.

"That's up to you. The last time I told you what to say, it didn't work very well. It's best if you think it through and handle it on your own. I'll go talk to Steve."

He got up then and left, leaving Dale with what seemed to be a monumental burden.

A few hours later Dale was in front of the cameras doing her spot on the five o'clock news. Her heart began to pound as she finished by giving the movie she was reviewing four peaches.

On cue, Steve Froebisher said, "I noticed in tonight's newspaper that one of our foremost movie critics took issue with your review of *The Great Fire* last night."

"Yes, he certainly did," Dale said with a smile. Her voice had more of its lilting southern charm than she usually allowed. "I've been reading Mr. Avery's column for a long time and I always learn something new. I didn't know before, that movie critics were supposed to review one another."

Froebisher laughed. "How would you rate *him*?"

Dale hesitated for a fraction of a second. She had said all she had planned to say. She hadn't expected Steve to ask a follow-up question. Suddenly words sprang from her mouth: "I'd give him one juicy peach, smack in the face!" she said, grinning sweetly.

The next day Dale was glad she had no film preview scheduled. She had no wish to encounter Sloane Avery. Though everyone had been much amused with her comments on the air the night before—even George Ellis had approved—Dale had mixed feelings. In one way she felt liberated, having finally had an opportunity to return the snipes Avery had been giving her in private and in public. But she also felt as though she were walking on eggs. She took no joy in feuding with anyone, especially not in public. And trying to match wits with Avery was a game she probably could not win. Back-biting and sarcasm were not natural to her, but Sloane Avery seemed to thrive on them.

She saw a movie at a public theater early that afternoon. On the way back she picked up the *Herald* and took it home with her. There she read Avery's negative review of the film she had just seen. Her shoulders slumped as she came to the last paragraph of his column.

I heard Miss Chastain's response to yesterday's column on the WNBS-TV news. She has good aim. After wiping the peach juice from my face, I had to acknowledge that she was

48

right to point out that movie critics ought to keep their critiquing to movies. While she may be much more professional than I in her conduct, I still await the day when the content of her reviews shows equal professionalism. I realize Miss Chastain is so charming it doesn't really matter to anyone what she says. But the consumer advocate in me demands that someone point out to her mesmerized audience that she barely knows what she's talking about. I know, y'all don't give a damn.

His comments really hurt this time. The remark about her reviews being unprofessional was the most deflating thing he could have said. It took some doing to lift herself out of her depression and appear bright and carefree on the five o'clock news. A number of her co-workers helped buck her up with supportive remarks.

Before they went on the air, George Ellis briefly advised Dale, Steve Froebisher, and Andrea Miles that, time allowing, some light comment ought to be exchanged among the three of them concerning Avery to show the station was standing behind Dale. As usual, there was little time to plan their off-the-cuff remarks, but Dale thought it a good idea when Andrea suggested they make some joke about sending Avery a towel.

Accordingly, after Dale finished, Steve said, "Good review, Dale. By the way, I read the paper tonight. It looks like Sloane Avery's face is still dripping from that peach you gave him last night!"

Andrea added, "Maybe you should send him a towel, Dale!"

"Oh, I'd be honored to give him anything he wants," Dale responded blithely. It was only when she caught the pained look on the floor director's face that she realized how her remark could be deliberately misconstrued. Dale, Steve, and Andrea retained their oblivious smiles as Steve introduced the commercial.

As soon as the cameras were off, Dale buried her face in her hands.

49

"Oh, Dale, you blew it this time," Andrea sympathized.

"I know. He'll make mincemeat out of me with that!"

After a long day's wait for his next column, however, Dale found after apprehensively reading it through, that it contained no mention of her at all. With relief she put the paper aside. Perhaps he had missed the show, she thought.

A week and a half went by. She purposely missed two private screenings she had been invited to. Instead, she saw each movie later when it opened at a public theater. Avoiding Sloane Avery, she hoped, would help to keep the antagonism between them at a minimum.

It seemed to work. There were no more jabs at her in his column, and neither she nor the anchorpeople made any remarks about him on the air. Maybe the "feud" was all over, Dale hoped.

She was mistaken. The day after she missed a third screening, Avery used a part of his column to print portions of what he called "the bagfuls of angry letters" he had received regarding his remarks about her. "Why don't you leave that little girl alone!" and "What misguided person at the *Chicago Herald* thought *you* made a good critic, Avery?" were two of the quotes he used. He finished his column by saying, "Look, I'm just as dumb as the rest of you. I like her too!"

Sitting home alone in her living room, Dale put the paper aside and grew thoughtful. Though she hadn't seen him in a while, a vague image of his large, overbearing frame came unbidden to her mind. She saw him offering her a bag of popcorn.

Her appointment with Dr. Whittaker, made a month ago, kept her from going to the next movie preview she might have attended.

"Well, Dale," the surgeon said after examining her once again, "your lump hasn't changed. I recommend that we do a biopsy."

Dale was stunned. "But the mammogram didn't show anything."

"I know, and that's a good sign. But mammograms do sometimes miss a malignancy. The only way we can be absolutely sure about your case is to do a biopsy—or just remove the lump. It's only a minor operation. We can do it under a local or you can be put to sleep. You won't even have to stay at the hospital overnight."

"Sounds like fun," Dale said in a weak attempt at humor, even as she felt the blood draining from her face. "I suppose once it's done, I wouldn't have to worry about it anymore." She felt like she wanted some reassurance about the outcome.

"Right," Dr. Whittaker agreed.

"Unless, of course, the results aren't good. . . ."

"That's unlikely, Dale. But we need to find out."

She took a long breath and slowly released it. "Okay. Let's get it over with."

Sloane Avery walked into the seventh-floor private theater for another scheduled preview. He was carrying a wet brown paper bag in his hand. Still wiping rain off his face, he looked around at the other reporters who had already arrived. Dale wasn't among them. She had already missed four screenings in a row. Had she decided never to come again just to avoid him?

It served him right, he supposed. He had wanted to give her a playful set-down, partly just to draw her attention. But somehow he had carried it too far. He was always so damned insecure around her. Now he had even used the power he had through his column to try to belittle her, still trying to make himself look superior.

Fortunately she had made it backfire on him. The public was clearly on her side, and he was glad. He hadn't wanted to hurt her career, but he might have. He wasn't quite in control anymore when it came to Dale. Feeling clumsy and ineffective around her made him angry sometimes. She never seemed to really see him. She never knew he was there, awkwardly admiring her, just waiting for her to notice. But why should she? He had turned his admiration into a defensive barrage of criticism.

Not feeling like talking with anyone, he began to walk to his favorite seat. Before he reached it, however, the door opened again. Suddenly she was there. As she moved into the room, she kept her gaze lowered, as if deliberately avoiding eye contact with anyone. He could easily guess whose eyes she was trying to avoid.

Nervously he rubbed his nose. He began to walk toward her then, not having a clue what he would say to her. He was a writer, he'd think of something, he told himself.

He was within a few feet of her now. His fleece-lined raincoat was still on over his suit, and he was beginning to sweat. But she looked all neat and trim in her little navy blue coat and matching umbrella, hardly a drop of rain on her even though it was pouring outside. How did she always manage to look like she just stepped out of a Marshall Field's display window?

"Hello," he said, stepping in front of her.

After nearly bumping into him, she looked up. He saw the blue of her eyes in a blur as he hurriedly averted his own gaze. That wouldn't do. He forced himself to look at her. As his eyes wavered over her beautiful face, he said, "Where've you been lately? I keep saving you the best seat and you never show up!" His voice came out sounding irritable.

Her brows drew together in a cross look. She turned away, muttering, "Why should you do that?"

"You need all the help you can get!" Sloane said. "No, wait . . ." She walked faster. "Wait. I . . . didn't mean that." He followed quickly behind her down the center aisle, catching her arm. "You know me by now. I'm always saying things I don't really mean."

"Does that include your column too?" she snapped, pulling her elbow from his fingers.

"You won that round. I still haven't gotten through all the letters from your angry fans." He smiled unsteadily. "Why don't we call a truce?" Taking the wet bag from his right hand, he offered a moist handshake.

She eyed him dubiously. Sighing with annoyance, she briefly put her gloved hand in his. In an instant she had turned away

52

and was moving up the aisle again. He reached and lightly took hold of her coat sleeve with his finger and thumb.

"No, no. You're going too close to the front. It's twice as far back as the screen is wide, remember?"

She paused and glanced at the hand pulling on her sleeve. "Maybe I like it up front!" she said argumentatively.

"Now, Dale, I'm only trying to help. You really ought to learn to take direction from those who are more experienced than you. Now . . . now, don't take that the wrong way." She was glaring at him and he didn't like the way her small hand was gripping her closed umbrella. "In some things *you* have more experience than I. If I had to appear on TV, for example, I might come to you for advice. You have one of the most pleasant TV personalities I've ever seen." It had cost him something inside to actually tell her that, but he was glad he had gotten the words out.

"Th-thank you." She eyed him as if he were a ventriloquist's dummy that had suddenly spoken on its own.

"You're welcome," he mumbled. He hoped the heat he felt rising to his face couldn't be seen in the dim lighting of the theater. "Let's, ah . . . sit down then. Back here."

She seemed a little numb as he took her elbow again and guided her to his favorite spot. He took off his coat and helped her off with hers. When they were seated, he gestured toward the screen and said, "You see, from this distance the picture's easy on the eyes. There's an overall sense of balance—no distraction from . . ." She had just crossed her legs, and her well-turned knee showing above her high boot caught his eyes. He forgot what he was saying. "So, how are things at WNBS?"

"Fine."

"Your peach rating system's a clever idea."

Suddenly she turned her bright blue eyes on him. They glinted with triumphant irony.

He made a half-grin. "Yes, I'm still sticky from the peach juice. You know, one of your fans sent me a shoebox full of moldy peaches? I didn't get around to opening it for a day or two. I was wondering why my office was starting to smell like a still."

She smiled. Sloane's heart soared. He felt like an actor at a successful opening on Broadway. The trouble was he couldn't think of anything to follow that story up with. They sat in silence for a few moments. He could feel his momentum quickly fading. How does a man keep a former Miss Georgia entertained?

He picked up his wet bag and took out a plastic container that had once held margarine. After taking off the lid, he looked at the contents—celery and carrot sticks. Dieting had required him to use such foods for snacks. After two weeks he was beginning to despise the stuff.

He held the container toward Dale. "Want some rabbit food?" he said, humor in his voice.

She leaned forward a bit and looked at the green and orange vegetables curiously. Smiling again, she said, "No, thanks."

"Great stuff," he said, and picked up a carrot stick. After chewing it for a moment he realized she was watching him, and he glanced at her. When their eyes met she quickly looked away. She began laughing silently, putting her hand over her mouth as her small shoulders shook. He didn't think anything he'd said had been *that* funny. "What's the matter?" he asked with a hesitant grin.

She looked as though she was trying to compose herself now. "Nothing . . . it's just . . . You called it rabbit food. It reminded me of *Harvey*—you know, that old movie with Jimmy Stewart?"

"Oh, yeah. Harvey, the six-foot rabbit." Sloane put away his vegetables. Harvey, huh? No, he didn't put her in mind of any handsome actor, not even Jimmy Stewart. When she looked at him she thought of a big, tubby, invisible rabbit. Why didn't he just give up now, he thought as the lights dimmed.

When the movie was over they walked out together. The film had been a reasonably good comedy, better than any he'd seen in a while. At least it had picked up his sunken spirits, and he'd noticed Dale had laughed quite a bit. As usual they didn't discuss the film, a rule he sometimes regretted having imposed that first time they'd met. But it was just as well, he thought as they rode down in the elevator together. It would only cause arguments, although they might have agreed on this film, and that would have been a pleasant way to end their time together today.

As they walked out onto the street, he said, "Well, the rain finally stopped!"

"Yes," Dale said.

Brilliant conversation, Avery, he told himself. "Were you invited to the screening next Thursday?"

Her bland expression changed slightly. "Yes."

"I'll see you there, then," he said. *And if things go well I'll ask you to have dinner with me on Saturday.*

"No, I won't be able to come Thursday," Dale said. They had paused together just outside the door before they went their separate ways.

"You shouldn't miss so many screenings," he chided.

"Well, it's—it can't be helped." She was trying to smile, but it wasn't convincing. He sensed some problem.

"Some big powwow at WNBS you're required to attend?" he asked good-naturedly, knowing he was probing. He was worried their public jabs at each other may have gotten her into trouble at her station after all.

"No. I'm scheduled for some minor surgery that day, that's all." She said the words lightly, but he noticed her hands were nervously fidgeting with the folds of cloth on her closed umbrella.

What she told him caught him by surprise. Surgery was the last thing he would have expected her to say. "Having a mole removed?" he asked in a joking way.

"No," she said with that same uneasy smile. She was edging away from him, anxious to move on.

"Wait." He put restraining fingertips on her arm. "You've got me concerned now. What sort of surgery is it?"

Her delicate brows drew together, her annoyance at odds with her sweetly formed features. "Why should you be concerned, Mr. Avery?"

"Call me Sloane, will you?" he replied in a voice that had also grown irritable in spite of himself. "I thought we called a truce. I'm concerned because I *like* you. I even said that in my column." Here he was, angry and defensive even though he could understand why she wouldn't trust him yet. He never seemed to be able to deal with her in a poised manner.

"I'm having a biopsy!" she said softly and with resentment.

He was perfectly still for a moment as he stared at her, genuinely shocked. "I see," he said quietly. "A breast biopsy?"

Her eyes showed her sudden discomfiture. She looked down at the ground and nodded. He wished he could put his arms around her and comfort her. Instead, he merely said, "I'm sorry. I didn't mean to embarrass you. It was an easy guess."

She nodded curtly, accepting his apology, but didn't look up.

He was quiet for a short while as his mind worked. "Do you have any relatives in Chicago?"

She looked up at him, not understanding. "No," she replied.

"Do you have someone to take you to the hospital and back?"

Her questioning expression cleared. "No, but I can take a cab. It's just a minor operation. It's the results that I'm worried about," she said with a nervous little laugh.

"Of course," Sloane said sympathetically. He was grateful she had opened up to him a little. "But you ought to have someone with you. I'd be happy to drive you."

His heart sank as she looked at him almost in horror. "Oh, no!" she said, and her radiant smile suddenly appeared, though there was an uneasy quiver in it. "Thank you, but, really, I'll be perfectly all right."

"You can't be sure, Dale. I had my tonsils out when I was in my teens and I was queasy and dizzy from the anesthetic for quite a while after I woke up."

"I'm having this done under a local," she said, "so I won't have any of the usual problems with a general anesthetic."

"A local? You mean you're going to go through it awake?"

"Yes."

56

Sloane felt himself growing pale. "Why, for heaven's sake? Can't they put you to sleep?"

"I chose to be awake. It's quicker that way and I avoid the problems you mentioned," Dale explained.

Sloane looked at her, dumbstruck. Finally he swallowed and said, "You're brave, you know that? Braver than me!"

She smiled at that. "Not really. I've always been a little afraid of being put to sleep. For me being awake is less scary."

He nodded thoughtfully. "It's funny, we always seem to be opposites. I'd still like to drive you. You may feel weak afterward; you can't tell. You ought to have someone with you."

Her expression was troubled as she studied the pavement at her feet. Sloane sensed she was seriously considering what he'd said. "It's a lot of trouble for you. . . ."

"Not at all!" he quickly contradicted her.

"But you'd have to take off from work."

"I can manage it. What time?"

"I'm supposed to be there at one. The surgery's scheduled for two," she said with reluctance, as if still hesitant about taking his offer.

"I can work around that. Where should I pick you up?"

She gave him her home address and indicated she wouldn't be going to the TV studio at all that day.

"I'll see you Thursday then," he said.

She nodded. "Thank you." There was shyness now in her voice and manner. Sheer impulse made him reach out and squeeze her wrist gently and quickly. Her beautiful eyes widened in confusion, but she smiled and said good-bye.

He turned away and began to walk down the sidewalk. *A biopsy,* he thought with concern. He hoped she would be all right. But how lucky to have been at the right place at the right time to be able to offer his help—and to have managed to say the right thing! Maybe now he could begin to make his feelings known to her.

About a block away, walking in the opposite direction, Dale was still wondering how it had all come about and why. Life was

57

becoming very strange lately: first to find out she had to have surgery at her young age, then to have a man she didn't like, who had publicly found fault with her, offer to drive her to the hospital! She assumed he was probably trying to make up for the things he had said in his column. But if he wanted to be friends with her, why did he write those things in the first place? Whenever she was with him he always seemed to have a dual nature, criticizing her one moment and offering her something to eat the next.

She came to a busy corner and stopped for a red light. How odd of him to have touched her wrist like that. A warm, prickly feeling ran down her spine as she thought of it. And the look that had been in his gray eyes, the sudden empathy and reassurance! Usually his eyes were like cold iron. What an unpredictable man.

She sighed fretfully as she crossed the street when the light changed. She shouldn't have agreed to let him drive her. He was probably right that she ought to have someone with her at the hospital, but she hadn't felt she knew anyone in Chicago long enough to ask such a favor. Everyone at WNBS was always so busy working on getting out the news anyway. Sloane Avery's offer had come out of the blue. The idea seemed awful at first; the surgery was enough for her to worry about without coping with his peculiarities too. But his persistence and common sense had finally made her agree. She figured it would just be a matter of his driving her there and picking her up later. They wouldn't be together enough for him to make her overly nervous. And he had been quite nice for a few moments there.

But then he had touched her wrist and left her wondering what exactly was going on. George Ellis's notion that Avery might be interested in her as a woman couldn't be . . .

No. How ridiculous! If he was attracted to her in some romantic way, he certainly wouldn't insult her every time he saw her. Would he?

Dale unbuttoned her coat. She was growing hot as she walked to the WNBS studios. The sun had come out bright and strong. A warm front must have moved over the city following the rain.

The city's climate, she was learning, was very changeable. There was a saying: If you don't like the weather in Chicago, wait a minute. It certainly seemed to apply today. And, she thought in exasperation, it seemed to apply to Sloane Avery's disposition as well.

Sloane arrived promptly that Thursday and drove her to the hospital's outpatient surgical clinic. They walked into the small waiting room and he went with her to the reception counter. He watched as Dale, who was wearing casual pants, a blouse, and a cardigan sweater, signed some forms. The nurse behind the counter attached a pink plastic bracelet to Dale's wrist, which listed her name, address, and other information. They were asked to take a seat and wait.

"Isn't this the sort of bracelet they put on newborn babies?" she said, trying to be cheerful in spite of her apprehension. She was grateful she was finally getting the surgery done with. When it was over and the results, she hoped, were good, she could forget it all and get on with her life.

"I wouldn't know," Sloane replied. "I noticed they had a box of blue ones up there too. Maybe you're right."

She smiled a little and glanced at him as he sat next to her. He had been very nice from the moment he'd arrived at her apartment—calm, pleasant, and patient. There was a solidness about him. For the first time, she had a sense of what it would be like to have someone to lean on in a time of crisis. It was odd; she hadn't expected to like having him along. But she shouldn't get too comfortable, she thought. It wasn't over yet. There was still time for him to become his usual self again.

"Would you like a magazine?" he asked, handing her one from the small table next to him.

She took it. As she absently leafed through it she said, "I guess this whole thing will take a couple of hours. You don't have to wait here with me until I'm called. You can go back to work."

"No, I arranged to take the afternoon off. They aren't expecting me back," he told her.

59

"Oh, you shouldn't have done that," she said.

"No problem."

"But you'll get bored waiting here. Have you eaten lunch? I think I saw a restaurant nearby."

He chuckled. "Don't tempt me."

She looked at him again. His appearance seemed to have changed slightly from when she first met him, though it had been so gradual she had barely noticed it. But today, when he had first come to her door, she had noted that his suit looked more than just rumpled. It looked poorly fitted, almost baggy. And his facial features appeared to have changed a bit. His cheekbones and jaw seemed to show more prominently. When they had first met she remembered how smooth and rounded his face had been. His big features had more definition now and the hint of potential, if craggy, good looks. Remembering his celery and carrot sticks, she wondered if he was dieting. She was considering asking him when someone called her name.

"Dale Chastain?" said a nurse in the doorway that led to the surgery rooms.

"Yes."

"Would you come with me, please?"

"Y-yes." Dale put aside the magazine and nervously clutched her purse. *Keep calm,* she tried to tell herself. *In a little while it'll all be over.* She rose from her seat and began to walk toward the nurse. After a few steps she turned to Sloane. "I'll see you later?" she asked, smiling wanly.

"Sure. I'll be here." His low voice sounded strong and reassuring. But as she gazed at him his gray eyes took on a strange inner light. They appeared silvery, almost shining. She had never seen him look like that before and she wondered why his eyes were that way now. Was it the light in the room, or . . .

"This way, Dale," the nurse reminded her. Dale turned and hurried toward the competent-looking woman in uniform. As they walked through the door and into a short hallway she said, "Your husband can come and visit with you in a few minutes. Now I'll be giving you—"

"What? He's not—" Dale began to explain, but the efficient, older woman continued.

". . . a hospital gown to put on. But first I need to ask you some questions to fill out your medical chart."

They came to a room which had five hospital beds in a row, partly separated by colorful curtains that hung on runners from the ceiling. Most of the beds were taken with others awaiting surgery. Each patient seemed to have someone with them, a relative or friend, Dale guessed. The nurse took Dale to the last bed, against the wall. She pulled the curtain to separate Dale's bed from the patient next to her.

A wooden chair was next to the bed and Dale was asked to sit down. After filling out her chart, the nurse gave Dale a Valium to swallow. She was told she could have further tranquilizing medication through an IV later on, if she felt she needed it. The nurse then handed Dale a large paper bag, similar to a grocery bag, with CHASTAIN written on it in big felt pen letters. Dale was asked to remove all her clothes and jewelry and put them into the bag. The nurse gave her a short hospital gown that tied at the back and gauze booties to wear. After she had changed, she was instructed to lie down on the hospital bed under the covers.

The nurse drew the curtain around the bed, and Dale dutifully did as she was told, feeling a little like an inmate entering a prison. After she was in the bed, leaning back on the two pillows, the nurse pushed back the separating curtain again and checked on her. As Dale declined the offer of an extra blanket, another woman in surgery attire came up and the nurse introduced her as Vicky, one of the nurses who would assist during Dale's surgery. After a few friendly words and a question or two, Vicky left, and Dale was alone for a few minutes. With nothing to do she studied the small blue and white floral pattern on her thin hospital gown and wondered how long the wait would be.

Then the nurse appeared again—with Sloane. He was told he could sit on the chair and keep Dale company until she was wheeled into surgery.

"I didn't know I'd be able to see you again," he said brightly as he sat down beside her high bed.

"No, neither did I," Dale said with somewhat less enthusiasm. She had forgotten what the nurse had mentioned on the way in. What they were supposed to talk about now, and for how long, she had no idea. It was one thing to have him drive her to the hospital; she had been prepared for that. But she really would have preferred to be alone just before the surgery than to have to make conversation with a man she hardly knew and understood even less. And to have him see her lying in bed wearing this ridiculous hospital gown besides! The nurse might have asked her if she wanted company, but in all her efficiency it apparently hadn't occurred to her.

"How do you feel?" Sloane asked.

"Okay. They gave me a tranquilizer a little while ago."

"That's good," he said. "You look fine." He smiled slightly and his gray eyes traveled over her reddish-brown hair, her loose curls somewhat mussed now from changing and lying on the pillow. His eyes glided over her face then, especially over her blue eyes, as she turned toward him against the pillow. She wished he wouldn't study her so closely. She hadn't put on much makeup that morning, figuring her usual amount would have only smudged through the ordeal.

"Thanks," she said. "But I'm glad I don't have to appear on TV right now."

"Oh, I'm sure all your fans would think you looked just as charming as ever, if not more so." There was a slight roughness in his voice she couldn't find a reason for. Feeling uneasy, she tried to change the subject.

"You said you had your tonsils out some years ago?"

"More years than I'd like to remember," he said.

"You're not that old," she said, smiling.

"No, I suppose thirty-six isn't so old," he agreed.

"Oh, is that all . . ." She stopped before finishing, her face coloring. She had guessed him to be at least forty.

"Yes, that's all," he said, looking a little insulted.

"Well, it's just that you s-seem sort of set in your ways."

He gazed at her, his eyes carrying more of their usual hardness now. "Set in my ways?" He shrugged uneasily. "I suppose I am. Living alone for more than a dozen years does that to a person."

"You never married?"

He lowered his eyes. "No."

She smiled. "Confirmed bachelor?"

His iron gray eyes rose sharply to hers. "Not at all."

"Oh." She felt peculiar suddenly. He had always struck her as a man who probably preferred the single life. To think of him contemplating marriage, even as a distant possibility, seemed a little odd. Maybe she misjudged him, but she had a hard time envisioning him with a wife. "Well, so you had your tonsils out when you were a teenager?" she said, feeling safer with their original subject.

"Yes. Is that what I seem like to you—a confirmed old bachelor?" His eyes pressed her for an answer.

"Not exactly. I don't know. . . ."

"Don't hedge."

"I never met anyone like you before."

"You're still hedging."

How did she get into this, she wondered. "Well, you don't seem like the playboy type, and you don't seem like a family man either, so . . ."

"So what's left but a confirmed old bachelor," he finished for her.

"Not old."

"But I seem older than I am?"

"A little. But there's nothing wrong with a man looking . . . mature." She was trying desperately to turn it into a compliment, but she knew it sounded lame.

"Mature? At least I sound more like Elwood P. Dowd now than Harvey," he said tartly, referring to the aging bachelor played by Jimmy Stewart in the movie.

Dale blushed deeply. She had hoped he hadn't completely understood what she was laughing at the other day, that she had actually envisioned *him* as the big white rabbit who leaned invisibly against lampposts. She wished she had been better at explaining away her laughing fit. He was more sensitive and inciteful than she realized. She didn't know what to say.

He seemed to be studying her embarrassment. "That's all right," he said. "I realize I'll never be mistaken for Robert Redford. I hadn't quite thought of myself as a walking ruin though."

"Oh, no . . ." she began, hoping somehow to amend the direction the conversation had taken, but she was interrupted by Dr. Whittaker, who had suddenly appeared at the foot of her bed.

"How are you, Dale?" the surgeon asked with a smile.

"F-fine." She smiled back weakly.

He glanced at Sloane. "And this is your husband, of course." The doctor stepped forward to shake hands.

"N-no . . ." Dale began.

"No, I'm the salty old bachelor type," Sloane said. He rose to take the doctor's hand. "Sloane Avery. I'm . . . a friend."

"Avery? The movie critic for the *Herald*?"

"Yes, that's right," Sloane said with a smile.

Dr. Whittaker looked a little confused. "I thought you two didn't get along."

"Actually, we don't," Sloane said. "But she needed a ride to the hospital and . . ."

Oddly, Dr. Whittaker looked a trifle embarrassed. "You know, my son—he's only ten—just adores Dale. He followed your little feud with great interest." The doctor smiled self-consciously. "He told my wife he . . . sent you a box of overripe peaches."

Sloane laughed. "I got them."

"Sorry. My son's a rascal sometimes."

"That's okay. Clever kid."

"I'm glad to have met you, Mr. Avery. Now, if you don't mind, I'll have to ask you to step away for a few minutes so I can check Dale."

Sloane's expression sobered. "Of course."

When he was gone, the doctor pulled the curtain around Dale's bed. He checked her breast once again. "Still the same," he commented. "How are you doing? Did the tranquilizer they gave you take the edge off?"

"I guess so," she replied. She didn't really feel any different from before. But she didn't feel overly anxious or nervous, either, so perhaps it had worked. Or maybe it was just that the conversation with Sloane had distracted her.

"Do you think you want more medication? It's available."

"No. I think I'm all right."

"Brave girl! It won't be that bad. The nurses will wheel you into the operating room in a few minutes. I'll see you there," Dr. Whittaker said. He pulled the curtain aside then and walked away.

Sloane was standing at a little distance. When the doctor was gone he hesitantly stepped toward her bed. "Everything okay?"

"Yes. They'll be taking me in in a few minutes."

He nodded. There was a new expression in his eyes she hadn't seen before. He looked almost contrite.

"I didn't mean to get into another tiff with you just before . . . You're not upset, are you? I wasn't serious."

He had taken her off guard. She said, "I'm sorry too. I didn't mean to imply that you were . . . that . . ."

He smiled. "You'd better quit while you're ahead."

Discomfited and tongue-tied, she could find no words to put right the unfortunate comments she had made on his appearance. Suddenly Vicky came up and handed Dale a plain plastic cap with an elastic band.

"Would you put this on, please? Tuck all your hair in. We'll be wheeling you in now."

Dale did as she was told. Another nurse appeared. As Sloane stepped out of the way, they put up the metal sides of the hospital bed. When Dale was ready and the bed was adjusted, they began moving her into the corridor. Turning her head, Dale looked past Vicky to get a glimpse of Sloane.

He was standing by the curtain watching, his broad face concerned and apprehensive. The expression in his gray eyes locked in her mind as they brought her into the small, bright operating room. She saw it still as they swabbed her with cold antiseptic and covered her with sterile towels. It was so strange, she thought. He looked as though he didn't want to let her go.

CHAPTER FOUR

When the surgery was over the nurses wheeled Dale into the recovery room. It was similar to the room she had been in earlier, with curtains dividing one patient's bed from the next. They adjusted her bed so she could sit up and offered her a choice of juice, 7-Up, or ice water to drink.

She leaned back against the pillows and let herself relax a moment. The words Dr. Whittaker had said when he was nearly finished with the surgery ran through her head and made her smile. "I've removed the lump, Dale, and I'm quite sure it's benign. We'll have it sent to the lab though." Tears had come to her eyes. Suddenly the surgery had all seemed worth it.

The plastic cap had been removed. Dale was fluffing out her hair with her fingers when a nurse brought her the ice water Dale had requested. The paper cup had a bent straw through which to drink. She was taking a sip when another nurse brought Sloane in.

He looked hesitant, as if not sure what he'd find. After he had studied her a moment, he smiled a little. "How are you doing?"

"Pretty well. I feel a little shaky and I've got a slight headache, but I can't really complain. The doctor said he was sure it was benign."

Sloane nodded. He looked as if he couldn't speak for a moment. "That's great," he finally said in a voice that was a trifle rough. "How long do you have to stay here?"

"A half-hour, they said. They're supposed to give me some directions about how to take care of the bandages and a prescription for a painkiller."

"Does the incision hurt?"

"No, but I guess it will when the local anesthetic wears off. I don't feel anything now." Without thinking, she put her hand to where the bandage covered her breast under the hospital gown the nurses had put on her again. Realizing what she had done, she was suddenly embarrassed. Sloane glanced away. Dale pulled the bedcovers up higher. "W-what did you do while I was in surgery?"

"I stayed in the waiting room and looked through some magazines."

"Oh. It must have been boring for you," Dale said, feeling bad that he had given up so much time for her.

"No." He made a self-deprecating chuckle. "I was too nervous to be bored."

Dale was a little startled at the statement. Sloane suddenly looked as though he felt he had said too much.

A nurse came in with the prescription and postoperative instructions and handed them to Dale. She read them over and then glanced at the prescription.

"Why don't you give that to me?" Sloane offered. "After I take you home I'll go and get it filled."

"No, Sloane, I don't want you to go to any more trouble. There's a drugstore not far from my apartment. I can go. . . ."

"Don't be silly! I took the afternoon off. Later on I'll go and bring you back some supper too. You won't feel like cooking."

He sounded as if his mind were made up. Dale made no more attempt to argue. She wondered why he was so intent on assisting her. Somehow she didn't think he would feel that guilty about the things he had written in his column. And now and then he seemed so genuinely concerned. It all made her a little uneasy.

When the half-hour recovery time was up, Dale drew the curtain and dressed herself, taking her clothes out of the paper bag which had been placed under her bed. A nurse cut off the pink identification bracelet and she was allowed to leave. Sloane drove her to her modern high-rise apartment on the Near North Side. He left again to get the prescription filled.

While he was gone Dale went into her bathroom and took off her sweater and blouse. What she saw did not look very pretty. A large white gauze dressing held on with wide tape covered most of her small left breast. The red-tinted iodine antiseptic the nurses had swabbed over her chest from neck to waist was still on her skin. She wet a washcloth and spent several minutes wiping it off. Soon her skin was its natural color again.

The large protective bandage remained, however, covering the outer side of her breast where the incision was and extending well over her nipple. She wondered what she would find underneath. According to the instructions, she was not allowed to remove the dressing until tomorrow.

Feeling a little neater now without the dried iodine on her skin, she grabbed a clean plaid blouse from her bedroom closet and put it on. She was finishing buttoning it when she heard Sloane's knock at her door.

"Here it is," he said when she had let him in. He held out a small white bag from the drugstore.

Thanking him, she took it. She began to open it, only vaguely noticing that his other hand was hidden behind his back. She was reading the label on the small bottle of pills when suddenly a dozen pink rosebuds bobbed in front of her.

"I, um, passed a florist on the way, so . . . I thought you might like . . ."

"Oh, no, you shouldn't have," she protested, even as a pleased smile lit her face. She took the cellophane-wrapped bouquet and smelled the blossoms. "They're beautiful. Thank you!" she said, looking up at him.

He quickly glanced away, but she could tell his eyes had been on her face. For a hard-boiled newspaperman, he certainly was ill at ease sometimes. He seemed incapable of even saying "You're welcome" at the moment. It made her diffident.

"Well, I'd better put these in water," she said. Turning away, she added, "I think I have something to put them in in the kitchen. It's one of those carafes, you know, that you buy wine in?" She was beginning to chatter now. Somehow she felt she needed to. It was a southern mannerism she had managed to subdue in the cold, businesslike North, but every now and then it reappeared, like her accent.

"I bought some burgundy about a month ago, mostly because I thought the bottle was pretty," she continued, laughing. They were in her small kitchen now. Reaching up with her right hand, she opened a high cabinet above the sink. An empty carafe was sitting on the shelf.

"You'd better let me get it," Sloane said, reaching up behind her. His hand accidentally touched hers near the shelf edge, and she felt his heavy, warm chest against her back as he leaned forward. She suddenly had a sense of how small she was next to him. An odd feeling engulfed her. She wanted to quickly get out of his way, and yet something kept her rooted where she was.

"Here," he said, putting the carafe down on the counter. He stepped away from her a little, and she sensed he felt as self-conscious as she did about their physical contact.

"Thanks," she said lightly, trying to sound as though she weren't aware of anything. Turning on the cold water faucet, she began to fill it with water. She unwrapped the roses and arranged them in the glass carafe. "That looks nice, don't you think?"

"Sure," he said rather curtly.

How strange. She felt at the moment as though she were totally in control, something she had never felt with him before. Underneath his lion's stance was there just an old yellow pussycat? Not old! She chided herself, remembering the trouble she had gotten herself into just before the surgery. He was a decade older than she, but definitely not old.

70

She took the flowers into the living room and set them on the glass-topped coffee table that stood in front of her modern white sofa. Opposite the sofa and matching chairs, which formed a circular arrangement around the low table, was a wall of long windows. From her fourteenth-floor apartment the view was that of the city streets and skyscrapers, the most prominent being the towering John Hancock Building.

"Nice apartment," Sloane commented, walking in after her.

"I like it," she said. "Where do you live?"

"Several blocks from here. I have a condo on Lake Shore Drive. My living room windows look out on the lake and Oak Street Beach."

"That must be pretty," she said enviously.

"During the day. At night you don't see much over the lake. No city lights like you must see."

"I never thought of that," Dale said. "At least people in other high rises can't see into your apartment though. I'm always careful to draw my drapes at night."

Sloane laughed. "Sounds like our spectacular views are hardly worth the high rent. So . . . how are you feeling?" He came around to face her now. His awkwardness of a few minutes ago seemed to have left him. "Maybe you should take one of those pain pills."

"No, I still feel all right. A little tired . . ."

She grew self-conscious as Sloane scrutinized her face. "You look beat. You've been through a lot, Dale. I think you ought to lie down."

"Well . . ." It was only four o'clock. She felt uncomfortable about going to sleep with him at loose ends in her apartment.

"Don't argue. Is that your bedroom?" He pointed toward a door off the living room. She nodded. "Come on, then." He actually took her by the hand and led her into her room. Suddenly she was nervous.

"W-what will *you* do?" They were standing next to her double bed.

"I'll plan out my column about the Oscar nominees," he answered very brusquely. "What did you think I'd do?"

Dale's pale face colored. She didn't dare tell him what had crossed her mind. She didn't know why she'd even thought of it. Again it seemed she had insulted him. When she managed to look up at him again, she noticed that his color had heightened a bit too. "Oh," she said. "Do you have paper and a pencil? There's some in my desk here if you need it." She motioned toward a desk in the corner of her room.

"I have a little notebook with me, thanks," he said.

"Want some coffee or anything?"

"No. Don't worry about me. Just get some rest. I'll go out around six and bring back something for dinner. Why don't you give me your key, so I won't have to disturb you?"

She went to her purse and gave him the key to her apartment.

"Okay," he said, moving to the door, awkward again. "I'll . . . be out here if you need anything."

"Yes. Thanks." She smiled hesitantly and began to close the wide-open door. Then, worried he might think she was anxious to push him out, she let go of the door. He gave an annoyed half-smile, took the knob in his hand, and pulled the door shut between them. Dale sighed with relief and exhaustion.

On the other side of the closed bedroom door Sloane was also sighing, more with irritation. What did she think, he was going to rape her? Did he seem that much of a monster to her? What a teeter-totter he'd been on today! One minute they'd get along fine, then everything would go wrong. She'd seemed to like him, and then she didn't. She was grateful for his help, thought he was old, loved the flowers, and didn't trust him near her bed. What did a man do with a woman like that?

He'd better learn to keep his emotions under better control, he chided himself. A few times he had let his feelings show too much. Wearing his heart on his sleeve would only leave him looking like a fool, at least at this point. He could tell she still had no interest in him. And he wished he didn't lose his cool so easily when he got physically near her. After all, he was thirty-

72

six, and he'd been around women before. Few that he'd cared about though. And none that he'd ever felt this way about.

He sat down on the couch and took out a small looseleaf notebook from his breast pocket. Finding a stub of a pencil in his pants pocket, he began to list that year's Oscar nominees, which had recently been announced. He tried to decide which he would choose as winners, but somehow his mind kept rechanneling itself to the beautiful young woman behind the closed door.

About six o'clock he went out, found a small restaurant with take-out food, and brought it back. He set the containers on the kitchen table and put on the automatic coffee percolator after some searching for the coffee in Dale's neatly stocked cabinets. He went to her bedroom door then and knocked softly. When there was no answer, he slowly opened the door and looked in.

She was lying on the bedspread in her blouse and pants, fast asleep. He walked over to the bed and looked down at her. Her beautiful hair was tousled and her extraordinarily long eyelashes curled gracefully at the tops of her cheeks. Her delicate wispy eyebrows and closed eyes had a sweet innocence, almost like a child. But her full lips, slightly parted in sleep, were those of a sensual woman.

He gave himself a mental shake. This was no time for such thoughts. "Dale," he said gently, and touched the dainty hand that lay across her waist.

The lovely eyes opened and the bright glass-blue color of them came as a pleasant shock. Sloane had to concentrate to ensure that his voice stayed matter-of-fact. "I just brought back some dinner. How do you feel?"

Her face was blank for a moment, then the light of her eyes seemed to dim. The soft curves of her face tensed. "Not too well, I guess."

"The anesthetic wore off?"

She gave a little nod. Her chest rose as she inhaled and then she seemed to stop herself. She smiled wanly. "It even hurts when I breathe."

"I'll get one of those pills for you." Immediately he left and went into the kitchen. He found the small prescription bottle and filled a glass of water for her.

When he approached her bed again she tried to sit up, but then fell back again, grimacing in pain. He set the bottle and water on the nightstand next to her bed. "Are you all right? Shall I help you?"

She tried to smile again. "I guess I moved the wrong way. Maybe if I lean more on my right arm . . ." As she began to push herself up again, he bent down and supported her back until she was sitting up.

After opening the bottle, he poured one pill into the palm of her hand. "You should have taken one sooner," he said, handing her the water. When she had swallowed the medication, he took the glass from her and watched as she slowly shifted her legs over the edge of the bed. "Maybe I should bring you your dinner in here?" he suggested.

"No. I'll go into the kitchen," she said, her voice soft. She stood up then, her face tautening again. Walking out of the room in front of him, she carried her body stiffly, as if afraid to move freely. It upset him inside to see her in pain. He felt so helpless.

In the kitchen he pulled out a chair for her at the table. At her direction he found two plates, cups, and silverware and set them out. He opened the containers of food then and sat down to eat with her.

"Hope you like stuffed cabbage," he said, dishing some onto her plate. "There's some salad in here." He pointed to another container.

"It smells good. Where did you get it?"

"At that little Eastern European restaurant down the street," he said.

They made innocuous small talk through the meal. Sloane was glad to see her eat well. Afterward he rinsed off the dishes while she finished her coffee. They walked into the living room and she sat down stiffly on the couch.

"Maybe you should go back to bed," he suggested.

"In a while. It's only seven o'clock. It seems too early."

74

"Do you feel better? Has the painkiller started to work?" he asked, taking a seat next to her.

She paused a moment. "I think so. At least it doesn't hurt when I breathe anymore."

They sat in silence for a few moments. She gazed at the roses on the table in front of them and murmured how pretty they looked. He made a comment about the view from the window again as darkness began to fall. It didn't seem to matter that they weren't saying much of anything. For once, he silently noted, they seemed to feel perfectly comfortable with each other and nothing really needed to be said.

It was like a little piece of heaven, sitting quietly next to her like this, Sloane thought. Outside, the skies were clear and limitless as night gradually fell on the city. The lights of the tall buildings were beginning to show and the faint noise of the traffic outside reached his ear. It gave him a sense of the staunch, efficient vitality that to him embodied the pace and spirit of Chicago. It was his city; born and raised here, he was at one with it. He wouldn't live anywhere else. And somehow the young woman next to him with her lilting southern drawl seemed to belong there too. Beneath all the soft warmth and charm was a Chicago-like toughness that enabled her to fit right in. But he liked the soft charm too. So, apparently, did her TV audience.

"You like living here?" he asked her. "Do you miss Georgia?"

She lowered her eyes. "Sometimes. Life isn't so hectic back home. But I like Chicago. I like to shop on North Michigan Avenue," she said with a little laugh. "I have a weakness for clothes, I'm afraid."

"I've noticed. I don't think I've ever seen you wear the same thing twice on TV," Sloane said.

"Why of course I have," she insisted. "I just wear different blouses with my suits, that's why it never looks quite the same."

"I still suspect that any man who marries you will have to spend a small fortune to keep your closet filled," he said a little waspishly.

"My salary is perfectly adequate to pay for my own clothes."

He had asked for that. "True," he agreed. "You—you do dress very beautifully." He didn't want to start sparring with her now. She wasn't feeling well, and things were so peaceful between them for once.

"Thank you," she said. He noticed she didn't return the compliment.

"What else do you like about Chicago?" he asked.

"I think it's very attractive—the skyscrapers, Lake Michigan, Grant Park. And then there are all the cultural advantages—the museums, the opera, the symphony . . ."

"How do you like the people?"

She was silent for a moment. Sloane suddenly felt fidgety. "Chicagoans are basically nice, I guess," she said. "A little brusque sometimes, but I think I'm getting used to it. In fact"—she paused and made a curious, sad smile—"when I call my mother on the phone, she says I sound like a Yankee. Of course, I studied with a speech coach for a while to lose some of my accent, but I didn't want to lose it all."

"You haven't lost it all, believe me!" Sloane assured her with a grin.

"No?" She looked up at him questioningly. Smiling back at him a little, she said, "It's hard for me to tell. I used to have to concentrate on not talking southern. Now it seems I have to think when I want to talk that way again." She sighed. "I don't know. I feel like I'm still a part of the South, and yet I'm beginning to feel that I can't go back there again, at least not to live. I've changed too much, even in three months. But I don't quite belong here either. Sometimes I feel a little lost."

"But you're wrong! I was just thinking you fit in very well here. Your audience adores you," Sloane told her, energy in his tone.

"Because I'm different. I'm a novelty here, and they think it's—cute. The word you've used," she said without malice.

"No, it's more than that. Your personality is very genuine and that's what comes across. Midwesterners are too down to earth to tolerate artificiality. You're as real as they come," he said.

76

A slight movement creased her forehead momentarily as she studied him. "I wish I could figure you out," she said. "You're always pointing out my shortcomings, and now you're telling me how good I am."

Sloane's eyes wavered a bit. "I'm . . . talking about your personality. I didn't say you knew anything about being a movie critic."

She smiled. "That sounds more like it."

Sloane lowered his gaze and shifted in his seat. He knew the calm rapport they had briefly shared was too good to last. She didn't even seem to believe him when he complimented her. "You shouldn't feel out of place in Chicago though," he said, trying again. "You do belong here." *Here with me,* he silently added.

She was looking at him with widening eyes. "Thank you. That's sweet of you to say so."

Heat began creeping up his collar. "Sweet? Me?" He laughed as if at himself. "You aren't feeling well."

She laughed too. "Sometimes I don't think you're nearly as mean as you'd like everyone to believe you are, Sloane Avery."

"Your accent's thick as molasses now," he derided her. He looked over her pale, strained face. "And I think you ought to go back to bed. You look pretty tired. You still have pain, don't you?"

She nodded. "I guess you're right." She leaned forward, about to get up. Turning to him, she said, "Thank you, Sloane, for all you've done."

"I wish you'd stop saying thank you," he told her, feigning impatience. He stood up and offered his hand to help her. She put her right hand in his and slowly got up. He followed her to her bedroom door.

"Will you be going now?" she asked. She almost sounded as though she would be a little sad to see him leave.

"I thought maybe I'd stay a while longer, if it's okay with you. If you can't sleep, you might want me to get you another pill or something."

77

"I'm sure I'd be all right by myself, but if you want to stay for a while . . ."

"Of course!" he said, brightening. She wanted him around! he thought with pleasure. "If you need any help changing . . ." he offered.

"Oh, no. I can manage," she said with a slightly embarrassed smile. She said good night before softly closing the door to her room.

"Yeah," he muttered. *Stupid! You shouldn't have offered to help her change!* Sloane chastised himself. Annoyed at his thoughtlessness, he went back to sit on the couch. She had been wary of him in her bedroom that afternoon. It was the worst thing he could have said to her. What must she think?

Everything was quiet for a few minutes. Sloane was morosely wondering if he should turn on the TV when the bedroom door opened and Dale peeked out. She looked quite embarrassed.

"Um . . . m-maybe you *could* help me. I can't get my left arm into the pajama sleeve. It hurts no matter how I try it."

Sloane was momentarily stunned. Quickly collecting himself, he rose and walked toward her. Pushing open the door, he found her wearing flower-patterned flannel pajama pants. The ruffled matching top was half on and half off. She had the right sleeve on and was clutching the front over her chest as best she could. He could see part of the thick white bandage over her left breast. Quickly reaching to pick up the left sleeve, he held it so that she could put her arm into it. But putting her left arm that far back seemed to pain her a great deal.

"I think you'll have to slip it over your left arm first, and then you can reach back easier with your right," he suggested hesitantly, knowing what that meant.

"I tried that," she said, "but I couldn't seem to grab it."

"I'll hold it for you."

"But . . . then . . ."

"I'll be behind you. I won't look, I promise," he said, trying to keep from sweating. This was too good to be true. He was dying to look. But he wouldn't, he sternly told himself.

She was deadly quiet for a moment. "All right," she said, keeping her eyes from his. Turning, and working very quickly, she slipped her right arm out of its sleeve as he stood behind her and took hold of the falling flannel. Her back was slender and smooth, her shoulders lovely and frail. He was touched by her delicate beauty.

Shifting the pajama top to the left, he held it forward so she could put her left arm in without moving much. Even so, it seemed to hurt her. He held the right side then, and she reached back to slip her arm in. As he let the fabric fall over her shoulders, he happened to glance up. Across the room was her dresser and mirror. Just before she pulled the garment around to cover herself, he unintentionally caught a glimpse of her, the sweet softly rounded breast and little pink nipple. She was exquisite! He felt guilty perspiration break out on his forehead.

As she was buttoning the top, he quickly stepped around to her left and turned her to face him. He didn't want her to discover that he could have seen her in the mirror. She apparently didn't know and he wanted to keep it that way. "Need some help with the buttons?" he said, trying mentally to calm his racing heartbeat.

"No," she said, backing away from him slightly as she finished. She looked wary and self-conscious.

Maybe he had seemed too forward again, but it was better than having her discover what had really happened. He stepped to the side of her bed then. With shaking hands he took hold of the quilted bedspread and pulled it off, letting it fall in a heap at the foot of the bed.

"Oh, I usually fold it. Well, that's all right," she said.

"Fold it? I can . . ."

"No, no," she said, smiling now. "It's okay."

He let the matter go. He wouldn't have known how to fold the damn thing anyway. Bending, he pulled aside the beige blanket and ivory eyelet-trimmed sheets for her. He caught a faint whiff of a floral fragrance. Sleeping in this bed would be paradise, he thought. For more reasons than one.

She took care getting in, clearly trying to minimize her discomfort. When she tried to lie back on the pillow, her forehead contracted in pain. He placed his hand under her back and eased her down.

"Thank you," she said softly as he arranged the covers over her. "Getting up and lying down is the worst."

"I hope you'll be better tomorrow," he said.

"I'm sure I will be. Good night." She smiled again as she looked up at him.

He smiled back faintly, contemplating for a fraction of a second whether he might kiss her good night. Reason and his deep sense of reality decided him against it. She would be shocked; she wouldn't understand. An instinct told him that she thought of him as some sort of neuter being. It didn't even seem to occur to her that he might be attracted to her as a man is to a woman. He might as well be her grandmother. He turned out her light and left the room, leaving the door slightly ajar so he could hear her if she called.

What does she think of me, really? he wondered as he looked out the window at the black outline of the John Hancock Building with its random sprinkling of lighted windows. She probably didn't think of him, he answered himself. Traffic weaved along the streets below. The city was still active and alive, but Sloane felt half dead inside just now.

But then again . . . She had been awfully skittish that afternoon when he first took her into her bedroom. She must have seen him as a man then. Not a man she was attracted to, obviously, but a man nevertheless. He felt better now, his momentary despair fading. There was hope. He wasn't done with himself or her yet. There was still a long way to go and work to be done, but there would come a day when he wouldn't think twice about kissing her, he promised himself!

He drew the floor-to-ceiling drape closed and went back to the couch. There was still his review of the Oscar nominees to finish and he'd better get it done so he could get it in as soon as he got to work. He had a lot to attend to tomorrow.

About ten o'clock he finished and peeked into Dale's room. She was asleep. He wondered if she'd be all right through the night. It was time he left. His eye fell on the long couch where he had been working on his column. Why not? he thought. There was an alarm on his digital watch. He could get up early, go home and shave, then go to the health club. And there wasn't any other place he'd rather spend the night.

He set his watch, then took off his tie and jacket and threw them over one of the easy chairs. There were a few throw pillows which he rearranged at one end of the couch to suit him. The only problem was, he didn't have a blanket. He supposed he'd have to make do with his suit jacket. Looking around the room, his gaze fell upon a basket next to one of the easy chairs, the one that faced the TV in the corner of the room. There was some sort of knitted material folded neatly in it.

He went over and inspected it. It seemed to be a rectangular piece, big enough to cover him, made in a wavy pattern of yellow, orange, and brown. It would do. As he lifted it out of the basket, two long knitting needles fell onto the carpet. Then he noticed there were large balls of yarn in the same colors at the bottom of the basket. So that was it. She must have made it herself!

He smiled as he took the colorful handiwork to the couch. After turning out the lights, he stretched out and covered himself with it, blissfully content at being enveloped by something she had made with her own hands. He'd settle for that for now.

Dale's eyes fluttered open. Dim light was filtering through the window drape. She looked at the clock on the bedstand. Almost five thirty A.M. After lying still for a few moments, she felt wide awake. She had slept soundly.

As she began to get up, pain on her left side reminded her of her surgery. She tried again, being more careful this time how she moved. Soon she was sitting on the edge of her bed. She felt much better this morning, she realized. It hurt only when she moved the wrong way.

She got up to go to her closet and get her robe. After some

81

difficulty she managed to get on the long, flowing cream-colored garment. Tying the belt at her waist, she walked to the door and opened it. She gasped as she saw Sloane Avery lying asleep on her couch.

What on earth? she thought. Why hadn't he gone home? Perhaps because he was concerned about leaving her alone when she was ill. She hoped that was why. It was kind of him, but she didn't particularly want men staying overnight in her apartment, even if they did sleep on the couch.

Quietly she stepped into the living room. In the dim light she had seen he was covered with something, and when she got closer she realized he was using her unfinished afghan. She saw the metal gleam of the knitting needles on the floor, and then she noticed the unraveled yellow yarn which made a squiggly line from the edge beneath his chin across the carpet to the yellow ball in the basket. She wondered how much of her work had been lost.

Sighing, she turned and went to the window to pull open the drape partway. The pale dawn light brightened the room a little. Suddenly there was a strange, high, intermittent sound coming from somewhere in the room. It disconcerted her a bit until she saw the large watch on Sloane's wrist. She watched him, a smile growing on her face, as it kept on ringing. He didn't seem to hear it at all.

Finally she walked over to the couch and carefully squatted down near his shoulder. "Sloane?"

"Mmmm."

"Sloane. Sloane! Your watch is ringing."

"Hmm?" Slowly his gray eyes opened.

"Wake up!" she said, laughing a little.

At the sound of her soft laugh his eyes went to her face, a look of wonder growing in them. They were silvery again. He stared at her as if mesmerized for a moment. "Am I still dreaming?" he mumbled.

"What?"

He shook his head sharply and rubbed his eyes with his fingertips. Pulling himself up, he leaned his shoulders against the pillows. "Dale, how come you're up so early?" He still sounded groggy, but he was awake.

"Because I went to bed early, I suppose," she answered. "I thought you were going to leave last night."

"I decided to stay in case you needed something. I was going to get up early and go. I didn't think you'd mind."

"That was thoughtful of you, Sloane."

"How do you feel?"

She smiled. "Pretty good!"

"I'm glad. Well, I'd . . . better be leaving. I—" He paused as he pushed aside the afghan. "What's this thread?"

"That's because it's not finished yet. It leads to the ball of yarn over there. See?"

His eyes trailed the wavy yellow line. "Not finished? Oh. Oh, I see, I've unraveled half of it." His face fell. "I'm sorry. I never noticed . . ."

"That's all right. It was only a row or two. I can fix it," she said.

He held the knit material more carefully now. "Here, maybe you'd better take this before I do more damage."

She took it off him and put it aside. He got up from the couch then and ran his fingers hastily through his mussed hair.

"I can make some scrambled eggs," she offered.

"No, I'll just go. I've been working out at a health club first thing every morning and then I eat afterward at a restaurant," he told her.

"Really?" she said with interest. He hadn't struck her as the type who worried about keeping in shape. "How long have you been doing that?"

"Almost a month now. It was sheer misery at first, but I'm getting used to it."

She chuckled. "Wouldn't you like a glass of orange juice at least?"

"Well . . . okay."

They went into the kitchen and Dale switched on the ceiling

83

light. As she got out a carton of orange juice and filled the two glasses he had taken from the cabinet, he asked, "Do you have to work today?"

"No," she said. "When I explained about the surgery they gave me two days off. I won't have to go back until Monday."

As they sipped in silence for a few moments, she made surreptitious glances at him. A full day's growth of beard shadowed the bottom half of his face. His hair was still mussed, incurably it seemed, and his wrinkled shirt draped loosely over his belt. He seemed thinner than she would have imagined. All in all, he looked like a hobo, she thought, straight out of the thirties, William Powell at the beginning of *My Man Godfrey*.

She knew she shouldn't laugh, but she felt a giggle rising within her. If she didn't suppress it, she might find herself in the same situation as she did when she thought he reminded her of Harvey. Unfortunately, she choked on her orange juice and began to cough.

"Are you all right?"

She nodded. "Just . . . went down the wrong pipe."

He set his empty glass on the counter. "I'd better go. Anything I can help you with before I leave?"

"No, I can manage fine today, thanks."

"Can I stop by and see how you're doing tonight? I could bring some dinner," he offered.

She thought a moment. "I have some steaks in the freezer. Frozen vegetables too. How about if I made dinner?"

"You may not feel up to it."

"It's all here, I won't have to shop. It won't be any problem," she said. She felt she ought to repay him somehow for all he'd done.

"You're sure?"

"Sure."

"Okay," he said, a quiet smile in his eyes. "I'll bring some wine."

"All right!" she replied, looking up at him. He did have nice eyes, she noted.

She followed him into the living room, where he picked up his suit coat and tie. Shrugging on the coat, he walked to the door.

"Have a nice day," she said as he was about to leave.

He just stared at her for a moment, his eyes full of ironic humor. "I'll try."

After she'd eaten some breakfast, she fixed the afghan and did a few other little odd jobs. Finally she decided the moment of truth had come. She found the instructions she had been given at the hospital and reread them to make sure. She went into the bathroom then, stood in front of the mirror, and removed her robe and pajama top. Working carefully, she eased the adhesive that held the large bandage in place off her skin.

When it was gone, she was relieved by what she found. Though the incision made a dark red line at the side of her breast, it was only about an inch and a half long. From the huge bandage they had put over it, she had envisioned something much worse. A neat little suture knot was at each end of the incision and it was covered crosswise by three half-inch wide strips of semi-transparent surgical tape, which she was not to remove yet.

Well, that's not so bad, she said to herself. Of course there would be a scar, but once it healed and the redness was gone it wouldn't be so noticeable. It would never be seen on TV in any case! She had her health, and that was what was most important.

Her instructions said she could take a shower, and she did so. Afterward she dressed in slacks and a blouse and walked back into the living room. Her gaze fell on the full-blossomed pink roses on the table, lovely in the morning sunlight. Sloane Avery had brought her flowers. It seemed comical to think of it, after all his needling and the disparaging comments in his column.

She sat down on the couch and looked at the roses, remembering how self-conscious he had been giving them to her. Then she remembered how embarrassed she had been when she couldn't get on her pajama top. She had to be grateful at least that Sloane had handled the situation like a gentleman.

Again, she had to laugh. Sloane Avery was one of the last

persons she would have described as having gentlemanly qualities.

Sloane was approaching the main entrance of the Herald Building, feeling good after his workout and a light breakfast. He only wished Dale hadn't seen him so grubby-looking that morning. When he'd gone home to shave, he'd been ready to kick himself when he first looked in the mirror. He was glad he had decided to finally do something about his clothes today, not that he was looking forward to it.

Suddenly, in the rush hour crowd, he noticed a stylish woman in her mid-fifties wearing a tailored red suit with black trim and a matching hat. She was moving toward the revolving door.

"Myrna!" he called. As she turned, he grinned. "Just the person I wanted to see!"

"Hi, Sloane," she said, breaking into a smile as she waited for him to catch up. A long black feather, which ornamented her hat, stylishly held its own in the sharp wind. "Why would you want to see me? No, don't tell me. You want to know what Christian Dior and Pierre Cardin are showing in men's fashions this spring. It'll be in my column tomorrow."

Sloane's smile changed to a partial smirk. "Maybe I *would* be interested," he said. Myrna Lowry, the *Herald*'s fashion editor, was tough and brassy in an elegant sort of way, and he liked her.

Myrna laughed heartily. "That'll be the day! I'll bet you still wear the suit you graduated high school in!"

"It's too tight on me," he said. She laughed again. "That's what I wanted to talk to you about," he continued. "I've decided to get some new clothes. In the past you've offered to go along with me if I would. I know you were just joking, but . . ."

Myrna's sharp hazel eyes brightened. "You mean you're actually going to enter a clothing store and buy something new? Why, I'd love to go! I've been itching to get my hands on your wardrobe for the past five years. Seeing you ambling around the building in your morbid old suits is . . ."

"All right, all right. So you've told me. When can you go with me? Today, maybe?"

The fashion editor's alert, attractive features were still for an instant as she apparently ran her schedule through her head. "Sounds possible. Around one?"

"That would be good. How about if I return the favor and buy you lunch?" Sloane said.

"Now, that's an inducement," she said in a mocking tone. "A hot dog at the dime store?"

"Myrna, you know I like to eat well. What do you mean?" he retorted.

"That's true, you do, don't you?" she agreed. "But I thought you've been brown-bagging it lately, for your diet."

"I'll make an exception today. Anyplace you name, Myrna," he said magnanimously.

"I don't know if the places I like would let you in with that shirt and tie combination, not to mention the dilapidated suit," she said. She looked with a hopeless eye at his paisley tie and striped shirt that were in colors that did not blend well. Her gaze fell to his baggy pants. "You *have* been losing weight, haven't you?"

"Seventeen pounds," he said, motioning them toward the revolving door.

They went into the imposing marble-floored lobby of the old Herald Building. "Shall I come by your office about one then?" he asked before they parted.

"Fine. I'll arrange to take the afternoon off. Outfitting you will be a major job."

"I'm looking forward to it," he said in a tone that meant exactly the opposite.

They met as planned and walked up North Michigan Avenue. After going up a few floors in a glass elevator, they had lunch at a Continental-style restaurant at elegant Water Tower Place. The menu had many tantalizing choices. Sloane settled for roast chicken, a baked potato, and a green salad, no dressing. No dessert either. He watched Myrna eat her chocolate eclair, telling himself he was full.

As she ate she kept eyeing his mismatched shirt and tie, wincing slightly. Finally, she said, "Sloane, how can you have lived this long and still know as little as you do about clothes?"

"It's just a matter of where a person's interests lie. Do you know who plays first base for the Cubs?"

"No," she admitted.

"Do you give a damn?"

"Okay, I see your point. So," she said, after pausing to sip her coffee, "how much do you want to buy? Or maybe I should ask how much do you want to spend?"

"Oh, I'm willing to spend whatever's reasonable. Money isn't a problem."

"Since you're a bachelor, I wouldn't think so. Not with your good salary. It looks like you haven't spent anything on clothes for the past ten years anyway," she said.

"I've bought new undershirts now and then," he said, smiling at her needling.

"Through a catalog, no doubt. What type of look do you want?"

"Look?" he said, his expression confused.

She smiled patiently. "You could try glancing at my column occasionally. Do you want your clothes to be conservative and businesslike? Or do you want to be trendy? Are you out to impress women?"

Sloane's brows drew together. Why did it have to be so complicated? "Well . . . conservative, I think. I don't mind if I look good to women too."

"That may be difficult," she said. "It's tricky to do both. A dark gray pinstripe suit is ideal for the business world, but most women wouldn't be particularly turned on by it. Actually, for your job, your clothes don't matter as much as if you worked for IBM, for example." She laughed at herself. "Obviously not! You've been a successful critic all these years dressed as you are. Do you have a priority? To dress for business or women?"

Sloane's color changed slightly. "Women, I suppose."

"Ah-ha!" Myrna said. "Is that by any chance why you're trying to lose weight too?"

"Maybe." He was becoming slightly irritated at her questions.

"Looking for a wife, I hope? I think you need one," she said, suddenly sounding rather motherly. Sloane knew she had a husband and two grown sons.

"*I* may need one, but a wife probably doesn't need *me*," he said a little sourly.

She looked at him in surprise. "Why do you say that? In spite of the way you dress, I hear you've had several women after you over the years."

"Yeah, that's true," he agreed, his eyes downcast, his voice world-weary. "There's a type of woman who is very attracted to power and fame. I may not be a household word everywhere, but in Chicago, at least, I'm something of a celebrity. Those women are more drawn to what I do than they are to me. I could look like King Kong and they'd be interested. And now and then there's always an aspiring actress who gets it into her head that I can somehow pull strings for her, which isn't true. I don't lead any of them on, but even so, some of them make me offers I—I haven't been able to keep myself from refusing. I'm getting damned tired of it all. I'd like someone permanent in my life, who really cares about me, and whom I really care about too."

Myrna's inquisitive eyes were glued to his face. "Have you met someone in particular, Sloane?"

He kept his eyes fixed on the tablecloth and said nothing.

"You have, haven't you!" she exclaimed. "Who is it? Anyone I know?"

Sloane shrugged enigmatically.

"Let's see, whom could it be?" Myrna wondered aloud, obviously relishing the puzzle.

"You'd never guess," he said, hoping to put her off the subject.

"I'd never guess? That's interesting. I know! Dale Chastain," she said with a grin.

Sloane looked up at her abruptly, his color changing again, his face in semi-shock.

"You're kidding," Myrna said. "It's not really her! I was just joking."

Sloane compressed his lips and threw down his napkin. He hadn't wanted anyone to know.

"So that's why you were picking on her in your column," Myrna surmised. "I couldn't figure it out; you'd never written about local people before. Are you dating her?"

"No, not really."

"Ah, but you'd like to, is that it? Is she attracted to you?"

"Probably not."

"Well, after what you said about her, I can understand . . ."

"Look, Myrna, I just want you to help me choose some clothes. I'd go to the letters from the lovelorn department if I wanted advice."

Myrna smiled to herself. "All right. Well, knowing you're trying to impress Dale Chastain makes things a lot simpler. All we have to do is dress you like Rhett Butler!"

"Very funny."

Two hours later in a rather exclusive men's store that Myrna had suggested, Sloane felt that he was being put through cruel and unusual punishment. He had always hated shopping, especially for clothes. He found stores oppressive somehow and never went near the huge and inevitably crowded department stores along State Street. He'd always get annoyed with pushy salespeople. He detested having to make decisions on items of clothing he'd need to wear for some time, when he had no knowledge of what was in style, what went together, and what looked good on him. He knew what a well-dressed man ought to look like—he saw them in movies all the time. But he had no idea how to go about making himself look like that. It was why he had asked Myrna along; she knew everything he didn't.

What he hadn't expected was that Myrna would be so unbelievably meticulous about it all—the quality of the material, the

90

shade, the cut, the pattern. So far they had selected only two suits. One suit an hour, Sloane calculated. He'd tried on dozens, and those only after careful selection. Even the salespeople were growing tired of Myrna's nitpicking. She had shocked them by taking the sleeve of each suit she looked at and crushing it hard in her hand to see how resilient the material was to wrinkles. When he had quietly objected to it, she said, "Listen, Sloane, with the sloppy way you take care of your clothes, you need something a steamroller couldn't wrinkle."

What could he say? She was right. Meanwhile, she'd also told him he needed new shoes, and she'd insisted that he put on a new pale beige shirt and dark tie from the store so she could better judge each suit he tried on. "Why don't you just throw those in the garbage," she'd said when he brought out the shirt and tie he'd come in wearing. And once she'd finally decided on a suit, she watched the store's tailor with a hawk's eye as he marked it for the necessary adjustments.

"Maybe two suits are enough, Myrna," Sloane suggested hopefully when the tailor had finished marking the second one, a dark blue wool with a barely visible plaid in its weave. "I'm getting a little tired . . ."

"Tired! We've only just begun!" she said. "*I'm* having a wonderful time. You asked for my help; you're going to get it! When Dale sees the new you, you'll be glad, believe me." He decided not to argue.

By closing time Sloane was bleary-eyed and exhausted. Myrna had, with infuriating preciseness, selected four three-piece suits, two blazers with coordinating trousers, two shirts for each suit and blazer, and he'd forgotten how many ties, all carefully chosen for shade, quality, and pattern. She had also helped him choose some casual clothing.

"Myrna, how do I know what goes with what when I get all this stuff home?" he asked while he was waiting for the salesman to return his credit card.

"Well, that should be obvious." She looked at him again. "No, I suppose it isn't to you. All right, I'll write it down for you at home tonight—make you a diagram. You're going to look great. You look better already with the new shirt and tie. Too bad you have to wait for the suits to be altered, but that can't be helped. One more thing though. You have *got* to get a better haircut. I'm going to give you the name of a place to go." She began opening her purse.

"I go to the barber in the building next to us. I thought he was pretty good," Sloane objected.

"Pretty good won't be good enough for these new clothes. Here," she said, handing him a card. "This place is marvelous. Now, you have to call to make an appointment. You can't just walk in like you can with a barber. In fact, you'll probably have to wait a week or more. When you call, ask for Marlene."

"Marlene! A woman?"

Myrna seemed to be swallowing a chuckle. "Sloane, even you must know that for the past decade or more there have been salons that do both men's *and* women's hair."

"You mean there'll be women customers too? No way, Myrna. I wouldn't be caught dead . . ."

"There'll be men there getting haircuts too. Don't be so old-fashioned!"

Old-fashioned! he thought stubbornly. And then he remembered Dale saying he was set in his ways. "I'm going to feel like a fool," he said grudgingly.

"You won't when you come out of there. Look, *I'll* call Marlene and make the appointment. That way I can prepare her for you!"

Dale had the table in her small apartment set and the steaks thawed and ready to go when her doorbell rang. She let Sloane in. He appeared carrying a bottle of red wine and a two-pound box of Auntie Kay's chocolates and presented her with both.

"Thank you for the wine, Sloane," she said, smiling, "but I didn't expect candy too." She was a little taken aback. It had been thoughtful of him to buy her flowers yesterday after her

92

surgery, but now chocolates too? He was beginning to behave like a suitor in some ways, and it worried her a little.

"That's the Plantation Assortment. I thought you'd like it."

"Plantation?" she said. "That's cute."

"It has more nuts than the other assortments do," Sloane explained.

"Oh, I see, like Georgia pecans? I didn't have anything much to serve for dessert, so this will be nice."

As she led him into her small kitchen he asked, "How do you feel?"

"I've been a little tired all day, but that's all. I thought I'd let you put the steaks on the broiler. Do you mind?"

An hour later they were finishing up their meal at a small, round polished wood table that stood in one corner of the living room. He was talking about his job, but as she listened Dale couldn't help eyeing his tie. It was of solid-colored charcoal silk, and looked rather elegant with its soft, expensive sheen. The thing was, it didn't fit with his old paunchy suit at all. He had taken his jacket off earlier, and now the tie looked a little more at home against the trim, tapered ecru shirt he wore underneath. The shirt was also unexpectedly fine and well-tailored compared to what she was used to seeing him wear. It accentuated very nicely his large masculine frame, with his broad shoulders and solid chest. She was sure now he was thinner than he used to be. The comfortable teddy bear look was beginning to fade.

But his hair was still unruly, as though combing it made little difference, and with that and his old rumpled suit, he was still Sloane. The classic tie and shirt were like a neat, freshly painted white picket fence around a yard of high weeds, and for some reason it bothered her. He was always doing things she couldn't explain, but she instinctively sensed there was something very basic that was changing here. Some mystic inner voice told her there might be more to it than she was ready or willing to deal with.

"That's a nice tie, Sloane," she said when there was a lull in their conversation.

She was surprised at his reaction. His eyes widened and he seemed speechless for a fraction of a second. "Thanks," he said softly, smiling a little now. He reached for his recently refilled cup of coffee. A drop spilled onto his cuff as he brought it to his mouth. At least the shirt looked more like it belonged to him now.

"I don't think I've seen you wear it before. It must be new." She wondered what made her prod him. It shouldn't make any difference to her if he had a new tie.

"It is."

Now she felt annoyed with him for not elaborating. "Would you like some more?" she asked, pointing toward the vegetable platter.

"No thanks. This has been great. Time for dessert." He got up and walked over to the coffee table where the box of Auntie Kay's had been left. He handed it to Dale as he took his seat again.

Dale removed the distinctive paper wrapping and carefully opened the glossy white box. "Mmm. Smells wonderful!" she said as she gazed over the assortment of chocolates, caramels, and special pieces. "I always wish I could tell what's inside the chocolate ones."

"You can tell by the shape and by the squiggles in the chocolate." He pointed with his finger. "This one here, for example, is walnut nougat. This has caramel inside. This long one here is coconut cream."

"Oh," she said with genuine interest. It astonished her that he seemed to be so well-acquainted with them. "It's going to be hard to choose."

"Well, I'll tell you the best piece in the whole box. This one right here." He pointed at one of the few colored candies, one that was cream-hued and round.

"That one? I think I'd prefer chocolate," she said.

"It is. Inside." There was restrained excitement in his voice, the way some men might speak of a new car they had just bought. "The center is chocolate fudge, very smooth and rich. It's out of this world."

He certainly sounded like he knew. "Maybe you'd like it," she said, moving the box toward him.

His face changed. "No. No, I'm not having any." He pushed himself back from the table a little. "You go ahead."

"But you brought them. You've got to have one, at least," she said as she picked the cream-colored one out of the box.

"Nope." He got up then and began removing their plates. "I'll put these in the kitchen for you."

She watched him. Obviously he loved chocolates and she had to admire his will power. After she had bitten into the candy, she had to admire his strength of character even more. It tasted every bit as heavenly as he'd said it would.

Dale followed it with the coconut cream and then decided she'd better exercise some will power of her own. They were deliciously addicting. She closed the box and carried the last few dishes on the table into the kitchen. Sloane was already scraping and rinsing those he'd taken in.

As they loaded them into the dishwasher, she asked Sloane, "You look thinner. Have you been losing weight?"

"Some, yes." He looked self-conscious.

"It looks good. Are you following a diet?"

"Yup."

"And that's why you didn't take any candy."

"You got it."

She laughed. "You must be trying to fatten me up, then, bringing me a two-pound box to finish by myself!"

He carefully eyed her figure, trimly clothed in navy pants and a clingy plaid gauze blouse. "No. You look just fine as you are. I bet you never gain weight." His gray eyes hovered over her bosom before coming up to meet her eyes. It made her breath catch in her throat momentarily.

It was the first time he had ever looked her over so blatantly, and it unsettled her. Beneath all the clever needling, all the intellectual sarcasm, and his good-Samaritan behavior of the last couple of days, there was a very basic man with all too typical male thought patterns. Except for his age, high intelligence, and rumpled-teddy-bear looks, it seemed he might merely be a restrained Gary Murdock. Was sex actually what had been on his mind all these weeks he'd been sparring with her? Was that why he had turned nice lately, why he was here now, chocolates in hand? After admiring his column all these years, especially his enlightened comments about women, she'd somehow thought he'd be above such obvious ogling.

She turned away, grabbed a wet dishcloth, and began wiping up the counter. Maybe she was being unfair, she thought. If she found him more sexy, instead of just big and sort of cuddly-looking, perhaps she wouldn't think twice about his looking at her that way. Over the years she'd gotten used to men's roving eyes. But from Sloane it seemed so unexpected.

"Is something wrong?" he asked, apparently wondering at her silence.

"What? No, you're right, I don't tend to gain weight. Just born with the right metabolism, I guess," she said breezily, covering her temporary distraction by pretending to be busy with the dishrag.

"You're lucky!"

"I know. Well, I guess we're finished in here. Would you like to sit in the living room for a while?"

What was she going to do with him for the rest of the evening? she asked herself as they walked into the next room. Watch TV? It was Friday night too. Neither of them had to work tomorrow, which meant he'd be in no hurry to leave. He'd better not have any thoughts of staying over like he did last night.

As she reluctantly sat down with him on the sofa, she reached over to pick up the TV listing book from last Sunday's *Herald*. Her eyes widened as she glanced over the Friday night offerings. "What do you know! They're showing *Gigi* tonight."

"Whoopdeedoo," Sloane said sarcastically.

"You don't like that movie? It won several Academy Awards back in 1958."

96

"Fluff and nonsense," he said. "Music's nice, I suppose."

"What about the acting? Louis Jourdan, for example, is wonderful."

"That skinny Frenchman?" Sloane said dismissively.

"What's his weight got to do with his acting ability? Besides, I think he's very handsome," Dale said, growing annoyed. *Gigi* was one of her all-time favorite movies.

Sloane made a belabored sigh. "Well, put it on. I'm ready for an after-dinner snooze anyway."

Why don't you go home then! she thought. She got up to turn on the TV.

It was about ten minutes into the movie. As she walked back from the television, she decided to take the chair where her knitting basket was. It was where she usually sat when watching TV, and she wanted to avoid Sloane and the couch. After the industrious way he'd studied every curve of her figure, who knew what ideas might be lurking in his head? She was irritated with his comments about the movie anyway. From the corner of her eye she saw Sloane glance at her as she took the chair, leaving him alone in the middle of the couch. She had a slight attack of conscience.

"I'm trying to finish this afghan to send to my grandmother for her birthday," she said, picking it up from the basket. "She'll be eighty next month."

"That's nice," he said dryly.

They watched the movie in silence for a long while, Sloane apparently deciding to stay awake. After a scene where young Gigi is tutored by her aunt in how to behave like a gentleman's lady, Sloane suddenly said, "I'd forgotten how good Leslie Caron was as Gigi. She's really charming!"

Dale glanced at Sloane, a faint look of betrayal in her eyes. *Charming* was the word he'd used to describe her in his column. It was the one nice thing he'd had to say about her. But now she realized it was a term he apparently used easily and lightly, and his having applied it to her suddenly didn't mean much anymore. As Dale's shoulders sagged a bit in disappointment, she tried to tell herself that what Sloane Avery thought of her didn't matter anyway. The pompous, sloppy, irritating man!

As they sat through the rest of the movie, Dale was glad the film had no love scenes. She didn't need to cope with that, too, alone with Sloane in her living room. As Maurice Chevalier's voice thanking heaven for little girls faded away at the end of the movie, Dale got up to turn it off.

"Aren't you going to watch the news?" Sloane said as she hit the Off button. "Put it on WNBS."

She did as he asked, wondering where he got the nerve to tell her what to do in her own apartment. She went back to her chair and her knitting.

"How about some coffee? I'll make it," Sloane said.

Dale sighed to herself. She was hoping he'd be getting ready to go home. Drinking coffee would only delay him. "Sure," she said. "The coffee can is out on the counter." Why did she always go along with what he wanted? she asked herself as he went into the kitchen. In spite of his abrasive manner and untidy appearance, there was a natural air of authority about him.

She heard the automatic drip coffeemaker start, and in a few minutes he came in with two cups and saucers. He put them on the low table, then came back with the coffee and filled each cup to the very brim. "Maybe you'd better sit here on the couch," he said. "You can't reach the table from over there."

He was right, she thought resentfully. She got up from her chair and moved to the couch to sit next to him, taking her knitting along with her as if for protection.

On TV Steve Froebisher mentioned that Dale Chastain had taken the day off, but would be back on Monday. They moved on to the sports report and then more news.

"The show's kind of dead without you," Sloane said as he picked up his cup and saucer. The hot liquid washed over the edge of the full cup and into the dish.

She paused in her knitting. "Thanks," she said, a little surprised at the sudden compliment. She saw him bring the cup of coffee to his lips. The steaming clear brown liquid must have

98

burned his mouth as he tipped it to his lips. "Sloane, be careful.
. . ." But it was too late. "Oh, no, you dripped coffee on your
tie."

"I did?" he said, looking down. Dale was already up, getting
a paper napkin in the kitchen which Sloane apparently hadn't
thought of bringing out. "Here," she said, coming back with it.
She sat down next to him again and began blotting the coffee,
which had already begun to soak into the silk material. "You'll
probably have to have it cleaned," she said, shaking her head.
"You shouldn't have taken such a large sip."

"They're such tiny cups, I misjudged. They hold only half a
teaspoon," he said. "I'm used to mugs."

The bone china cup did look small in his big hand. He put it
back on the table. "It's all I brought with me from Georgia. I'm
sorry about your tie," she said, glancing up at him as she made
one last dab at the streak of wetness in the material.

His gray eyes had a smiling, intimate quality as he looked
down at her. The unusual inner light she'd seen before was
coming into them again. "Don't be sorry. It was worth it," he
said softly.

She drew her hand away then, realizing she had been touching
his chest as she blotted the tie. Looking away, she crumbled the
paper napkin into a ball in her fist. Suddenly she felt his fingers
closing over her other hand.

"Thanks for your concern," he said.

"Th-that's all right," she said quickly as her heart began to
pound. Why was he holding her hand? He picked it up and
looked at it closely, gently moving his thumb over the soft
smooth skin of its back. A warm tingling sensation crept up her
arm. Involuntarily she held her breath at the feeling.

"Such a little hand," he said. He turned it over and studied
her palm. "I wish I could read fortunes. I'd like to know who's
in your future."

With a tentative movement she pulled her hand away from
his. "Why would you want to know that?" she said, a slight

sharpness in her tone. The subtle reactions within her were confusing. She didn't want to deal with it.

He was silent for a moment. "Just curiosity." His voice was indifferent now, ever so slightly annoyed. Leaning forward, he took a few gulps of coffee and set the cup down. "I guess I ought to be going." He rose from the sofa and Dale did, too, putting aside the afghan. "Thanks for dinner."

"You're welcome," Dale said in automatic response. She felt a little disoriented. Though she had been hoping he'd leave soon, he was doing it so abruptly now she felt as if she had offended him. She hadn't wanted to do that exactly. It was just that he made her so unsettled.

She followed him to the door. He said, "I imagine I'll be seeing you around." His tone was cold.

"Sure." She didn't know how to respond to that.

"Good-bye."

"'Bye." After he'd walked out, she stood there looking at her closed door for a moment. She felt like she'd gotten the brush-off. Never in a million years would she understand that man.

Outside, in the hall, Sloane waited morosely for the elevator. He still hadn't gotten to first base with her. She was as wary as a cat around him and it had made him angry again. He wanted to show her he didn't care if she rejected him. As if that would make any difference to her.

The trouble was he did care, more and more with each time he saw her. She was like a glittering little jewel, always just out of his reach, beautiful, delicate, and rare. Just touching her hand made him feel like a klutz. What a combination they made— Tinkerbell and the Cookie Monster. Well, he wasn't giving up yet, not after all he'd invested today in a new wardrobe. But he had to wonder if it was even remotely possible for the Cookie Monster to turn into Prince Charming.

On Monday Dale went back to work. Her co-workers were solicitous, most having heard that she had had to have surgery. As soon as she could she called Dr. Whittaker's office. "Oh, yes,

Miss Chastain, I was about to call you," the secretary said. "Your biopsy report is negative." Smiling joyfully, Dale thanked her and hung up. Dr. Whittaker had said he thought her lump was benign, but now it was certain. Now she had nothing more to worry about.

She was looking over her week's schedule when Gary Murdock came over to her desk. He was carrying a rose wrapped in green florist's paper.

"Hi. I heard you had some surgery. How'd it go?" he asked, as if he'd been concerned about her. She was surprised after the argument they'd had.

"Just fine."

"That's good. I got this for you."

"Thank you," she said, not a little astonished.

"Glad to see you back. Someone said it was a breast biopsy?" he asked, sounding innocent.

"Yes," she said, drawing out the word. She put the flower down on her desk.

"I hope things turned out okay."

"I just found out for sure it was benign."

"I'm glad. You don't look any the worse for it," he said, leaning insidiously against her desk and leering down at her attributes.

"Yes, well, the biopsy did leave an ugly red scar," she told him, keeping herself from smiling. Maybe she'd found something that would finally put him off. She thought he'd given up on her, but obviously he hadn't.

"Wouldn't bother me, sugar," he said, grinning comfortably. Her cheeks reddened. "How about lunch today?"

She took a breath to brace herself. "I thought you said you weren't going to waste your time on me anymore."

"Spoken in haste, sweetheart," he said softly, even a little wistfully. "I got impatient, that's all. But I'm willing to wait as long as it takes. And maybe you were upset, knowing you had that surgery to go through."

Oh, good grief! Dale thought. *That wasn't the problem at all. The male ego can certainly find excuses!*

"I'm really hung up on you, Dale," he went on. "I don't admit that to a chick often. But you're a special lady."

I thought he just said I was a chick.

"And someday you're going to be my lady. I've got my mind set. And when Gary Murdock sets his mind on something, things happen. It's only a matter of time. How about lunch?"

"No thanks, Gary. And I think you'd better give up your—"

"Come on, sugar. What have you got to lose? Lunch is safe. I can't seduce you then! It'll be nice." His tone was easy and rather persuasive.

Dale wasn't buying it. "I'm not interested, Gary. Sorry."

He bowed his head and was silent a moment. "All right. I'll wait." He picked up the flower and put it nearer her hand on the desk. "Meanwhile, enjoy your rose." With that he got up and walked away.

She picked up the red flower and looked at it. Lately it seemed as though men were coming out of the woodwork with roses for her. Gary Murdock's change in approach worried her. She thought he had looked upon her mainly as a sexual conquest, but now he'd sounded as though he had some real feeling behind his pursuit. Unfortunately she had absolutely no feeling for him.

The phone rang once again and Dale was beginning to think it was her morning for interruptions. "Hello?"

A rather hesitant, somewhat distant, male voice responded. "Dale? It's Sloane. I just wanted to know if you got that final report about your biopsy yet."

"Why, yes," she said, a little surprised. A warm feeling came over her in spite of his cool tone. It was sweet that he had called to ask, especially in view of the way they had parted the other night. "I just phoned my doctor's office about it. They said I'm fine."

"Good. Good," he said. She heard the faint tone of relief in his voice. "Well . . . good-bye."

Again she found herself a little startled. "Good-bye. Thank you for asking," she hurried to add.

"Well, after going through the surgery with you, I just . . ." His words trailed off. "I have to get back to work. Be seeing you."

"Okay," she replied, smiling at his abruptness.

"Okay, good-bye then."

"'Bye." She was laughing a little as she hung up the phone. He was the most unpredictable person. As she pondered a moment, she thought that, odd as it seemed, she'd rather have Sloane Avery in love with her than have Gary Murdock. But with her career taking total precedence in her life, as it had for the last several years, she did not particularly want anyone in love with her.

Over the next few days there was much discussion about resuming plans for Dale's postponed trip to England. The director of *Ivanhoe* was to go back to work on location in a day or two. Dale anxiously held her breath, waiting for the station manager and George Ellis to make up their minds.

At last one evening on both the five o'clock and the ten o'clock news, Dale made the following announcement after her nightly review. "I'll be flying next Tuesday to England," she told Steve and Andrea in their planned on-the-air chit-chat. "To Manchester; It's close to the Lake District, where I'll be visiting the *Ivanhoe* set and interviewing the director and the stars, John Trevor and Velvet Hunt. I'm really looking forward to it," she said with a bright, genuine smile.

The only thing that dampened her enthusiasm was a few days later when George Ellis informed her that her crew would consist of Hal Santini, serving as her sound man, and Gary Murdock as cameraman. Well, she couldn't hope for everything to be perfect. At least the crew would be flying out a day ahead, so she wouldn't have to be on the long flight with Gary trying to impose himself on her. England was going to be beautiful even with him around, she assured herself.

* * *

An unfamiliar man looked back at Sloane Avery from the full-length mirror that was a sliding door to his bedroom closet. This man looked fit, trim, immaculate. Even debonair.

What had happened? Sloane asked himself uncomfortably, reaching out of habit to push his hair back from his forehead. As he ruffled his fingers through it, it felt as though there were very little left of it. Marlene had certainly done a job on him. "I'll give you a cut that takes advantage of your natural wave and will never look mussed. You can just shake your head and it will fall into place," she'd told him. What could he say? He'd have been foolish to say no to that, particularly after Myrna's recommendation.

Everyone had teased him when he'd come to the office that afternoon. Myrna was the only one who seemed to approve wholeheartedly. "It's because they're not used to seeing you look good," Myrna had told him. "It probably makes them a little nervous—you seem like a different person. But in a few days they won't remember what you used to look like. Some will begin to treat you differently too. Being well-dressed influences people, whether they're aware of it or not. You'll have to go through an adjustment, but you'll get used to it."

Myrna's words ran through his mind as he looked at himself. Adjustment was right. He had gotten his altered suits from the store yesterday, and nothing he'd worn today was old and familiar to him. Except for his hair. And after his appointment with Marlene that morning, even that was taken away. The longish brown hair that used to fall over his forehead was clipped short and stood away from his scalp as though it had been slightly curled. He'd thought it looked silly.

And then there was his suit, pressed and perfect above his shiny new shoes. He had put on the blue one with the faint plaid in its weave. Following Myrna's written instructions, he'd worn the solid pale blue shirt and bold plaid tie that she said coordinated with that suit. He supposed they did; they looked good together. But not on him. He felt like a live mannekin. It had been all he could do just to walk out on the street that way, looking so obviously slick, as though he were deliberately trying to attract attention to himself. Though he'd had to admit as he walked downtown, no one had particularly noticed.

And so along with the new wardrobe came his new haircut, and now, Myrna had told him, he was finished being made over. Finished was the truth! Where, pray tell, was the old Sloane Avery beneath all this finery? How could he be himself looking like this?

Had he made the right move? he wondered morbidly. What would Dale think? Dale. That was another problem. How could he pack all this stuff in suitcases and keep it looking good?

He'd better call Myrna.

CHAPTER FIVE

Excited and filled with a sense of adventure, Dale found her way to the correct international airline counter. It was mid-afternoon. She had been to the massive maze that was O'Hare Airport a few times before, but never to begin a trip across the ocean. Taking a place at the end of the line for the ticket counter, she set down her suitcase, tote bag, and raincoat, slightly out of breath from physical exertion and anticipation. She unbuttoned the jacket of her wool tweed suit and tucked in the coordinated green-blue blouse which had pulled out from the waistband a bit.

After several minutes in the slow-moving line, a number of people extended the queue behind her. She was checking her plane tickets and passport once again when she heard: "It's always nice to run into an old friend in a long line."

The voice was bewilderingly familiar. So was the face, she discovered when she looked up. And yet, for a few confusing seconds, she couldn't place the gray-eyed man staring down at her with such a delighted smile on his lips.

"Mind if I cut in front of you?" he said, edging in as the woman ahead of her moved forward with the line. He was carrying a suit bag and a medium-size suitcase. He set the suitcase down next to Dale's matching red luggage and draped his suit bag over all three. It was about this time that Dale finally realized what was happening.

"Sloane . . . I didn't know you!" she said, her voice weak and her expression almost gaping. "You look so different." She smiled slightly. "I mean, you look so . . . *neat* . . . and . . ." She had almost said *handsome* but caught herself.

He smiled and averted his eyes from hers. "After eight or nine hours on the plane, I imagine I'll look more like my usual self," he said, as if slightly embarrassed.

"That blazer is just beautiful," Dale said, almost reaching out to touch the fine material. It was a solid dark blue jacket, which he wore with gray pants, a burgundy tie, and a white shirt with blue and burgundy pinstripes. It was conservatively casual, with the deep wine-red giving it a splash of color. The contrast of the white in his shirt with the dark colors and his naturally deep skin tone was especially striking.

But Dale could see Sloane's well-groomed appearance was not just a matter of color coordination. The clothes fit him beautifully, giving his once bulky figure a very masculine grace and elegance of line in spite of the fact that he was still quite a large man. The cut of the coat emphasized his broad shoulders by tapering smoothly all around to his narrow waistline. The lapels and tie stood out slightly from his deep chest, giving a hint of pride in his bearing.

Perhaps the most astonishing change was his hair. Gone was the unruly hair that seemed to have a mind of its own. Ordinarily Dale preferred longer hair on men, but it was clear this shorter style was perfect for Sloane. Not only did it look neater on him, but it was much more suited to his broad face and large facial features. Suddenly he looked as intelligent as he was. And, Dale noted, now he looked as young as he really was too.

After taking a few moments to analyze all the outer changes in Sloane, her increasingly unsteady heartbeat made her realize she had better begin to monitor her own reactions. Why was she suddenly so breathless and at a loss for words? Why did she feel so shaken, and so shy? He was still only Sloane Avery, the man she had wished out of her apartment over a week ago.

She swallowed. Bending, she helped Sloane push their luggage ahead as the line moved forward. She had been kidding herself, hadn't she? He had never been *only* Sloane. He was the brilliant movie critic whose column she had admired for years before she ever met him. And, though she tried hard to ignore it, he had become even more than that. All at once she didn't want to analyze herself anymore. What was he doing here anyway? she wondered in sudden, illogical annoyance.

"Are you going to Manchester too?" she asked him, a quiver of panic running up her spine at the possibility.

"Why else would I be in this line carrying luggage?" he said.

"But . . . why? Oh. I suppose your paper sent you to cover *Ivanhoe* too." She looked up at him for verification. He shrugged nonchalantly and she took it to mean yes. "Are you staying in the Lake District then? Windermere?"

"Probably."

Probably? That was an odd answer. Wouldn't his paper have made lodging arrangements for him as her station had for her? Well, it wasn't any of her business. She just hoped they wouldn't be at the same hotel. She didn't want any distractions from her work. Having to deal with Gary Murdock was enough; she didn't need Sloane Avery trying to hold her hand too. She remembered the last time he'd been in her apartment. Worry puckered her forehead. This was too much to deal with—her first trip abroad, her first big reporting assignment, and now a suddenly appealing Sloane Avery was going to be close by.

"Have you been to England before?" she asked.

"Several times. The Lake District is one of my favorite spots. I vacationed there a couple of years ago."

"Really?" she said with envy. "This is only *my* first trip."

"Well, I'll have to show you around a little!"

They pushed their luggage forward for the last time as they finally came to the counter. Sloane handed the agent his ticket and passport. "The lady and I would like to sit together," he said, indicating Dale with a gesture of his hand.

Dale was taken by surprise. That they might sit together on the plane hadn't even occurred to her. With no time to consider the idea, she handed over her own ticket. *Oh, good Lord!* she thought. *Eight hours next to Sloane Avery!* What sort of state of mind would she be in when they arrived in England? She pictured herself exhausted from lack of sleep and her brains scrambled from coping with him for eight hours straight. It quickly was occurring to her that perhaps she ought to object. But she could think of no polite and acceptable reason to do so. Besides, the ticket agent had already made the arrangement and was writing up their boarding passes.

Their cargo luggage was weighed and put on the conveyor belt. Dale and Sloane picked up their remaining baggage and found their way to the proper terminal gate. They waited there for some time until it was announced they could board the plane. At last they were settled in two seats between an aisle and a window. Having stowed his own luggage, Sloane helped her push her tote bag under the seat in front of her.

Both watched out the window some minutes later as their plane moved to a runway and then, at last, took off. The distractions of boarding and getting under way over with, Dale's mind began to dwell on Sloane's unexpected presence. She looked over at him. The seat belt signs had just gone off, and he was unfastening the heavy black band around his hips. The movement of his hands at the buckle attracted her eye. She felt a sudden physical sensation in her abdomen, astonishing her, like a flame that had spontaneously kindled. Oh, this was going to be more than she was prepared to deal with, she thought in a wave of silent panic. She swallowed and caught a grip on her unruly sensual reactions, but she couldn't take her eyes from his hands.

She didn't know why she hadn't noticed them before. Perhaps it was because the crisp cuffs of his shirt, which extended just the right length beyond his jacket sleeves, set off his large masculine hands beautifully. She hadn't realized they were so handsomely formed, with long, molded fingers and broad, angular backs that had a smooth sprinkling of dark brown hair. After thinking a moment, she remembered vaguely that his fingers used to be more fleshy and soft-looking. Apparently the general slimming of his body had also extended to his limbs. Now there was no other way to describe his hands but sexy.

As he finished unbuckling the seat belt, her eyes traveled up his shirt front to the collar. Her heartbeat quickened again and she was aware of a slight, helpless, sinking feeling. The sharp white of the collar had the same contrast with the smooth, dark skin of his strong neck. The effect was so sensually tantalizing, she almost felt as if she had been stung.

She was still mesmerized as he turned his face toward her. Only half aware of his gaze, her eyes moved up to his firm jaw and chin and then to his mouth with its manly contours. His lips were neither too full nor too thin and looked hard and set, but not so much so that it kept her from wanting to reach up with her finger to see how they would feel to the touch.

Suddenly her senses told her he was aware of her stare and her eyes rose to his. The look in the gray depths told her he was more than aware. There was a sureness in his eyes and a profound happiness she'd never seen in him before. It was as though he felt he had won some triumph over her. Quickly she drew her guard back into place. She purposely moved her gaze over his hair, studying the top and sides.

"You got a new haircut, didn't you?" she asked with very casual interest.

His expression changed slightly, but he didn't appear to be fooled by her sudden, half-yawned question.

"Yup. Do you like it?"

"Yes, it's very becoming on you."

"I'm glad you approve." There was a new self-assurance and intimacy in his eyes as he said the words.

"Anyone would," she said, her voice slightly shaken and irritable. "W-where did you have it cut?"

He named the place and her eyes widened.

110

"That's where I go," she said.

His complexion seemed to pale slightly. "I'm glad you weren't there that day," he said rather cryptically.

"Why?"

"Well, to tell you the truth, I'm used to barber shops, where a man can get a haircut like a man. I felt pretty silly just walking into that place—women everywhere, and hanging plants all around to bump into."

Dale had to smile, her self-consciousness ebbing. She could just picture him walking into the smart salon just off North Michigan Avenue. Remembering the way he used to look, it certainly wouldn't have been his type of atmosphere. "Tell me about it. Who cut your hair?"

"Marlene. You know her?" Dale shook her head. "She came out and introduced herself when I got there," he continued. "She had this wild hairdo and outfit on—all purple and green, her outfit I mean—dangling earrings, and inch-long fingernails. I didn't think she'd be able to pick up a pair of scissors."

He paused to smile as Dale put her hand over her mouth and began to laugh. "Go on," Dale said, trying to compose herself.

"Well," he continued, warming to the tale, "she took me back into that big room with all the mirrors and plants and chairs and had me sit down. It wasn't a regular barber's chair. After fingering my hair and deciding what she wanted to do, she put one of those plastic capes over me. Then we had to go into another room where she laid me back in one of those sinks and a girl in a miniskirt washed my hair. I didn't see why they needed to do that. I mean, I could have washed it myself when I got home."

Dale was now shaking with laughter, visualizing it all. He went on anyway, apparently enjoying the fact that he was entertaining her.

"After that they led me back to the room with the mirrors. That was really embarrassing, wet hair and a cape and I had to go past all those women customers. Anyway, Marlene sat me down in the chair again and gave me the haircut. Finally I was allowed to go. After leaving half my paycheck there, of course."

It was a moment before Dale could speak. "It is rather expensive, I agree. But it was worth it, wasn't it?"

"I don't know. I'm not looking forward to going back."

"There were some other male customers, weren't there? There usually are when I've been there," she said.

"A few. They looked as ridiculous as I felt."

"Oh, Sloane!" she said, laughing again. In spite of his new appearance, she could see he hadn't changed. She was glad. It made her feel more comfortable, like putting on an old shoe. And yet, when she looked up at him, his striking new looks still unsettled her. He wasn't handsome, not in the classic sense of the word. But his change in appearance allowed the full force of his masculinity to show through, and that, Dale was beginning to realize, was devastating. She supposed the pure, unadulterated manly essence of him had always been there beneath the excess weight and old clothes. When watching the love scene in *The Great Fire* with him she had become acutely aware of it. She had managed to attribute her reaction to other reasons then. Now she was forced to recognize the truth.

Two flight attendants came down the aisle pushing a cart of soft drinks and alcoholic beverages. "Like anything?" one of them asked.

Sloane turned toward Dale, who was next to the window. "I'll buy," he offered.

"Maybe some wine?" Dale said. Soon they both had glasses of California Chablis.

"You weren't at the screening last Tuesday," Dale said after taking a sip. "You must have been invited."

"The editors decided to call a big staff meeting that afternoon. I couldn't get out of it. Did you miss me?"

Words caught in Dale's throat. "No . . . I mean . . ."

"Pining away, I can tell," he said mockingly as he lifted his glass to his lips.

"Well, I never know what I'm going to run into with you," she tried to explain honestly. "Sometimes you're pleasant, and sometimes you pick me apart."

"Don't take it seriously. It's just . . . sort of a self-defense," he said, half mumbling the last words.

"Self-defense? Against *me?*" What on earth was he talking about?

He was silent for a long moment, looking into his wineglass. "You're beautiful, Dale. Not every man has the confidence to go up to an exceptionally lovely woman and talk to her with grace and composure. Some of us expect to be rejected, so we try to look like we're doing the rejecting first."

She stared at his profile, startled at his revelation. It was as though he were laying himself open before her. In a way, she didn't want to know what he had told her. They weren't that good friends to be admitting such things. "Why would you think I'd reject you? The first thing I told you when we were introduced was that I admired you," she said.

"Admired my column. Not me. There's a big difference there," he said, turning to look at her.

Nervously she lowered her eyes from his intent gaze. "I . . . don't understand."

"Maybe you'll catch on before this trip is over." She glanced up to find him draining his wineglass in a large gulp. He seemed a little angry suddenly.

Dale looked out the window for a while. Both were silent. But Sloane soon broke the morose quiet with words she could hardly believe.

"You know, I saw you years ago on TV in the Miss America Pageant."

She looked at him in astonishment. "*You* watch beauty contests?" She would have thought he'd look down his intellectual nose at them.

"Are you kidding? They're a bachelor's dream! If I'm out, I put them on my video cassette recorder."

She smiled. "And you remember *me?*"

"You were first runner-up; why shouldn't I? I had picked you out during the parade of states anyway."

"Oh, you're just saying that," she chided, not quite trusting him.

He turned his gray eyes on her, a small flame of indignation in them. "You were wearing a long blue dress that matched your eyes. And your hair was longer than it is now. It fell over your bare shoulders. You were like a graceful little doll walking up the runway." He grinned. "And when you introduced yourself in the microphone you smiled and chattered in that adorable accent. I could hardly make out what you said. You looked damn good in your bathing suit too. When you played piano so beautifully, I thought you had it made!"

Dale's eyes were sparkling as she looked at him. "You remember all that?" she said, genuinely flattered.

"And at the very end, you cried a little when they called you out of the ten finalists as first runner-up, as if you were amazed they'd chosen you at all."

"I was," she said. "Mostly I was just relieved it was all over."

"You really *didn't* want to win?"

She was thoughtful. "I entered the contest hoping to get scholarship money because my parents couldn't afford to put me through college. I had two older brothers they were already putting through. I told myself I didn't really care if I won or not, but in the end I think I did want to win just a little. But I was surprised I got as far as I did."

"I thought you should have won."

Dale's face broke into a misty smile. "That's sweet, Sloane."

"You probably lost only because you weren't tall enough. You did look like a shrimp next to the others."

She laughed. "Five foot four is short by beauty contest standards. Maybe you're right."

"I'm glad you didn't win though." Suddenly he seemed serious as he looked at her.

"Why?" she asked, her smile fading.

"I think it would have changed you, all that sudden fame and fortune when you were so young. I like you the way you are." His voice had softened and his eyes were lost in hers.

She blinked hard. "That's one of the nicest things anyone has ever said to me. Thank you."

The last word was only a whisper. Suddenly and totally unexpectedly, he was leaning over her, his face growing large as it loomed in toward hers. And then his warm lips tentatively brushed her cheek near her mouth. She stared at him, stunned, her lips breathlessly parted. What was he doing? Her heart began pounding within her small rib cage and her face flushed with color. She felt like she did when she was fifteen and on her first date.

He smiled just slightly as he watched her face, his eyes silvery and adoring. Again he moved toward her, his mouth aiming for hers this time. "No . . ." she said weakly, but the word was swallowed as his mouth fixed moistly onto hers, warm and consuming. He reached out with his hands and took hold of her upper arms, first to keep her from backing away and then to pull her closer. The armrest was between them, but he still was able to press her stunned and yielding feminine form against his chest. His arms curved around her. His mouth feasted on hers, like a man long famished. Smothered by his hard, possessive kiss, she began to feel like a person drowning. Her small hands clutched his lapels, as if needing to grasp on to something under his masculine onslaught.

He pushed her back then, his body moving toward hers until she was against the back of her seat, her head pressed into its cushiony upper portion. She might have tried to move away, but her still fastened seat belt kept her in place. Continuing without abatement was the firm, insistent back and forth movement of his lips over hers, drinking in all they could of her without becoming blatantly intimate. Whatever tiny part of her mind could still think was glad he was keeping some reserve.

She felt his breath on her cheek and the forward pressure of his broad hard chest against her hands, which by now had flattened against him. She had instinctively wanted to push him away, but somewhere in all this the instinct had been forgotten. Now she was aware of the thudding of his heart. One of her hands had somehow slipped beneath his coat and was pressing against the thin material of his shirt. The heat radiating from his skin just underneath felt like fire under her fingers. She began to tremble.

As if momentarily spent, he drew back from her a few inches. He was breathing hard, catching his breath. But as he looked down at her, there was a wild freedom in his silvery gaze that at once frightened her and yet infused her with a similar exuberance.

"W-why . . . did you . . . do that?" she asked between breaths.

The light in his eyes died a little. "For a reasonably intelligent woman, that's a pretty stupid question. Why do you think?" he railed at her in his old way.

"You're attracted to me?"

He shook his head hopelessly, but there was a trace of humor in his eyes. "You're just now figuring that out?"

"I've been trying to figure you out since I met you," she said defensively. "Even now you're yelling at me!"

"Yelling? This isn't yelling. I'm just amazed that a beauty queen who must have had a string of male followers needs to be physically assaulted before she realizes a certain man has been crazy about her for months!"

"But you've always been so disdainful," Dale said. "Right now you're telling me how stupid I am. And with all those things you said in your column about me, why should I ever assume you'd be attracted to me?"

He made an exasperated sigh. "Didn't you listen to what I said a few minutes ago about wanting to reject you before you rejected me?"

"You're rejecting me?" she said in confusion.

"No!" he practically bellowed. He lowered his voice then, but there was anger in it. "Don't be so obtuse! You just don't want to understand, do you? You'd rather not deal with the fact that an overweight, average-looking man could desire a woman who looks like you, a woman who could have anyone!" he finished bitterly.

She stared at him a long while. Perhaps all along she had been looking past him a bit, seeing him as a bristly teddy bear she'd constantly been forced to deal with rather than as a man who might be attracted to her. But she'd always had a high regard for intelligence, rating that quality above all in a man. Had he been nicer to her in the beginning, Sloane's outstanding mental capacity, which she had long admired, might have outshined his rumpled looks. But his defensive attitude hadn't allowed that to happen.

She reached out and lightly placed her hand on his coat sleeve. "You're not overweight and average-looking anymore, Sloane. There's no use in considering that now," she said in a gentle voice.

Sloane's gray eyes widened, the angry hardness vanishing instantly. He glanced down for a moment at his jacket and tie, as if reminding himself how he was dressed. He looked up again hesitantly.

"I'm still no Paul Newman."

She smiled. "Paul Newman's married."

He nodded. His expression grew whimsical. "I'm . . . not."

"No," she said, drawing out the word in her soft southern way.

His eyes showed a slight astonishment. "You're flirting with me now, aren't you? Aren't you?"

She grinned coyly. "Maybe."

He leaned closer. "I'd like to think you are." He reached up to touch her cheek with his fingertips, caressing its downy softness. He moved toward her then, his eyes on her full, parting lips. But before he reached his destination, he stopped sharply, swore softly, and then reached down to push the movable armrest up between the seat backs. "I don't want to have that digging into my waist again," he said. "While we're at it, why don't we release you from this," he added as he unbuckled her seat belt, "so you aren't so . . . constrained." He looked up into her eyes then, the intensity of his gaze suggesting much more than his careful words.

117

Dale's heart jumped unsteadily. She wasn't quite ready for this new Sloane, but there was something very magnetic about him. His newly polished elemental form created a whole new chemical equation between them. She didn't quite know how to handle the reactions it was causing, those silent little explosions that kept her nervous system jumping.

"I can run away now," she said, referring to her unfastened seat belt. Her jittery blue eyes wandered over his face, half-fearful, half-anticipating what was to come next.

A smile crept into his eyes. "I have a feeling you won't." He pulled her into his arms, his hands reaching beneath her open suit jacket and around her back. Her breasts came up against his chest. The warmth and pressure of his hard body against her sent a silent rapture through her, taking her breath away.

"Sloane," she said as he bent his head to kiss her, "remember we're . . . on a plane . . . a public place." The sense of reckless masculinity she felt within him frightened her a little. She didn't know for sure what he might do.

"I know," he said softly, his mouth hovering about an inch from hers. "How come you're so breathless? I'm not holding you that tightly."

She lowered her eyes, suddenly feeling more shy than she ever had in her life. "When I left Atlanta to come to Chicago, I never dreamed one day I'd be . . . k-kissing Sloane Avery, the famous critic."

"Oh, Dale," he said. "When I first saw you on the news I knew right away you were that little Miss Georgia I'd rooted for. I've dreamed of holding you in my arms, but I never thought it would happen either!"

He pulled her body closer against him as his lips came down warmly and urgently on her trembling mouth. The manly feel of him enveloping her made her let go of any last reserve. Her arms came up around his neck and she kissed him back wholeheartedly. She was deeply attracted to him, she realized; it was there all along beneath their snipes at each other, beneath Dale's attempt to stifle her feelings whenever they did appear. Now she was thrilled to be in his arms, to know he desired her and to realize that it was possible she could return his feelings equally.

His lips were moving away from her mouth, along her cheek and down her long slender throat, spreading hot little kisses along the way. Beneath her jacket his strong hands were gently kneading her soft back muscles, gradually moving forward to the sides of her rib cage. For a man who'd just claimed to be unsure of himself around her, he certainly seemed to know what would put her on fire. She was clearly not the first woman he'd ever held in his arms!

His mouth came back to hers, pressing gently against her lips, then with increasing pressure coaxing her mouth open. A new intimacy flamed between them as he investigated the honeyed recesses within. Her hands caressed the strong column of his neck above his collar, the tips of her fingers reaching up into the coarse, thick volume of his hair. She was beginning to feel as if she were vibrating beneath his touch.

He pulled away from her slightly. Breathing erratically, he said, "We'd better stop before I go into orbit! Where did you learn to kiss like that?"

"Where did you?" she countered with a grin.

He smiled ruefully. "Maybe we'd better not answer those questions."

With a little smile she reached over to the extended tray that held her wineglass and picked up the small napkin the flight attendant had left. "You've got lipstick on your mouth," she said, and began gently wiping the faint smear of coral from his lips. He sat still for her, obviously enjoying her ministrations.

"Oh, it must be smeared on me too," she said, putting her fingertips to her mouth when she was finished with him.

"A little," he said. "It looks good. You look sexy a little disheveled." He reached up to muss her hair.

"Sloane!" she protested, laughing as she reached up to pull his offending hand away. "I'd better go to the rest room and make myself a little more presentable."

119

"Why? You're not on TV now. I like seeing you this way for a change." His eyes took on a predatory gleam.

"You do, do you? Well, I'm not going to play to your prurient interests, Mr. Avery," she said, teasing him. "I'm not that kind of girl."

"I think you could be if you tried. You just proved that." His voice was low and suggestive.

She put up the tray in front of him so she could get out. Taking her purse and rising from her seat, she said, "I'm not trying just now. Would you let me out, please, sir?"

"*Sir?*" he repeated with a smile. "Don't assume being polite will draw the same from me. It'd be more fun to have you crawl over me."

She stared at him, grinning and startled. "I didn't know you had such a wicked side to you. But never mind. I believe I'm thin enough to get by without you rising from your chair, like any true gentleman would."

As she began to try to edge between his long legs and the seat in front of him, he surprised her and got up to move into the aisle.

"Thanks," she said with a bright glance at him as she moved past him. "I'll be back in a minute."

He caught her by the arm, bending to bring his mouth near her ear. "Don't bother putting on any more lipstick."

It made her heart race. She smiled but couldn't quite bring her eyes to his. She moved away from him then, down the aisle, without looking back. Her legs were a little weak, she noticed.

In the rest room she looked into the mirror at her flushed face and wide, unusually bright eyes. Her hair was still mussed from his fingers. What had he done to her? She was losing her composure. A new sense of wildness in her was pushing aside her innate sense of propriety. Kissing a man so wantonly on a plane where anyone passing by could see! And yet she didn't care. She was having the time of her life. Permeating her whole being was a sublime sense of sheer devil-may-care joy she had never felt before, not even when she was crowned Miss Georgia, or when she'd learned she'd gotten her job in Chicago. Those events had carried responsibilities with them. Being with Sloane was just plain fun. Like tasting ice cream for the first time, she thought as she wiped the remaining lipstick from her mouth. She never would have guessed this would happen with him. And now it seemed they were on their way to becoming—She stopped her thoughts before using the word *lovers.* Was that where this would lead? Is that what she wanted? Things were moving so fast.

She was used to flirting. She'd done it all her life, it seemed. But it had always been innocent. She'd kept herself away from men who wouldn't play the game her way, like Gary Murdock.

She'd better be a little more careful how she let things proceed with Sloane. She hadn't looked for any entanglements with a man. There was her career to think of first. Until now it hadn't been much of a problem. She hadn't met anyone who had made her think twice about her priorities, and she'd never been one for casual sexual involvements. Yes, she was expert at flirting and she'd learned how to kiss over the years since her first date, but when it came down to brass tacks, she was really rather inexperienced.

And Sloane Avery was moving toward the brass-tack level pretty quickly. What would come next? she wondered as she put away her comb and gave her appearance a final glance in the mirror. Her face looked paler now. A new sense of gravity had come over her.

She gave Sloane a polite, rather tentative smile when she reached their seats. He stood up and let her slide next to the window.

"You look all prim and proper again," he said, eyeing her combed hair and careful expression as he sat down. "You also look a little wary now. Why?"

She was surprised at his straightforward question. "I do? I—I don't know."

"You had a little time to think about what was happening

121

between us, and now you're wishing you hadn't kissed me like that?" he said, as if guessing what was in her mind.

Dale blushed and glanced away. "Like what?" She wished she could keep her cool better than this.

"So wholeheartedly."

She gave him a wavering glance and looked ahead again. To her mortification, she couldn't think of a thing to say. She felt him take her hand in his.

"I hope we'll have even better kisses than that, Dale. Don't stop to think about it. No need to invite unnecessary uncertainties between us," he said, sounding very level-headed.

She gazed up at his face, so manly and intent as he regarded her. "You're very sure of yourself all of a sudden," she said, almost in wonder.

He smiled a bit. "It's partly façade. Inside I'm as jumpy as you seem to be. But I do feel pretty sure, from the way you kissed me, that you're rather attracted to me. A very welcome surprise, I might add."

Dale inclined her head, a smile hovering on her lips. "This has all been a surprise to me too."

He leaned closer, his forehead almost touching hers as she continued to look down. "So don't stop and analyze it. Just enjoy it," he whispered. Even his voice was sexy now.

Her heart began to race again. She lifted her gaze to his, her eyes fixed on him. "You're scaring me a little, Sloane," she said softly.

He studied her for a moment, his gray eyes infused with silvery light. "Maybe you're confusing fear with excitement. I don't think you're afraid. You're just excited. Like me."

Slowly she grinned in pleasant astonishment. He was remarkably sensitive. And clever. "You seem to know the right thing to say to a woman."

"I do? I hope I'm finally learning what to say to *you*."

Another good answer, Dale thought. A woman could get used to this in a hurry. Once he let go of his defensive posture, he

122

managed to use his instincts well. But he gave her no more time to think; his lips were edging toward hers.

She drew her head back slightly, laughing a little nervously. "Sloane, give a girl a break!"

"You know you want to kiss me again," he said with soft assurance.

"How do you know?"

"Because you didn't put on any more lipstick."

She closed her eyes in delighted consternation, then melted against him as he took her in his arms.

After an hour of whispered banter interspersed with many kisses, they were forced to come back to reality for a time. The flight attendant brought them their dinners.

A while after they had finished eating, a movie was shown. Neither Dale or Sloane bought the earphones necessary to hear it. There were no movies they hadn't already seen. But as the film came on the screen they found themselves watching it and talking shop.

"You even gave this one a poor review, didn't you?" Dale said to him. "I thought it was such a good mystery!"

"Why?"

"Well, I couldn't guess whodunit," she said with a grin. "And the sets and costumes were marvelous—a good roaring twenties atmosphere. And the photography was wonderful."

"I agree it was a well-mounted film. But a good mystery has to have crispness and clarity. If the relationships among the characters aren't precisely defined, if we aren't always sure where we are at all times, our attention begins to wander. At least mine did. You say you couldn't guess who did the murder. A better question to ask yourself is, did you care who did it?"

"Well . . ." she began to argue. "Uhm . . . Okay, I see what you mean. The plot *was* kind of a hodgepodge. How come I never know what's wrong with films until you tell me?" she said in some distress.

"You're too easy an audience. You just let it all pass by you. If it looks pretty and has some sort of resolution, you feel you've been satisfactorily entertained. Except for *The Great Fire,* of course. For some reason you tore that to shreds—one of the few good movies I've seen lately!"

Dale didn't respond. After a thoughtful moment she asked, "How well do you know Velvet Hunt? You said she was a friend of yours."

He nodded. "I met her a couple of years ago. The *Herald* sent me to Hollywood for a week to do some interviews with actors and directors. She had just become popular with her first big picture and I interviewed her. I was one of the few who gave her performance a good review and she was appreciative of that. We've . . . kind of kept in touch since then."

A question that had come to Dale's mind before troubled her now. In view of what was happening between her and Sloane, she decided to see if she could get it answered. She put on a smile, as though teasing him. "In what way was Velvet appreciative?"

Sloane eyed her for a fraction of a second, as if he didn't understand. Then he smiled a little and shrugged. "She said thank you. What did you think? Velvet Hunt would do anything more for a man who was a sloppy thirty pounds overweight?"

Dale grinned, relieved inside. "Her male companions have usually been pretty handsome," Dale agreed. "Like John Trevor."

"Yes," he said with a heavy sigh. "She'd do better to find some who were less handsome and more honest. Her string of broken affairs is taking its toll, I'm afraid. She's too damn gullible."

He seemed to be concerned about the actress, Dale sensed. "You apparently know her pretty well."

He shrugged again. "It's not hard. She's rather an open book. Not like you. You're a little more complicated," he said with a smile.

"You always give her good reviews," Dale said, letting the last remark pass. "Do you really think she's that good an actress?"

"I think time will show that she's an outstanding actress. She's like Marilyn Monroe. Nobody thought Marilyn could act when she was first becoming a big name star. Now that she's gone, almost everyone recognizes what a remarkable talent she had. Velvet has some of the same qualities, but they're being over-looked because her screen sexuality is so powerful. People don't want to see her for anything more than a sex symbol. I don't understand why. Maybe it's partly because of her poor judgment in her personal life. It only tends to focus attention on her sexpot image."

Dale did not pursue the subject any further. Satisfied that Sloane's interest in Velvet was only career admiration and human concern, Dale had grown bored discussing the actress. Try as she might, she could not see the gem of talent in the beautiful but vacuous blonde that Sloane seemed to see, and she was tired of thinking about it.

"There's been something I've wanted to know for ages, Sloane. What's your all-time favorite movie?" She smiled, eager for his answer.

"How do you know I have one?" he said after thinking a moment.

"Every critic does," she said.

"Very well. What's yours?"

"I won't tell until you do." She wasn't going to let him be evasive.

"I bet I can guess," he said. *"Gone With the Wind."*

"You're no fun! How did you know?"

"That film is a lot of people's favorite, and since you're from Georgia and you seem partial to pretty, romantic, gushy movies —"

"Oh, all right," she interrupted irritably. "So what's your favorite?"

He paused, as though bandying clever replies through his head. Finally he said, "That's classified information."

"What! Everyone tells what their favorite movie is!"

"Where is that carved in stone? The great Sloane Avery doesn't have to do what the masses do," he said, regally lifting one eyebrow.

125

"Oh, for heaven's sake! I know, you don't have a favorite movie. You hate them all and are afraid to admit it!"

He laughed. "No, I have a favorite." An easy, predatory gleam came into his eye and he leaned toward her. "Maybe when we've gotten to know each other a little more intimately, I'll tell you."

"How intimately?" she said, backing away a hairsbreadth.

"Oh . . ." he said, smiling and possessive as he put his arms around her beneath her jacket, "I'll let you know."

"You're imposs—" His lips had fastened onto hers before she could finish the word. In a moment her body was locked tightly against his again. She was beginning to feel at home in his arms. He kept her there, softly kissing and cajoling, gently teasing and laughing with her. The time, so pleasantly spent, passed so quickly, they were amazed when the movie was over.

Blankets were passed out and most passengers settled down for a few hours of sleep. Dale removed her suit jacket and so did Sloane. After Sloane had covered himself with a blanket, he looked over at Dale, snugly huddled in hers. She was about to close her eyes to try to sleep when she caught his glance.

"Come on, Dale," he said softly. "I want to sleep with you."

"What?" she whispered back in alarm.

One strong arm crept out from under his blanket. It went around her shoulders and pulled her against him. His other hand went under both their blankets to move to her waist.

"Sleep in my arms," he whispered, his lips pressed against her forehead as she warmed to his embrace.

"Sloane . . ." she said on a breath-hushed sigh. Her hands moved slowly up his shirt front to his shoulders, feeling the warmth and hardness of his body without his crisp suit jacket in the way. She brought her lips up to meet his, instantly losing herself in the moist warmth of his mouth.

As he responded to her kiss, his hands moved up and down her slender back beneath the blanket. She could feel the massaging strength of his fingers through the silken material of her blouse. His mouth began a series of caressing kisses down her neck, and her eyes closed as she smiled with the pleasure of it. He made her feel more sensual than she ever knew she was.

His hands, meanwhile, had moved to her sides, the heels of them grazing the sides of her breasts. The sensation, or perhaps the anticipation, made her quiver. Then, while one hand moved to her back again to keep her near, the other gently moved over her right breast, feeling out its firm, tender contours through the thin material of the blouse. The bra she was wearing underneath was made of a light, stretchy material, and she knew it would not conceal the evidence of her tautening nipple. Indeed, she gave a slight involuntary gasp as she felt his thumb seeking out the little nub with a small circular motion through the slippery fabrics.

She was too embarrassed at her body's obvious reaction to say anything. Sloane's mouth was leaving the smooth, delicate skin of her neck to go back to her lips. After a short gentle kiss he whispered unsteadily, "Oh, Dale, you're too much for me. I wish we were somewhere else." She could feel his heart pounding in his chest. He kissed her lightly again, then her cheek, then her nose. "Maybe we'd better just try to sleep."

She gave him a trembling little smile and nodded. He was too much for her, she thought. The arm around her back drew her more snugly to him as she settled her head against his shoulder at the base of his neck. But beneath the blanket his hand remained at her breast, now resting warmly over the feminine swell of softness, rising and falling with each gentle breath she took. As he laid his head against his seat's high backrest, she closed her eyes. How much more intimate could they get? she wondered.

CHAPTER SIX

They landed safely in Manchester about 11:00 A.M. local time. After going through customs, they found their way to the car rental at the airport, where a car had been arranged for Dale.

When they walked into the small office, the agent behind the counter was dealing with another customer, so they had to wait. "Are you renting a car too?" Dale asked Sloane.

"Well, if I need to," Sloane answered rather cryptically.

"How else will you get to the Lake District?"

"I believe there's a train that goes to Windermere. Or maybe I can get a ride from someone . . ."

"Your paper didn't arrange transportation for you?" she asked in surprise.

"My coming here was kind of a last minute thing," Sloane explained.

"Oh." Dale was thinking she was glad she didn't work for a newspaper. "What will you do then? Oh, I guess you could ride with me," she said, brightening. But then, as she looked up at his smug facial expression, she began to wonder if he hadn't planned it that way.

"Clever of you to think of that after standing here ten minutes!" he said. He grinned a little, but sounded disgruntled.

Dale's complexion reddened momentarily. She shouldn't have been so slow to catch on to him. "You figured on coming with me all along, didn't you? Isn't that being a little presumptuous?"

"Well, I did wait until you invited me—which took long enough! After getting to know each other so well on the plane," he said in softer, slightly suggestive tones, "I didn't think you'd mind."

"It's not that I mind, exactly. But you might have just asked me for a ride instead of manipulating me to fall in with your plans!" Tired from jet lag, she found herself growing angry as she expressed her thoughts. She was beginning to wonder if his whole trip hadn't been arranged to coincide with hers. He probably had enough clout at the *Herald* to get himself a journalistic junket when he wanted one. No doubt he'd heard her on TV when she said what day she was leaving. It would have been easy to find her; there was only one plane per day going from Chicago to Manchester.

At her strong indictment he looked chastened for just a moment. Then his expression became fixed and slightly irritated— more like his old self. "I can rent my own car if you prefer."

She paused before answering. There was a small involuntary movement in her lower lip and chin. "Yes, why don't you?" she said coolly. Immediately she looked away, her heart pounding with the knowledge that she had just given him a decisive setdown. Harder than necessary, perhaps. She really didn't mind driving him. After all, she was in a foreign country for the first time and the company of a more experienced traveler would have been welcome. But from the day she first met him he'd shown a definite talent for maneuvering her into doing things his way, and it was time that stopped. Especially after the increasingly physical attraction between them that became so apparent on the plane. She had to make some show of control. And, perhaps, she was just a little afraid of what he was doing to her emotionally. She needed some distance. Those long hours sitting with him had been . . .

"May I help you?" the car rental agent said.

Dale was stirred from her nervous rumination. "Oh, yes." She stepped up to the counter. "I'm supposed to have a car reserved here." She handed him the appropriate papers.

As the agent turned away to look in his files, Sloane, who had followed her to the counter, said, "You know how to drive a stick shift? Most cars here are standard."

"Yes, I can drive a stick shift," she said evenly without looking at him.

"On the left side of the road?"

"I'm . . . sure I can manage," she said. She put some testiness into her voice to hide her insecurity. Coping with driving on the left side of the street a long distance with unfamiliar road signs was one thing that had worried her quite a bit. But having driven once on Chicago's infamous Dan Ryan Expressway, she'd told herself she could handle anything.

The rental agent came back with some papers for her to sign, a small map of Manchester, and a set of car keys. Sloane watched silently and morosely as she signed the forms. He had certainly lost the ball, he was chiding himself. One poorly judged move on his part and she had changed toward him quicker than lightning. He'd put on his new clothes, his new self, and for about ten hours now everything had gone swimmingly. It had seemed too good to be true. He guessed it was. What did he do now? The perfect opportunity to continue this real life fantasy with Dale was quickly slipping from his grasp. And he was worried about her driving alone.

The paperwork taken care of, the young rental agent led her out of the office to a dark green subcompact parked just outside the door. Sloane followed them.

"Here you are," the young man said in clipped British tones as he handed Dale the map and keys. He turned to Sloane then and said, "I'll be with you in just a moment. Will you want a rental car?"

Sloane's eyes were on Dale, who was walking around to the other side of the small vehicle. "I'm not sure yet," he said to the agent. He raised his voice then. "Dale, you'll find the steering wheel on the *right* side of the car. Unless you'd like *me* to drive . . ."

He watched Dale stop gracefully in her tracks. She glanced up at the two men then, looking annoyed with herself, and retraced her steps. As she opened the car door on the right side to get in, Sloane moved briskly to assist her.

"You're sure you want to do this on your own?" he said, putting every ounce of respect he had into his voice. He knew at this point he'd better not risk even the remotest possibility of insulting her driving capabilities.

"Yes," she said snappishly.

"The ignition is right here," the rental agent said, stepping forward, forcing Sloane to edge back against the open door. "The light switch is here, car instructions should be in here . . . yes, they are," the young man said, opening the glove compartment.

Dale was watching as he pointed everything out. Suddenly Sloane saw her face grow a little pale and panicky. "Oh, the gear shift is in the middle . . . I mean, I'll have to shift with my left hand. I never thought of that."

Sloane cleared his throat authoritatively. "I've driven in England before. I'd be happy to—"

He was interrupted by the agent leaning over her. "I think if you just practice it a few times while the car is parked, you'll catch on quickly."

You don't have to be so damned helpful! Sloane silently reproached the young man.

"It works a little stiffly, doesn't it?" Dale murmured worriedly. She was pushing the round knob of the stick shift into its various positions, apparently having to force it into the third and fourth gears.

"It's a new car. Sometimes they need breaking in. I'm afraid I don't have anything older available," the agent said regretfully.

Sloane edged himself forward and peered down at Dale. "There's a time to use common sense, Dale," he said quietly and carefully. "This car won't be any trouble for me to drive. I have more strength in my left arm than you do. And we both have

131

to get to the Lake District. If two go together, one can read the map while the other drives. It's just more sensible."

"Oh, all right!" she said in a sudden soft explosion. Sloane and the agent hurried out of her way as she quickly swung her legs out of the car. "Honestly! How do you always manage to get everything to suit you?" she said with fiery energy as she walked past Sloane.

"I'll put our luggage in the car," he said obeisantly, all the while secretly smiling to himself. As she got in on the passenger side, Sloane and the agent began loading their luggage into the trunk and back seat. The young agent looked a little confused by the turn of events, but said nothing.

At last Sloane got behind the wheel and backed the car out of the parking place. As he began to go forward, however, the car stopped and started awkwardly as he was shifting.

"I thought you said you could drive this car!" Dale said. She was grabbing the armrest on her left as the car bounced.

"Well, I have to adjust to using my left hand too! At least *I* can shift the gears," he said tartly, impatient with himself. He didn't want to look inept in front of her. In a few moments he had gotten used to the clutch and to shifting on the left, and the car moved smoothly out onto Manchester's busy streets.

"Now," he said, reaching into his coat pocket, "we have to get on the right motorway. Here's a map of England I had on my last visit." He handed her a used-looking map. "I think it's the M6 we want. Better check. Look on the map of Manchester the agent gave you and see if you can figure out how we find it."

"Why didn't we look at the maps before we left the airport?" she said, wide-eyed and growing dry-mouthed as she watched him maneuvering at a fast pace through busy streets on what seemed to be the wrong side of the road.

"I was too distracted figuring out how to handle *you,*" he muttered, watching the speeding traffic.

She looked up from the map she had opened. "*Handle* me? Is that what you call it?" she said.

"It was for your own good! I didn't want to see you try to drive up there alone. I know how difficult it is from having done it myself. I was afraid because of our little, er, tiff, that you'd be stubborn about it. I'm glad you weren't." He thought a little compliment might help.

She was silent as she went back to studying the maps. He hoped it meant he'd said the right thing for a change. "Yes, it looks like it's the M6 that goes to the Lake District," she said after a few moments. "Have you seen any signs for it?"

"No. I also don't have a clue where I am in this city."

While Sloane kept up with the traffic, Dale quickly studied the Manchester map. Soon she found the street they were on. After figuring out the roads that led to the M6, she directed Sloane which turns to make.

A while later things were much more relaxed as they were breezing along through the lovely green English countryside along the M6, a wide six-lane divided thoroughfare. Even though it was raining a bit, Dale's eyes were bright as she took in the quaint farms, rolling verdant fields with grazing sheep and cattle, and occasional small towns they were passing. Sloane glanced at her, glad to see that she was apparently enjoying herself.

"You're a good map reader!" he said, hoping to get on an even keel with her again.

"Thanks," she said with a smile. "You're a good driver."

"We make a great team!" he said.

She didn't reply and looked out her side window again. *Oh, well, at least we're in the same car,* he thought.

After a couple of hours they got off the M6 and onto a road that led to Windermere. It was a surprise to see the amount of bustle and traffic that congested the narrow old streets of the stately town when they entered it. After driving around they located Dale's hotel, but then had trouble finding a spot to park. That finally accomplished, they walked up the steps and into the lobby of the well-kept turreted old building.

"Miss Chastain," the middle-aged reservations clerk repeated as he looked through a file. "You say you're with the American TV station . . . WNBS?"

"Yes, from Chicago."

"Here it is. Just as I thought. The other members of your party have already arrived and checked in. The names are Murdock and Santini, is that correct?"

"Yes, they were supposed to have a room together and there was to be a separate room for me."

"A separate room? Oh, dear. No. No, our records show a request for one room for three."

"No, I'm sure our secretary asked for two rooms. I can't stay in a hotel room with two men," Dale said with a grin.

The man looked troubled. "I do understand the problem, but I can't give you another room. We're all booked up. Every room in the hotel is taken. They've started filming that movie again, you see. We had a brief respite, but now the movie people have come back again, and all the reporters too. And our busy tourist season is just beginning. I'm afraid you'll have a difficult time finding a room anywhere in Windermere without a reservation."

"Oh, no," Dale said.

"I'm very sorry about the mistake," the clerk said. "Perhaps you can get together with your party and make some arrangement."

There was no way she was going to share a room with Gary Murdock and Hal Santini. "Are the nearby towns less busy? I have a car."

"You can try, but at this time of year hotel reservations are always advisable. And with the movie . . ."

"I see," Dale said worriedly.

"What about the bed and breakfasts?" Sloane said. "Wouldn't some on the outskirts of town have rooms available?"

"Well, yes, you might have some luck there. In fact, that may be your best bet."

Sloane turned to Dale. "Why don't we try that? I need a room too."

"That's right, you do," she said. "I guess you didn't anticipate this either."

"It'll work out. Don't worry."

134

"Hi, Dale, see you made it!"

She turned to find Gary Murdock coming up to them. Behind him was Hal Santini.

"Hi. Hello, Hal. I made it, but they don't have a room for me. Somehow the reservations got mixed up."

"There's an extra bed in our room," Gary said, a glint in his eye.

"I'll find someplace else. This is Sloane Avery," she said, gesturing to Sloane. After introducing them, she said, "We met on the plane coming out. Sloane's been sent here too."

"All the media are here. We've run into reporters from Germany, France, and Australia besides other Americans," Gary said. "By the way, we talked to the film's publicist, and she's happy to have you interview anyone you want. They'll allow us to film the actors at work too."

Hal, a quiet man in his early forties who had a wife and five children at home, smiled. "They were filming a jousting scene this morning until it started raining again. We got some footage of that."

"That's good," Dale said. "I'm glad they're so cooperative. What's your room number? I'll phone you when I find a place to stay."

Hal told her, then said, "Gee, I hope you can find a place. If not, you can take our room. We could camp out in the lobby, I suppose."

"Oh, I imagine we'll find something," Dale said.

"We?" Gary said. He eyed Sloane then, who had been quietly observing them all.

"I need a room too," Sloane said coolly. "We're sharing a car, so Dale and I might as well stay at the same place if we can."

"Sharing a car?" Gary said, his voice growing cold also.

"I couldn't work the stick shift, so Sloane offered to drive me," Dale explained hurriedly. She sensed some suspicion stirring and wanted to quell it. Gary Murdock was enough of a problem to handle without adding jealousy to his character.

Murdock looked darkly annoyed. "I told Ellis you should

135

have come with us," he complained. "But, no, he wanted you on the air one more night, and left all the preliminary work to us. If we'd all come out together, we wouldn't have had these problems!"

"I know," Dale said placatingly. "But George Ellis isn't someone I like to argue with. We'll make the best of it!" She smiled at Gary, hoping to calm his easily aroused anger. She had to work with him the next two days.

Her smile worked. The belligerence in Murdock's lean, chiseled face faded and his eyes brightened. "You bet we will, sugar!" he said, grinning securely now.

Oh, no, she thought. She'd overshot her mark. She'd only meant to calm him down, not encourage his advances. It certainly took next to nothing to encourage him.

When they had said good-bye to her co-workers and had gotten back into the rental car, Sloane said, "Isn't he a little young for you?"

"Who?" she said with a sigh.

"That Murdock fellow."

"I guess he is a couple of years younger than me. But he's not too particular. Anything reasonably attractive in a skirt is fair game for him."

His hand about to turn the inserted ignition key, Sloane paused to look at her. "You sound like you don't like him," he said, a nuance of surprise in his voice.

"No, I don't much. But I have to get along with him nevertheless."

"And that explains the flirtatious smile?" Sloane said, still looking at her with his hand poised at the ignition.

"Flirtatious!"

"What did *you* think it was?" he countered.

"Friendly," she said.

Sloane made a wry chuckle. "I wish you'd smile at me that way more often."

Dale made a long sigh. Men! They read anything they want to into a pretty face. Sometimes she wished she were the type of

136

woman men never noticed. "Are you going to turn that car key sometime in the near future?"

Sloane started the motor. But before shifting to reverse, he said, "Why do you let him call you *sugar*?"

Dale lifted her eyes heavenward. "You saw the type of person he is. Do you think if I asked him to please stop calling me that, he would?"

Sloane's large gray eyes studied her. "Does he bother you?"

Dale looked at him, startled by the gravity of his tone. "Sometimes, but it's nothing I can't handle," she assured him quietly. Sloane's eyes were so intense and concerned, she had to avert her gaze slightly. The way he looked at her sometimes took her breath away.

"You let me know if he gets out of hand, Dale," Sloane told her, his voice sounding wonderfully masculine. A little thrill crept up her spine. He certainly was a man who could take care of a woman if necessary.

"All right," she said, smiling flirtatiously now. "But whom do I call on when *you* get out of hand?"

His intent look dissolved into a greatly amused grin. He didn't answer. Obviously pleased with himself, he backed the car out of the parking spot.

They drove around the outskirts of town in the increasingly heavy rain, looking for the traditional bed and breakfast sign that indicated a home had rooms to let. Some had No Vacancy signs posted. Others had no rooms open when they stopped to inquire. They decided to try going farther out and took the road that went alongside broad and beautiful Windermere Lake.

Soon they came to the smaller town of Ambleside, a quaint, lovely old English village. After trying several more places without luck, they finally came upon a small inn outside of town which did have a vacancy. Dale's heart sank, however, when the accommodation was described.

"We have a small room with a double bed. Would that be suitable?" the young woman told them in the tiny lobby.

"Just one room?" Dale asked.

137

"That's all that's left, yes. But it does have a double bed."
Apparently the young woman was assuming they were married.

"That might do," Sloane said, casting a twinkling eye at Dale.
Dale breathed an impatient little sigh and walked out.

Following her to the parked car in the rain, he said, "We may have to settle for that, Dale."

"It's only mid-afternoon. We still have time to look," she said irritably. "If you think because of a few kisses on the plane that I'm going to share a double bed with you, you're badly mistaken!"

"Okay," he said with a smile. "Look, we're both cold and wet and hungry. Why don't we stop for something to eat?"

They drove back into the center of Ambleside and found a small, wood-frame restaurant, painted white, whose window was filled with a delightful display of meat pies, pork pies, sausage rolls, roast chickens, not to mention scones, cakes, and various fruit pies. They ordered a large pot of tea served with milk, and sampled an assortment of goodies until they couldn't eat anymore.

Dale felt much better afterward, realizing she had been getting irritable from a combination of hunger and jet lag. They set off again in the continuing steady rain, heading out of Ambleside northward along the road that followed Rydal Water. After trying a couple of more bed and breakfasts without luck, they came upon one on the road a little way past a medium-size old inn that displayed a No Vacancy sign.

It appeared to be quite an old house built of roughly hewn gray stones of differing sizes. Its construction resembled the ancient stone fences Dale had noticed separating the fields in the countryside between towns. It was a square, two-story house with a small newer addition at one side.

They knocked on the thick wooden door. An elderly white-haired man answered and invited them in out of the rain. They walked into a small entryway which had a desk and phone. Dale noticed a door that led to the quaint-looking kitchen off to the right.

"Do you have any rooms available?" Sloane asked.

"Yes, we just had a family leave unexpectedly. Child was sick. My wife's getting it ready now. It has a double bed and two small twin beds. Might be more than you need, but it's available," he said with a smile.

"I think that would suit us," Sloane said, eyeing Dale.

Dale looked much less sure.

"Let me see if my wife is finished changing the linens," the proprietor said. "If she is, you can go up and have a look at it." He went through what appeared to be a sitting room on the left, and disappeared.

"Sounds good, doesn't it?" Sloane said to Dale when he was gone.

"We need *two* rooms, Sloane," Dale told him in a no-nonsense tone.

"I don't think we're going to be able to find a place with two rooms. It's getting late. We're lucky to find this."

Dale's brow contracted fretfully. Then it cleared. "I know—I can take this one, and you can go back to the inn in Ambleside that had the double bed."

"A nice solution, but we have only one car between us," Sloane said.

"Well, you can take the car. Gary and Hal have a rental car too. I can have them pick me up tomorrow."

Sloane was silent for a minute, his expression set and his mind obviously working. "What are you thinking?" she asked, growing impatient and suspicious.

"I'm thinking that, one, that room at the inn may have been taken by now. And, two, this is too good to pass up. Look at it from my point of view, Dale. If you were a man, wouldn't you want to share a room with Miss America? No, I'm staying here with you," he said. "At least this room has *three* beds," he pointed out cheerfully.

Dale's fair complexion was growing dark pink with anger. "Of all the . . . You're no gentleman!"

"I never claimed to be," he said. "Neither was Rhett Butler, if you recall your favorite movie."

"I don't give a damn about Rhett Butler!" she said, anger bringing her accent back in full force. "I . . ."

"You better watch your language, or I'll send Mammy after you!" he said with a grin.

"Oh, hush your mouth!" she spat at him furiously.

He only grinned more. "I love it! You'd make a good Scarlett! Remember that scene when she slapped Prissy?" As a fiery new light came in her eyes, he took a step back. "Don't even consider it, Dale. You slap me and I'll take you over my knee!"

She felt as if she were a fuse about to blow. "Don't you threaten *me*, you . . . you wolf!" she said. She went back to the door and opened it.

"Now, wait a minute. Don't go off in a huff." He came up and put his hand on the door, preventing her from opening it any farther. "After the way I took care of you when you had your surgery, don't you trust me? We've stayed under the same roof overnight before." His tone was suddenly all reason and goodwill.

Dale looked out the partially open door at the pouring rain. It was beginning to look like she had no choice. It was as though he had called upon nature to help him outwit her. It was true, though, that he had behaved very nicely that night at her apartment. But just to ensure her security, she thought, perhaps she ought to try using a little psychology.

She slowly closed the door and contritely looked up at Sloane. "You're right. I'm doing you an injustice. You were a perfect gentleman in my apartment, and I do trust you. I know you won't so much as lay a hand on me." *There, let him cross that line!* she thought.

He looked at her blankly for a moment, but then his eyes began to narrow in glinting humor. "I get slippery when I'm buttered up, Dale. I'd try a different approach, if I were you."

"You are the most unscrupulous, most impossible—"

Her tirade was interrupted when the proprietor returned. "I

just helped my wife put on the last bedspread. The room's ready if you'd care to see it."

"I'm sure it will be fine," Sloane said. "Why don't we just sign in?"

"Certainly." The elderly man brought out a registration book and opened it. Sloane wrote his name and address and then handed the pen to Dale. She was so angry, she could hardly see to write.

"Oh . . ." the man said, his voice dropping as he read what they had written. "You're not married, then. We usually don't allow that sort of thing here. This is our home, you know."

Dale's face colored with embarrassment now. She glared at Sloane for getting them into this situation. He glanced at her, taking in her vehemence, then said to the proprietor, "I know it looks questionable, but Miss Chastain and I are only forced to resort to this because of circumstance. We're both reporters from Chicago. In fact, Miss Chastain is a well-known TV newswoman there." The white-haired man glanced at Dale and seemed impressed. "We happened to meet on the plane. The hotel where she was to stay made a mistake and didn't have a room for her. I invited her to come with me and look for another accommodation. Believe me, Miss Chastain would prefer a separate room. . . ."

"I certainly would!" Dale muttered.

"But we've been looking all afternoon and this is about all we've found. You know how busy it is with the movie . . ."

"Indeed, I do," the proprietor said. "So you won't be using the room to . . . as a . . ."

"No!" Dale said. "We certainly won't!" She stared up at Sloane, wanting him to get the full emphasis of her words too.

"Well, then, since it's raining, I guess I can let you stay," the proprietor said. "But just between you and me, I think I'd better tell my wife that you're married," he told them. "She's pretty old-fashioned. For myself, I wouldn't really care too much what you young people do nowadays, but, well, enough said." He picked up the registration book. "I'll just cross out your name,

141

Miss Chastain, and put Mr. and Mrs. in front of the gentleman's name. There. No one will be the wiser, will they?" he said with a smile.

Dale hesitantly smiled back. She was uneasy with this little white lie; it went against her grain to agree to a falsehood. But under the circumstances she didn't see what good it would do anyone to argue.

The proprietor introduced himself as John Bates and led them through the sitting room. He took them up a small, very narrow flight of steps to their room. Breakfast would be served downstairs at 8:30, he said, and they were free to relax in the sitting room in the evening if they liked. The W.C., he pointed out, was just across the narrow hall from their room.

Dale peeked in. "Is there a bath or shower anywhere?"

"Yes, if you require it. You have to go outside. It's in the small addition at the back of the house."

Great, Dale thought drearily. She'd have to go out in the rain to take a bath!

"How old is this house?" Sloane asked with interest.

"Over two hundred years," Mr. Bates said. "These thick old stone walls have stood the test of time, all right. Let me know if you need anything," he added cordially and then went back downstairs.

Dale glanced down the hall and noticed two other doors farther down. Apparently Mr. and Mrs. Bates had guests in those two rooms. She followed Sloane into the room they had been given. There was a small sink with hot and cold running water and an old mirror above it next to the door. Inside there was a double bed, which took up most of the small room, a twin bed against the far wall, and another beneath a large, curtained, recessed window. There was a little sealed-off fireplace, two padded wood chairs, a tiny three-drawer dresser, and an inexpensive plywood armoire to hang clothing in.

The first thing that struck Dale, besides the amount of furniture jammed into the room, was that nothing matched. The carpeting was patterned and multicolored, each bedspread was

142

a different color, one white with flowers in the center, one solid pink, one beige. The drapes over the window curtains were rose-patterned. As she closed the door, she saw, hanging from hooks on the inside of it, two empty hot water bottles, one red and one green.

"What are these here for?" she wondered aloud.

"In case you get cold at night, I guess. But you can use me instead," he offered.

She felt like throwing one at him in exasperation. "You better not take one step out of line," she warned him. "My daddy taught me a few things to defend myself when I was young. If you don't behave, I'll kick you where you won't forget it!"

Sloane chuckled and sat down on the edge of the double bed. "We should string up a blanket with a rope, like in *It Happened One Night*. Except we don't have a rope."

"If I had a rope, I'd find something better to do with it," she said.

"Dale! Mr. Bates would be shocked if he knew you went in for *that* sort of thing!"

She didn't understand for a moment, but then her cheeks reddened. "I meant I'd wrap it around your neck!"

"I'd rather be kicked where I won't forget it. You have a nicely turned knee." His eyes were alight with humor.

"You're certainly enjoying this situation!" she said, controlling her increasing anger. "Why do you keep goading me?"

"You'll pardon the cliché, but you're cute when you're mad." He was looking up at her, delight in his gray eyes.

She studied him for a moment. *What a hypocrite!* she thought. "Sloane, I'm not a toy put here for your entertainment. How can you write such brilliant articles decrying the way women are portrayed in movies, and then treat me the way you do?"

His smile faded. He seemed taken aback. As he sat in silent thought for a few moments, his expression grew a trifle chastened. "I think I'm sensitive to women—intellectually, at least. But what's going on here is at a different level. I guess you're right, I have trouble reconciling the mental with the physical."

"I don't know what you're talking about," she said impatiently.

"I mean that all your sputtering and sparks turn me on. It only makes me want to tease you more, see what you'll do next. It creates an electricity between us that I find exciting. Don't you feel it?"

Dale didn't answer. She felt confused now. She knew exactly what he was talking about, remembering the way his banter with her on the plane had pumped her adrenaline. But things hadn't gotten so out of hand then; they were only sitting together on a plane. The situation was quite different now, the potential consequences of his suggestive remarks so much more possible.

He lowered his eyes, because of her lack of positive response to his question. "You could give me credit for discussing it with you," he said quietly. A touch of self-mocking humor entered his voice. "At least I'm willing to acknowledge my flaw. It takes a man to admit he's still part male chauvinist."

She studied him a moment and thought, *It's true.* Some men she'd met were totally unaware of their chauvinist attitudes and didn't understand what the fuss was all about. Others vigorously denied having any such attitudes even when it was pretty clear they did. Sloane, however, was that rare individual who was mature enough to openly examine himself and admit to a flaw if he found one. Admit it even to a woman. He had a basic sense of self it took some people a lifetime to achieve. She had to admire him for it.

"Yes, it does," she said softly, looking over his husky frame and strong, masculine face. He was a man through and through.

He looked up, half in surprise. "You agree?"

She nodded.

Grinning slowly, he said, "Friends?"

"Friends."

He stood up and put out his hand. "Should we shake on it?"

She smiled and put her hand in his.

"How about sealing it with a kiss?"

"Now, Sloane . . ." She was in his arms before she could finish her objection. With gentle insistence his mouth eased down on hers as he drew her to him. His hands slipped under her jacket at her waist and moved caressingly upward to the sides of her breasts. She knew she should resist more, but she liked it too much. It had been several hours since she'd been in his arms on the plane, and she realized now she was missing his touch. How quickly she had come to need it.

"Maybe this Mr. and Mrs. Avery business isn't such a bad idea," he murmured softly, brushing his cheek against hers.

What? she thought. *Is he saying we should get married?* A flush of surprise, almost alarm, swept through her. She hadn't expected him to make any remark like that—not so soon—and not him. She continued to think of him as a settled bachelor type and couldn't quite picture him with a wife. He must have been joking or just making an idle comment. He couldn't mean it; they didn't even know each other well enough to be speaking of marriage!

His mouth was moving hungrily over her lips now. As her arms rose to his shoulders to steady herself, his hands slid down to her soft derriere. After exploring her rounded contours, he pressed her more closely against him and, for the first time, she could feel his growing arousal. It unsettled her even more. She hadn't been aware that he could become aroused so quickly. It excited and frightened her at the same time. She tried to draw away from his seeking mouth. "Sloane . . ." she said breathlessly between kisses, "we've got to bring our luggage up . . . and . . . unpack."

"Always have your nose to the grindstone, haven't you?" He nuzzled her in amusement, still holding her in his arms.

"With you around, it's wise," she said, trying to sound clever and cool. Gently she pushed herself away from him. He gave her forehead a little kiss and let her go.

They went down to the car together and brought their luggage up to the room. It was still raining, but beginning to let up a little. They hung their suit bags in the armoire. Dale opened her tote bag then and took out her hair dryer. Her hair was damp from the rain, and she thought it would be prudent to dry it and stave

145

off a possible cold. She'd wash it later tonight before she went to bed.

As she looked around she saw only one electrical outlet, inconveniently placed near the floor by the double bed. She also noticed another problem: The outlet had three holes; the plug adapter on her dual-voltage dryer had only two prongs. All she had to do was flip a switch on the dryer to adjust to 220 volts, but how could she plug it into the wall?

"Oh, no, I won't be able to use my blow dryer," she lamented. "What'll I do about my hair? We'll be taping tomorrow."

"What a calamity!" Sloane said as he walked up to her.

"Don't joke! You're the one who says I keep my job because of my looks. Oh, I won't be able to use my travel iron either! I'm going to look like a mess."

"Now, don't panic," he said calmly. He knelt down and looked at the outlet. "What you need is a different plug adapter. The one you've got is for the Continent. There's probably an electrician in Ambleside who'd have one. I'll drive in and look for one while you finish unpacking."

"You will? Gosh, that's nice of you, Sloane," she said.

He rose to his feet and smiled at her. "Aren't you glad you're rooming with me?"

She couldn't help smiling back as she made an exasperated sigh. "No comment!"

He grinned. "I'd better hurry before the stores close."

While he was gone she quickly finished unpacking. She eyed the small mirror over the sink and wondered how she'd be able to do her makeup properly. Everything was beginning to seem like a monumental hassle. She realized then how long she had gone without enough rest. Leaving Chicago in the late afternoon had deprived her of a good night's sleep. Thinking about it made her feel drained suddenly. She decided to lie down and nap until Sloane returned.

She took off her suit jacket and hung it up in the armoire. It felt cold and damp in the room, she noticed, no doubt due to the weather. Choosing the small bed by the window, she pulled aside

146

the bedspread. Underneath was a pillow in a clean floral-patterned case. She was surprised the bedsheet matched. As she pulled aside the orange blanket on top, she found a green one underneath, and under that a pink comforter. They certainly liked to keep their guests warm! Chuckling to herself, she crawled underneath them. Her body shivered, for the sheets were cold, even with all the heavy blankets on top of her. Even so, she lay back and soon dozed off.

"You sure look cozy!" The words woke her a while later. She opened her eyes to find Sloane smiling down at her. "I got your adapter," he said, and held up a rather large white plastic thing with three metal prongs coming from one side of it. The other side had two holes to fit her plug.

"Thanks! Will it work?" she asked, lifting herself up on her elbows.

"It should." He picked up the hair dryer that was lying on the double bed and walked over to the wall. "The electrician put a special fuse in it." He plugged it in and she heard the welcome hum of her dryer working.

"Oh, that's wonderful, Sloane!" She laid her head back on the pillow, thinking that that was one problem off her mind.

Sloane unplugged the dryer and set it down. He walked to Dale and sat on the edge of her small bed. "Tired?"

"Aren't you? Those couple of hours sleep on the plane weren't enough. You look a little worn out," she said, studying the shadows under his eyes. "Maybe you should rest from the jet lag, too, before we go out to eat."

"Sounds like a good idea," he said. He kicked off his shoes and removed his jacket and tie. To her astonishment, he began to pull her covers aside.

"What are you doing?" she said, tugging them back.

"I thought there wouldn't be any harm in us napping together," he said lightly. "Like we did on the plane."

"But this bed's too small. Sloane, you get out of here!"

But he was in, forcing her over to make room. He pulled her to lie comfortably in his arms and then drew the covers over

147

them. "I'm too beat after running into town again to try anything serious, Dale. I just want to be close to you for a while." His voice was soft and tired in her ear. She felt the heat of his big body against the length of hers, warming her bed and making her grow irresistibly languid and sleepy.

"All right," she said, resting her head against his shoulder. "Just for now, for a little while."

He chuckled comfortably and shifted a bit, drawing her closer, his hand near her breast. Bending his head, he brushed her lips with his, then lay back again on the pillow they shared.

"Sloane," she chided him sleepily, feeling the gentle warmth of his hand at her breast, "we don't want to make a lie out of what we told Mr. Bates."

Half asleep now, she barely heard his drowsy voice. "Don't we?"

CHAPTER SEVEN

Sloane felt something warm and soft moving against him, edging half on top of him, drawing him out of a deep sleep. A sweet, insinuating pressure over his upper thigh almost nudging his masculinity brought him fully awake. He opened his eyes and found his nose being tickled by reddish-brown curls as Dale continued to make herself comfortable against him in her sleep.

He heard her soft sigh as she finally settled down. Beneath the covers he could feel her arm resting carelessly across his abdomen. Carefully exploring, so as not to wake her, he slowly moved his hand from where it had been resting just below her breast. It moved over the smooth material of her blouse to her waist, where he encountered the soft, but heavier material of her skirt. Rising up over her hip, his hand moved to her thigh, gliding over thick folds of material until suddenly his fingers touched silky nylon-covered skin. She had turned more toward him, lying on her side, bringing her knee up so that her thigh crossed his, he realized. But she had done it in her sleep. He was reluctant to consider how she would react to this situation when she awoke.

Well, it wasn't his fault, was it? True, he had invited himself to share her bed for a nap, but he couldn't help it if she was a restless sleeper. His errant hand couldn't resist the smooth warmth of her thigh. He glided his fingers down to the delicate turn of her knee and then up again, slowly feeling and caressing every inch as his heart rate began to rise. When his fingers reached the edge of her skirt, he slipped them beneath the bunched material, moving all the way up to her panty line.

He could feel tiny beads of perspiration breaking out on his forehead and the involuntary swell of arousal just above where her thigh lay so provocatively against him. He swallowed convulsively and his breathing grew husky. This was beginning to be more than he could safely handle. If he had a caveman's freedom to act on his desires, he would roll on top of her this moment and ardently press her into the sheets.

But he was civilized, he reminded himself. And he had promised she could trust him. Yet, he kept wondering if perhaps he could arouse her in her sleep, so that she would be willing.

. . .

But that wasn't fair. Even if he succeeded, she might regret it afterward, and he didn't want her to regret anything she did with him. Especially not lovemaking.

Reluctantly he drew his hand away from beneath her skirt. He came up and gently grasped her upper arm. "Dale," he said softly. "Dale, it's"—he glanced at his watch—"after seven. We have to go out and find somewhere to eat."

"Hmm?" She lifted her head sleepily from his shoulder.

"Time to get up," he said, his voice full of warmth. She looked like a child, rubbing her eyes, her beautiful hair mussed. He couldn't resist giving her some soft kisses on her cheek and mouth. She kissed him back in sleepy innocence.

"Gee, I was really sleeping soundly," she murmured, brushing back her tousled hair and shaking her head as if to clear it.

"Yes, you were," Sloane said ruefully. He slowly began to sit up, which, because she was partly on top of him, forced her to do the same. As she adjusted her position, he watched her become aware of just how she was lying against him. Her face suddenly showing acute embarrassment, she drew away from him, moving her thigh off his. She quickly sat up then, pushing the covers away. Seeing the disarray of her clothes seemed to increase her discomfiture.

Sloane knew he should have looked away and pretended not to notice, but he couldn't take his eyes off her. He didn't think he'd ever seen a woman look so sexy and sweet. Her blouse was half out of the waistband of her skirt and somehow the top two buttons had come undone. He couldn't take credit for that, but wouldn't stop himself from enjoying a glimpse of lacy bra and soft shadowy cleavage. As she immediately became preoccupied with rebuttoning her blouse, Sloane turned his gaze to the smooth slender thighs her hiked-up skirt left uncovered. She was sitting with her legs bent to one side. Something caught in his throat as he admired how graceful and beautifully formed her limbs were.

"You're sure giving yourself an eyeful!" she said in annoyance. She pushed herself to a kneeling position and smoothed her narrow skirt back down to knee level.

You don't know how much will power I've already used! he retorted silently. He covered his frustration with, "You should have won that contest on your legs alone!"

He put his feet over the edge of the bed then and got up. She made no reply to his comment, but quickly got off the bed herself the way a lucky mouse might scurry from a cat.

After combing her hair and clicking her tongue over her wrinkled skirt, she put on her suit jacket. Sloane slipped on his suit coat and followed her down the narrow steps into the empty sitting room.

"Before we leave, I'd better call Gary and Hal in Windermere to tell them where I am."

"Knock on the door here and ask Mr. Bates if you can use their phone," Sloane said. He pointed to a closed door which apparently led to private quarters.

The knock was answered by a gray-haired prim-looking woman with glasses, who couldn't have been anyone but Mrs. Bates.

"Hello," Dale said with a smile. "I was wondering if I could use your phone for a moment."

"Are you Mr. and Mrs. Avery?" Mrs. Bates asked.

"Yes," Sloane quickly said to cover Dale's hesitation.

"I thought you must be," the elderly woman said with a polite smile. "You may use the phone on the desk in the entryway. There's a phone book for the Lake District there if you need it." Having delivered this information she promptly closed the door.

"C'mon, Mrs. Avery!" Sloane said in amusement as he took Dale's arm.

"Oh, hush!" she said crossly, moving with him toward the phone.

When they reached it she looked up the number for the hotel in Windermere and dialed. Sloane listened glumly as she asked to be connected with Gary Murdock's room.

"Gary? Dale. Listen, I'm staying at a small bed and breakfast. It's between Ambleside and Grasmere on the road by Rydal Water . . ."

As she described the place and gave her address and phone, Sloane walked restlessly to the door. He opened it slightly to peek out. At least it had finally stopped raining.

"What time do you and Hal want to pick me up tomorrow? Nine thirty? Okay. No, I'll let Sloane take my car. He won't have any way to get around on his own otherwise. Yes, he's staying at the same place here. No. No, Gary." Sloane turned and glanced at Dale. Her voice was growing annoyed. "I can take care of myself, as you well know. No, we aren't. It's none of your business!"

"Want me to talk to him?" Sloane said, ready to take the phone from her.

"Shhh," Dale said to him, shaking her head. Sloane turned away, growing angry. Why didn't she let him take care of that adolescent Casanova? He didn't want to see her dealing with men like that.

"Yes, I know, Gary." Her voice was more soothing now.

"Thanks. Yes, okay. See you tomorrow." She made a tired sigh and hung up.

As they walked out the door together, Sloane said sarcastically, "Did he call you *sugar?*"

She sighed again. "What of it? He seems to have a crush on me. He's jealous of you."

"Why do you put up with it? You don't have to answer all his questions. You don't owe him explanations," Sloane said.

"I told him that, didn't I? I do have to work with him. And I don't owe *you* any explanations, either."

Sloane grew silent. It hadn't occurred to him that she could look upon him and Murdock in the same light. But he was behaving much like her petulant young co-worker, wasn't he? No wonder she was getting annoyed with them both. He'd better curb his tongue a little more from now on.

As she began to head toward their car in the tiny parking area next to the old house, he touched her arm and said, "There's that old inn just up the road." He pointed to a long white building not too far away. "We could walk over there."

"That would be nice, since it's not raining anymore," she said in a more amicable tone.

As they walked down the sloping gravel driveway to the paved road, she took his arm. It gave him a quiet thrill to feel her willingly attach herself to him, just as though they actually were Mr. and Mrs. Sloane Avery. She didn't really want to be angry with him, he sensed.

Though it was early evening, there was no sign of encroaching darkness. He remembered from previous trips that the sun rose early and set quite late in England in the spring and summer because of the northern latitude. When they reached the road they paused to look back at the old stone house in which they were staying. It was set at the bottom of a green, forested hill. At one side was a large flower garden, beautifully kept, and in back of the house, up the slope a bit, was a line of full-blossomed red rhododendrons. On the other side of the road, in the still of the evening, they could hear the gentle rippling of Rydal Water, a wide stream at that point. Beyond it was a lovely, quiet, green forest. All about in the distance were wooded hill tops.

After a short walk along the two-lane paved road, they came to the small hotel. It was also an ancient-looking building, part graystone, the rest whitewashed, with a number of narrow chimneys extending from its gabled roof. The inn, they discovered, had a formal dining room and a pub. They chose the casual atmosphere of the pub. After finding an empty table, they went to the bar at the back, where roast beef with Yorkshire pudding, steak and kidney pie, and other English favorites could be ordered. After getting their plates of food and glasses of ale, they made their way back to their table.

Just before sitting down, Sloane barely noticed a beautiful blonde waving at him. He looked again and smiled. It was Velvet. She was sitting at a table with John Trevor, Sloane noticed with displeasure. After setting down his plate he waved back at Velvet and nodded to Trevor.

"Look who's here," he said quietly to Dale when they had taken their seats.

"Oh," she said, eyeing them curiously. "Why would they come all the way out here? Aren't they staying in Windermere?"

"Probably trying to escape reporters," Sloane said.

"Yes," Dale said, sounding momentarily depressed. "And if I'm going to do my job as a good reporter, I should go over to them and see if I can set up an interview for tomorrow. I really hate to bother them."

"Velvet probably won't mind," he said a little reluctantly. He remembered Dale's last interview with the actress. He hoped he could trust her to be kinder to Velvet this time. "I don't know about Trevor though." His tone indicated his dislike of the actor. Sloane's impression of Trevor, from having met him once briefly, was that the movie star was an egotistical stud dignified by a British accent. The man might be handsome with an appealing screen personality, but he had no moral character to speak of. And Velvet had fallen prey to him.

As Sloane gazed at Velvet with serious eyes, he realized she was smiling at him. She turned to say something to John Trevor and then rose from her seat. "You're in luck, Dale," Sloane said. "It looks like she's coming over to say hello."

Velvet walked across the small room, her luxurious long curls bouncing as was her T-shirt–covered bosom. Even in old blue jeans she was a knockout, Sloane thought.

"Sloane," she said when she reached the table, "I'm so surprised to see you. Did your paper send you?"

"Um . . . not exactly." He purposely kept his eyes from Dale's. "You look great."

"*You* look fantastic," the young actress gushed, her bright eyes gleeful. "It took me a minute to recognize you when you walked in. Your clothes are beautiful, and you've lost a lot of weight, haven't you? Aren't you sneaky, doing all that since the last time I saw you. I'm going to have to watch myself with you, you're so *handsome*. Isn't he?" She turned to Dale while Sloane blushed under all this praise. Dale murmured something polite. "You're Dale Chastain—the TV interview in Chicago, right?" Dale nodded. "It's nice to see you again," Velvet said.

"Nice to see you. My station sent me here to get some coverage of the movie you're doing. Do you think I could tape an interview with you tomorrow for TV?"

"Oh, sure," Velvet said with a smile, though her exuberance seemed to wane a bit.

"Do you think John Trevor would mind if I interviewed him too?"

Velvet's voice faltered. "Well, I—you'd better ask him. He's sitting over there."

"All right," Dale said. "I'll go now."

While Dale walked over to Trevor's table, Velvet took her seat next to Sloane.

"How are things going with you and him? Any better than the last time I saw you?" Sloane asked with concern.

"Yes, things have been pretty smooth lately. No bad disagreements during the last few weeks."

Disagreements? Sloane thought. They were arguments that

155

had often stopped production on the movie. "Has he said anything more about leaving his wife to marry you?"

"No, but I don't want to pressure him. He has his two children to think of," Velvet said. "He . . . visited his wife while I was in Chicago. He told me afterward."

"Nice of him. Are you sure he really intends to get a divorce, Velvet?" he asked as gently as he could. He didn't want to upset her.

"Yes, Sloane. They don't get along at all. He says they argue every time they see each other," she assured him, her eyes having a childlike quality, that earnest belief in Santa Claus. It was that impressionable quality that always brought out Sloane's protective instincts. He wished she could take better care of herself. The movie industry and its people were too dangerous a world for her.

"But, Velvet, he argues with *you* too. Maybe he's not capable of a stable relationship with any woman," Sloane pointed out softly.

Her expression grew troubled. He could tell that she was weighing what he'd said. She always did. She seemed to trust him instinctively. "But we always make up afterward," she said, and then her face reddened slightly. It was well known how she and John Trevor made up. Their open affair had become notorious. Sloane guessed there was something about Trevor's lovemaking techniques that kept her addicted. He wondered enviously what it was that enabled a selfish egotist like Trevor to keep two women, if not more, on a string. If he'd liked the man at all, he might have asked him.

After her silent inner agitation the young actress said, "I love him, Sloane. I . . . can't help it." Tears came into her eyes.

His heart sank. She was still in emotional disorder. He wished he could help. Reaching over to take her hand, he said, "Now, now, don't cry. Things will all work out somehow. Are you sleeping any better than you were?"

"Yes, a little. It's such a relief to have you to confide in, Sloane. You're so understanding," she said with a sniff.

"I'm glad you think so," Sloane said. Something drew his eye away from Velvet. He looked up and found Dale standing by their table, her beautiful eyes expressionless, watching them.

"Oh, I'm sorry, Dale," Velvet said, letting go of Sloane's hand and rising from the table. "I didn't realize you'd come back. Did you talk to John?"

"Yes, he agreed to an interview," Dale said with a politeness that sounded a bit rigid.

"Oh, good! Well, we'll see you tomorrow then." She turned to Sloane. "Will you be . . ."

"I'll be around where you're shooting tomorrow," he said.

"Great!" she said, smiling her brilliant smile now, her eyes still bright from the tears. "You look so good, Sloane, I'm going to kiss you," she said in her breathy screen voice, giggling a bit.

Sloane grinned sheepishly and felt himself coloring again as she bent over him. Putting her arms around his neck as he sat at the table, she gave him an exaggerated kiss at the corner of his mouth. "Mmmmmwah," she said as she did so. "Well, for heaven's sake! Sloane Avery, the fearsome critic, is blushing," she said, laughing as she drew away. "Isn't that cute?"

"Adorable," Dale said in a wry voice.

"Well, see you both," Velvet said, and whirled around to go back to her table.

"She's like a little kid sometimes," Sloane said, wiping the corner of his mouth with a napkin in case there was lipstick on it.

"First little kid I've seen with a thirty-eight-inch bust," Dale muttered.

"Yeah, she's got that too," Sloane had to agree.

"I'm sure you must have seen plenty of it when she was leaning over to kiss you," Dale added.

With amusement he studied the southern beauty sitting next to him. "You know, you sound a tad jealous, Dale," Sloane said, unable to keep satisfaction from showing in his voice.

"Why should I be?" she said a little too coolly as she cut the meat on her plate.

"Beats me! You can kiss me anytime. I take all comers," he said, grinning.

"I'll just bet you do."

"How did it go with Trevor?"

"He was very nice actually," she said. "I told him I was a TV reporter and he asked me to sit down for a minute, which I didn't expect. He was quite charming."

"I can imagine," Sloane said with sarcasm. What was the matter with women? he wondered. Didn't honesty and reliability count with them? Handsome looks and an engaging manner seemed to be the only traits they cherished.

Sloane may have just managed to climb to the lower plateau of good looks. But he knew he still fell flat when it came to being suave and charming. Beneath the glossy new book cover was the same old book.

The clearing sky was just beginning to grow dark as they walked back to the bed and breakfast over an hour later. Sloane had taken her hand and Dale hadn't objected. In fact, it was reassuring to Dale after witnessing Velvet's little performance at the pub.

Actually, the flashy kiss didn't bother her so much as seeing them holding hands before they knew she had returned. What was between Sloane and Velvet? she wondered as they walked along in the chilly evening air. Was it just some sort of warm friendship as he had told her on the plane? Velvet, after all, was with John Trevor, and Dale had heard all about their tempestuous affair. And she couldn't quite picture Sloane trying to steal her away from the actor. Sloane's looks may have improved markedly, but he could never match John Trevor's black-haired, blue-eyed perfection.

Still, she wished she knew what was between them. It made her uneasy. Sloane had clearly been pursuing Dale—had even hinted at marriage—and to suddenly see him holding another woman's hand during what appeared to be intimate conversation was unsettling. Dale wasn't sure how serious he truly was about her, but she had thought she could trust him not to seek the favors of another woman at the same time. Well, maybe she was reading more into it than there was, Dale told herself as they entered the old house.

On the way in they met Mr. Bates. Dale asked if she could take a bath tonight, and he gave her a key to the new addition. Sloane indicated he wished to follow suit.

"Maybe we could take a bath together," Sloane suggested as they walked up the stairs to their room.

"Shh! The people downstairs might hear you," she whispered in embarrassment. They had passed two middle-aged English ladies peacefully talking on the old couch in the sitting room as they came in.

"It would make their evening more interesting speculating about us," he said innocently as they walked into their room.

"Oh . . ."

"Hush my mouth?" he finished for her.

"Yes!" She smiled in spite of herself. His humor was growing on her.

"You want to go first or should I?" he asked.

"You go." That way, she thought, he might go to bed afterward and fall asleep while she was taking her bath, thereby lessening the chances of any more dangerous sensuality rising between them.

He seemed surprised, but said, "Okay!" After grabbing one of the two unmatched towels in the room and the small bar of soap provided, he left.

In less than a half-hour he was back again. His short hair was damp, but he had dressed in his street clothes to pass through the sitting room. Dale meanwhile decided to forget appearances and had changed into her pajamas and long robe.

When she went outside and entered the "new" addition, which she guessed was about twenty years old, she found a small room with a long bathtub. At one end, near the faucet, there rested what at first looked like an enlarged old-fashioned telephone receiver. She quickly figured out it was a hand-held shower

159

attachment. She was glad she would have an easy way to wash her hair. Everything was clean and serviceable enough, but there was one major drawback: No heat. She was freezing when she stepped out of the tub to dry off, her wet hair hanging about her face. Shivering, she hurried back into her pajamas and got into her warm robe.

After rushing back into the house and up to the room, she found Sloane sitting up on the double bed, reading a paperback. He was wearing a dark blue robe, which looked new and expensive, over his pajamas.

He chuckled when he glanced up at her. "You look like a wet kitten."

Dale's brows knotted. She knew what she must look like with no makeup and wet hair. She didn't like to have anyone see her this way, but what could she do? "I was hoping you'd be asleep," she said.

"No such luck. You'd better dry that hair, or you'll get a chill. There's no heat in the room."

"There isn't?" she said in dismay.

"Nope. I noticed there was an electric heater downstairs, but nothing up here. These old buildings don't have central heating, you know."

"No wonder they give you hot water bottles!" It *was* cold, she thought as she picked up the hair dryer from where it lay on the bed next to him. It was still plugged in.

"I borrowed it briefly. Hope you don't mind," he said.

She glanced at his dry, neat hair. "No, that's okay." She tried to take it over to the mirror over the small sink, but the cord wasn't long enough.

"I think you'll have to dry it here by the bed," Sloane told her.

"Then I can't see what I'm doing." She pictured her hair looking like hash when she was finished.

"Got a mirror in your purse? I can hold it for you," he said. He shifted his long legs around to sit on the edge of the bed.

Dale went to her suitcase and took out a round, plastic-framed mirror she used for travel. After handing it to him, she kneeled on the floor in front of him since the electric outlet was by the baseboard of the wall. She showed him how to hold the mirror so she could see, and started the dryer going.

After she had been working on her hair for several minutes, she looked up at Sloane. He was staring at her, that absorbed, silvery look in his eyes again. It made her catch her breath. He seemed to be drinking her in. She glanced away and continued with the dryer, pretending not to notice. In a few more minutes she was finished and switched the appliance off. Looking in the mirror, she ran her fingers through the loose, smooth waves, making sure her hair was dry.

Sloane's large hand came near her cheek. Time seemed to be suspended for a moment as she felt his long fingers slowly glide through her hair at the side of her face. Goose bumps rose on her arms and back, and she didn't breathe for a second. The palm of his hand warmly cupped her cheek then. He put the mirror aside and bent toward her. Her heart began to beat more forcefully. In the next instant his lips were on hers, masculine and magnetic. She couldn't make herself pull away, yet she knew she was on the edge of a potentially powerful situation, alone in a cold room with him and a double bed.

Soon his hands had come down beneath her arms to lift her up into his lap. "Sloane!" she objected with a breathless, nervous little smile. "What are you doing?"

"Giving you a comfortable seat," he murmured in his low voice.

"Maybe a little too comfortable," she said.

"I think you'll be happy here." His big hand slipped beneath the lapel of her robe to feel her breast through the flannel of her pajamas.

Her eyes made a gentle, sensual wince at the soft pleasure of his touch. "Sloane, don't . . ." she said, making a weak effort to pull his hand away.

"You like it." He nuzzled her cheek with his nose.

"But you shouldn't . . ."

"Why?"

161

"Because we're alone here and . . ."

"That's the most appropriate time to do things like this—when we're alone. We can't do it on the movie set tomorrow," he said with amusement.

"You know what I mean." She tried to sound annoyed while his gentle fondling made her feel like she wanted to melt.

"How's your surgery healing up?" he asked.

"Fine. They removed the stitches . . . oh, Sloane, don't . . ." He had found the nub of her nipple through the material and was giving it very special attention.

"Does it hurt?" he asked.

"Hurt?" He was so incredibly gentle, she thought dreamily.

"Your incision."

"Oh—no." She was beginning not to think straight anymore.

"Maybe you should let me see it," he whispered. His fingers moved to the buttons of her pajama top.

"Sloane!" Her hand flew to his to stop him unbuttoning her.

"I'll kiss it and make it better," he murmured naughtily while nibbling on her ear.

She couldn't help but laugh softly. "You're unscrupulous! You'll say anything to get your way with a woman!" The fires of excitement in her eyes belied her chastising words. Beneath her restraining hand he had already undone one button, she realized. But she seemed to have lost track of the idea that she should actually stop him. Playing with him was too much fun.

"You're a flirt!" he accused her gently, enjoyment obvious in his voice. "A little southern tease! Your eyes are alive with anticipation. They brighten with every objection you make."

"They do not."

"How do *you* know?" he teased back as she felt the second button come undone. "You turn me on, you know that? You know how to fan every spark."

She was amazed at his words and her eyes said so. Within herself she really didn't know what she was doing except reacting to him. "You make me this way," she said.

His busy hand stopped a moment and he gazed at her face, his

162

eyes a little wide, their gray hue almost iridescent. "I wish you knew how I long to believe that, Dale. Don't just tell me what I want to hear. I know there must be other men in your life." His tone of voice showed he hoped there weren't.

Her eyes were large as she stared at him. "What do you think I am, Sloane? I have the feeling you're quite a bit more experienced than me. When I said it's because of you that I'm responding this way, I meant it. You—you're a little dangerous."

Sloane looked like a man amazed at his own success. "Me, dangerous?" he said with a grin. "I'm happy you think so. I didn't think you had much of an opinion of me until that plane ride."

She lowered her eyes. "I'd still like to know what you think of me. You really believe I always carry on like this with a man?" She felt a trifle insulted.

"You often seem innocent, but, being so beautiful, I figured you had to have had some experience with men. It's not that I'd mind it, I mean. I could accept it. I'm no innocent either. But the idea of me making any sort of impression on you when you could have your choice . . ."

"The bulk of my experience has been learning how to keep men in line—like Gary Murdock. I haven't really wanted any involvements yet. My career is very important to me and I don't want any emotional distraction until I reach my goals. But you've kind of snuck up on me." She smiled a little, but it was a troubled smile.

"You really find me attractive?"

"It seems I do. I've tried not to think about it. If I am attracted to you, it's really going to disrupt my life."

"We're both in the same business, more or less. Why should it? I won't interfere with your career." He seemed eager to reassure her.

Her smile looked a little vulnerable now. "You're really attracted to me, Sloane? After all those things you wrote?"

"I've already told you I am. Why do you think I came on this trip? My paper didn't send me here."

"I heard you tell Velvet . . . You mean you—"

"Took a few vacation days, hoping I'd spend them with you."

She grinned. "Sometimes I thought you seemed to have it all planned out. Like when we were renting the car."

He nodded. "I nearly blew that. But it looks like things are working out after all," he said, his voice lowering softly. He brought his lips near hers.

"Oh, no, Sloane," she murmured weakly, and then their lips met. She felt a warm electricity between them as her mouth clung to his. His arm around her shoulders brought her closer against him and her arms went around his neck. She could feel from the cold air on her skin that her pajama top had fall open as he pulled the tie of her robe. She moaned softly when his hand tenderly caressed her bare breast. Her skin quivered in a sensual frisson at his touch. She began to breathe unsteadily, catching the masculine scent of his skin with every shallow breath.

In a while he moved his mouth from hers, forsaking the sweetness of her lips for a new pleasure. His yearning gaze lowered to her uncovered breasts as he continued to caress her.

"How beautiful you are," he murmured huskily, his eyes devouring her warm, rounded curves. The inviting pinkness of her delicate nipples drew his lips.

"Ohhh . . ." she whispered in deep pleasure. Her hand moved up the back of his head to press him closer. She could feel his tongue working on the raisinlike nub, giving her delightful little shocks. Lifting her toward him then, he moved his mouth away from her moistened nipple to the side of her breast. She smiled as he did what he said he'd do, and kissed her healing pink scar.

He drew his face back up to hers. His lips near her cheek, he warmly murmured, "All better now."

She laughed lightly, and as her eyes smiled into his, he eased her off his lap and pressed her down gently onto the bedspread. He gazed down at the soft slopes of her breasts as she lay there, sweet and unobjecting. He pulled apart the lapels of his robe and the tie came undone. Next he tugged at the buttons of his light blue silk pajamas.

A thrill ran through Dale as she took a heady gaze at his uncovered chest. It was broad with surprisingly muscular contours, and deep, giving a beautiful resonance to his voice. And there was a soft thickness of dark brown hair. Almost a little frightened by his manliness, she reached out hesitantly with her fingertips.

"Touch me, Dale. Please, touch me." He eased his body closer to meet her hand, and her fingers sank into the soft hair over his breastbone. She smiled a little at the tickly feeling and then ran her fingers through the hair over the warm skin beneath. The reverberation of his quickening heartbeat went through her fingers. His chest began to heave unsteadily as his breathing grew heavier. She could feel the tenseness within him, sensing he was holding himself back.

He broke through his own silent restraints then and moved toward her. As she felt the heat of his skin pressing down on her breasts and abdomen, his mouth fastened hungrily onto hers. Easily he parted her lips and his tongue explored her honey sweetness.

His heavy weight was fully upon her now and she felt small and deliciously helpless. Her arms went round his back beneath his pajamas and she stroked his smooth, heated skin as they continued their ardent kiss. He moved slightly and edged his thigh between hers. In the bliss of their embrace some primordial instinct urged her to bend her knee and capture his thigh between hers.

Her heart was pumping rapidly now and she could feel his was too. His breathing labored and shaky, he said, "Let me make love to you, Dale. Let's finish this. Let me love you!"

The words and his inflamed voice made her stop all movement. Through their clothing she could feel his pressing arousal against her, so near to that feminine place it sought desperately for release. Suddenly her mind seemed thrown against the wall of reality. How had she let this go so far? She wasn't ready to sleep with Sloane. She didn't want an affair with any man, not now, and perhaps never. The idea of sex without a commitment went against her instincts and her upbringing. Suddenly she was alarmed. This was all too quick and . . . wrong.

"Sloane, no." She pushed against him. "I—I can't. Please, let me go."

His gray eyes filled with acute pain. "Oh, Dale, don't say no. I want you so much."

Her eyes brimmed with stinging tears of unquenched need. "It's not that I don't want you, Sloane. I've—I've never felt this way before, never wanted any other man so much. But it's not right for me. Not now, not here like this without thinking what we're doing. I'm not like that. I'm just not!" Her voice broke and she sniffed back tears.

He drew away from her then and shifted onto his side, leaning on one elbow. His head was bowed. She sensed his deep frustration and disappointment. Yet there was no regret in his voice as he said, "I'm sorry."

She was sitting up now, clutching her robe around her. But she felt moved to touch his hand and say, "Don't be sorry. It's my fault too. I should have stopped us sooner. I didn't mean to cause you pain."

He took hold of her fingertips and lifted his large gray eyes to hers. They had a melancholy sheen to them now. With sad humor he said, "It's all right. I'd rather be rejected by you than by anyone else."

"Oh, Sloane, don't take it as a rejection. I wanted to sleep with you. I think you know that. But things are happening so fast between us. I never have a chance to think. I can't just jump into an affair with you. I think there should be a definite commitment between people if they're going to start sleeping together. It's too important a thing to just fly into casually. And I don't think either of us is ready for any sort of commitment yet."

He lowered his eyes to the bedspread. "No?" His tone sounded as though he would have had a different answer to that question.

She stared at him, her eyes widening, speechless. *Oh, God, he really meant that hint about getting married,* she thought. This was too much to deal with just now. Things were going much too fast for her.

Gathering up her long robe, she moved toward the edge of the bed. "We'd better get some sleep now," she said with a shaky smile. "Thanks for being so sweet, Sloane. Some men get very disagreeable when they're refused. You *are* a gentleman."

He made an ironic smile. "Yeah. Bully for me." He gazed at her in disappointed longing. "How about a little good-night kiss?"

"Just a little one?" she asked warily.

"Just a little one. On the cheek, if you like."

She smiled and leaned toward him. Putting her hand at the open collar of his pajamas, she kissed him warmly but briefly on his cheek. His heated breath fanned her skin as he grasped her upper arms and said, "If you get cold over there in your little bed tonight, you know where you can come."

The very words and the intense way he said them aroused her. She felt hot prickles along her spine. "I know," she whispered on a breath, and then hurried away from him.

Her bed felt cold all night.

CHAPTER EIGHT

Dale awoke the next morning to the bright light of day streaming through the window over her bed. It was about seven thirty, but the sun had already been up for hours. It was Sloane's watch that woke her. As before, he was sleeping through its queer little beeps.

Hurrying out of bed in the cold room, she slipped on her robe as she went to the double bed.

"Sloane. Sloane, wake up!" She shook his shoulder until his eyes opened. "How do you ever wake up at home?" she asked, laughing.

"Two alarm clocks," he mumbled in a groggy voice. After running his hand over his face, he opened his eyes fully and looked up at her. "Morning, beautiful!" he said with a smile.

"Good morning," she smiled back. There was a different atmosphere now from last night, she sensed. More down to earth. Their heated passions had gotten lost, but the warmth remained.

By eight thirty they were dressed, and they went down to breakfast together. Sloane was more casual than he had usually been since his metamorphosis, wearing navy pants, an open-collar plaid shirt coordinating nicely with the pants, and a white pullover sweater that looked expensive. Dale was still puzzled and dazzled by his new array of clothes. How could a man who had once been so sloppy make such an obviously well-organized change to designer-type clothing? She hated to ask him, since doing so would reveal her lack of confidence in his sense of style. Maybe someday she'd find out.

She wished she could have dressed more casually today too. But her job required her usual tailored attire. She put on a coral-colored spring suit with a lighter peach-hued blouse. The suit bag had kept the garments well enough that she hadn't had to use her travel iron.

As they walked down the steps they found the sitting room had been rearranged into a breakfast room. Some furniture had been pushed aside and three small tables had been set up with place mats, paper napkins, and silverware. The two English ladies were already seated by the front window and a young couple with a small child were seated at another table. Sloane and Dale had no choice but to sit at the table near the door, where Dale had spoken to Mrs. Bates the night before.

They sat down on the hard wood chairs. On the table was butter and marmalade and a few slices of thin white bread. Dale noticed Sloane eyeing them hungrily. There were also cups and saucers and two juice glasses. Mrs. Bates was nowhere to be seen, but it wasn't quite eight thirty yet.

"I wonder what we'll have?" Dale said.

"It's pretty standard at bed and breakfasts," Sloane told her. "Usually cereal, one egg sunny-side up, sausage and bacon, toast, and coffee or tea. Once in a while you get half of a broiled tomato or a piece of fried bread on your plate too."

"Fried bread?" Dale asked. It didn't sound too appetizing. "I wish I could have some grits. That's one thing I like about breakfast back home in Georgia."

"I don't think you'll get them here," he said with mild humor. "I tried them once on a trip down south. I, um, pretty much decided I could live without them."

"You didn't like grits? Did you put butter on them?" she said.

"I can't remember."

169

"They're really good with butter. If you had stayed that morning for breakfast, I would have made you some. I finally found a store in Chicago that sold them."

"Gee. Up until now I'd always regretted turning down that breakfast."

"Oh, Sloane!" she said in perturbed amusement.

All at once the door opened and Mrs. Bates appeared, wearing an apron and carrying a pitcher of orange juice.

"Good morning," she said to them. "Would you like juice?" Both nodded. As she poured she asked, "Do you care for cereal? I have corn flakes and a wheat cereal." Sloane asked for corn flakes.

"I'll have the wheat cereal," Dale said as a tiny drip from Mrs. Bates's pitcher fell onto her left hand. Dale picked up the napkin to wipe it off.

"Oh, I'm sorry," Mrs. Bates said. She glanced at Dale's hand again. "Where's your ring, Mrs. Avery? Haven't misplaced it, I hope."

Dale stared at her blankly. Sloane, meanwhile, quickly moved his left hand to his lap. Just as Dale realized what the woman was talking about, Sloane said, "I bet you left it on the sink upstairs when you washed your hands." He looked up at Mrs. Bates. "She's always doing that," he said impatiently. "Someday she's going to lose it."

Dale sat silently with her eyes lowered. When Mrs. Bates had moved on to the two English ladies on the other side of the room, Dale whispered disapprovingly, "You certainly know how to lie with a flair!"

"Only to save a lady's honor," Sloane said.

"Oh, hush."

Shortly, Mrs. Bates brought them their bowls of cereal with a pitcher of milk. When they had finished that, she brought out two plates of hot food. It was just as Sloane had predicted: one fried egg, one large sausage which had a consistency of mashed potatoes when eaten, a small broiled half-tomato, one slice of bacon which seemed to be a cross between American-style bacon and Canadian bacon, and toast. They also got hot coffee.

"What are you going to do today?" Dale asked as they ate.

"Watch you work."

"Thanks. Aren't you going to do any interviews for your paper as long as you're here?"

"I suppose I ought to," Sloane said with a sigh. "I could at least take this trip as a tax deduction then."

"Your paper wouldn't reimburse you?"

"I doubt it. The trip wasn't their idea."

"They don't want to support your dalliances?" Dale teased. "I can't imagine why."

"No. And I haven't gotten to dally with anyone yet either," Sloane complained.

"Maybe you should look for someone instead of watching me work," she suggested impishly.

"Is that what you'd like me to do?" he asked. He looked at her as he waited for her reply.

"No," she said quietly.

"Then maybe you shouldn't work today. Spend the day with me instead," he said with a grin.

She sighed. "Sloane, I can't do that. *I* was paid to come here."

"You can use me as a fringe benefit!"

"Sloane," she said, looking around, "will you hush. The others will hear." She glanced again and saw Mrs. Bates, who was removing empty cereal bowls at another table, regarding them from behind her hawkish glasses.

"I'll hush if you spend the afternoon with me," he said in a softer voice.

"I don't know if I can," Dale said. "We might be taping all day."

"Do you have to get permission from Gary Murdock?" he asked sarcastically.

"No. My crew follows me."

"Good. Then give yourself the afternoon off."

171

"Sloane," she said, growing annoyed now, "I have to do my job."

"One shouldn't sacrifice one's love life for one's job," he said, as if speaking sage words of wisdom.

"Oh, eat your sausage." Dale knew he was baiting her. She didn't understand how he always managed to pull her into these bantering conversations.

"Is everything all right here?" Mrs. Bates asked as she was passing by on her way to the kitchen.

"Fine," Sloane said. "Mrs. Avery's just crabby because she's been missing her grits."

Mrs. Bates's eyes narrowed down on him with a severe, questioning look. Her back straightened. Apparently the English woman didn't know what grits were and thought he was using some suggestive American expression. She turned and walked primly through the door.

Dale couldn't help laughing. "Now see what you've done?" she said to Sloane.

"Mrs. Bates seems to have a dirtier mind than I do," he said.

Gary Murdock and Hal Santini arrived at the Bates's bed and breakfast at nine thirty as planned. Dale was waiting for them outside when they arrived. Sloane had not come out to wait with her. She sensed he wanted to avoid Murdock and she was glad. She didn't want any problems.

Dale and her crew drove with their equipment to a tiny lake, called a tarn, south of Keswick and Derwent Water. Here they found the dressing room trailers, movie filming equipment, and actors and production crew of the on-location set of *Ivanhoe*. It was a fine, sunny day, growing comfortably warm, and the movie makers were busy taking advantage of the favorable weather. The little tarn looked peaceful amid the grassy fields surrounding it and the rocky hills in the distance.

They found the publicist, a personable woman of about forty-five, who told them the jousting scene was being refilmed, as most of what was shot yesterday had not come out well due to the rain. Dale and her crew were allowed to tape a scene between

172

Velvet Hunt and John Trevor being filmed near the tarn. It was the scene where Trevor, as Ivanhoe, has won the tournament and is kneeling before Rowena, played by Velvet, so she can place the victor's wreath of chivalry on his head. Then, because of the severe wounds Ivanhoe received during the joust, he faints at her feet.

As Dale watched, however, she noticed that Velvet, wearing a long blue twelfth-century gown, seemed nervous and kept forgetting her lines. John Trevor appeared annoyed and impatient, complaining that his armor was uncomfortable and that Velvet was unprepared. Dale felt the tension growing on the set. Was this the beginning of another of their famous arguments? she wondered.

While she stood there watching as Gary and Hal taped the unsteady performance, she turned and saw Sloane approaching them. Since the filming was going on, they could not speak, but Dale exchanged a smile with him. He stood a short distance away from her and her crew, apparently not wanting to interfere with their work.

At last the scene was shot satisfactorily and the director, Ian Michaels, called for a break. Velvet, who looked near tears, walked off in one direction and John Trevor in another. As Dale approached Ian Michaels for an interview, she noticed Trevor walking toward one of the trailers, which probably served as his dressing room.

Michaels, an energetic, amusing, gray-haired man, was very accommodating. Dale got an excellent interview with him. When she and her crew were finished, Dale looked around for Velvet. She spotted the beautiful young blonde some distance away near a tree—with Sloane.

They appeared to be in a very serious, even intimate conversation. Sloane's expression looked almost ardent with concern. It disturbed Dale to see him so preoccupied with another woman. As for Velvet, the actress still appeared upset. She was looking up at Sloane as if hanging on every word, as if everything he said were carved in gold. Dale knew that Velvet was about twenty-two, but she appeared even younger now, like a teenager seeking advice from her counselor about her future. What was between them?

"Looks like Avery's getting a good interview over there," Gary Murdock said with suggestive sarcasm. He had come up behind Dale as she watched them.

"Yes, it does." Dale made her voice sound mildly interested, though a growing hurt was beginning to knot her stomach. "We'll just have to see if we can talk to her later. Think we should try knocking on John Trevor's door?"

Dale, Gary, and Hal Santini walked over to the large modern trailer she had seen the actor enter. Trevor seemed in none too good a mood when he opened the door to them. Reminded of his promise for an interview, he let them in. Once the TV camera was rolling he quickly warmed to the task of answering Dale's questions in his most charming manner. Dale sensed he was anxious to keep a good public image, possibly to make up for the bad publicity he had received from his affair with Velvet and his notorious temper. Dale did not try to question him on either subject, no matter what her news director would have wanted.

All in all, Dale came away with the feeling that Trevor thought mainly about himself, that he was the most important person in his own life. Handsome and charming though he had been, Dale felt a faint distaste in her mouth as she left the trailer. Nevertheless, she had another good interview to take home.

Once outside again, Dale quickly saw that Sloane and Velvet were still talking by the tree. Dale set her shoulders and walked up to them. Gary and Hal followed. Sloane glanced at them as they came near, and the look in his eye was like an insult to Dale. He might as well have said out loud, *Go away. Don't bother us now!* He was behaving like an overprotective father, Dale thought. Or lover?

Dale's resentment showed in her eyes, but Sloane's expression did not change. "Velvet?" Dale said when she had reached them. She kept her voice pleasant. When Velvet turned to look at her, Dale could see she had been crying. "You . . . promised us an

174

interview, but . . . we can do it later if this isn't a convenient time," Dale said. She found she didn't have the heart to push the matter.

"Oh, sorry, I can't. I have to see my makeup lady. They'll be shooting the next scene in a few minutes," Velvet explained, managing to smile at the end.

"Maybe later then?" Dale said.

"Yes, sure. I'd better go now." The actress looked up at Sloane. "Thanks." She touched his sweater lightly at his abdomen and then turned to walk away.

When she had gotten a little distance, Sloane said angrily, "Why don't you leave her alone?"

"I have my job to do, Sloane. Last night she agreed to an interview," Dale said hotly.

"Why don't you butt out of this, Avery," Gary Murdock suddenly said. "Dale doesn't need you telling her what to do."

"She doesn't need you either," Sloane shot back. Sloane was angrier than Dale ever knew he could be. All at once he seemed to have the force of a bull within him. Protecting Velvet's interests obviously aroused his intense feelings.

"Come on, Gary," she said, pulling on the surly young cameraman's elbow, "maybe we can get an interview with that actress who's playing Rebecca."

"I'm glad to see you can walk away from him," Gary muttered as they moved away from Sloane. "I was beginning to think you were hung up on Avery."

"I'm not," Dale said irritably, knowing it wasn't quite the truth.

"I saw the way you smiled at him when he showed up here," Gary said. He sounded jealous again.

"I just smiled to say hello. It didn't mean anything."

"You see he's trying to get something going with Velvet Hunt?" Gary snickered. "How he thinks he can compete with John Trevor is beyond me."

"Shh. Someone may hear and we'll lose our welcome here. Forget about Sloane Avery, will you? Stay out of his way."

"Okay," Murdock said, "but I hope you follow your own advice."

For once Gary might be right, Dale thought as they walked back toward the spot where the previous scene had been shot. The director was arranging about twenty bit actors to form a crowd around John Trevor's stand-in, who was lying on a wood stretcher. The beautiful, as yet unknown actress playing Rebecca was being told what to do, and Dale didn't feel she could interrupt to try to get an interview.

Dale and her crew watched and taped some of the set-up for the scene. Finally John Trevor appeared and replaced his stand-in to play the wounded Ivanhoe being tended to by Rebecca, Rowena, and others in the crowd. Velvet appeared at last, all traces of her tears covered by makeup.

Later, as they began to film the scene, a new problem developed. Dale watched as one of the movie crew came up and said something to the director about the generators. Hal quietly speculated to his co-workers that it must be the film unit's electrician who had discovered that the gasoline-powered generators that provided electricity to the company were not working properly. Snatches of conversation Dale managed to overhear indicated that yesterday's rain may have damaged them somehow.

After forty-five minutes with everyone standing around waiting to see if the electrician's crew could get the generators running again, the director finally cancelled production for the rest of the day. Dale managed then to get her interview with the dark-haired actress playing Rebecca. By the time that was finished, most of the cast had vanished, either to their trailers or elsewhere. Dale realized she'd probably have to give up for today. She had gotten three good interviews, however, and some tape of the actors at work on a scene, so she felt she had accomplished quite a bit at that.

Gary suggested that he and Hal go over to try to get some footage of the men working on the generator. The tape would be used with a voice-over added by Dale later when she put together her final report. Dale agreed and parted company with them for the moment to see if she could spot Velvet. She walked back toward the trailers near the parked cars. It was then she saw Sloane leaning against their rented car.

"Waiting for someone?" Dale said coolly as she continued toward the trailers, all of whose doors were closed.

"I'm waiting for you." He sounded annoyed as he folded his arms over his broad chest.

"I'm still working," she said. She was a little surprised, however, that it wasn't Velvet he was waiting for.

"Everybody's gone back to their hotels in Windermere. You might as well take the afternoon off."

"Velvet too?" Dale asked.

"She left with Trevor," he said matter-of-factly.

"Oh."

"It's past noon. Why don't we have lunch somewhere?"

She considered refusing, but found herself walking up to him. "I'll have to tell my crew I'm leaving," she said.

"They're big boys. They'll figure it out."

Dale looked at the grass at her feet. He was probably thinking as she was that Gary might give her a problem. He'd guess, even if she didn't say it, that she was leaving with Sloane. She didn't have a ride other than with him or her crew. Yes, it was best to just leave. Otherwise she might wind up with another argument on her hands, or, worse, having lunch with Gary. Besides, she wanted to know if Sloane had anything to say for himself concerning Velvet.

She nodded her head, indicating her acquiescence yet showing no eagerness for Sloane's suggestion. She didn't know what to think of Sloane just now. He opened the car door and she got in.

Sloane drove to the delightful little town of Grasmere, which was situated on a lake of the same name. All distances in the Lake District were short by car, so it was not long before he pulled into a small parking area by an old inn called The Swan. It was a long two-story white building with a large painting of a swan on the front, serving as a reminder of old coaching days.

The historic building had obviously been refurbished inside and was richly decorated with antique furniture, brass and copper pieces, and beautiful dried plant arrangements. They went through the lobby to the restaurant, a handsomely proportioned and decorated room.

After they had looked over the menu and given their order to the waitress, Sloane said, "Did you know that Wordsworth lived in Grasmere for a time?"

"Really." Dale's mind was still stewing and she could drum up little interest in history at the moment.

"I see you're impressed," he muttered. "What's the matter, Dale? Still annoyed with me because I didn't want you to interview Velvet?"

"Yes." She looked at him straightforwardly.

"You could see she was upset. It was a bad time to interview her, both for her sake and yours."

"You're so thoughtful, Sloane," Dale couldn't help but say rather sarcastically.

Her reply seemed to annoy him. "Well, the way you conduct an interview, you may have upset her even more."

"Ah, now we have it: It's *her* welfare you're concerned about, not mine. I don't want to hear any more about how you did it for my sake as well."

He shifted in his seat. "Okay, but you saw she was crying."

"I don't deny that."

"Well, what are you angry about?"

Dale took a deep breath to gather herself together. "Let's say I'm confused, Sloane. I . . . kind of thought my interests would have concerned you at least as much as Velvet's." After last night, she would have thought they would have concerned him more.

"Of course I'd be concerned about you. But Velvet had the greater problem this morning. And you know how to take better care of yourself than she does."

Was that it? Dale wondered. Was Sloane a pushover for helpless, tearful women? "And you felt you had to look after her?"

178

"If you saw someone drowning, wouldn't you do what you could to try to help them?"

"A few tears is far from drowning. Are you sure you aren't exaggerating her problems?" Dale said.

"I've known her a lot longer than you have."

"A lot better, too, obviously," Dale said, a sting in her tone.

"Now, don't *you* exaggerate things," Sloane warned her.

Dale rubbed her fingers over her forehead. "I just don't know what you expect me to make of the situation, that's all."

"There's nothing to make out of it. Velvet was upset because of another argument she'd had with Trevor, and she came to confide in me."

"Why you?"

He shrugged. "Because she seems to trust me." He grinned a little. "And I give good advice."

Dale wanted to ask what else he was good at giving her, but stopped herself. "Advice about what?"

"Her . . . problems."

"What are her problems?" Dale pestered him. She didn't like his vague answers.

"I can't discuss that, Dale. Velvet has a right to her privacy. And with you being a TV reporter, it would be even less appropriate for me to repeat anything she's told me in confidence." Sloane told Dale this in a sobering tone of voice.

Dale felt as though her chair had been pulled from under her. He certainly could make clear how things stood when he wanted to. "I see you don't trust me," she said when she had recovered.

"As you've told me, you have your job to do."

"I just review movies, like you," she said.

"Yes, but it would impress your boss if you could come back with some juicy tidbit about a well-known actress, even if Froebisher or Andrea Miles were the one to actually report it on the air."

She swallowed and looked down. Of course that was true. Yes, she could understand why he felt he couldn't discuss Velvet. But why was Velvet so important to him that he would make himself available to her and be so careful about protecting her? Was he in love with her? Seeing that her troubled affair had grown so shaky, did he hope his feelings might be returned if he stood by patiently, ready to help Velvet in case she broke off with Trevor? The actress was so beautiful, any man would desire her. And so vulnerable too. Some men liked that quality in particular.

"Don't misunderstand, Dale," he said, looking at her. Dale realized her face was revealing her sad, uneasy thoughts, and she quickly masked her emotions. "I'm not saying it's wrong for you to do the best you can in your work. Gossip is hot news and it's your job to report it if you come across any. But I would be betraying another person if you heard it from me."

"Yes, I see," Dale said. She forced a little smile. "You make a good friend, Sloane. Velvet is right to trust you."

"I'm glad you see it that way. I thought you would understand."

He did? He really thought she would understand why he was playing the Rock of Gibraltar for Velvet? Especially after he had mentioned marriage? He was being a little foolish, Dale thought.

Their lunch plates were brought and Dale ate her steak and kidney pie in silence for a while. Sloane seemed to note her quiet attitude and kept trying to make conversation on one innocuous subject after another. Finally he ventured: "Why don't we go for a drive this afternoon? Maybe do a little hiking. There are a lot of paths in the countryside to walk along."

"I'm not dressed for it." Dale was feeling she'd rather spend time by herself somewhere. Some surprisingly strong emotions were churning within her and she wanted to sort them out.

"Our bed and breakfast is just up the road a few miles. We can go back and you can change into slacks. You brought some along, didn't you?"

"Yes."

"Good. So that's settled then. Okay?" She could hear the hesitancy in his voice. It somehow made her feel better that he sounded so unsure of her reaction.

"Okay."

180

Dale changed into tan slacks, loafers and socks, an orange short-sleeved blouse, and a cream-colored cardigan sweater. They were on their way then, spending some time driving through the beautiful countryside from lake to lake and small town to small town. Eventually they found themselves around Ullswater Lake. Sloane pulled into a car park and they began a walk along a well-used path through delightful woodlands. Eventually it led along one steep side of a ravine with a river below. They met several other sight-seers as they walked.

In a while they came to Aira Force, a secluded seventy-foot waterfall situated between precipitous rock walls. It was quite impressive and Sloane and Dale watched it in the shady coolness of the valley for a while. They turned then and followed the trail back to their car.

Sloane drove along Ullswater for a bit and then turned up a small paved road which led through rich green farmland. There were white sheep with lambs grazing in some pastures. Sloane pulled off the road along a fence that had a gate. Pedestrians could walk through it to follow the path that led into the large enclosed meadow.

As Sloane opened the car door to get out, Dale said, "You're going to walk through here? Isn't it private property?"

"It's a public footpath. People walk anywhere they like around here."

"We won't scare any sheep?"

He laughed. "This meadow looks empty. Come on."

They were alone now. There was not another car to be seen coming from either direction on the small road, nor any other hikers either. As they walked through the gate, Dale felt a sense of quiet and peacefulness all about her. The path through the thick, lushly green grass was easy to follow at first, but it soon diminished to a bare hint of an indentation in the rich, rolling carpet of lawn. Since the gate where they had entered was easy to spot, Dale was not worried about getting lost. The meadow was dotted here and there with trees and bushes. As they walked they soon came to a small stream flowing through a tiny ravine about three feet deep. There were small rocks along the bottom, but the banks were soft and grassy. A flat little bridge of wood planks had been built over it at the place where the vague path crossed the stream. It was a beautiful spot.

"This reminds me of some of the sets in *Finian's Rainbow*." she told Sloane with a smile.

"It does," he agreed. "You see? Sometimes real life can match the romantic stuff they put in movies."

Romantic stuff, Dale thought with amusement. Just the way a man would put it! They had gradually fallen back into being easy with each other again over the last couple of hours. Dale had put aside her nagging doubts about his friendship with Velvet for the moment. In fact, she was beginning to think she was probably reading too much into what she had seen going on between them. After all, he was spending the afternoon with her, not the actress. And Velvet was apparently with John Trevor. What was there to worry about? Nothing seemed to have changed since yesterday or the day before.

Nothing except that Dale was beginning to admit to herself that her feelings for Sloane were quite serious, and growing deeper by the hour. She was beginning to wonder whether she was falling in love. It was hard to tell and rather frightening to contemplate. She had never really been in love before. And his hints about wanting to marry her made it all that much more monumental. But she found the prospect very exciting too. There were moments in the last few hours when she actually felt that her feet weren't quite touching the ground as she'd walked with Sloane, holding his hand.

They crossed the bridge. After that the path became too obscure to follow. It was growing warm in the bright sun, and Sloane pulled off his sweater. Dale decided to shed hers also. Sloane suggested they walk over to where some medium-size trees stood together on a slight rise, along with an assortment of low bushes and wildflowers. When they reached the tallest tree, Sloane sat down beneath it and pulled Dale along beside him on the soft grass.

182

They sat for a while in silence in the shade dappled with patches of sunlight. The gurgling of the small stream could be heard a short distance away, and some distant bird was chirping.

"I was hoping we'd find a spot like this—romantic, no one around," Sloane said.

"Why?" Dale asked, amused suspicion in her voice.

"Why do you think?"

"I'm a little afraid to guess."

He laughed as he fondled her hand. "You're not afraid. Underneath that plantation propriety is a definite naughty streak."

"Not *that* naughty. Remember last night." Her voice was soft and southern, her eyes watching his with impish lights.

He drew closer and sighed. "I remember all right. Frustration is hard to forget."

"I'm sorry."

"Don't be sorry. Just kiss me again. Like you did last night." His arms enveloped her in masculine warmth and her lips took to his like a soft magnet. She felt how badly she needed his kiss and she drank it in fully, opening her mouth to his, allowing the silken intimacy to intensify her longing for the manly strength of his body.

The memory of how it had felt last night to have him lying on top of her, his weight pressing her into the bedspread, raced through her mind. She reminded herself not to let things escalate to the point they had then. She wasn't ready to make love with him yet, and she didn't want to have to refuse him again at the last moment, leaving them both hurting.

He tore his lips from hers and spread kisses over her cheek and chin to her throat. Here he took more time, nuzzling his lips against her tender skin, the moist heat seeming to ignite sparks through her body.

She moved her hands over his chest, feeling his masculine contours through his thin shirt. When she came to his open collar, she hesitated a moment, then edged her fingers beneath it to touch the heated skin of his neck. Her hand went around the back of his neck then, feeling the strong muscles working as

183

he continued to press his eager mouth along her throat. As he reached her collarbone, she felt his hand come up to the button between her breasts. She thought, *No, I mustn't let him.* But in an instant the button was undone, then the next and then the next. She felt the soft material of her blouse being pushed away from her body. Her breathing quickened, but no objection ever came to her lips. How she hungered for him to touch her again.

He moved so that he was kneeling, his hips on his heels, in front of her. As she clung to him she kissed his neck, then felt the front opening of her bra come undone with a quick twist of his fingers. She basked in the smooth, delightful feel of his hands moving slowly up the front of her rib cage, over the lower, pendulous curve of her breasts. Then she felt the slightly rough heat of his thumbs pressing on her nipples, rubbing them, teasing them until she gasped in delight as the pink nubs hardened beneath his touch. It was a tingling feeling he was creating within her, a soft electricity that started at her nipples with the caressing friction of his hands and permeated her breasts and then her body. She leaned in toward him, her hands at his shoulders for support. While she buried her face in his neck, he continued the seductive movement of his hands over her swelling breasts.

"You really enjoy it when I touch you like this, don't you?" he said in a rough, assured tone. "You thrive on it!"

"Oh, Sloane," she said, her voice sounding helpless and sensual. "You're wicked to tease me."

"I'm not teasing." He smiled as he looked down at her face. "At least not with words, Mrs. Avery."

She smiled back at the name he had used. Did he really want to marry her? she asked herself, pride and happiness showing in her eyes. Sloane Avery, the brilliant critic she had admired for so long? He took his hands from her soft breasts to unbutton his shirt. When his broad chest was uncovered he put his hands around her slender back beneath her arms and slowly pulled her to him. A deep warming awareness of their masculine and feminine differences seemed to infuse the close atmosphere between them as her rose-tipped breasts pressed into his chest. She closed her eyes at the feel of it, of her super-sensitized nipples pushing into the dark hair and then losing their pert shape against the hardness of his chest.

His arms slipped tightly around her and he pressed her very closely against him. Her upper torso gracefully arched toward him. She would have been off balance except for his holding her. Feverishly his lips met hers again, claiming her mouth to explore it. The growing heat between them and an increasing restlessness made them writhe together in kindling passion.

All at once he released her, panting for breath. He reached for the sweater he had tossed beside him and spread it over the grass. He took her gently then by the upper arms and made her lie down upon it.

"Sloane . . ." she said weakly.

"I know, Dale. You're not sure. I—I'll stop whenever you ask me to. But you know how I want you, darling. Let me—let me just touch you a little more."

His voice was so needy and earnest, she did not object when he pressed himself down on top of her, bare chest against bare chest. Was it so wrong? After all, he wanted to marry her, and she was thinking more and more that that was what she wanted, too, whatever it meant for her career.

She felt the weight of him relax over her as he kissed her again, and her eyes slowly closed in sweet bliss. Her arms moved over his back to hold him in her embrace. Oh, yes, this was what she wanted.

As they kissed and caressed, their bodies began to move against each other in a primordial rhythm that at once frightened Dale and intensified her already pulsating arousal. As he had the night before, he pressed his thigh between hers, forcing her legs apart. Instinctively, she brought her knees up around him, wanting to know what it would feel like to lie with him. As she did so she could feel the firm evidence of his own arousal. By the urgent way they were both breathing and the heat rising between them, Dale sensed something would have to give soon.

She ought to ask him to stop, she told herself. But then she argued, *Was that being fair to him?* She had allowed things to go this far again. Wasn't she being a tease, letting him touch her, yet all the while intending to back off at the moment of truth? She shouldn't use him that way. If she refused him again, leaving him deeply frustrated once more, she might lose him altogether. And besides, it was very likely that she might marry him, astounding as that fact was. Why not give them both the fulfillment they so desperately wanted?

Was she finding excuses to do what she ordinarily would never even consider—allowing intimacy with a man when she wasn't sure what their future together held? She honestly didn't know. Maybe she was rationalizing, maybe not. She couldn't tell anymore what was common sense and what was pure desire.

Sloane suddenly rolled off her to lie on his side next to her, their bodies still touching. He was breathing hard, as was she. Beads of perspiration had broken out on his forehead. With a shaking hand he reached out and with a circular motion massaged her abdomen. Her soft skin quivered in reaction. His hand moved to her waist and unbuttoned the fastening of her slacks.

"Sloane . . . no . . ." Her objection was only a whisper.

"Shh. Please, let me." His hand undid her zipper then. In a moment his fingers were inside finding their way beneath the elastic waistband of her pink bikini-style panties.

"Sloane!" she softly cried as she felt the invasion of his fingertips into her soft feminine recesses, already deliciously moistened by her intense arousal. Her breathing increased to short gasps as he quickly found that most sensitive point of her body. With sure delicate movements he stroked it. In seconds she felt an undeniable need, a heat, a pressure begin in her lower extremities and rush through her body. "Oh, Sloane . . ." she breathed as the pleasure warmed her muscles and calmed her agitation, all the while arousing her senses.

Never stopping the work of his hand between her soft thighs, he bent over her and kissed her nipples, using his lips and tongue to arouse her further. She ran her hand tremorously over his shoulder as she felt her sensual motors heating up beyond remission. Making little moans, she writhed in pleasurable agony beneath him, arching her chest toward him to press her breast against his seeking mouth, moving her hips in an urgent undulating rhythm.

Soon she was aware that he was pulling off her clothing. In a few moments she was lying there in the soft thick grass wearing only her open blouse and her panties. But as he leaned over her again, her only thought was, "Sloane, will someone see us if we . . ."

"There's no one even near here," he said, his voice heavy with desire. "The grass is high and there are bushes around us. No one would ever know, darling." He grinned a little. "Not even Mrs. Bates."

Dale smiled back, her lips tremulous, her gaze full of confusion. Her eyes were darting like candle flames over his face. "You—you want me, Sloane?" She wanted him to reassure her somehow.

His eyes darkened and then grew silvery and shone into hers. "It seems like I've been wanting you forever. I ache with it. I've needed your affection so badly, Dale. And never more than right now. Please, darling . . ."

Her fingers trembled as she put them to his lips. She didn't want him to beg. "All right, Sloane."

She felt she had heard what she needed to hear. He hadn't used the word *love*, but she guessed that for a man like him it was a difficult word to say. And perhaps he was hesitant to use it because she had never used it. Once she had given herself to him, no doubt their shyness at expressing their emotions would disappear.

Eagerly he took her hand and kissed it. With feverish fingers he removed her flimsy panties, then unbuckled his belt and pushed away his own garments. Her heart nearly stopped when she saw his virility. His manliness unbridled was a little frightening. All at once she had second thoughts about giving her body up to such an intense and secret intimacy, with a man she suddenly felt she hardly knew. When he moved over her small form

187

she instinctively put her hands up against his chest, as if to protect herself.

"You aren't afraid, are you? Of me?" His gray eyes searched hers.

"A little."

His eyes were suddenly filled with empathy. "You're so frail, I must seem like a monster to you. Just think if I hadn't lost weight. I would have scared you out of your wits." There was a trace of humor about his mouth.

She couldn't help but smile back. At such a delicate moment he had managed to put her at ease. "No, you wouldn't have," she whispered. She put her arms around his waist and urged him closer.

Her eyes widened then as she looked up at the sky. She was feeling him enter her, so gently, filling that void that was aching within her. Her eyes closed as she heard his low moan at the pleasure of it. Her arms tightened around him, hugging him as he began a rocking movement against her. Now she gasped in delight at the sweetness of it. The flames of rekindling arousal licked through her. She began to move her pelvis in unison against his, creating a beautiful mesmerizing friction that grew and grew. Her hands moved restlessly over his back, nervous, excited, unsure what was to happen. Would this change everything between her and Sloane? she wondered with growing anxiety. How would they feel toward each other after this?

It was hard to think clearly. She couldn't with Sloane's masculine body overwhelming her. His urging thrusts within her, his huge chest deliciously weighing on her breasts, his heated deep kisses, were her whole world right now. There was nothing else, only this little hidden patch of meadow, Sloane's body united with hers, and the raging passions that flamed between them, building and building. She could hardly bear the tension within her, binding her to him for the desperate promise of release.

All at once she felt a suspension within her, as though she had been let loose on a new plateau where she could run freely. All conscious thought ceased in that momentary wait before the final fulfillment. Her fingers glided tremorously over his back in anticipation of the unknown as she unconsciously held her breath.

Then it came, a wild flight of ecstasy that made her grip Sloane tightly as she softly cried out. Her small body quaked beneath his as she clung to him. In the midst of it she felt the intensity of his own passion as he spent himself in several final climactic thrusts. Her body relaxed and she lay quietly in his arms, her eyes closed, recovering.

Sloane's masculine voice broke the silence. "Oh, Dale, you were made for love!" he said in a vibrant whisper. "You're beautiful!"

Her cheeks grew pink. She was realizing what an intimate aspect of themselves they had just experienced. Now they had a whole new knowledge of each other. It made her uneasy, a little embarrassed. In some ways she still felt she hardly knew him. Yet it was the most fulfilling moment she had ever known. "You're . . . beautiful too," she said, smiling while a tear streamed down her cheek.

"I feel a little odd sitting here having afternoon tea, after our . . . activities in the meadow," Dale said, glancing at the elderly woman who had brought them the tray of tea and biscuits. Dale's pulses were still irregular and jittery.

They had driven the short distance to Glenridding, the nearest town on Ullswater, and had stopped in the lounge of an old hotel to have afternoon tea. Sloane had told Dale it was an English custom she shouldn't miss. In view of how they had spent the last hour, however, it seemed a little too quaint and proper, there in the quiet sitting room with its overstuffed chairs, the English bone china, and elegant tea service.

"I don't," Sloane said. He looked comfortable with himself. "You're an exquisite lover, Dale. An exquisite woman!" There was a caring, warm gleam of satisfaction in his eye.

"Sloane!" She glanced across the room at the middle-aged couple sitting in easy chairs with a small tea table between them.

They kept on sipping their tea and didn't appear to have over-heard anything.

Grinning, Sloane leaned forward to the small table in front of the love seat on which they sat together and picked up the tea pot. "More, Mrs. Avery?"

She held out her cup and saucer, her hands still a bit tremor-ous. "Yes, please."

"Milk?"

She nodded.

After pouring some milk into her cup, he picked up a small plate. "Have a biscuit."

"They look like cookies to me," Dale said, taking one. She was trying to be nonchalant, but she couldn't get over the fact she had actually made love with Sloane Avery. In a meadow!

"They look like cookies to me, too, but they call them biscuits here. We can order some scones and jam if you like."

"Could we? I think I'm hungry."

He laughed. "Worked up an appetite this afternoon?" While she was shushing him he called over the lady who had served them and asked for scones.

A few minutes later, when the scones and strawberry jam were set before them, Dale said, "Now, these look like biscuits."

"I don't care what they're called, I just like to eat them," he said as he spread jam on one. She watched him curiously and was about to speak, when he said, "And don't you dare remind me about my diet!"

She chuckled, for that was exactly what she was thinking. "Okay, I won't." After taking a bite of her own scone, she asked, "You don't need to lose much more weight, do you?"

"Another ten pounds wouldn't hurt."

"Really?" she said with surprise. "You wouldn't be too thin?"

"Bless you for saying that!"

She smiled. "I think you look good as you are. At least you did . . . you know . . . a little while ago." As she blushed, her eyes roved over his broad chest, covered up again by his shirt and white pullover. When she looked up at his face, she found his gray eyes fixed on her, an odd, yearning look in them.

"You mean that?" he said. There was a nuance of surprise in his tone.

"Yes," she said, her smile growing shy for some reason. She lowered her eyes slightly from his. "You're built like a football player, big-boned and . . . and m-muscular. Maybe it's not natural for you to be thin."

"You're cute when you stutter."

His unexpected words brought her gaze back to his. His eyes were shining. It made her heart skip a beat. "You said I was cute when I was mad."

"You're adorable all the time," he said. He leaned toward her and put his hand lightly on her thigh, then kissed her long and softly on the mouth. Time seemed to stand still. His breath gently fanned her cheek as her lips melded with his. The feeling between them was so tangible and so exquisitely tender, it left her spinning slightly when they drew apart. From the corner of her eye she caught the other couple in the room glancing at them. "Sloane," she softly chided as she stroked the back of his hand, "we're not alone here."

"No. We will be tonight though," he whispered.

She bowed her head. His words excited her more than she wished to admit. Her fingertips continued to stroke his large, angular, very masculine hand. Tonight. She had no doubt he'd want to keep her warm tonight. What was all this really leading to? She had never wanted to get herself involved in an affair with a man, but here she was, suddenly in the midst of one. She had never liked the idea of an affair because it seemed so nebulous a relationship, a commitment that wasn't a commitment. She ought to bring up the subject of marriage to him. But did she want to marry him? It was clear she was deeply attracted to him sexually, but did she love him? What about her career? She had totally forgotten it in the last few hours with Sloane. She felt as though her life had just taken a sharp turn and she didn't know in which direction.

"Tell me what you're thinking." His low voice invaded her silent pondering. She looked up to find his luminescent eyes studying her. Feeling too vulnerable and confused, she laughed lightly, unsteadily, as she felt fevered tears start in her eyes. She'd just given herself to a man when she wasn't sure what her feelings for him were. And he still hadn't said he loved her. This was a little more than she could think through just now.

She found a way to avoid answering his question as her gaze fell on Sloane's other hand in his lap. The edge of his sweater sleeve caught her eye and she laughed again, slightly uncontrollably. As she reached for his arm, she said, "Oh, Sloane, look at this! You got jam on your sweater."

Quickly she grabbed her napkin and set about making him neat again.

Dinner that evening at a small restaurant in Ambleside was a heady and amusing affair. Sloane continued to make it clear during their table banter that he wanted to share a bed with her that night. Dale was collected enough by then to be able to parry these comments with clever responses. It threw her a little, though, when he said, "I'm glad you kept your word."

"My word?"

"Don't you remember? You said it over the air. Your whole TV audience heard you."

"What are you talking about?" she asked, totally at sea.

"I'll quote you—in fact I taped it because I wasn't home until late that night. You said: 'I'd be honored to give him anything he wants.'"

Embarrassment heated her skin as she remembered her ill-chosen response that evening when Andrea joked about sending Sloane a towel. "I didn't mean that the way it came out."

"Maybe it was a Freudian slip," Sloane suggested wickedly.

"I doubt it. I didn't like you much then. In fact, I was surprised I didn't see some needling remark about it in your column the next day."

"I'm not *that* crude," Sloane said. "Not in public print anyway. And I didn't want to take advantage of you."

"How kind."

"I thought I was." He looked self-satisfied. It bothered her a little. It was almost as though their lovemaking that afternoon had been the fulfillment of a bet he'd made with himself to see if he could make her keep her 'word.' "

After dinner they came back to their bed and breakfast. It was about nine P.M. and Dale suggested they sit downstairs for a while before going up to their room. They were sitting on the couch looking at an English magazine together when Dale heard the phone ring. In a moment Mrs. Bates appeared by the entryway.

"Mr. Avery?" she said. "There's a call for you."

Sloane looked puzzled, but got up to answer it. Dale could hear his voice talking softly from the little hall where they had registered the day before, but she couldn't make out what he was saying. In about five minutes he came back into the room. His expression was troubled.

"Dale, I have to go out for a while. I'm taking the car. I'll . . . be back later."

"All right." She reacted automatically, taken by surprise. "Is something wrong?"

"Nothing for you to worry about," he said quickly as he turned to leave, apparently in a hurry.

"Where are you going?" she asked as he went through the door.

He never answered. In the next second she heard the outside door open and close. Moments later the car engine started and then faded off into the distance.

Dale was at a loss. What on earth could it be? Couldn't he have at least taken a moment to explain? A name crossed her mind: Velvet. She shouldn't jump to conclusions, she told herself. She had no good reason to assume Velvet had called him. But she couldn't think of anyone in the Lake District for whom he would rush off except poor helpless Velvet, who always seemed to need so much advice. Dale didn't think there was anyone else in the area he really knew other than herself and the actress. He had no co-workers from his newspaper there. In fact, he was on vacation. Earlier he'd shown little interest in meeting the movie people, and she didn't think he'd made any appointments to interview anyone. Who else . . . ?

She heard a noise and turned to see Mrs. Bates hustling into the room. "I just wanted to turn on the electric heater here," the lady said as she walked to the space heater. "It's beginning to get chilly."

"Mrs. Bates," Dale said with some hesitance, "that phone call—Sloane didn't have time to explain—who was it?"

Mrs. Bates stood up after bending to adjust the heater. "She didn't say. It was a young woman, I believe, though her voice was rather childlike. Sorry I can't tell you any more than that."

"No, that's enough. I know who it was now," Dale said, feigning a calm smile. "Thank you."

"Have a nice evening," Mrs. Bates said as she left the room.

Dale's smile disappeared as soon as she was gone. So. Sloane *had* rushed off to see Velvet. And to hold her little hand, no doubt. Poor little girl was probably crying again because John Trevor looked at her cross-eyed or some such thing. Didn't Velvet have any friends? Couldn't she confide in her makeup woman or her hair stylist, Dale thought in jealous annoyance.

She was being unkind, Dale chided herself. Maybe Velvet got more reassurance from Sloane than from anyone else. Dale remembered from her own surgery that Sloane was remarkably strong and comforting. He was someone who made himself available to lean on in a crisis. If Velvet had problems, why shouldn't she seek out someone like that?

But what did Sloane get out of it? Satisfaction in helping others? Perhaps. But after he had offered his assistance to Dale when she had her operation, she had later realized it was probably because he was interested in her and meant to pursue her. Did he have similar hopes for Velvet?

Dale restlessly got up from the couch. She had already run all that through her mind this morning after she had seen his protective behavior with the actress. She had even speculated he might be in love with Velvet. But Dale had forgotten it all after his ardent lovemaking in the meadow. His mind seemed to be only on Dale then—and all through the rest of the afternoon and dinner too. He'd never stopped giving her the message that he wanted very much to sleep with her tonight.

Maybe she should have been more receptive instead of just bantering with him as usual, she thought fretfully as she paced about the room. Perhaps she should have admitted she wanted to make love with him again too. She was surprised that even though she had shared such a deep intimacy with him, they still couldn't seem to express their true feelings to each other. They had gone back to hiding behind silly repartee. She could have at least told him how terribly attracted to him she was. If he'd known her feelings for him were serious, maybe he wouldn't have rushed off to Velvet. Even though Dale had let him make love to her, she wondered now if perhaps she hadn't been responsive enough. Had he been disappointed?

Well, he was gone and there wasn't anything she could do about it now, Dale told herself with a sigh. She might as well just go have her bath and then wait for him to come back.

Two hours later Dale was in her pajamas and robe, pacing between the beds in her room. It was almost eleven thirty. He ought to be coming back soon. How long could he spend talking to a vacuous movie star? Unless they were doing more than talking.

Don't think that way, she scolded herself. She didn't want to appear like a suspicious and scowling wife when he did get back. He had given her no reason to assume the worst.

She took another turn about the room, trying to find something with which to occupy herself until he returned. Coming by the armoire, she opened it, only half thinking about what she was doing. Inside, she saw her clothes hanging beside his. It gave her a warm, reassuring feeling. Smiling a bit, she ran her fingers over his suit jacket, feeling its fine material. She moved on to his blazer and his shirts, sensing through them his masculine presence in the room, even though she was alone.

There was a hat rack above the clothes and she happened to glance up there. She saw a folded sheet of paper with some odd markings on it. Curious, she took it down and looked at it. It was some sort of diagram. Glancing over it, she saw it was a listing of descriptions of several suits and jackets and shirts with lines drawn between, apparently to indicate what was to be worn with what.

Dale chuckled. So he *did* have some help in arranging his wardrobe. She hadn't realized a store clerk would go to all that trouble, but perhaps in a better men's shop they did. No, wait. There was a little message scrawled at the bottom followed by a rather flamboyant signature.

> Don't you dare try playing mix and match after all my work. I wouldn't do this for just anyone, you know. Enjoy!
>
> Myrna

Who on earth was Myrna? Another old friend? At least she had good taste in clothes, Dale thought sardonically. She put the paper back on the shelf. How interesting: a woman who had gone to the trouble of planning his whole wardrobe. How many other women were going to spring from the corners of Sloane's life? Perhaps Dale wasn't an *old* enough friend to really know his true character. Perhaps he had added her as the newest addition to his collection. A group of pretty marionettes on strings—was that what he had? Was he pulling Velvet's strings now?

Oh, who gave a damn! Hot with sudden anger, she pulled off her robe, turned out the light, and got into her small bed. She lay there fuming for some time. When her anger subsided, she felt completely confused. What was true and what wasn't? She didn't know what to think of Sloane anymore. Though the experience had been wonderful, she was beginning to very seriously regret having given herself to him that afternoon.

As time wore on in the quiet, cold darkness, she closed her eyes to try to sleep, but sleep wouldn't come. Soon she began to wonder what time it was. At one point she even got up to turn on the light and look at her watch. Two thirty. It would be rather naive to continue to hope that his relationship with Velvet was innocent, whatever he said. He had been with her for over five hours now. At this time of night where could they be but in some hotel room, no doubt Velvet's if she was on the outs with John Trevor at the moment.

What difference did it make where they were? Dale told herself as she blinked back cold, sick tears. She turned off the light and went back to bed.

When she heard Sloane come in about a half-hour later, she lay still, with her face turned resolutely toward the window and pretended to be asleep.

CHAPTER NINE

About five hours later Dale awoke to the high beeps of Sloane's watch alarm. She didn't bother to wake him up this time. In a short while the beeps stopped and he was still asleep. She dressed, combed her hair, and got ready to go down for breakfast at eight thirty. When she left the room she slammed the door hard. Let that be his morning wake-up, she thought with a resentment that was like icy steel.

As she turned to go down the short flight of steps, she was surprised to see Gary and Hal in the sitting room. They were looking up at her, having taken seats at the table where the young couple with a child had sat yesterday morning. When Dale walked into the room, she saw the other two tables were taken by the other guests.

"You two are up early today!" Dale said, feigning a pleasant smile to cover her crabby mood.

"Already had breakfast too! There was a little restaurant in Windermere we decided to try," Gary said. "You look tired."

"I . . . didn't sleep well. How are you, Hal?"

"Fine, which is a surprise after being out so late last night."

"Where did you go?" Dale asked. She took a seat at the table.

"Yesterday afternoon—after *you* disappeared—" Gary said

accusingly, "we went back to the hotel and ran into Alan Thornton and his crew. WAAB sent them out to cover *Ivanhoe.* You notice they seem to be copying what our station does lately?"

"Yes," Dale agreed. She was surprised that another Chicago TV station had come to the Lake District. "So you went out with them last night?"

"Yeah, we just walked around Windermere. Found a nice old pub. Actually, we weren't out that late."

"It was late enough for me," Hal said.

Gary's expression became smug all at once. "And you'll be interested to know, Dale, whom we happened to see going into a hotel as we drove by: Sloane Avery and Velvet Hunt!"

"Really?" Dale said with disinterest while she felt her stomach twisting with hurt.

"It was about ten thirty or so, wasn't it?" he said, turning to Hal for a moment. Hal agreed. "We saw them walking kind of leisurely up the sidewalk and then they turned to go into the fancy hotel where she's staying. He had his arm around her."

Dale couldn't breathe for a moment. Her lips trembled as she tried to keep her face composed. She was glad to hear Mrs. Bates's voice distract the men.

"Did you gentlemen want breakfast here?" the lady asked, looking at them in some confusion.

"They're my TV crew," Dale hurried to explain. "They're staying somewhere else and just came by to pick me up."

"Oh," Mrs. Bates said. She was apparently impressed. "I remember now my husband said you were a TV person. Would you like some coffee while I serve Mrs. Avery breakfast?" she asked the men.

"No, we just had some, thank you," Hal said pleasantly. He apparently didn't notice the name she had called Dale. Dale meanwhile had grown very tense. She hoped Gary hadn't caught it either.

"All right. I'll have your breakfast in a minute," she said to Dale, and walked away.

"*Mrs. Avery?*" Gary said, narrowing his eyes on Dale.

"That's just a misunderstanding," Dale said, beginning to fidget. "Because we came in together, she assumed . . ."

"But if you and Avery have separate rooms, why would she still assume you were married?" Gary said.

Whatever explanation Dale might have come up with, it was nullified as they heard the door at the top of the stairs open. All looked up to see Sloane coming out of the very same room from which she had come.

"You bitch!" Gary said under his breath. "You wouldn't let *me* near you, but you'd spend two nights with a big-name critic. And I thought you were something special!" His tone was ugly and getting louder.

"Be quiet!" Dale whispered harshly to Gary while Hal looked embarrassed.

"You even lied and said you were married!"

"It wasn't like that."

"What's going on here?" Sloane said in a low, clipped voice as he approached the table. He looked like he hadn't had enough sleep.

All were tensely silent for a moment until Gary said in snide angry tones, "Quite the ladies' man, aren't you, Avery? Two beds in one night!"

Sloane seemed to loom taller and larger as he stood by the table looking down at them. There was not a noise in the room as the other guests became aware a scene was brewing. "What do you mean?" Sloane said with deceptive softness.

"I mean you were with a certain well-known actress at a hotel in Windermere last night, and then you came back to your . . . *wife* here," Murdock said. He made a disdainful gesture toward Dale.

"You have big eyes and a little mind, Murdock. What are you doing here?" Sloane's voice seemed to carry a threat in it.

"Come to pick up my esteemed co-worker," Gary said, sending a hard glare at Dale, "who everyone thinks is so sweet and wholesome."

"Maybe you should wait outside," Sloane said.

Murdock grinned unpleasantly. "You gonna make me?"

"Want me to?" Sloane shot back.

Dale rose quickly from her chair. "Come on, let's go!" she said with all the authority she could muster. "It's getting late and we ought to be at the movie set. Hal?"

Hal got up from his seat and took Gary by the arm, pulling him from his chair as the young cameraman glowered at Sloane. "I'll fix you!" Murdock swore. He turned to Dale. "I'll fix both of you. Refusing me for him—a guy who's two-timing you. You'll be sorry."

"Come on, Gary!" Hal said, and the two walked out. Dale began to follow along behind, aware that everyone was looking at them, including Mrs. Bates, who was standing by the kitchen door holding a breakfast tray.

When they reached the little hallway, Dale was caught by the arm as Gary and Hal went out the door. "Dale . . ." Sloane said.

"Let me go," she said, wrenching her arm from his grasp.

"We need to talk."

"I don't want to hear anything you have to say. Go talk to Velvet!" She went out the door then and slammed it in his face.

Dale sat in the backseat with some of the camera and sound equipment as the three of them rode to the same on-location set as was used the day before. Hal drove the car and Gary looked out the window in a sullen, petulant silence.

When they arrived on the set Dale quickly learned that the generators were working again. As the weather promised to remain fine, it looked as though it would be a good work day. They spent some time interviewing the prop lady and some of the bit actors while everything on the set was made ready. Gary was uncommunicative and difficult at first. Hal, to Dale's surprise, gave him a good talking-to. "I don't want my job jeopardized because you and Dale had a fight!" he told Murdock. "Together the three of us have to produce something worthwhile to take back to the station with us, so let's just do it!" Gary was cooperative after that, though he said nothing to Dale other than what was necessary to their work.

While they were talking to the prop lady, Alan Thornton and the WAAB-TV crew arrived. Dale exchanged small talk with Alan for a little while when both were free for a few moments. As she was chatting with him, she saw Velvet come onto the set, apparently just having come from Makeup. She was wearing the same blue gown she had worn yesterday. "Excuse me," Dale said to Alan and quickly rushed toward the actress, wanting to get to her first.

"Can we have our interview now?" she asked Velvet. Her job required her to be pleasant to the young woman. She kept telling herself she wasn't jealous of the curvaceous blonde, that she didn't care whom Sloane took up with. But Dale found it was costing her a great deal to be kind to the actress.

"Oh, sure." Velvet looked tired, even with her perfectly applied makeup. Dale could guess why.

"Could we step over here?" Dale led her away from the movie set a bit. They stood by the edge of the small lake while Hal and Gary readied their equipment. Dale might have had enough gumption to ask the actress what she did last night, but with Gary Murdock there she didn't want to. She didn't want to risk his snide I-told-you-so looks.

They did the interview. Dale asked easy, innocuous questions about Velvet's costumes, whether she liked England, and if she had another picture lined up after this one. Velvet was able to respond to these well enough, though she was somewhat unsure what she would do when *Ivanhoe* was finished. All in all, it was an adequate interview.

Shortly after that John Trevor came on the set. Dale watched as Velvet walked up and said something to him. He seemed not to be speaking to the actress, however. After glaring at her he walked away. Everyone seemed to be in a bad mood this morning, Dale thought.

They began filming the scene where they had left off yesterday —Ivanhoe wounded on the stretcher with everyone gathered around. While Hal and Gary were recording the scene, Dale turned and saw Sloane standing some distance away. He had apparently just arrived. She quickly turned around again. Why had he come to England, Dale wondered. For a vacation? To pursue her? Or Velvet? Both?

Suddenly her attention was drawn back to the actors on the set. Velvet apparently had forgotten her lines again. John Trevor was snarling some very uncouth language at her. The director called a halt to the filming and asked for a half-hour break. He went to Trevor then, perhaps hoping to quell the actor's tantrum. Velvet, meanwhile, had rushed away. Dale's eye followed her as she went straight to Sloane. He took her in his arms as she fell crying on his shoulder.

Dale had had about enough at that point. The film's publicist came up to her crew and also the WAAB crew. Gathering the two groups together, the publicist asked if they would please not show any tape they might have of the flash of temper between Velvet and John Trevor. It was just a minor thing due to overwork, the publicist insisted. She said it would be unfair for the news media to blow it out of proportion. She also hinted at legal ramifications if they did use it.

Dale made no promises and she noted that Alan Thornton didn't either. It was somewhat out of their hands, in any case. Their news directors would decide what would be shown. The publicist left then. About fifteen minutes later she came back and made the announcement that everyone not connected with the filming of the movie must leave. The director, Ian Michaels, had asked for a closed set today.

"Well, I suppose that's that," Dale said to Alan.

"You probably have enough taped already," he said with envy. "You've been here a day or two, haven't you?"

"Yes," Dale said. "We're scheduled to fly home tomorrow noon. I'll be glad to get out of here!" She went on to tell him whom she had interviewed yesterday. Alan seemed impressed.

"Fast work! You might as well take the day off. I'm going to see if I can coax them to let me and my crew stay."

"I think I will take the day off," Dale said. "I need a little rest." She glanced up at Gary, who with Hal was standing by

203

with Alan's crew. Gary was staring at her with an odd, cunning look in his eye. Dale ignored it.

She spoke quietly to Hal and asked if he would drive her back to her bed and breakfast. Of course, he agreed. As they walked off the set, she saw Sloane following Velvet into her trailer dressing room. Dale's heart was heavy and dejected as she got into the car with Hal. When they pulled away she saw Gary Murdock taking Alan Thornton aside to speak to him.

"Poor Alan," Dale said idly to Hal. "I don't think he'll get to cover much today."

Hal dropped Dale off at the bed and breakfast and then he left to drive back to the set. As she said good-bye, Dale suggested that if the set was still closed, which she expected it would be—she had often wondered why the publicist had given them such freedom earlier—that Hal and Gary ought to get some footage of the Lake District scenery. It might be needed for lead-ins when her report was aired. She had enough for two or three reports and hoped the station would make good use of it.

On the way in she saw Mrs. Bates. She apologized for the behavior of her crew that morning. Mrs. Bates stiffly accepted the apology. Her opinion of TV people had clearly gone down.

With a sigh Dale went upstairs and changed from her suit into slacks and a blouse. She went outside then, crossed the road, and found a footpath she had noticed yesterday when she and Sloane had driven back after lunch to change. The path led to a footbridge that crossed Rydal Water and led through a wood on the other side. Dale spent the next few hours walking by herself, grateful for the solitude and beauty around her. It was like a balm on her strained nerves.

She wondered where Sloane was now. Still with Velvet? She wouldn't doubt it. Unless he was asked off the set too. If Velvet was claiming him as her protector for the moment, he probably wouldn't be, however. *Well, I don't care!* Dale told herself. In the next second forlorn tears were clouding her vision. She sat down on a log then and gave way to long, agonized sobbing. *Why not cry?* she thought stubbornly as she got out a handkerchief to wipe her eyes. Hadn't she been used and abandoned? Maybe tears would help get Sloane Avery out of her system for good.

About mid-afternoon Dale came back from her wanderings. She was tired, had a headache from crying, and decided she'd like to take a nap. As she crossed the road to go back to the bed and breakfast she noticed three men standing in the building's small car park. As she got closer she saw it was Alan Thornton and his crew. When they noticed her walking up the driveway, she was surprised to see them readying their camera and sound equipment.

Alan approached her, microphone in hand. "Hi, Dale. I have some information I wanted to confirm with you." Dale drew her brows together, wondering what it was all about. Was this a joke? She noticed the camera was rolling then and automatically cleared her expression. "I understand you're staying here at this bed and breakfast while you're in the Lake District covering the making of *Ivanhoe?*"

"Yes," she said, her mind still in confusion as to what on earth Alan was doing. The way he questioned her, filling in details a listener would need to know, was as if for a news report.

"I've talked with Mrs. Bates, the lady who runs the bed and breakfast. She told me that you signed in as Mrs. Sloane Avery and that you and he are sharing a room. Is it true? Are you and your former adversary really married?" he asked with a grin. "Was your public feud just for publicity?" Alan's smile seemed genuine, as if he were remembering that he was the one who had introduced her to Sloane.

Dale's face grew white. Suddenly she realized what a story it would make back in Chicago. The image of Gary Murdock taking Alan aside flashed in her mind. Gary must have told the TV reporter enough to peak his interest, knowing he was setting her up. She saw with cold frightening clarity that she was indeed trapped, enmeshed in that lie she had so reluctantly agreed to. "I . . . um," she stammered. "I . . . have no comment."

Alan laughed. "No comment? Is this a secret marriage?" Alan

seemed amused, as if honestly not understanding her reaction. It apparently didn't occur to him yet that it might not be true. In one shattering moment Dale could feel her ingenuous, wholesome public image about to be destroyed.

"I can't say any more," she said, and began to move quickly toward the house.

"Wait, Dale." She heard Alan running to catch up to her. He had left his microphone behind with his sound man. "I'm sorry to do that, but news is news. Why don't you want to talk about it? Chicago would love to hear that you married Sloane Avery. I was surprised when Gary told me. Does your station know yet?"

"No."

"Great! WAAB will get it first then. I already phoned my station. It'll be on the noon news in a little while back home."

"What! That—that I married Sloane?" Dale's face showed her great alarm.

"Yes."

Her shoulders slumped and she leaned against the door.

"What's wrong?" Alan asked.

Dale wet her dry lips. What else was there to do but tell him the truth and hope he would act as a friend and cover it over somehow. It would be found out soon enough that she and Sloane were never married. "Alan, it's not true." Quickly she explained how the entire situation came about and the lie they had agreed to with Mr. Bates. "It's true, Sloane and I have shared a room. But . . . there's nothing between us." *Not anymore there isn't*, she thought, and decided her answer was truthful.

"God, Dale. I'm sorry! Why did Gary . . ."

"Gary has his reasons. He and I don't get along well."

"I see." Alan looked down at the ground. "I'll do what I can to put a good face on it, Dale, but"—he looked up again—"you realize I'll have to tell the whole story now. I already reported that you and Avery are sharing a room."

"I know, Alan. News is news."

It seemed like the worst thing that could have happened, but it wasn't. Within an hour, apparently after the news was broadcast over WAAB, the small bed and breakfast got several phone calls from Chicago newspapers and TV and radio stations. After a few such calls Mrs. Bates was prompted to tell Mr. Bates about the media attention. Mr. Bates apparently had an attack of conscience then and told his wife the truth, that Mr. and Mrs. Avery were not really married.

Dale found all this out when Mrs. Bates knocked on her door and coldly informed her that she and Sloane Avery were no longer welcome guests. Dale was ordered to pack and leave immediately. As she followed the woman downstairs to try to ameliorate the situation somehow, the phone kept interrupting the abrasive conversation that followed. Dale heard the woman tell two long-distance reporters: "I'm asking Sloane Avery and that Chastain woman to leave! They lied about being married and shared a room. I won't have such unchaste behavior in my home!"

In the midst of this Sloane walked in.

"Ah, there you are," Mrs. Bates said as she put down the phone for the third time in Dale's presence. "I want you and your *girlfriend,* to put it nicely, out of here in half an hour! You TV people are the most ill-bred persons I've ever met. I'll never open my house to a reporter again." She walked out of the room then and shut the door sharply.

"What's going on?" Sloane asked. "Why is Alan Thornton outside?"

Dale told him all that had happened, beginning with Gary Murdock's tip to the rival station and ending with the numerous phone calls from reporters. "Everyone in Chicago will know about that little lie to fool Mrs. Bates! But *you* needn't worry. It'll probably enhance your reputation—no one will ever think of you as a stodgy critic again. Meanwhile, *I* wind up looking like a tramp!" Her eyes became glassy.

Sloane seemed dazed for a moment. "Dale, I'm—I never dreamed this could happen. It seemed so harmless. This is all my fault. I'll tell them. Don't cry." He moved to put his arms around her.

She pushed herself out of his grasp. "Don't give me any of your comfort. Save it for Velvet!"

"Dale, you're wrong about Velvet."

"You spent half the night with her. Gary and Hal both saw you with her. How can you stand there and tell me there's nothing going on? You agreed to lie about us being married so we'd share a room, you led me to believe I meant something to you to get what you wanted, you can lie about Velvet too!"

"I've never lied to you, Dale! I can't always tell you everything, but I've never lied to you."

She turned away from him. "I have to go up and pack. I've never been thrown out of a place before," she said as she began to climb the stairs.

He followed and both packed their clothes in hurried silence.

"What will you do?" he asked as she shut her suitcase.

"Catch the first plane home."

"Shall I drive you to Manchester?"

"Yes, would you?" she said in a clipped tone.

Sloane paid Mrs. Bates for the room. She took the money in silence, apparently finding it beneath her dignity to even speak to them anymore. Sloane and Dale walked out then, only to find the WAAB camera rolling as they went to their car and put their luggage in. Dale glanced at Alan. He stood aside and made no attempt to interview them. Dale felt it was his way of doing what he could to keep from embarrassing her further. She was grateful for that.

They got in the car and Sloane drove to Manchester. As they rode along the M6, he said, "Why didn't you tell Alan you and I *were* married?"

"And repeat the lie? Something like that is too easy to check. All they'd have to do is call City Hall," Dale said.

"We might have been married elsewhere."

"I'm sure in time they could find out the truth. What good would it have done anyway?" she said.

208

"It might have avoided a scandal. This could cost you your job, Dale, if the public becomes disappointed in you. They've got you on a pedestal. They won't like seeing you step off it."

"I didn't step off voluntarily!"

"I know. It's all my fault, as I said. But . . . I suggested we get married, didn't I?" He sounded as though he were repressing some annoyance. "If you had shown more interest in the idea, we probably could have gotten married somewhere, and the whole thing might have blown over without much fuss. Now . . ."

"Gotten married?" she said in astonishment. "How was I to know you were serious? You said it so off-handedly, I assumed it was one of your jokes." She didn't want to admit she had begun to believe him. "Besides, when would we have married? You weren't even around when I needed you." She remembered having left him on the set with Velvet clinging to him that morning.

"You always act like you *don't* need me," he said a little angrily, keeping his eyes on the road.

"Well, I wouldn't want to be married to you in any case," she retorted.

His profile looked like it was carved of granite. "I get the picture," he said icily. "But it might have spared your reputation."

"I don't think you give a damn about my reputation. I'm sure it was far from your thoughts in that meadow. I don't want my name linked with yours in any way. It would only be one of a growing chain," she said.

He turned to look at her sharply. "What do you mean?"

"I think you know." She turned her gaze away from him, out her side window. Velvet, Myrna . . . how many others might there be? she wondered as tears stung her eyes.

Neither said another word until they reached the airport in Manchester. Here they found there was just enough time to make a flight that left for New York in half an hour. From New York there were several connecting flights to Chicago.

As Dale was getting her ticket Sloane said, "I wish I could go

209

with you so you wouldn't have to face all the reporters in Chicago alone."

"I was wondering why you didn't bring your luggage in. I forgot. You're on vacation," she said snappishly. She took her completed ticket from the airline clerk and began to walk in the direction of her flight's gate number.

"It's not that," Sloane said, following her. His voice carried a great deal of regret. "I planned to go home when you did. The only reason I came to England was to be with you. But . . ."

When he hesitated without finishing, Dale said, "Let me guess: Velvet?"

He looked at her as if he didn't know what to say. "Yes, I have to stay at least one more day because of her. But, Dale, it's not at all what you think." His large gray eyes seemed to plead with her to believe him.

He looked so sincere she was tempted to trust his word. But after all that had happened, Dale couldn't. If he cared for her as much as he'd intimated, he wouldn't be letting her go home alone. He'd be standing by *her,* not Velvet.

"I don't care what your relationship with her is, Sloane," Dale said, hurrying her pace. "Whether or not you've gotten her to sleep with you, the way you did me—and I don't doubt you've tried—she's still obviously more important to you than I am. So go back to her and let her cry on your shoulder some more. Maybe you'll get lucky and Trevor will dump her for good. Then you can be right there to pick up the pieces."

"You're misinterpreting the whole thing, Dale," Sloane said. His voice was hoarse, his eyes fiery with some withheld emotion.

"Am I?" she said, out of breath from rushing. "I don't care. I've got more important things to worry about now." Like her job, she thought as she glanced at her watch. "I'd better not miss that plane."

They got to the gate as the last passengers were boarding. She took the tote bag Sloane had carried for her from his hand. "Thanks," she said, irony in her tone.

"Dale, I'll be back in Chicago in a day or two." He caught her arm and sounded as though he meant to reassure her.

She pulled away from him. As she walked toward the plane she said over her shoulder, "Fine. Don't look me up."

Sloane hid his agitated feelings behind a tight mask as he watched the plane take off. What a tangled web he was in. Mostly of his own making too. A year ago who would have believed he'd be caught in knots between two beautiful women? Both needed him; only one wanted his help. Neither loved him.

And he? He'd only lately admitted the truth to himself, and it was pretty devastating: He was desperately in love. Of course he'd known for a long while that he cared. But this? This was heartache and misery and every other lovesick emotion he'd seen portrayed in movies over the years. His new appearance had turned their "friendship" completely around. But other people kept getting in their way. If he could only manage to hang on to her a little longer, maybe he could make her his yet. His love allowed no choice but to try.

CHAPTER TEN

"For a woman who had so much affection and respect from her public, you certainly have handled yourself poorly," George Ellis said, his face and voice more stern than Dale had ever seen him.

"But, as I explained, it was all because of that mix-up with my hotel reservation in Windermere. I had no choice but to share a room with Sloane Avery," Dale said. "I can't stand the man."

Ellis sighed and leaned back in his chair as he sat behind his desk. "Whether you and he had a relationship or not is irrelevant at this point. The problem is, it *looks* like you decided to have a quick affair. Nowadays even that may have been tolerated by your audience, but that lie about being married gave a sordid overtone to the whole thing. It makes you look cheap, like you were trying to cover up something illicit. The way to have an affair these days is to do it openly and behave as though you were proud of it!"

"I'm sorry I wasn't sophisticated enough to handle it properly," Dale said tartly. "I didn't want to room with him, but it was raining, and there were no accommodations . . ."

"And Mrs. Bates's scruples had to be appeased," Ellis finished. "I can see how it came about, Dale. *I* believe you. The

212

question is, will your audience if we tell them? And should we tell them, or ignore it and hope it's forgotten quickly? You know, Dale, that if you lose your audience, you lose your job."

She swallowed hard. Her throat hurt. "I know."

"What will Sloane Avery say to the press when he comes back?"

"I have no idea," she said coldly, feeling anger churn within her.

"When is he coming back?" Ellis asked.

"He told me he was staying there at least one more day."

"Will you see him when he returns?" George Ellis asked with slightly more delicacy.

"I don't intend to!" she said curtly.

"That may help your credibility. What have you told the press so far? Just said *no comment?*"

"Yes," Dale replied. "I thought that would be best."

"It was." The news director was thoughtful for a few moments. "You had that feud going with him some time ago. The public seemed to enjoy that. If we could turn this into an amusing extension of that, it might do the trick. But it would be chancy. Do you want to go on the air tonight?"

"Tonight?" she said with alarm. "I . . . don't know if I'd be able to be clever and humorous about it yet."

"Okay. We can tell the newspaper reporters who keep calling that you have jet lag. It might be best if we wait until Avery gets back anyway, to see what he tells the press. Apparently he's been able to avoid them in England. But he won't escape them here. You'll have to go on tomorrow night in any case. If you wait too long, it'll look like you're hiding."

"Yes, I understand," Dale said softly.

"By the way, we're firing Gary Murdock," Ellis said.

"That's a relief," Dale said. "Though I'm sorry he's out of a job."

"Don't feel too bad. I heard he's been offered a job at WAAB —a return favor for the hot tip they've made such good use of.

I think they'll be sorry though. *I* wouldn't want to hire someone who'd stab a co-worker in the back."

Dale spent the day preparing her report on *Ivanhoe*. The news director liked the interviews she had gotten and decided to spread her report over three nights to make the most use of it. Dale suspected it was also to make her appear as though she weren't shying away from the scandal that had come about because of her trip.

Sloane arrived in Chicago late that afternoon. She knew because she watched WAAB that night. A tape was shown of him coming from customs in the O'Hare Airport terminal. A reporter tried to question him, but Sloane said nothing and ignored the microphone.

He did not remain silent for the *Herald,* however. The morning edition carried a front page article that featured an exclusive interview with their prize-winning critic. Dale read it at work the next day.

The *Herald* naturally told the story in as favorable a light as possible, but it appeared Sloane didn't really need their help. After an introductory paragraph summarizing events, the article read:

> With so many conflicting reports from the various media about what really happened at Mr. and Mrs. Bates's bed and breakfast near Ambleside, England, the *Herald* contacted Sloane Avery at his home last night to get his side of the story.
>
> "It happened that Miss Chastain and I took the same flight to Manchester," he told the *Herald.* "As it seemed logical to travel to the Lake District together, I drove her to Windermere, where she was to meet her crew. There was some mix-up and her hotel didn't have a room for her. I'm sure that can be verified, but no one appears to have bothered. I didn't have any room reservation, so we set off together to find separate accommodations elsewhere. Unfortunately with the tourist season and the attraction of the

movie being made, there were no rooms to be had. All we found was the place near Ambleside, which offered a room with three beds. Believe me, Miss Chastain did not like the set-up at all, but she had no choice."

Avery was asked if he minded the situation. "I'm a red-blooded American bachelor," the critic jauntily replied. "I'll share a room with a former Miss Georgia anytime."

"So what happened?" he was asked. Mr. Avery replied, "After our public feuding a while back, Miss Chastain can hardly stand being in the same city with me, much less the same bed."

"What about the report that you registered as Mr. and Mrs. Sloane Avery?" the *Herald* asked. "We registered individually under our own names," Mr. Avery maintained. "The owner, Mr. Bates, foresaw his wife wouldn't approve, so he winked and changed it to look like we were married."

Finally, Sloane Avery was asked if there is any romantic entanglement between him and Miss Chastain. Tongue in cheek, he replied, "Actually, she's hopelessly in love with me, but she knows I'm too good for her."

The article was accompanied by a photograph of Sloane taken when he was still thirty pounds overweight. His hair was rumpled and his tie slightly askew.

Looking at the photo, which apparently was drawn from the newspaper's files, Dale felt odd. It was like running across the snapshot of someone who had moved away long ago.

It seemed he had handled things well, Dale thought as she perused the article again. Sloane's approach fit in with George Ellis's idea of handling the hot potato with humor. But Dale hadn't enjoyed their last public clash, and she certainly did not relish dealing with this.

Quickly she leafed through the rest of the paper. When she came to the Hollywood gossip column, she noticed Velvet Hunt's name. Velvet, it was reported, had briefly broken off her affair with John Trevor during their on-location work in England. But the break-up was short-lived, the gossip columnist reported. After two days apart, the two stars were sharing the same hotel room again.

Dale wondered just what Sloane had to do with all that. Had Velvet broken with Trevor for the comfort she found in Sloane's arms? Was that why John Trevor had been in such a temper—was he jealous of Velvet's obvious affection for Sloane? Had Sloane tried to steal her away? Perhaps his sudden good looks had made him newly appealing to Velvet. Dale remembered how the actress had smothered him with praise that night at dinner. Perhaps Sloane had made a play for her, but Trevor had won her back in the end.

What difference does it make? Dale asked herself angrily. She put the paper aside. *You have work to do!* she told herself as tears started in her eyes. She wished she didn't have such a propensity to cry lately. She was lucky she hadn't fallen for Sloane, that she had learned the truth about him before she had completely lost her heart to him. *No, I'm not in love with him,* Dale assured herself as she straightened her desk. A few moments of thoughtless passion may have made her think she was, but she knew now she had let her own wayward desire mislead her. No, it was the threat to her career that she was upset about. That, and the fact that she had been gullible enough to give herself to a man after he'd made a few idle remarks about marrying her.

Dale was raised in the Bible Belt and had been brought up with traditional moral values. It came home to her now that the old-fashioned idea of actually waiting until the wedding night to make love might have some sense to it after all. But it was too late to be regretting her foolishness now. She could only learn from her mistakes.

Her phone rang. She hesitated to pick it up. Even though her calls were being screened by the secretary so she wouldn't have to talk to reporters, she still dreaded the phone. If it was the station manager or George Ellis, it meant she would have to discuss her situation again and what she would have to do to remedy it. It wasn't something she was eager to face. And then, of course, it might be someone else calling—someone she did not want to talk to, but who was equally involved. Someone whose solid strength she missed and could never rely on again.

"Hello?" she answered, trying to put self-assurance in her voice.

"Dale? It's Sloane. I tried to call you at home last night, but . . ."

"I unplugged my phone," she said tersely, though her heartbeat was quickly escalating.

"I don't blame you. I'm getting sick of reporters too. How are you?"

"Fine," she said.

"What about your job?"

"I still have it. For the moment, anyway," she said sarcastically.

"Dale, if there's anything I can do . . ."

"You've done enough," she said. Remembering the front page article she'd just read, she recanted a bit. "You handled the *Herald* interview pretty well. Thanks."

"Sorry about that *hopelessly in love* line, but I thought . . ."

"No, it's okay," Dale said. "The humor should help to deflate the issue a little. My boss wants me to try using the same type of tactic on the air. I wish I were as clever as you . . ." She trailed off, realizing she was telling him her troubles. Like Velvet, she wanted his comfort.

"Don't try to be too clever, Dale. It might work against you. You have a natural wholesomeness. Just let that shine through. Make me out to be the ogre. I won't mind. I deserve it."

His words and voice were so kind she had to choke down the lump forming in her throat before she could speak. "M-maybe I will," she said, trying to sound a little tougher.

"Good! Can we meet for lunch, Dale? Or dinner? I want to see you."

"No. I don't think it would be wise for us to be seen together.

217

Besides, I told you when I got on the plane not to look me up. I meant that."

"Why not?"

"You know why."

"No, I don't."

She sighed impatiently. "Because you're involved with a certain actress." Dale glanced around, wanting no one at her office to overhear. "I'm surprised you didn't make the gossip column."

"I'm not involved with her, not the way you think anyway," Sloane said. "Let me see you and I'll explain what I can about her."

"Your explanations don't ring true. And I don't have the time. I have my career to keep intact. Don't call me here again," she said, and hung up before he could reply.

That night at five o'clock Dale appeared on the air. Looking as fresh and sparkling as she knew how, she introduced the first segment of her edited taped report featuring the interview of *Ivanhoe*'s director. While the tape ran on the air, she went over with Steve Froebisher and Andrea Miles what they would say. The three had discussed it late that afternoon with George Ellis.

The tape ended and Dale, live on the air again, mentioned that tomorrow night she would show her interview with John Trevor. She turned to Steve and Andrea with a smile then, though her hands were clenched tensely in her lap beneath the desk.

"You made a little news yourself while you were in England," Steve said with a casual grin, "concerning a possible romance between you and Sloane Avery. We saw Avery's account in the *Herald*. Are we going to hear your side of the story?"

Dale increased her smile, as though she thought the whole thing was a good joke. "Mr. Avery's account was pretty accurate. All the hotels near the movie set were so crowded we were forced to share a room."

"With *how* many beds?" Steve asked, raising an amused eyebrow.

"Three," Dale said, laughing. "There was one left over," she hastened to point out.

Andrea asked, "What was it like having to be in close proximity to a man you'd recently had a public spat with?"

"Let's just say the feud hasn't stopped," Dale replied.

"That's being diplomatic," Steve said with a chuckle. "But what about this statement Mr. Avery made?" He picked up a copy of the *Herald* and read: " 'She's hopelessly in love with me, but she knows I'm too good for her.' "

Dale grinned again, a tense grin, but the stiffness did not come across on camera. "Oh, it's true! I believe I've said before that I've always admired him," she said, loosening her southern drawl. "But he's right. He's *so* far superior to me, that I'm just obliged to leave him free to find someone more his equal."

Steve and Andrea laughed, while Andrea murmured, "There can't be many women who'd fill that bill!"

They broke then for a commercial and Dale walked off the set. George Ellis came up to congratulate her, saying it had gone even better than he'd expected. Earlier he had decided against mentioning the lie about being married. "I'm glad we didn't," he said now. "It would have drawn attention to the wrong thing. Avery made a good explanation in the paper anyway. You did great, Dale!"

Over the next few days the station watched its mail carefully. Reaction to Dale's scandal and her TV explanation was mixed, but largely favorable. It seemed her audience was no longer quite so sure of her, but willing to give her the benefit of the doubt. In spite of this positive sign, however, George Ellis warned her that her job was still at risk. Ratings were high now because of all the publicity. It remained to be seen if she could keep her audience when the gossip died down.

But the gossip was very slow to die down. The public seemed eager for news of the bickering couple, and the Chicago newspapers supplied whatever new shreds of the story could be found. It was verified that Dale had not been able to get a room at the hotel where her crew had stayed, which lent credence to Sloane's explanation of events. The *Herald* also interviewed Mr. Bates by phone, and the man admitted that he had been the one to suggest they register as a married couple. But an interview with Mrs. Bates by another paper was not so positive. She complained of the newspeople's unruly behavior at breakfast, and she continually referred to Dale as "that woman."

Dale knew that Hal had been approached for his view of the events, but he had not said a word to anyone, for which Dale thanked him. Gary Murdock, now working for WAAB, did not remain silent. He told the newspapers that Dale was not what she seemed on the air, that he believed she and Sloane did have an affair, and that Sloane was also involved with another woman whose name Murdock either did not mention, or the paper decided not to print.

In response, Dale's station manager issued a press statement saying that Gary Murdock had been fired by them for uncooperative and surly behavior while on the job.

And so it continued, only gradually waning as all news sources were used up. Dale finished her series on the filming of *Ivanhoe* and continued to do her nightly movie reviews. This required that she go to most preview screenings in order to keep ahead of the movie release schedule. And that of course meant that she saw Sloane at the seventh-floor private theater on State Street.

On all these occasions Dale scrupulously avoided him. If he came up to her and said hello, she nodded her head in acknowledgment and walked away. If he tried to sit next to her, she would move to another seat. And yet every time she saw him she wished she could run into his arms and let him hold her against his large masculine frame. He continued to look good, more handsome than ever. It appeared he might still be losing weight, for he looked more lean and athletic every time she saw him. But Dale continued to tell herself she wanted nothing to do with him.

Sloane, for his part, could understand her coolness. But he hadn't thought it would last so long. He'd thought, after the intimacy they'd shared in England, that she might give him another chance. They'd been back in Chicago for several weeks now. It was the middle of summer. Velvet was still in England. Dale, he'd thought, would have seen that he and the actress were not in close contact. How could they be with an ocean between them? But Dale, it seemed, had a long memory.

A ray of hope came in the form of an unexpected phone call from an independent Chicago TV station, WXN. "We're trying to put together a movie review show with two critics called *Private Screenings,*" Raymond Marek, the show's producer told Sloane. "Each week the critics will give their opinions of four films. We want to do a half-hour pilot. If the show becomes successful, we're hoping to put it into syndication eventually. Since you're the top movie critic in Chicago, we of course wanted you to do the show."

"For television?" Sloane felt queasy at the mere thought of talking coherently in front of a camera.

"Yes, we'd tape the shows. There would be lots of preparation before we actually began to record it, however. Have you ever done TV?"

"No. Well, once. I was interviewed for a news report. They were doing a series on interesting professions. I was terrible."

"Perhaps they didn't prepare you properly," Marek said. "I hope you'd be willing to try a pilot for us anyway. If the show catches on, it would enhance your name recognition and there could be some good money in it too."

"I know," Sloane said with a sigh. He really wasn't interested, but felt the pressure of knowing that it was a career opportunity he oughtn't pass up. "Who's the other critic?"

"We're not sure yet," Marek said. "We thought of Dale Chastain. She has a wonderful TV presence. But I understand there are some difficulties between the two of you, so I thought I'd get your reaction on the matter first."

Sloane's face brightened. "Well, I'll tell you, Mr. Marek— she'll probably cream me on a TV show with her smile and southern spunk. But I won't do the pilot unless she agrees to be the other critic."

"All right," Raymond Marek said with satisfaction. "We'll have to see what we can do."

Sloane was on pins and needles until he heard further on the matter. At present he was getting nowhere trying to rekindle the spark that had flamed between him and Dale in England. But working together on the projected show might be the catalyst that would put new life into their frozen relationship. At last he got another call from Raymond Marek a few days later.

"I finally got hold of Dale Chastain and offered her the job. She wanted to refuse. I asked her to think it over for a few days before giving me a final answer. I'm afraid it doesn't look too hopeful, Mr. Avery," Marek told him.

"Did she lose interest when you told her she'd be working with me?" Sloane asked matter-of-factly.

"Well, yes, it appeared that way. I told her that the public interest in the incident between you and her would only increase the ratings for the show, but . . ."

"It didn't help," Sloane surmised. "I may be foolish, but let me see what I can do. She still speaks to me on rare occasions."

Sloane planned carefully for the next screening, both his wardrobe and his strategy. When he arrived at the theater he looked conservative but very elegant in a light gray three-piece suit, a pale blue shirt, and a gray, navy, and white striped tie. He had checked that morning to make sure there were no coffee stains on anything. He still had a problem with that, not to mention numerous cleaning bills.

When he walked in he saw Dale already seated toward the front. He'd noticed she had been sitting up front often, perhaps because she knew he couldn't tolerate watching a movie so close to the screen. He took his usual place and made no attempt to speak to her.

When the movie was over, however, and everyone was getting up to leave, he walked toward her. As Sloane moved against the direction of the main group of reporters, he bumped into Alan Thornton and said hello. He'd noticed that Alan had seemed to go out of his way to try to remain friendly with Dale and himself. Sloane hurried toward Dale then. Her eyes downcast, she was keeping toward the tail end of the exiting crowd, probably hoping to avoid Sloane that way. She seemed a little surprised when she looked up at the tall man who suddenly blocked her path.

"Dale, I just want to talk to you for two minutes." She said nothing and tried to move past him. He firmly grabbed her arm. "Two minutes!"

She stood still. "What do you want?"

"I think you should do *Private Screenings* with me."

"Why?" Her tone was not amicable.

"Because I think we'd work well together. And you need the job security. Your current job still isn't certain, is it? This would give you something to fall back on if WNBS decides to let you go. And it's always possible the show could be a hit," Sloane said in his most businesslike manner.

She lowered her eyes, as if his words were making sense in spite of her antipathy toward him.

"You don't have to worry about me. I'll do my best to stay out of your way when we're not doing the show," he added.

Dale looked up at him suddenly. The bright blue of her lovely eyes disconcerted him a bit. She was so damned beautiful. "Why do you care if I do the show or not then?" she said. "They could find someone else to work with you."

Sloane hesitated a moment, searching for the best answer. "Because you and I complement each other. I have the prestige and you have the personality. You could show me how to be smooth in front of a camera."

Dale lowered her eyes again, as if disappointed with his answer somehow. He'd thought he'd managed to find impersonal business reasons and still flatter her too. But it seemed he must have said something wrong somewhere. "It's just a pilot, Dale. Maybe the station won't pick it up. What is there to lose trying it out?"

"The public is going to wonder why we're working together when we aren't supposed to like each other. They might wonder again what *did* happen in England," Dale said.

"We won't have to pretend to like each other," Sloane said. "I have a hunch that Marek wants us because of our antagonism.

223

It would make the show more interesting than having two people who are polite to each other and agree on everything."

She seemed to weigh seriously what he said. A small flame of hope kindled in Sloane's eyes as he watched her thoughtful expression.

"We can just be us, then?" she said.

"I'm sure that's what they want. And if that's what we give them, I don't think anyone would suspect a romance between us. And you'll always have the advantage—we'll be working on your turf."

She smiled slightly at that. It was the first time she'd smiled at him in weeks and it nearly brought tears to his eyes.

"All right. I guess it's a chance I shouldn't pass up," she said. "I'll tell Mr. Marek I'll do it."

Sloane stifled the great sigh of relief he felt welling within him and discouraged the grin that came to his lips. He said, "Do you think anyone would make anything of it if we go down the elevator together?"

She looked around the small, empty theater. "I guess not," she said with another little smile. They went down to State Street together and then went their separate ways. Sloane felt a foot taller all day.

Dale adjusted her position again, never feeling quite comfortable sitting on the two cushions the director, Mark Cutter, had given her. She was sitting opposite a very narrow aisle from Sloane in a bogus, empty, movie theater balcony. Around them was the darkened warehouse atmosphere of the large studio in which they were taping. The cushions were to make Dale's shoulders more on a level with Sloane's. The cameramen, Cutter, and producer Raymond Marek had all agreed she looked too diminutive opposite Sloane's large frame. If she appeared like a twelve-year-old next to him, they said, it would lessen her impact on camera.

Sloane had come in wearing his gray three-piece suit and Dale had worn a pastel green suit with a dotted blouse. After Dale was given the cushions, Sloane still looked overbearing next to her, so the director asked him to remove his coat. He looked less challenging in his vest and shirt-sleeves. At last, it was decided, they looked balanced together on camera.

They had been sitting there for two hours now, taping in fits and starts. The director was trying to get a good take on the ad-libbed cross-talk between them after a clip of the first film had been shown. Sloane was still very nervous and stiff, and too polite. Dale wished she could help him relax.

"Sloane," she'd said quietly when Mark Cutter was advising the cameramen again, "they told you to look at *me*, remember? Try to forget the cameras."

"How can I forget when that one is always staring me in the face?" Sloane said. He motioned toward one in front of Dale that was aimed at him. Similarly, one near him was aimed at Dale as he and she leaned toward each other over the aisle.

"You should try to get involved with what you're saying. Remember on the plane that discussion we had about the movie that was shown? You disagreed with me and gave a beautiful explanation why. Do the same now. Get mad, if you want. I know you think my opinion of this film is silly. Tell me!"

His expression grew troubled. "I don't want to put you down."

She laughed. "You never had second thoughts about it before. I think I can take care of myself at the moment." Having decided to do the pilot, she wanted the show to be a success, for herself, and, she had to admit, for Sloane too.

"All right, let's try it again," Cutter said, coming back to them. "When the clip is over, face the screen, Dale, then turn to Sloane—just like before."

Dale watched the clip for the fourth time on the small TV monitor. When it was almost finished, she looked straight ahead, as if she were watching the movie screen ahead of them. On the finished tape, Cutter had explained, the movie would look as though it were being projected on the screen.

She turned then to Sloane. "I think we can see from that scene how unbelievable these characters are," she said to him. She was referring to a statement she had taped earlier when she had introduced the clip of the crime drama they were reviewing. "They are two-dimensional, going through their paces like rats in a maze. And none of them are likeable. I thought this was a tiresome, mean little picture and I can't recommend it. Sloane?"

Sloane was keeping his eyes on her now and appeared this time to have actually heard what she'd said. Up until now he had been too disconcerted to really respond to her. "I think that was the *meanest* review you've ever given!" Her bright gaze returned his humor. His gray eyes responded by coming fully to life. "I liked this picture," he went on. "It was clearly modeled after the old detective movies of the forties, only the story line has been changed to fit current times. Sure, it's tough, but the crimes— murder and drug-running—are tough. I thought it was slickly made, fast-moving, and engrossing."

"But," Dale countered, "none of the characters in this film had the charm or screen presence of old stars like Bogart or Cagney or Alan Ladd."

"You want charm, go see a musical!" Sloane said.

"Respond to my point," Dale insisted. "Do you think any of these actors could equal the tough guys of the forties? *I* like the old films, too, and I say this one doesn't compare."

"All right, I'll concede these actors don't match Bogart or Ladd, but the story, the pacing, and the style make this movie worthwhile all the same."

"So we disagree on this one. Shall we go on to the next?" Dale said.

"That's a take!" Cutter said jubilantly. Raymond Marek also nodded his approval. "Great, both of you!" Cutter said. "That's what we want! Now, Sloane, you'll nod to Dale, responding to her suggesting we go on. Then you read your introduction of the next film from the TelePrompTer. Can you see it all right?"

"Yes," Sloane said. He sounded like he was catching his breath. "I just try to do this the way she read the first one?"

"Right. When you finish, look up at the screen as if you were going to watch it."

Dale's heart sank a little as Sloane read. He had grown stiff again, looking toward the camera as he went through the introduction he had written.

"Cut," the director said before Sloane had finished. "All right, let's do it again. Try to relax, Sloane. Put some variation in your voice. You're speaking in a monotone."

Sloane tried again, but it wasn't much better. When Cutter stopped him again, Dale said, "Pretend the camera is a person. That's what I used to do when I started."

"A person, huh?" Sloane said sardonically as a makeup man came to dab perspiration from his forehead. "With one big eye?"

"Use your imagination."

"I haven't got any."

The makeup man finished. The director had Sloane begin again, but soon interrupted him again.

"You're reading better now, but you still look stiff. It's okay if you smile now and then," Cutter said.

"What am I supposed to be smiling at?" Sloane asked with a weary sigh.

"Just try to look like you want to be here. You had it a minute ago when you were responding to Dale," the director said.

"I'll make him smile," Dale said mischievously. She reached across then and dug her fingers into Sloane's side beneath the lower edge of his vest.

"Hey!" Sloane said, reacting to her tickling with a broad grin. "Stop it!" He grabbed her small wrist. "How can I be dignified with you . . . ."

"You're too dignified. Be your old sloppy self. Anybody have a bag of popcorn?" Dale joked. She was genuinely enjoying having the upper hand over Sloane for once.

Sloane was obviously enjoying it, too, for he was laughing now as he continued to half-heartedly try to push away her wiggling fingers.

Cutter was grinning as he said, "Okay, let's settle down, you two. Sloane? Try it again."

Sloane straightened his tie and vest, but as he began reading, his voice was lighter, his expression had warmth, and his eyes were alight. He was still rather stilted, but it was much better.

The rest of the taping went more smoothly from then on, and the director predicted the pilot had a good chance of success when they finished a few hours later.

"Thanks, Dale," Sloane said as they walked out of the studio together, "for helping me through it. It makes me appreciate even more what a beautiful job you do on the news every night."

He said all this with such sincerity, it made Dale's reply catch in her throat a bit. "Thank you. I'm glad I could help."

"Look, why don't we go have an early dinner somewhere? There's time before you have to be at the station for the five o'clock news."

Dale hesitated before answering. She wanted to be with him. More than anything she would have enjoyed spending the next hour with him, talking over the pilot, laughing together some more. They might have been like they once were together, the way they were in England before—before Velvet had caught his interest. Dale didn't want to chance going through that again, almost falling for him and then watching him spend all his time with another woman.

No, for all his openness and down-to-earth qualities, Sloane Avery was still a dangerous man to get involved with emotionally. Dale had been shaken to find how entrenched in him her feelings had been, having realized it fully when he had forsaken her to stay one more night with Velvet in England. Dale was thankful she hadn't fallen completely in love with him. She didn't want to expose herself to the possibility again.

"No, Sloane, I have to go to the studio now," she told him. She swallowed convulsively as she watched his expression fade to disappointment and the light go out of his eyes. Sometimes she could almost believe that he did care for her. Maybe he did, though he'd never really said so. In any case, he cared for Velvet more. "I'm glad the pilot went well. I hope we can do more shows together," she said, and then left him.

The pilot was a success and was quickly bought by WXN. Dale and Sloane were contracted to do more. They began taping one a week. Quickly they fell into a pattern, using their natural inclination to disagree about films to advantage, creating stimulating shows which the Chicago public immediately liked.

But the clever banter they had for the camera always failed off-camera, Sloane noted with continuing dismay. As soon as each taping was finished, Dale became polite and businesslike with him. Apparently she wanted to remain on good enough terms with him to continue doing the show, but had no interest in recapturing their former, albeit brief, closeness. Every week his hopes were crushed anew.

Sloane was growing tired and impatient with the situation after two months. He wanted the rapport, the energizing eye contact they had on-camera full-time. He wanted much more than that too. He had had enough of taking slow, careful steps to win her again. A new approach was definitely in order, he decided.

From the time he got up, Sloane was on edge the morning of the next *Private Screenings* taping. It showed in his disposition when he arrived at the studio. He was no-nonsense and ready for work, all remains of camera-shyness gone. And it showed in his ad-libbed repartee with Dale.

"As you can see, this is an intense, sensual film, in the tradition of *The Postman Always Rings Twice* and *Body Heat*," he said after a clip of the last film of the day, a romantic thriller, was shown. The movie footage was a night scene at a beach house with a man and woman preparing to make steamy illicit love in the moonlight. "It's a film aimed at adults for a change, rather than teenagers. And it deals with adults doing things they know they should not be doing. It's an intriguing, complex story of lust and treachery, and I found its moody, sexually charged atmosphere mesmerizing. I highly recommend it. Dale?"

He turned to her as the camera continued to roll on this first take. Dale seemed slightly discomfited. He could see it in her eyes, though she was quick enough to respond.

"I'm surprised you liked this one so well. You seem much easier on films lately than you used to be," she said.

"And you're finally getting tougher on them! But what could you find to dislike about this movie?" Sloane knew he was giving her a hard time, but he felt that trying to outwit her intellectually might be his one remaining weapon. It was the only way he could put her off-balance.

"I'm only giving it a qualified recommendation," Dale said. "While it was well-acted and smoothly paced, I thought its atmosphere was too unrelentingly oppressive."

"You find sexual tension oppressive?"

She seemed at a loss for words for a fraction of a second. "But this was so brooding and devoid of any positive feeling."

"Unrequited need makes a person that way," Sloane said. His tone was getting a bit harsh.

"The people in this film weren't unrequited. By the second half of the picture they were in bed every fifteen minutes," Dale retorted.

"Lucky them!" Sloane said with a smile he didn't feel. He realized his own emotions were getting the better of him and he kept himself in check.

"I think we're digressing," Dale said firmly. "As I say, I recommend that our viewers see this film, but with the admonition that not everyone may care for the driving, obsessively sexual thrust of the film."

Sloane was amused. "I like your word choice. I think you enjoyed this picture better than you want to admit." He could see the angry spark in her eye, though she said nothing further. The director called it a take.

After a round-up of the four pictures they had reviewed, in which they recapped their yes and no votes for each, they were finished with that week's taping. Dale rose from her two-cushioned seat and began to leave. The lights were turned off and it was rather dark in the large studio. She was wearing a light yellow summer dress, and Sloane could see her moving as if through shadows toward the large metal exit door. Quickly he nodded good-bye to the director and crew people who were putting away equipment, grabbed his suit jacket, and followed her.

"Not even going to say good-bye today?" he said as he caught up with her.

"I used up all my civility toward you on camera," she said curtly. She maintained her pace and did not look at him.

He followed her through the door, then possessively took hold of her upper arm in the empty hallway outside.

"Let me go," she said.

"I want you to tell me what's bothering you today," Sloane said.

"What's bothering *me!* How about you? You kept badgering me all day, making fun of me on-camera. We're supposed to be two professional critics. We're not doing this show to needle and ridicule each other."

"Mark Cutter didn't mind. He knows the audience loves it when we argue," Sloane said.

"Well, I think you carried it too far today," Dale said. She turned to go.

Sloane restrained her, taking hold of her shoulders. He pulled her back toward him. "You've lost your sense of humor, Dale. And I think I know why. You're frustrated. Like me."

"F-frustrated! What do you mean?" The glimmer of the hall ceiling lights wavered in her eyes, giving her a vulnerable quality suddenly. It made Sloane feel stronger and more confident.

"I mean sexually—you and I working together, trying to ignore all those feelings we had for each other in England, pretending we don't need or even like each other. I don't know about you, but I'm damned tired of it. I want us back together, in every sense of the word." He stared down at her, feeling his passion

231

infusing his eyes, for his lids felt tense and wide. He waited, as if at the edge of a cliff, for Dale to make some response.

She seemed confused, yet she never took her eyes from his. It was as if she were fixed by his intense gaze. "I don't want to get involved with you, Sloane."

"Why?"

"Velvet Hunt," she said.

He sighed sharply and gripped Dale more tightly. "How many times must I tell you, there's nothing between me and Velvet. She loves John Trevor. She's just a friend to me and that's all."

"And Myrna?"

"Myrna. Myrna Lowry, you mean?" he said. "What about her?"

"I found that diagram she made for you. She picked out your whole wardrobe for you, didn't she?"

"Yes."

"Then you have some sort of relationship going with her," Dale said as if it were fact.

Sloane laughed ironically. "She's the *Herald*'s fashion editor and happily married for thirty years or more. She did me a favor and went shopping with me, that's all."

Dale looked doubtful, as if she didn't know whether or not to believe that.

"Check tomorrow's paper. You'll see her name on the fashion page," Sloane said. "Can't you try trusting me for once?" He pressed her against him, feeling himself melting with the joy of her fragile, pliant body touching his once again. Her lips were soft and full as she looked up at him with troubled, apprehensive eyes. He couldn't suppress the overwhelming desire to kiss her. Enfolding her in his arms, he allowed himself the full pleasure of her lips. He could feel her body trembling within his warm embrace. At first she was unresponsive, her mouth seemingly numb. But after a few moments her lips surrendered to his coaxing and she kissed him back hungrily.

"Oh, Dale," he whispered against her cheek. "I've missed

kissing you, holding you like this. You've missed it too. Admit it, darling."

She lowered her eyes and nodded imperceptibly. It wasn't much reassurance, but it was enough to give him the nerve to tell her what he had intended to tell her all day. His heart pounding against his ribs, he said in a husky, barely restrained voice, "I love you, Dale. I . . . *love you!*" She looked up in sudden astonishment, but he continued. "I want us to be together always."

Dale's quivering lips seemed to stumble for words. "Love . . . me?"

"Yes! You don't have to look so shocked. I told you I was crazy about you," he said in irritation born of the fear of her rejection.

Her eyes studied his face earnestly. "You really love *me?*"

He smiled. "Yes!" He watched and waited as she seemed to mentally digest that fact, wondering in deep anxiety what her response would be. After a full minute it began to seem like she didn't have any. Heart sinking, he said, "Do you think you could tell me how *you* feel?"

As if his voice had shaken her perplexed contemplation, she looked up at him, her eyes full of hesitance. "I . . ." she began, but then words seemed to leave her. In a moment she blurted out, "I don't want to have an affair, Sloane. I have my career, and I don't want anything to . . ."

"I'm not talking about an affair!" he interrupted testily. "I want us to be married."

Her eyes widened in astonishment. "Married!" she said in a bare whisper.

"Married!" he repeated, growing angry. "You don't have to act as though the notion were so peculiar. I love you and I want to marry you! I told you that in England."

"You never said you loved me," she said, defensiveness in her tone. "Sure, you muttered something about us marrying—and then you stayed on an extra day to be with Velvet. How do you think I should react?"

"You could say yes," he said adamantly. "I didn't tell you I loved you because I wasn't sure how you felt about me. And I must have said a hundred times now that there's nothing going on between me and Velvet."

She put her fingertips to her forehead and shook her head. "How do you expect me to believe that?" she murmured.

"Because I love you dearly and I wouldn't lie to you," he said, taking her hands in his.

Dale seemed totally befuddled. "I never thought that after all we've been through you'd seriously ask me to be your wife." She sounded almost meek. "Sloane, look, I—I'm flattered that you asked me to marry you."

"You really look like it," he mumbled.

"But I'll have to consider all this, how I feel and . . . and what I want to do." She was gradually backing away from him as she spoke. Her voice, weak and hesitating, seemed to reflect a genuine confusion of thought. "I have to leave now to go to work. I'll talk to you."

"When?"

She paused in her slow, backstepping retreat. "I don't know."

"Can I call you tonight? After the ten o'clock news? Or I could stop by when you get home. Can I pick you up and drive you home?" Eagerly he put forth each possibility that flew into his mind.

Dale put her hand to her head again. "No, no, I—I need some time to myself. I have to go now." She turned and moved to the outside exit door nearby with an air of numb determination. Just before she pushed it open, she glanced back at Sloane. After looking at him unsteadily for a moment, she said, "'Bye," in a slight voice. Then she was gone.

All day Sloane had wondered how she would react. He had hoped for joyful surprise, but had mentally armored himself for a sarcastic rejection, or perhaps just humiliating amusement. He had never envisioned her becoming almost catatonic.

He was nearly thirty-seven now. Through the two decades

since his adolescence, Sloane had now and again thought that by the time he reached his late thirties he'd have learned how to handle a woman. At least he'd hoped to have found some way to win the one woman who was meant for him. Marriages, it used to be said, were made in heaven, but this one was certainly having trouble finding its way to earth. How come it never happened this way in the movies?

CHAPTER ELEVEN

Dale stood on the terrace and looked across Lake Shore Drive to the Sunday crowd on Oak Street Beach. Farther out she could see graceful sailboats gliding through the blue waters of Lake Michigan. It was a warm, sunny day, one of the final days of the fading summer. Perhaps the last good opportunity to take advantage of the beach, she thought, feeling somehow restless.

She had in fact put on her white bikini bathing suit. They had just decided to go down to the beach, and she was waiting for Sloane, who had gotten detained by a phone call. She had stepped out onto the small terrace off of the bedroom in Sloane's spacious condominium.

She gazed down again at the people on blankets, like small ants from the height of the balcony, stretched out in the sun. Children were running through the sand. It looked idyllic, but somehow today it didn't appeal to Dale as much as she'd thought it would when Sloane first suggested it after brunch. She imagined it would get hot sitting in the sun, and she felt too lazy to swim. Why go down there, when it was so private and quiet up here? she thought.

Behind her she heard the open and close of the sliding glass door. "Who was it?" she asked, turning to Sloane.

He walked up to where she was standing by the white railing. Her heart began to spin when she gazed at his tall masculine frame clad only in snug blue bathing trunks. He was sublimely lean and muscular now, his daily morning workouts having reshaped his body to its full potential. And his physical potential, it had turned out, was close to perfection in Dale's estimation. Flat, hard stomach muscles, a marvelous sculpted chest with luxurious dark hair, wondrously strong shoulders and arms, tantalizing thighs, and though it wasn't visible to her now, a charming rear—he was everything she had once only dreamed of.

"A reporter," Sloane said, answering her question. "I got rid of him. I would have thought we'd be old news by now. Ready to go?"

She sighed. "I guess so." Her tone carried no enthusiasm.

Sloane angled his head in a questioning attitude. "Don't you want to? I thought that's what we decided to do."

"I know," she said. She was gazing out toward the beach again. "It looks kind of crowded down there though. And people might recognize us."

"We'll wear sunglasses."

"Well, okay," she said with a long sigh.

Sloane grinned. "We don't have to." He lifted one hand toward her. "Is there something else you'd rather do?"

"Oh, I don't know."

"Dale," he said, sounding a little exasperated, "what is this problem you have making up your mind lately? Now you can't even decide whether you want to go to the beach."

"You'll just have to learn to be patient, that's all," she said, tilting up her chin.

"I've had to learn that over and over with you." He looked at her with a touch of resignation. "Well, are we going to the beach?"

"I guess I'd rather not."

"At least you decided—after I went to the trouble of putting on my suit."

"You complain too much."

"I do, do I?" he said with a hint of amusement. "So, my dear, how would you like to spend the afternoon?"

He sounded like Clark Gable in *Gone With the Wind,* Dale thought with secret excitement. Her pulse began to escalate. "I'm . . . not sure. What would you like to do?" she asked, looking up at him. Some instinct made her widen her eyes ingenuously.

The expression in his gray eyes changed slightly at the way she gazed at him. She sensed he knew she was flirting and it made her heart beat faster. His eyes made a purposeful inspection of the length of her slim, graceful, barely covered body. He shifted his weight and leaned against the railing.

"You really want to know?" he said.

"Yes."

"I'd like to take you inside and pull down that little bikini bottom."

A small involuntary gasp parted her lips. His words enflamed her. "Sloane, you're so bawdy!"

"And you love it," he said.

"How dare you, say such a thing!"

"Don't put on your southern propriety with me. I know you."

She pouted at him and then turned toward the railing and looked out at the lake. She still wasn't quite used to bantering with him at such a heady level, knowing the consequences. "Well, what *are* we going to do for the rest of the day?" she asked innocently.

He put his arms lightly around her, turning her to face him. "I have a feeling you have something in mind."

Dale lowered her eyes to his chest, feeling shy for some extraordinary reason. After searching her head for something to say, she told him, "You'd better not lose any more weight, Sloane. You look wonderful just like this." She ran her fingertips lightly up his chest, watching her polished pink nails get lost in his thick springy hair.

"I don't think I should either," he said. "I'm getting tired of having my suits altered." He grabbed her exploring hands. "And I wouldn't want you to think I was too skinny."

"No," she said, her voice very breathless.

"What are you up to?" he asked, adoring amusement in his eyes and voice. He put his hands at her back and edged her closer to him.

"Up to?"

"All this bashful touching and not saying what you want. It's not quite the way you ordinarily flirt. You're usually a little more sure of yourself."

Dale glanced down self-consciously and then up at him again. She didn't know what to answer. Flirting had been easy when she was merely interested in a man. It had been natural to flirt with Sloane once she'd discovered he could be so attractive. But her feelings were much too strong just now to be playful and superficial. She didn't know how to flirt with someone she had only recently discovered she was deeply in love with. And she certainly wasn't used to telling a man she wanted him to take her to bed. She wanted Sloane to take the initiative, the way he always had with her from the beginning. She had managed to get him on the right track, but now he was toying with her.

"Come on, darling." His voice was sensual and coaxing. "Tell me what you want."

She took one of his handsomely formed hands from the curve of her waist and brought it up to cup her breast. "This," she whispered.

"Again?" Flames smoldered in his eyes as he watched her face. She turned a rosier hue from embarrassment. It only made him smile. "After last night and this morning?" he went on. "Do you have some plot to wear me down, blitzing my body and mind so you can walk all over me on our show? What an unprofessional tactic!"

"Oh, hush," she said softly, her face coloring more with his teasing.

"So there was a reason why you didn't want to go to the beach. Why didn't you say something before we changed?"

"It was when I saw you in your bathing suit that . . ." She finished the sentence with a little shrug that mutely explained the rest.

"Really?" he said. "My body turns you on?"

She nodded and leaned down to kiss the large hand she held at her breast. Sloane bent his head then to touch her lips with his. As his mouth moved moistly against hers, she felt a little tug at the nape of her neck, then another at the middle of her back. Her bikini top came loose from her body. Sloane edged back slightly to let it fall into his hand, then he tossed it onto a lounge chair in the corner of the terrace.

Feeling the wind run across her bared nipples, she brought her hands up to cover herself. "Sloane, we'd better go in. Someone might see."

"We're sixteen floors up. Who can see?" he said, putting his arms around her.

"Some reporter with a telescopic lens," she said. She glanced in back of him. "Or one of our neighbors might come out on their balcony."

He made a regretful sigh. "I suppose we have to bow to the conventions of society. I hope the reporter managed to catch you like this though," he teased. He was looking at her small hands pressing into her soft flesh. "You're adorable in that pose."

"Come on, Sloane," she said, and urged him toward the sliding door. He opened it for her when they reached it and they went in. As he closed it again she went to the hidden pull cord and began to close the sheer white floor-to-ceiling drape.

Suddenly she felt a sharp pull at the back of her bikini bottom and gave a little cry of surprise. As he knelt behind her he slid the panties down her smooth slender thighs, stopping to gently bite her soft white derriere. "Sloane!" she squealed, catching on to the drape to keep her balance.

He pushed the panties down her shapely calves to her ankles. She stepped out of them then and turned to face him. His forehead was at the level of her breastbone. He leaned forward to kiss her silken skin while she stroked the back of his head and played with his hair.

After a long deep breath, she said, "I love you, Sloane." She felt odd at having finally said the words out loud. Her soft voice seemed to hang in the quiet pale blue room.

His eyes grew glassy for a moment. He rose to his feet and took her into his arms. "I hoped you did," he said, his voice husky. "I'm glad to hear you say it."

She brought her arms up around his neck, smiling with quiet joy, and rose up on her toes to kiss him. "Please take me to bed," she whispered.

Now, oddly, it was easy to say. She felt that finally, after several weeks of emotional turbulence, everything was growing steady between them. They were becoming emotionally attuned to each other.

"You don't have to say please," he told her softly. He picked her up in his arms as if she weighed nothing and took her to the large bed. It was still unmade from that morning. They had been living together only a brief time, but Dale already found herself falling in with Sloane's casual attitude toward neatness. Why make a bed when you were in it half the time? became her rationale.

The sheets felt cool as he laid her upon them. Sloane took off his bathing suit and stretched out his long frame beside her. The removal of his swim trunks clearly showed he was ready whenever she was. As he began to stroke her torso and kiss her breasts she knew she would not keep him waiting long.

She ran her fingers through his hair and then lightly over the back of his shoulders as he teased her nipples with his mouth and tongue. A delicious prickly sensation coursed through her. She felt heat infusing her body from head to toe. That something which was so much fun could be so fulfilling continued to amaze her.

Dale closed her eyes at the pleasurable feel of her breasts swelling beneath his expert touch. The rose tips were nublike now, pert little centers of sensation receptive to the sweet suction and movement of his mouth. His lips left them, however, to move along her soft skin to her stomach. Numerous little kisses around her belly button made her giggle and her skin quiver with delight.

He grinned at her light laughter and leaned down on one arm beside her again. As he bent his head to kiss her mouth she put her arm about his strong, large rib cage and pulled him closer. Drawing one leg up, she rubbed the inside of her thigh along the outside of his while her mouth opened for him to explore.

She was fully enjoying the masculine feel of his body against hers, when suddenly he increased her pleasure one hundredfold. His hand found its way to her lower extremities and all at once she felt his fingertip gently stroking her most sweetly sensual spot.

"Oh, Sloane . . ." she moaned, and edged even closer to him. "Don't stop. It's wonderful," she breathed.

"I wouldn't dream of stopping," he said with a grin. "Just let me know when you can't take it anymore."

She smiled in the midst of her lulling bliss. As he continued the magic of his hand between her thighs, she realized she couldn't let the sensual tension he was creating within her build much more. Her blue eyes rose to his, shining and glistening with the pleasure he was giving her. Her lips were wet and full from his kisses.

"Sloane," she said in a silky, urging voice, letting her slow natural accent drip like honey on her words, "I can't take it anymore."

Sloane's silvery eyes were bright with flame. "You little hussy," he said in low, loving, masculine tones. "You even flirt when you're doing this."

"I am not," she protested, even as she brought her pelvis forward to engage with his. Her hands on his tightly firmed buttocks now, she slid her thighs around him as he rolled on top of her. "Oh . . . Sloane . . ." she cried in low, gasping tones, reveling in the feel of his heavy weight on her and the manly hardness within her.

"You're a dream lover, Dale," Sloane murmured in her ear. "More exciting than a man could imagine. Stay with me always?"

"Of course I will, Sloane." Warmly she stroked his back as his body gently moved back and forth over hers. "I think I'd die without you now." Her voice broke a little as she said the words. "Don't *you* leave me."

He rose up on his elbows slightly to look down at her face. "Are you out of your mind?" he said, his voice full of love. "That's why I wanted to marry you so badly. So you couldn't get away from me!"

She smiled up at him while a small tear streamed from the corner of one eye back into her hair. They kissed eagerly and then more and more heatedly as the passions within them grew overpowering.

All at once she felt she had climbed to the top of a mountain . . . and at the top there was a rushing silence for a brief moment. And then . . . an explosion. Her body pulsated and writhed beneath his. Tidal waves of ecstasy shook her soul. In the midst of it she smiled with joy; she felt his intense trauma and violent release while she gripped his strong body in the circle of her arms. After his passion was spent, he continued to move against her, producing within her one burst after another, like fireworks, until her body was completely sated and she begged him to stop.

He moved off her then and lay beside her, pulling her gently against him, his arm languidly around her back. After a very contented sigh, he nuzzled and kissed her forehead, then lay his head back on the pillow.

"I'm glad I met you while I was still reasonably young," he said. "I don't know if I could take this otherwise."

"You seem to manage just fine," she said, gently playing with the hair on his chest as she lay with her head on his shoulder. "I'll buy you some Vitamin E if you're worried."

"Great. I suppose you'll mix it with my grits in the morning."

"You still don't like grits?" she said, looking up at him. She had been making them for their breakfast every day along with toast and eggs.

He smiled as if he had told himself something snide and witty and then said, "No comment."

"You'll learn to like them," she assured him.

"Being married to you, I expect I'll have to," he murmured and then closed his eyes to sleep.

Dale snuggled against him. She felt like drifting into a nap also. But before she fell asleep her mind reflected on all that had happened in the last weeks: Sloane's proposal, which had taken her so completely off-guard, her confusion of feelings and resistance, Sloane's persistent pursuit until, last weekend, they had been married in the small chapel of a large church on North Michigan Avenue. The press and public had been astonished, and the couple had been pursued by reporters.

But no one had been more surprised than Dale that she had actually wed Sloane Avery, the man she had so long admired, fought with, and had so many doubts about. He had convinced her somehow; she couldn't even quite remember now how he had done it. She should have known he always managed to get his way.

But lying with him now, so peaceful and satisfied after making love, she wondered why she had been so concerned that she was doing the right thing. There of course had been the question of his relationship with Velvet. Dale still wasn't sure what had happened in Windermere. Sloane continually denied any affair with Velvet, and Dale knew he couldn't have seen her for some time now, since Velvet was still in England.

And then there had been Dale's embarrassing suspicion of Myrna. Sloane had introduced her to Myrna a few days ago at his office. Not only had Dale been completely reassured on that point, but she had even liked the woman.

Dale also wasn't sure she wanted to be married yet, and she wasn't certain what exactly her feelings for Sloane were. As far as her career, marriage had made little difference so far, except for giving her more publicity. The other question, her feelings for

244

Sloane, had been the heart of her dilemma. She had known she was deeply attracted to him, more than to any other man she'd ever met. But she'd had to stifle that attraction when she'd suspected he was involved with Velvet, mainly to protect herself from hurt. And in any case, she had never been sure that that attraction was love. She wasn't sure she knew what love was then.

Even when she had stood before the minister with Sloane, both their families in attendance, she didn't know if she truly loved him. At that point she had been very mixed up emotionally, trying to be logical about her future while Sloane was calling or visiting her day and night, doing everything he could to convince her to go through with a wedding. In the end she had decided to follow her gut reaction, which kept telling her: *Don't pass this man up!* Something deep within her knew she belonged with Sloane, even if her mind was never sure.

It was only yesterday she'd realized she did love him. It had been a difficult week, moving into his home, living with a man for the first time, visiting with relatives who had briefly come in for the wedding, all the while keeping her work schedule and appearing composed and happy on the air. She knew everyone watching was probably wondering how and why she had come to marry Sloane Avery, her old adversary. The press had pestered them, too, lifting verbal eyebrows again at their explanation of the bed and breakfast episode in the Lake District.

But last night Sloane had taken her to the elegant restaurant at the top of the Hancock Building, across the street from the church where they were married, to celebrate their first anniversary. They'd been married exactly one week. He had been handsome and witty and sweet, in his way, and she had realized then as she looked at him over the candlelight, that she in fact loved him a great deal. The odd feeling in the pit of her stomach and the lump in her throat that made it hard to swallow her gourmet meal were physical proof, if she'd needed it. Her heart had told her enough. They'd made love afterward, here in Sloane's bed-

245

room where they were lying now, and she could feel tangibly then how happy she was with him.

Sloane's bedroom, she thought, glancing around the nicely furnished, slightly messy room. It was hers, too, now, she reminded herself. And here she was, lying in his . . . *their* bed again. After they'd made love this morning, too, before breakfast.

Weekends were nice, she thought as she grew more and more drowsy. In moments she was blissfully asleep on her husband's shoulder.

Life was beautiful over the next few months. Public surprise at their marriage soon died down after both had gotten a spurt of approving and congratulatory fan mail. Sloane continued his column, Dale's job at WNBS seemed secure, and *Private Screenings* went into national syndication because of its growing popularity.

"It's like that old adage about Fred Astaire and Ginger Rogers," the *Herald's* TV critic quoted Sloane when he asked him to explain the success of *Private Screenings.* "I give Dale class, and she makes me look sexy." When the same reporter asked Dale to respond to that for his article, she said, "I think it's just the opposite. I give *him* class. And *he's* the one who thinks about sex all the time."

Thus even after marriage, their public bantering continued, not that Sloane or Dale wanted to stop what had created success, and happiness, for them. In fact, when a temporary complacency developed between them during their first few weeks of marriage, the director of *Private Screenings* had grown somewhat alarmed.

"You've gotten too comfortable with each other," he told them at one of the show's taping sessions. "You're too easygoing. Somehow you've got to get back that argumentative annoyance between you. The audience is going to get bored seeing you so tolerant of each other's viewpoints—especially you, Sloane. Work on it!"

Later, in bed that night after they had made love, Dale told Sloane, "I think I know what's wrong. You're not frustrated anymore. You're so appeased with sex now, you've lost your grouchiness."

"You may be right," Sloane said, sounding comfortable and sleepy.

"You know what we should do?" Dale said. She turned toward him within the circle of his arm as they lay together under the covers. "We should abstain for at least a day before we tape the show."

"What?" Sloane said, suddenly annoyed.

"See? Just the idea bothers you. I think it would work."

It did. Putting Dale's idea into practice made Sloane irritated with her for an entire day because she held herself away from him. His mood always continued through the taping the next day.

"You're manipulating me with sex!" Sloane would tell her.

"I'm glad I finally discovered *some* way to do it," she'd tease him back.

His temporary grouchiness was always easily remedied at the end of the taping day, however, at which time Sloane would agree it was all worth the wait—both for the successful taping and the increased passion due to their brief abstinence.

During this period Dale felt there was only one real shadow that came between them, though Sloane did not seem aware of it. From time to time there were phone calls from Velvet. In all, there had been about five. Sloane would always speak to her privately, moving into another room with the phone if Dale was nearby. He would later explain that Velvet still had personal problems that he felt he could not discuss with anyone else.

"Not even your wife?" Dale once asked.

"You're a newswoman, Dale. I'd like to, but it would be putting us all on the spot. It's better this way. I don't want to chance breaking Velvet's trust."

Velvet's trust! What about mine? Dale thought but did not have the courage to say. While he always assured Dale that he and Velvet were merely friends, Dale still felt compelled to question what kind of friendship it could be. Since she had met him,

247

Dale could never remember a time when Sloane did not come to the beautiful actress's defense, whether it was regarding her questionable acting ability or maintaining her privacy. Though what secrets an actress who openly had affairs with married men could have was another interesting question.

What was it Sloane felt he had to help Velvet keep secret? Was it the brief affair between the two of them in England that Dale always suspected? Was he still hoping to win her? Had Dale been only his second choice after losing Velvet back to John Trevor?

These questions would plague Dale for days after each call from Velvet. But in each case, time would go on, Sloane would continue to live with and make love with Dale as usual, and she would begin to think she was making too much of it. And each time, after Dale had ceased to worry, Velvet would call again.

Dale knew from newspaper and TV gossip that Velvet had gone home to California after *Ivanhoe* was finally finished. She was at work on another movie being filmed in Hollywood, and she was still living with John Trevor. Their affair was reportedly as stormy as ever, and Trevor had still not divorced his wife though it was often predicted he would.

Dale kept trying to assure herself that since the actress's life remained in turmoil, Velvet merely called Sloane for advice. "She just needs someone to listen to her problems," Sloane had told Dale after one call.

"Why doesn't she go to an analyst and have him listen to her problems?" Dale had replied.

"She does," Sloane said. Immediately he looked as though he had said something he hadn't intended to.

"If she has an analyst, why does she continue to call you?"

"Because I asked her to," Sloane answered in some irritation. "She's a friend. Don't you keep up with your friends?"

Dale had nodded her head acquiescently. She didn't want to argue with him or show her jealousy. She couldn't prove anything; she only had suspicions—suspicions her mind may have blown out of proportion.

So Dale continued day to day, taking joy in her life with Sloane and doing her best to repress her doubts. One day, however, the tenuous balance changed. Another call came from Velvet.

The gorgeous film star had reason to stop in Chicago briefly and wanted to know if she could see Sloane and Dale while she was in town. At least, Sloane told Dale that Velvet said she wanted to see them both, for as always it was he who had talked to her over the phone. Sloane had eagerly told the actress that of course they would see her, and a date to have dinner out was agreed on. When he had hung up, he told Dale about the arrangement.

"But, Sloane, I can't be out late that night. I have to be at the station to do my review. It's a week night, remember," Dale said.

"You have time in between the five and ten o'clock newscasts," he said.

"But . . . you said dinner at eight at that expensive French restaurant. With cocktails first and all the courses, we'd be there for hours."

Sloane looked troubled. "I should have thought of that," he said. "I'm sorry. But you could come and leave when you have to, couldn't you?"

"Yes, I suppose so," Dale said reluctantly.

"Would you like me to call her back and change the arrangement?" Sloane offered.

Dale thought it over for a moment. How could he change it? Have dinner earlier? Velvet's schedule might not allow for that. And she'd probably want to stay up late talking to Sloane anyway. Dale would probably have to leave them alone together in any case. "No," she told him. "It's all right."

Velvet arrived in Chicago as planned. Sloane and Dale met her at eight at the restaurant. He seemed very happy to see the actress again, and Dale pretended to be. Velvet was glowing in her white fur coat and hat, for it was mid-winter now. Beneath that was a violet knit dress that clung to every curve. Her blond hair fluffed out beneath the fur hat and fell gracefully to her shoulders. When she saw Sloane she hugged him and gushed, "You're getting handsomer by the minute!" She turned to Dale and said, "Marriage must suit him."

"It does," Dale replied with an apt smile. She only hoped that with the actress's penchant for married men, it didn't make Sloane more attractive to Velvet.

The maître d' led them to a quiet table. They talked about *Ivanhoe* and the new movie Velvet was working on. She had flown to Chicago to do a nationwide daytime syndicated talk show that was taped in town, and she would be leaving the next morning. She mentioned the hotel she was staying at, the Ritz-Carlton near Water Tower Place and not far from where Sloane and Dale lived. Dale wondered if Sloane would accompany Velvet back to the hotel after dinner was over and Dale had left for work.

An hour and a half slid by without Dale saying much, leaving the conversation to her husband and Velvet. Before dessert was served, she had to leave for the ten o'clock broadcast. Smiling apologetically, she rose from the table and expressed regrets to Velvet about having to leave early.

"I'm sorry you have to go too," Velvet said, sounding sincere. "I'm afraid I've monopolized the conversation. I hope we have more time to get to know each other next time."

"That's all right. I hope we see you again soon. In fact, have Sloane bring you up to our condo after dinner tonight," Dale said with a nervous smile. It was an awkward situation to leave her husband alone to a tempting dessert and a stunning actress. And Velvet's warmth toward her had been unexpected.

Dale walked around the table as Sloane stood up. He kissed her lightly on the mouth and said, "See you later. Be careful driving in the snow. I'll take a cab back."

Dale smiled at him and walked away without looking back.

She did the ten o'clock broadcast as usual and drove home as a light snow continued to make the streets a little slippery. After parking her car in the residents' garage under the building, she took the elevator up to their condominium apartment.

They had been talking lately of buying a home somewhere. Dale hoped they would soon. She liked Sloane's apartment, but she had grown up in a house in Savannah, and she felt she would have more of a sense of permanency in a home with a mortgage and a fence around it. Tonight she didn't have a sense of being settled at all. Somehow she felt her whole world could suddenly be taken from her, with one consenting smile from a beautiful blonde in white mink.

Dale reached the apartment door and unlocked it. When she walked in, everything was dark as they had left it. She had hoped Sloane might have come home already, perhaps brought Velvet with him. But he hadn't. Well, it was only an hour and fifteen minutes since she'd left them. In a French restaurant with dessert, coffee, and possibly an after-dinner drink to go, that wasn't much time.

After turning on the lights, she took off her winter coat and boots and put them into the hall closet. She went to the kitchen and put on some coffee in case he did bring Velvet back. Dale sat down in the living room then and picked up the best seller she'd been reading.

An hour went by and then two. It was almost one A.M. now. A heavy, cold feeling came over Dale. She remembered another night in England when she had waited for Sloane to come back. He had been at a hotel with Velvet that night, and he probably was now too. *Oh, God,* she thought in despair. *What are they doing?*

Blinking back the tears starting in her eyes, she threw aside her book and got up from the couch. "I can compete with her. I know I can!" Dale said to herself as she went to the bedroom. "He must love me too. A little."

She was reminded then that they had a *Private Screenings* taping tomorrow. Sloane wouldn't expect to be able to come home to her and make love. "What a miserable idea," she whispered to herself in anger. "Why did I have to start that? It only gives him more reason to . . . go to her." How foolish to play such games with the man she loved, even for the sake of their TV show. Perhaps tragically foolish.

She'd just have to try to make up for it, she told herself. Even if it was too late. Though she knew that if he was too tired, it probably meant that he and Velvet . . . She didn't allow herself to finish the thought. She went to her lingerie drawer and brought out a lacy black shortie nightgown with matching black lace panties. She had bought it a few days ago and hadn't worn it yet. It had been intended as a surprise for their five-month anniversary night, but it would serve Dale better now.

An hour later, when Sloane finally returned, alone, Dale was waiting anxiously in their bedroom. She had put her long robe over her nightie and had been pacing back and forth when she heard him come in.

Not wanting to show her anxiety, she waited in the bedroom until he found her. She stretched across the bed and pretended to be leafing through a magazine.

"Still up, Dale? You shouldn't have waited. You'll be tired tomorrow," Sloane said when he walked in the room.

"So will you," she said, and forced a smile. "You took Velvet to her hotel?"

"Yes. We got started talking and the time just flew. I didn't realize it was so late. I'm sorry." He took off his jacket, tossed it on a chair, and then sat near Dale on the bed.

"That's okay," she said. Her tone was easy, though inside she hurt. "Velvet told you all her problems again?"

"Yes," he said, sighing. "I don't know why she doesn't get out of that damned relationship with Trevor. It's plain as day he's no good for her." As he spoke his tone grew angry. Or was it jealousy he was feeling? Dale wondered fearfully.

Her hands shook slightly as she reached up to loosen his tie. "You'd better come to bed," she said softly. He slipped off his vest as she took off the tie and unbuttoned his shirt. She slid her hand underneath to stroke his chest. Her fingers warmed to the heat of his skin as she moved over the strong muscular contours. "S-Sloane? Will you make love to me?"

252

He looked at her in surprise. "Now? It's so late, we wouldn't get much sleep. And aren't we taping tomorrow? What about . . ."

"I decided I don't like depriving myself of you just for a stupid old TV show," she said, trying to conjure up her southern ways. "We'll just have to learn how to *act* annoyed with each other, that's all." She untied the belt of her robe then and let it slip from her shoulders to reveal her sexy lingerie.

Sloane had looked like he was about to say something, but it apparently flew from his head when he saw the black transparent lace that barely covered her torso from low on her breasts to her hips, held up by fragile spaghetti straps. She could see his eyes drinking in her roundly contoured white cleavage and the hints of pink peeking through the lace.

He swallowed and said, "I'm not much of an actor, but I'm willing to learn."

Dale tossed aside the robe. Curling her legs around beside her, she leaned toward Sloane. The loose black material had slits up the sides. It fell away from the warm rise of her hip to fully reveal the tiny black lace panty. Sloane's kindling gray eyes did not fail to take in this, too, she noticed with pleasure. Perhaps she had been wrong about him and Velvet. He certainly wasn't disinterested in his wife.

Provocatively she slid her hand up his chest under the open shirt, pausing to stroke his nipple. "Will you make love to me, Sloane? It was all I could think about while I was waiting for you to come home."

He smiled, gathered her near him, and pressed her down onto the bedspread. After a searing hot kiss that made her mind reel, he said, "This isn't by any chance because you're still worrying about something between me and Velvet, is it?"

Pinned beneath his big masculine body, his heated breath on her cheek, she managed a trembling, "Maybe . . . just a little."

He shook his head and grinned. "You're silly. But I love it!" He shifted the thin straps and pulled down the black lace to bare her breasts then. He gazed hungrily at the soft white mounds rising gently toward him with each breath she took. Leaning in, he started at her slender throat, making a line of hot eager kisses. He worked his way down over her soft, sweet-smelling skin and vulnerable contours to one taut little nipple. As he nibbled on the pink nub, sending delicate shock waves through her body, he reached lower and tugged off the next-to-nothing panties. When he had put them aside, he slid his hand over and then between her smooth thighs. She felt a delicious burning sensation at that special place his fingers were so near but were avoiding with maddening playfulness. Soon she ached for him to touch her.

"Sloane . . ." she whispered, looking up at him with begging eyes. Then, gently, with unerring precision, he stroked her exactly as she wanted it, for he had become an expert at pleasing her. "Oh . . . ohhh . . ." she cried and clutched at his wide shoulders. "Oh, yes! Yes! Oh . . . now, Sloane! Please . . ."

Perhaps it was the reassurance that he wanted her and was so anxious to please her that made her passion come to full bloom so quickly that night. Neither ever got all their clothes off. Dale's warm fingers, trembling with anticipation, worked at his belt and zipper. Pushing his clothing away, she reached for his rounded muscular buttocks and urged him to her. Thick moans of pleasure escaped them both as she felt him enter her.

She put her arms around him tightly as his big body moved ardently back and forth over hers. He was hers now. No one could take him from her in these moments. He was hers alone and no one would come between them. She would make this moment last forever.

But their pulsating need was such that before very long it was all over, their frenzied desires assuaged in one deep, endless moment of profound ecstasy. Later, her body relaxing after such intense fulfillment, she cuddled next to him under the covers in the warm darkness and whispered, "You're wonderful, Sloane. The best."

"How do you know?" There was mock suspicion in his voice.

"No one could possibly be better," she said. She heard his low chuckle as she snuggled closer in his arms. He belonged to her completely, she felt. He couldn't possibly experience with any other woman what they shared together, she and Sloane.

The next day she still felt secure about her husband, though doubts about Velvet kept creeping into her mind in spite of the exquisite and heated way they'd made love last night. She didn't think he could have made love to her like that if he'd just come from the arms of another woman. But Sloane, as well she knew, was a very virile man, and she could never feel absolutely sure.

The *Private Screenings* taping was difficult. The director's constant prodding eventually drew a sufficient amount of genuine irritability from Sloane, but not from Dale, that day. Dale felt too loving and eager to please Sloane to retort to him with any of her customary finesse. Her gentle pliability allowed him to verbally walk all over her, and she just smiled and took it.

She didn't want to fight with him, not even for the show. She wanted only to keep him and cater to him, so that he wouldn't have any reason to be tempted by another woman. Waiting for him last night had been too scary.

After the unusually long taping session, Dale and Sloane were having an early dinner at a well-known German restaurant in the Loop.

"Are you feeling all right, Dale?" he asked suddenly while spreading a piece of rye bread with butter.

"Sure," she said with a smile. "Why?"

"You were so quiet today. Neither Mark nor I could get a rise out of you."

She lowered her eyes a bit. "I know. I just wasn't in the mood to argue."

"Maybe we should go back to our old method of creating antagonism," he said in a half-joking way.

She looked up quickly. "No. I—I don't want to keep away from you anymore, not even for a night."

He was looking at her now with a very unusual expression, something like concern combined with awe. "You don't have anything to tell me, do you?"

Dale was puzzled. "Tell you?"

"Are you pregnant?"

"Pregnant!" She began to laugh. "Why do you ask that?"

"Because your disposition is so odd. It's not impossible, you know. We haven't been very careful about taking precautions. Are you sure you're not?"

"I really don't think so," she said with an amused grin. She hadn't noticed any particular signs that she was. After a few moments of silence between them, she asked, "Do you want children, Sloane?"

"I think I might. I haven't really thought much about it. How about you?"

"I've been so career-oriented, I always put off thinking about it," she replied.

"It's probably something we ought to begin to consider. For one thing, it would make a difference as to the size of house we want to buy if we're going to have a family."

She nodded slowly at the enormity of the question. "I guess you're right." Now she had a new problem to think about.

But, in a way, this issue tended to wipe away her fears about Velvet's hold on her husband. Dale felt very secure now, knowing that Sloane was thinking of possibly starting a family. It meant he must be looking upon their marriage as something permanent, not something he would dissolve if Velvet suddenly decided she wanted him.

Maybe she and not the actress had been his first choice after all.

It was two months later when the phone rang about eight thirty one Saturday morning. Dale answered it in the kitchen, where she was making breakfast.

"Dale? It's Velvet. Is . . . is Sloane there? I need to talk to him." Her distant voice sounded distraught and weak.

"Well, yes," Dale said, not knowing quite what to do. Since she had answered the phone this time, she'd thought of offering to talk to the actress herself and make Velvet's problems more of a family affair among the three of them. But Velvet sounded so upset she decided to let Sloane handle it. "He's dressing. Just a minute and I'll get him."

She called to Sloane and he picked it up in the bedroom. When she heard the click she reluctantly hung up her phone. She would have liked to listen in, but her conscience wouldn't let her. The bedroom door was open, however, and she could hear Sloane's side of the conversation.

"What's wrong?" she heard him say, and then a tragic-sounding, "Oh, Velvet!" After some words of reassurance he said, "Just keep a grip on yourself. I'll fly out today if I can."

He hung up then and immediately dialed another number. Dale overheard him make a flight reservation for noon. Her heart began to pound with apprehension when she heard this. She walked into the bedroom as he put down the phone.

"What's going on, Sloane?"

He looked very sober and concerned. "I have to fly to California. Velvet's . . . got a serious problem."

"What is it?" Dale said, her tone indicating she expected a complete answer.

"I suppose it will all come out anyway," Sloane said. "She's going to have a baby. She just found out yesterday from the doctor and got so upset, she couldn't sleep all night. Trevor left her a few days ago."

Dale felt a little limp suddenly, truly sympathizing with the actress's plight. Then a frightening thought crept into her mind. "How far along is she? How many months?"

"About two, she said."

Dale's hand went to her abdomen, for she suddenly felt faint and sick. Her voice was an agonized whisper as she said, "It's yours, isn't it?"

Sloane's expression changed. "Mine? What are you talking about?"

"Two months ago when she came to Chicago you took her to her hotel and didn't come back until late. You went to bed with her, didn't you? Then you came back to me. You went from her to me without the slightest bit of conscience!" She felt nausea and revulsion rising within her as she glared at him.

"That's ridiculous! How can you even think that?" Sloane said, looking angry.

"It's not hard! You stayed out with her that night in England after you'd made love with me in the afternoon. You were seen going into her hotel with your arm around her. And then you spent an extra day with her when you could have flown home with me. *I* was the one in trouble then, but you chose to be with her. And now you're running to her again. You're in love with her, aren't you? Why don't you admit it? I was only a substitute for the woman you really wanted." Her voice was becoming hysterical.

"You're being totally absurd!"

"I am? Then stay home! Don't fly to California," she begged.

"Dale, I have to go to her. She needs someone. You don't know the whole situation."

"Why does it have to be you?"

He sighed. "Because I seem to be the only one she really trusts."

"Because it's your child she's carrying, you mean!"

"No, Dale. She must be pregnant by John Trevor," Sloane said as if his wife were trying his patience.

"Then why didn't she call *him?*"

"Because he's left her! He's not good for her anyway. He'd never give her the kind of support she needs right now." Sloane's voice was rising.

"And you could. Because you love her so much more than he does. And now's your chance to prove it to her, by coming to her rescue when he's deserted her. I'm sure she'll take you now, Sloane, whether it's your child or not," Dale said tearfully.

"It's not! And you're all wrong about this whole thing," Sloane said, his voice hoarse with suppressed anger. "I love *you.*"

Dale was silent for a moment while she wiped away her tears. She took a breath to calm herself sufficiently to say, "I believe

258

you honestly mean it when you say you love me, Sloane. But you love her more. You're proving that now." Dale's reddened eyes grew sadly wistful. "You were probably in love with her before you even met me. But she never quite returned the feeling, so you married me instead. And now you have your best chance yet to try to win her." Dale straightened her back to show some last shred of pride. "Well, go ahead. I only want you to be happy. Pack your bags and run to her."

Dale rushed from the room then. Behind her she heard him say, "I don't have time to discuss this now, Dale, but you're wrong. We'll talk about it when I get back." As if annoyed, he went into the bedroom again and she heard him taking down a suitcase from the bedroom closet.

Unable to stand any more, Dale went to the hall closet, grabbed her boots, and pulled them on over her pants. She put on her winter coat and scarf and left the apartment without a word. She didn't want to see him leave.

After wandering the streets of Chicago aimlessly for several hours, she came back to the apartment in the early afternoon, emotionally exhausted. Their home was silent and empty. Sloane had left.

CHAPTER TWELVE

Dale's phone rang. "It's Mr. Avery again. He wants to speak to you," the WNBS switchboard operator said. "Are you in?"

"No." Dale put down the phone and closed her eyes as she sat at her desk. She'd left him a note saying she was moving out to live alone again, and that she wanted a divorce. Why couldn't he just let things be and have their lawyers settle it all? After he'd run off to be with Velvet, what more did he think they could have to say to each other?

She'd packed her clothes and moved out of their condominium the same day he'd flown to California. After staying at a hotel for a couple of nights, she found a furnished apartment to sublet. It was comfortable and close to work. When the divorce was final and she'd decided what to do with her future, she would find someplace permanent to live—perhaps back in Savannah or Atlanta.

But, for now, the furnished apartment would do. She'd taken great pains to keep her address and home phone secret. The only way Sloane could contact her was at work, so Dale had asked the switchboard to screen her calls. Five days had gone by and she hadn't seen or spoken to Sloane. But he had been trying to call her since early Monday morning.

Dale did not go to any movie previews that week. She hoped to avoid them as long as possible, seeing movies in public theaters instead. She had also contacted her lawyer about getting out of her contract to do *Private Screenings*. Luckily, a taping of that show hadn't been scheduled this week. She had come to love doing the show with Sloane, but now she felt it would be impossible to work with him.

After Thursday morning Dale received no more phone calls. On Friday, however, she got a letter at the station. The envelope was typewritten with no return address. She'd assumed at first that it was a fan letter. When she opened it her breath caught in her throat as she recognized Sloane's scrawled handwriting and hasty signature.

"Dale," it read,

> I've given up trying to call you. I don't suppose they'd let me in if I went to the station to try to see you. That note you left on the dresser is incomprehensible to me. You want a divorce just because I flew to California to visit Velvet? Considering all the time it took you to decide to marry me, couldn't you think about *this* a little more? Can't we talk it over? This affects me as well as you, or hadn't you thought of that?
>
> You never did have much empathy for my point of view. Looking and behaving the way I did, I could always forgive you. But you and I have been married over seven months now, and I think I deserve better than this. I always thought you were sensible and level-headed. How can you leave me over a groundless jealousy of an actress I see only two or three times a year? You owe me a better explanation, Dale. Can't you at least write me another two-sentence note? God bless you, Sloane.

Dale shut her eyes tightly and choked back tears. Each sentence had antagonized her until she had come to the close. It was like him to change tone so abruptly. He did have some warm feelings for her.

But to Dale it was clear that he cared more for Velvet, even if he did see her only occasionally. The fact that he would run to the blonde so quickly showed his feelings for the actress didn't wane while they were apart. Dale wasn't willing to share her husband with anyone. Groundless jealousy! How could he think she would believe it was groundless? He was the one who wasn't being sensible.

She opened her desk drawer and took out a piece of stationery. Picking up a pen she wrote:

Sloane: I have read your letter. It seems to me that you are blind to my point of view. Yes, we've been married more than seven months. Don't you think you might have at least asked how I would feel about it if you flew off to see another woman before you made your plane reservation? A married man isn't free to come and go as he was when he was single.

But you never thought of your wife. Velvet claimed your attention and in minutes you were set to fly off to her, never considering what I'd think of the matter—never mind that she was pregnant, possibly by you. I've watched you rush off to comfort her too many times to think there was nothing between you and her. You've always put her first when you had to choose between us. As your wife, I think *I* deserved better.

But I'm not angry anymore. I'm just a little heartsick that you married me when you really loved her all along. You shouldn't have done that, though I believe you meant well for everyone concerned. The best thing now is for us to divorce. Then maybe you can marry Velvet. I wish you happiness. Dale.

A tear slid from her eye as she sealed the envelope. Writing this letter to him had been difficult, but perhaps now the air would be clearer. She hoped he wouldn't make any objection to a divorce. It was best for them both, she told herself.

Dale's lawyer continued to try to negotiate a way out of her obligation to do *Private Screenings*. The TV station and Raymond Marek were forcefully objecting to letting her out of the contract, however. Her lawyer predicted they would have a difficult time.

She heard nothing more from Sloane for several days. In the middle of the following week, while she was being pressured by the producer to show up for the *Private Screenings* taping the next day, she received another letter from Sloane.

"Dear Dale," it said.

> Thank you for your letter. Relax, I'm writing strictly for business reasons this time. Take some friendly advice: Don't try to get out of your contract for the show. It will give you a reputation as being difficult and unreliable. And it would be a very foolish career move to walk out of a TV program that's a hit and is giving you national recognition.
>
> I know you want to leave because of what's happened between us. For the sake of both our careers, why don't we adopt a business-first attitude? It's just a job. If we've come this far, I'm sure we can still work together, even under present circumstances. I promise I won't speak of personal problems. It may be difficult seeing each other at first, but we're both adults. Let's try behaving like we are and fulfill our contract obligations. Best, Sloane.

Well! Dale thought. He certainly wasn't wasting any more emotion on her. Maybe he was of an easier mind now since she had given him written permission to go ahead and marry Velvet. Not even a God bless you this time. A twinge of pain hurt her stomach and her eyes filled with tears. All right, she thought. If he could be so casual about it all, so could she. She supposed that was what he meant by behaving like an adult.

He was right about breaking her contract. She knew it would

injure her reputation in the broadcasting world. And her career was what was most important to her, especially now that she was going to be divorced. Her career was all she had. She'd have to continue to do *Private Screenings*.

Dale felt stiff and numb the next day when she showed up for the taping. When she saw Sloane it took a moment of concentration to compose herself. She thought he showed some strain too. He said little to her, as he'd promised. He looked as though he hadn't been sleeping well, though he was handsome in her eyes nevertheless. She wished she could have gone up and put her arms around him as she was used to doing. But they were divided by a huge invisible canyon now. It pained her to think she would never touch him again.

The taping was very difficult. Both were stilted and the ad-lib talk between them was joyless and without energy. Though their marital problems were not generally known, it was soon clear to everyone on the set that something was desperately wrong in their relationship.

When they finally finished, Dale began to walk out. She was upset because the show had gone poorly, and because she would be going to her empty apartment tonight instead of home to Sloane. It was hard to accept after seeing him again.

"Dale." She heard his voice behind her. She turned. "How about having dinner somewhere? Or a cup of coffee at least." His face, she noted, was expressionless.

"No! You said you wouldn't . . ."

"This is business. Obviously things didn't go well today. If we turn out many more shows as dead as this one was, *Private Screenings* will be canceled. I don't think either of us really wants that. I thought if we talked things over a little, maybe we could become easier with each other again."

Dale was suspicious. He had used a casual approach with her on other occasions, only to have his real intent appear before she knew what was happening. It was his method for getting his way. She wasn't falling for it this time. He'd broken her heart once too often.

"No, Sloane."

"But . . . what about the show?"

She swallowed. "I don't care about the show. That's why I didn't want to do it anymore." It wasn't the truth, but it was what she needed to tell him.

He appeared stunned. "But it means a lot to your career."

"I believe in myself enough to think that my career will survive a failure. It may even leave me free for a better opportunity. As you said in your letter, it's just a job. Good-bye, Sloane." Leaving him apparently speechless, she walked away.

To everyone's surprise, the next taping improved greatly, in energy level at least. Sloane had not tried to contact her since the last show. From the beginning of the taping session a rigid coolness formed between them. They became intensely annoyed with each other. It didn't stem from any single remark or insult. Like two hornets, they grew sharp and determined and the stinging barbs flew faster sometimes than the recording equipment could catch them.

The show the following week was even more treacherous. Mark Cutter, the director, had to ask them to tone themselves down and show at least a hint of politeness toward each other.

Dale was at a loss to explain what was happening. She didn't understand it herself. As soon as she saw Sloane he was in a bad mood, it seemed, and everything he said appeared calculated to make her resentful and recriminating. His acid wit was in excellent form, and he never hesitated to use it to belittle her. "Our audience can see you're petite in every way," he'd said as the camera rolled, "including critical stature." "You're beautiful but banal, Dale. You couldn't tell a good movie from a video game!" They were back to where they were when they first met, only much worse. Dale, who had filed for divorce last week, was more convinced than ever now that it was the right thing to do.

"Dale," George Ellis said the next day as he stopped by her desk, "we're sending you to England again. I hope you'll manage to be a good girl this time," he said, a hint of a smile at the corner of his hard mouth.

"England?"

"It's one of those publicity junkets movie production companies put on to promote a new film. This time it's for *Ivanhoe*. There, I see the invitation on your desk. They sent me one too. Didn't you open it?"

She glanced at the pile of unopened mail. She had come in a little late. "No," she said, picking up the letter.

"Well, I just squared it with the station manager and you're going. They'll be showing a preview of the film for reporters in Windermere. All the actors are supposed to be there for interviews. They offered to pay your expenses, of course, but just to keep things on the up and up, we'll pay your way. They offer to provide a taping crew though. We thought we'd take advantage of that. So you'll be going alone this time. Okay?"

"Okay," she responded. She had been taken wholly by surprise. It would be good to get away, she supposed, thinking it over later. But she'd just as soon not see the Lake District again, or interview a pregnant Velvet Hunt.

Uneager as she was to see Windermere, Dale was glad when its quaint old buildings came into view. She had arrived safely, driving by herself this time from Manchester. She had taken the precaution of ordering a car with an automatic shift ahead of time.

She found her hotel, and her reservations were in order. It was early afternoon. In a couple of hours there would be a preview showing of *Ivanhoe*. She took some time to unpack and rest, then drove to the theater. After showing her special pass, she went into the large, darkened room and walked up the middle aisle. She moved up several rows and took a seat on the right.

When her eyes had sufficiently adjusted to the dim light, she looked around a bit at the gathering audience. Her heart stopped when she saw across the aisle and two rows up the shadowy outline of her husband's shoulders and head. Her hand went to her lips. *Oh, no,* she thought. It had occurred to her he would be invited, but when she hadn't seen him on the plane, she had assumed he decided not to come. Perhaps he had flown to Manchester yesterday or even earlier. It was a good excuse to see Velvet again.

Her legs slightly unsteady, Dale rose quietly from her seat and went all the way to the back row, where she took a seat in one corner of the theater. She had no desire to see or speak to Sloane. Especially not here in England where she had first become aware of her feelings for him and made love with him; where, once again, Velvet was near and she would have to endure watching him pursue the actress. She couldn't bear that. She had to avoid him at all costs.

Ivanhoe was a mediocre movie. At least Dale thought so, though she knew she wasn't in any state of mind to judge it impartially. It seemed a movie without emotion, perhaps because the two leading actors were having to suppress all their real-life feelings in order to do the film. The costumes and sets were pretty, and Velvet, of course, was breathtaking. It was no wonder Sloane loved her, a young woman so wonderfully beautiful. How could he help himself? Dale thought as tears filled her eyes.

She hurried out of the theater when the credits first started to roll up the screen. She went to her car and drove back to her hotel.

There was to be a large dinner reception that evening for reporters and those connected with the film at one of the big hotels in Windermere. Dale decided not to go. It was one of the free affairs designed to induce invited reporters to think highly of the movie and its stars, so as to encourage their good reviews. The only thing Dale was required to attend, besides the movie, was the interview session the next morning.

She went to bed early. After long hours in bed with little sleep, she dressed the next morning in a peacock blue linen suit and a coordinated striped blouse with a frill down the front. It was early spring, more than ten months since she had last been to England. This year the weather appeared to be better, however, and unusually warm. Her spring suit seemed appropriate. She hoped the bright color would make her appear whole and happy.

which in truth she was far from being. But she wanted Sloane to think she was. He would no doubt be at the interview session.

Dale drove to the hotel where it was to be held, where the reception had taken place the night before. She walked into a large room with many round tables of about ten chairs each and took a seat at the nearest vacant set-up. One chair at each table was to be left empty, so that the actors and director could table-hop from one group to another.

As she waited for the many milling reporters to take their seats, she happened to see Sloane across the room. He was leaning against the wall, talking to—why was she surprised?—Velvet Hunt. Velvet was wearing a stylish, loose-fitting scarf dress, no doubt to disguise her still secret pregnancy.

As she watched them, Dale saw Velvet's eyes meet hers while she spoke with Sloane. Suddenly Sloane turned and looked directly at Dale. Dale couldn't breathe for several seconds, the air locked in her lungs, as her husband's gaze held hers across the room. Her eyes grew determined then, and hurt, and she turned away abruptly.

Not daring to look in that direction again, she shifted in her seat to face the other way. In a few minutes she heard Sloane's voice behind her.

"I didn't know you'd be here."

She turned and looked up. Sloane's gray eyes were hard upon her, filled with a spectrum of feelings she couldn't begin to fathom. Prominent, however, was the resentful defiance she'd seen in his face at the last few tapings of *Private Screenings*.

"Obviously not," she said, her lips trembling slightly.

"What do you mean by that?" he replied curtly.

"If you knew I was here, you probably would have been a little more discreet about whom you could be seen talking with."

His jaw clenched. "I never thought you could be so hard-headed."

"I never thought you would be so . . ."

"What?"

Insensitive, cold, untrue—she could take her pick. But she

said, "I don't know. I don't want to see you. Please, go away," she said, barely keeping her voice from breaking.

"Tell me one thing first." His tone was low and harsh. "Did you ever have any feeling for me at all?"

The question took her aback. "What difference does it make?" she said, trying to copy his taunting manner.

"None, I guess," he said in icy tones. "Not anymore. I've decided not to contest the divorce. You're free again. It's what you wanted all along, isn't it? To be free of me."

She didn't know what he was talking about. "Oh, go back to Velvet!" she said. If he didn't leave soon, she feared she would break into sobs. He gave her one final glare and then walked away. Dale watched him weave his way between the tables back to the beautiful actress. She saw Velvet look up at him and take one of his hands in both of hers.

Unable to bear it, Dale turned away then. With shaking fingers, she dug into her purse and took out a handkerchief to dab her eyes and blow her nose. She'd have to pretend she had a cold.

The chairs beside her were soon filled with other reporters. Then the interviews began. The producers came to her table first and then the director. She asked Ian Michaels if she could tape a private interview with him sometime, and he agreed.

John Trevor came by next. Another reporter at the table asked Trevor if it was true that he had reconciled with his wife. Trevor answered with a smile that it was true. Dale felt a stab in her heart. It meant Velvet was free for Sloane—Velvet and her child, they would both be his now.

Had Sloane wanted a child more than he had said he did, Dale wondered. When she had seemed less than eager for the idea, did it make him want Velvet's baby, whether it was his or not, all that much more? If Dale promised to give him a child, would that bring him back?

No, she knew it was far too late for that now. She should have tried harder to understand him better. He didn't always say what he meant, she'd learned that.

Eventually Velvet came by her table. Dale could see how the men around her were affected by the stunning blonde. They tended to stumble over their words and grin too much. When Dale was Miss Georgia she remembered men behaving that way around her, she recalled wistfully. Had she lost her beauty too? She was twenty-seven now. Suddenly she felt old sitting near the young, lovely, pregnant actress, who was smiling so delightedly at the men around her. Dale had a terrible sinking feeling. She wanted to crawl into bed, pull the covers over her head, and cry for a week. How could she ever have thought she could compete with Velvet Hunt for Sloane's affection? It was a lost cause from the beginning. She should have realized it sooner.

"Dale?" Her ruminating was interrupted by the sound of her name. She looked up to see Velvet looking hesitantly at her. "Dale, I'll be moving on to the next table soon. Did you want to ask anything? You've been so quiet."

"Oh, yes. I need to . . . can I tape an interview with you . . . afterward, I mean?" Dale said, caught off-balance.

"Sure! How about in half an hour? The taping crew is up in Suite 206. Should I meet you there?"

"Yes. Thank you." Dale was a little bewildered. Velvet had been so thoughtful. Perhaps she was feeling guilty for stealing her husband.

In a half-hour Dale went up to Suite 206. It took all her will power to pull herself together, put on her TV personality, and interview Velvet for the cameras. It seemed this time Velvet was almost going out of her way to help Dale do it smoothly. It threw Dale a little. She was given the tape of the interview afterward to take back to Chicago.

"Do you have a minute?" Velvet said as Dale walked toward the door to leave.

"A minute? Yes, I suppose so."

"My suite is just down the hall. Can I talk to you for a little while? It's . . . very important," Velvet said in her honeyed voice.

Dale tried to steel herself. She had seen many movies where the other woman has a heart-to-heart talk with the wife of the

270

man she's taken. Dale never dreamed she would have to play such a scene herself. Worse than that, Velvet was being so sweet, as if she felt sorry for Dale. It was galling. "Of course," Dale said coolly.

Velvet's suite was small but beautifully decorated. They sat down together on a flowered couch. Dale stiffly declined Velvet's offer to order tea or coffee from room service.

"Sloane flew out a day early," Velvet began. "He knew I was already here in England to promote the movie, and he wanted to see how I was doing."

"That . . . comes as no surprise." Dale's glassy eyes were focused on some point across the room.

"He told me that you and he were breaking up," Velvet said. "I was shocked. I thought you made such a perfect couple. And when I asked him why . . . well, he didn't want to tell me, but I finally gathered it was because of me. He said you didn't understand that he and I are just friends."

Dale had difficulty believing what she was hearing. Slowly she turned her widening eyes toward the young actress.

Velvet smiled a little. "It's true, Dale, honestly. There's never been anything—what shall I say?—amorous between Sloane and me. That's probably why he is such a good friend. That's why I've trusted him. He's the only man I've met who seems to see me as a person first and not as a sex symbol, or whatever it is I've become. Everyone else around me is either connected with my career somehow or they . . . they just want . . . me," she said, lowering her eyes briefly.

"It's taken me quite a while to realize that, of course." Velvet's smile became slightly tremulous. "All I've looked for all my life is to be loved. Mostly what I've found is men who want to use me one way or another. I just mistook it for love. That's where Sloane was different. He had no stake in my career. He never took anything from me. All he ever offered was friendship, and I guess that was why I always sensed I could trust him."

She hesitantly studied Dale's frozen expression. "Am I making sense? Do you understand any of this?"

271

"N-not really," Dale said, feeling all at sea.

Velvet moistened her lips worriedly. "I don't want to bore you with the whole history of my life. Let's just say I didn't come from a good family and I wanted to become a movie star to escape. I was too trusting of people I shouldn't have trusted, men I shouldn't have gotten involved with. To cope, I began to take prescription drugs from my doctor—sleeping pills, tranquilizers, other pills to pep me up again. The first time I met him, I took a pill while Sloane was interviewing me. He said then I was asking for trouble doing that. I should have listened.

"While I was getting hooked on pills, I met John Trevor. I had just broken off an affair. I suppose I was on the rebound, but I fell hard for John. I—I can't tell you everything that happened, but we had a miserable relationship. He treated me very badly. But I couldn't break away somehow. I was getting lost in the drugs and I needed someone to cling to.

"That night that I called Sloane—when you and he were staying together at that bed and breakfast? Sloane said you never believed him. What happened was, John and I had a terrible, terrible fight. He called me names, said he was sick of me. I—I wanted to kill myself. I had the pills to do it. All I could think of was to call Sloane. Of course he came. He stayed on the next night, too, because he knew I wasn't ready to be left alone.

"Sloane convinced me to see an analyst then. I did. I was starting to get better, even though I was still living with John. I managed to give up the drugs. Finally John left me for good. He never did intend to marry me. I know that now. Then I found out I was pregnant. It sent me into such a tailspin, I'm afraid I had to call Sloane again. My analyst was out of town. But I'm all right now. I think I've finally learned I don't have to be attached to a man to feel that I'm worth something. I think that's what Sloane had been trying to tell me all along."

She looked questioningly at Dale. "Does this explain what happened? Do you understand now about Sloane and me?"

"Yes, I think so," Dale said, stumbling for words. "Wh-what about . . . the baby?"

Velvet smiled. "I'm going to keep it. My analyst says she thinks I can handle it. I'm even looking forward to it now."

"But I mean, who's the father?" Dale asked, her cheeks reddening at being compelled to ask such a thing, but she had to know.

"John, of course," Velvet said. "Not that it matters much to him. Oh, you didn't think? . . . Oh, no, Dale! Sloane never told me you thought it was his."

Dale covered her face with her hands for a moment. "I'm so sorry," she said with embarrassment. "But that night you had dinner with us in Chicago, he stayed late with you at your hotel. It was just about the time . . ."

Velvet's hand reached toward Dale. "Yes, I can see why you might think that. No, Dale, we just talked. Really. When he and I are together, I just start pouring out my problems and he listens. And then we just talk and laugh. When he leaves I always feel so much better. He really is just a wonderful friend. That's why, lately, I was glad to be able to listen to his problems, even though it turned out I was the cause of them. He misses you so, Dale. It's all he talks about. Did you see how thin he's getting? Last night at the reception he hardly ate a thing. And he was so hurt this morning after he went over to talk to you. He says you don't love him. That's not true, is it?"

"No," Dale said. She was on the edge of a sob. "I love him very much. I thought he didn't love me."

Velvet smiled and touched Dale's wrist. "I'll tell you what to do." She named the location of a bed and breakfast near Grasmere. "I think he left before the interview session was over. He's probably there brooding and dejected. Go and see him."

CHAPTER THIRTEEN

Dale couldn't navigate her car fast enough to match her impatience to see Sloane. She only hoped he'd be there when she found the place. Seeing a sign with the name of the bed and breakfast Velvet had mentioned, she turned off the main road outside of Grasmere and drove up a hill toward a large stone house surrounded by rhododendron trees and a garden.

She parked her car in the drive in front of the house, which looked newer than the one she had stayed in on her last trip. A middle-aged man was working in a flower bed near the front door.

"Excuse me," she said, taking him to be the proprietor, "can you tell me if Sloane Avery is staying here?"

"Mr. Avery? Yes. He went out for a walk up the path in the wood about fifteen minutes ago." He pointed to a dirt path near a rhododendron tree some distance away. In back lay a wood that extended upward to the top of the hill. In other directions were meadows and the town of Grasmere could be seen resting quietly down below in the valley.

"I see," Dale said. "I'm his wife. I may be staying here with him. He wasn't expecting me to be here yet," she said, trying to sound as though there had been some minor change in their plans.

"Fine," the man said. "His room has a double bed. You'll be comfortable there I think."

"Thanks," she said with a fluttery smile. She hoped she'd be comfortable there with Sloane tonight. She prayed that after all that had happened between them, he would still want her.

Following the proprietor's directions, she found the trail and soon was in the midst of a lovely forest with ferns and rich lush grass alongside the dirt path. The only problem was that she was still wearing high heels to go with her tailored suit. The uneven trail slowed her speed. She'd never catch up with him at this rate, she fretted.

The path straightened at one point and she looked ahead as far as she could see. Sloane was nowhere in sight. Should she go back to the house and wait for him? she wondered. But he might be gone for hours.

Putting her hands at the sides of her mouth, she called as loud as she could, "Sloane!" If he could hear her, perhaps he would come back. "Sloane!" she called again.

She kept walking farther up the path, not knowing what else to do. There was so much welling inside her that she wanted to tell him, and she couldn't even find him. She was growing so frustrated now that tears were stinging the backs of her eyes.

All at once she heard the noise of twigs breaking. Ahead of her a tall figure emerged from the trees beyond a bend in the trail. It was Sloane.

He paused in his tracks when he saw her. Dale began to hurry toward him, her heart ready to burst with a mixture of joy and anxiety. She stumbled once or twice because of her shoes, but in a minute she was standing in front of him, breathless and eager to speak. But no words came from her mouth. She was in such a dither, she didn't know what to say first, or how to say it.

Sloane was looking down at her, his eyes a blend of surprise and confusion. He'd thought he'd heard someone call his name. It had sounded like Dale, but he couldn't let himself believe it was. He had turned back anyway to investigate. And suddenly here she was. How did she get here? Why?

Suddenly she clutched the lapels of his wool tweed jacket. "Sloane, I'm sorry. Velvet explained everything. Can you ever forgive me?"

His hands automatically went to her waist. He could feel her slender body trembling. There were tears in her beautiful blue eyes. "Of . . . course . . ." he said, still in shock. "What do you mean? What did Velvet tell you?"

"That you and she are just friends, as you always said. I'm sorry I didn't believe you, Sloane. It was wrong of me. She told me all about her dependence on drugs and how you kept her from taking her own life. . . ."

"She told you all that?" Sloane said with concern.

"Yes. I won't repeat it to anyone. I can see now why you didn't want me to know. If it had become public, it would have caused her even more stress. It was right of you to protect her. I should have trusted you—the way she does."

Sloane was gripped by conscience. "No, Dale. I should have talked to you before flying to California. I was a bachelor so long, I forgot I had no right to act so independently once I was married. And I was wrong to expect you to understand about my friendship with Velvet. I realize now that if you had run off to see some other man, claiming he was an old friend, I wouldn't have understood. I should have tried to see it all through your eyes."

They stared at each other, silent for a moment. Was she coming back to him? After all that had happened, he was hesitant to ask. He couldn't take it if she was still going to reject him. Instead, he waited for her to speak. But she was hesitating too.

"I . . . Velvet told me you were staying here. The man said you'd taken this path, so I followed," she said.

Don't beat around the bush, Dale. What are you here for? his inner voice cried. "I heard you call me," he said aloud.

Dale took a breath before speaking again. He held her lightly, his hands remaining at her waist, and he could still feel her shaking. "V-Velvet said that you missed me," she blurted out all at once, as if she had only enough courage to say the words fast.

"Of course I miss you!" he said. His voice sounded irritated, as it always did when he was unsure of himself.

"But you've been so angry with me lately. Even this morning," she said in a wavering voice.

"Because I thought you didn't want me. You even filed for divorce," he said defensively.

"But I did want you."

"You have a hell of a way of showing it," he blustered out. "You didn't even care about *Private Screenings* anymore, after we'd worked so hard on it together. You were going to just scrap it all and go your own way. You were breaking every tie between us."

"But, Sloane, it was because I thought you were really in love with Velvet and wanted to be with her."

He shook his head. "Dale, I'm very fond of Velvet, but she's naive and unstable. I've never been in love with her, and I certainly wouldn't want to be married to her." His voice grew husky. "You're the one I love! You're the only woman I've ever loved. It's been killing me to think it took so long to find you; if I lose you, I know I'll never want anyone else. You're the only woman I want to spend my life with, and I've been miserable without you." He could feel hot tears springing to his eyes. He didn't want to cry in front of her, but he couldn't help himself.

Suddenly he saw through his blurred vision a tear running down her soft cheek. She clutched his lapels tighter and drew closer to him. Looking up, she said, "I don't want anyone else but you either. I've been so unhappy without you, Sloane."

He slid his arms around her and gathered her against him. His body shuddered with a silent sob as, finally, he held again the woman he adored. He closed his eyes as he felt her arms slip around him beneath his jacket. She was crying on his shoulder now and he ran his hands over her back to comfort her, all the while trying to control his own deep emotion. Who would have thought this day would turn out to be so wonderful?

He smiled now as he felt her warm feminine body leaning against him. An insidious heat permeated his bones. He wanted her lips now; he needed to kiss her. He bent his head and she lifted her mouth to meet his. She was so willing, it warmed him even more. Her mouth was soft and moist like honey, and without hesitation he found himself drinking all he could from her. He needed this. Oh, how he needed her love. It had been so long.

A murmur of pleasure came from his throat as he pressed her closer against him. She was kissing him back so hungrily. This was heaven.

He broke away from her lips, partly to regain his breath. "Oh, darling," he whispered. His eyes moved over her exquisite face, the shimmering blue eyes, the tiny nose, the full lips, slightly swollen now from his hard kisses. "I love you!" He watched her smile up at him, that dazzling smile of hers. She would be his again. And she would stay his. He'd do everything he could to make certain of her trust and love.

He wanted something tangible to prove it to her now. Through her clothes he grew consciously aware of the frail, soft body beneath. Suddenly need arose within him. Yes, he wanted to show his love, to give substance to this renewed marriage that was so quickly coming to bloom again. For a man and woman, a husband and wife deeply in love, there was only one way to fully manifest their feelings.

His hands shook slightly as he moved them under her suit jacket to the ruffle at the front of her blouse. When he felt the swell of her breasts, he pressed the palms of his hands softly against them and gently squeezed. He watched her eyes slowly close in pleasure. It reminded him of how she looked when
. . .

Growing feverish now, his hands found the front buttons and undid them. He pushed the silky material aside. There underneath he took joy in seeing once again her sweet rounded breasts, the pink nipples barely hidden beneath her thin lace bra. Her cleavage was rising and falling more and more quickly as her breathing grew faster. His heart soared as he realized that she was as eager as he.

Quickly he unfastened the front hook of her bra and pushed it aside. "Touch me, Sloane. Please," she whispered as she began to undo his shirt buttons. Warmly he cradled her breasts in the palms of his hands, then reached up with his thumbs to squeeze and caress her nipples. They grew firm and erect under his touch. He bent to put his lips to one and teased it further with his tongue. She was so deliciously sexy to look at and touch. Kissing her breasts always aroused him as much as it seemed to stimulate her.

His heart was pounding against his ribs now. "Dale, I want you, darling," he said, straightening up and pressing her against his chest.

"I know, I know," she said in an aching whisper.

She had gotten his shirt undone and he could feel the wondrously soft, warm mounds pressing against his bared skin. His breathing was quite erratic now. The need in him was growing unbearably intense. All at once the greenery around him reminded him of the fact that they were outdoors.

"We'd better go back to the house," he said reluctantly, glancing down the well-worn path. His body told him he couldn't wait that long.

"Why? Remember our first time?" she murmured, and reached up to kiss his cheek lovingly. He lowered his face toward hers again and in the next moment their mouths met in a kiss that seared his very soul. She clung against him as her lips parted, allowing him to seek out her silken recesses. It made him even more desperate to have what their kiss only promised.

Dale's breathing was ragged and shallow now, and she grew lax and easy in his arms. As if her knees were giving way, she began slipping downward. He supported her as she drooped to the soft thick grass at the side of the path. Her arms, still clinging around his neck, urged him down on top of her. His large frame molded itself over her small form. Feeling her willing body

279

beneath him aroused him to the limit. He smothered her face with kisses and fondled her body with his hands.

"Oh, Sloane . . ." she moaned. Her knee rose up to rub against his thigh. Her hands came between their bodies to unfasten his belt. He rose up on his arms to allow her to complete the task. There was no stopping now. His need was imperative and Dale's desires were obviously just as urgent.

He reached down to push up her skirt, running his hand along her smooth slender thigh. It was then he realized there was a minor obstacle in his way—that modern invention called panty hose. He simply broke the thin material with his fingernail.

He heard her sublime moan of pleasure when he gently found his way to her. Immediately he felt the profound comfort of being one with her again. Their bodies united, their souls met in the fervent ecstasy that made them oblivious to everything but each other. He pressed her into the lush grass.

The wind whisked fragrantly through the trees above them. Except for the chirping of birds there was stillness all about them as he moved back and forth over her, their bodies rocking together in that ageless rhythm known since the beginning of time. His breathing was labored and heavy, uniting sometimes with her higher gasps. She was stroking his back beneath his shirt and jacket, digging her fingertips into his skin with each wave of pleasure he brought her. He fought to keep control of himself in order to give her complete satisfaction, but he was losing ground quickly to his raging need. It had been too long since he'd made love to her.

All at once she made that certain little cry he'd learned to wait for. He smiled with joy as he felt her grip him suddenly and then her slender body writhed in pulsating movements beneath him. He allowed his own passion full release while she was still quivering in his embrace. He felt the life force flow between them. His chest heaving for air, he immersed himself in the intense satisfaction of her love.

They lay still for a few moments in the pristine silence of the woods. Sloane moved off her then. Cautiously he glanced around, but the path was empty in both directions. He looked down at Dale as she lay there all delightfully disheveled.

"You sure know how to make a man forget himself!" he said with a loving grin.

She smiled back and pushed a hand through her mussed red-brown hair. "I do?" She was still a little out of breath. "You led me astray!"

"Brazen little hussy!"

"Oh, hush!"

He leaned over to kiss her lightly. "I wouldn't trade a second of what we just shared. Not for my life," he said with feeling.

"I wouldn't either, Sloane. You're wonderful." She began to kiss him back.

"Hey," he said, laughing as he held her off a little. "Maybe we'd better go back to the house first."

She smiled warmly. "Okay."

After adjusting their clothing properly back into place, they slowly walked along the trail to the house. Sloane's arm was around her shoulders and hers around his waist.

Dale felt whole again, happy and serene. Everything was going to be all right now, she knew it in her heart. But there was still a question or two she hoped he'd explain.

"Sloane, why did you ask this morning if I ever had any feeling for you? How could you doubt that I did?"

"Well," he said, "if you think about it, I had to talk you into everything we've done together. I had to coax you into letting me take you to the hospital for your surgery. I more or less finagled our rooming together at that old bed and breakfast. I had to convince you to do *Private Screenings* with me, and then I all but begged you to marry me. I hadn't realized the depth of your doubts about Velvet and me. It seemed to me that you were jumping at the first excuse you could find to divorce me. I thought I had pushed you into marriage and you'd come to regret it."

"Poor Sloane. I'm sorry," she said, giving him a hug. "But I thought you had grown indifferent. That second letter you sent me was all cold business advice."

"That was just a tactic to try to keep you from leaving the show. *Private Screenings* was the only remaining contact I had with you. I thought if I pretended to be all business, you would think I wasn't going to try to regain your affection and you'd relax about continuing to work with me. Then I hoped I might find some surreptitious way to win you back."

"Like you've done all along," she said with a chuckle.

"Would you ever have noticed me if I hadn't wormed my way into your life?" he asked.

She looked up at him. "I'd noticed you before I even met you. Realizing I could love you did take a while though. I'm glad you pursued me as conscientiously as you did, so we didn't waste all that time."

"Me too," he said meaningfully. As he gazed down at her she was struck again by the sparkling clarity of his eyes. He was so manly and handsome to her now, she wondered how she could have ever thought him a teddy bear. She noticed now his face seemed a little gaunt.

"You've lost more weight, haven't you? Velvet was concerned. She said you haven't been eating much."

He lowered his head. "I didn't feel like eating. I was too heartsick. I felt I didn't want to face life without you. Velvet kept trying to buck me up all day yesterday and this morning."

"I'm glad she talked to me the way she did," Dale said.

"I am, too, even though I'd told her not to bother. I thought it was too late. Fortunately she didn't follow my advice this time," he said with a poignant laugh.

"She's learning to think on her own," Dale said.

"Yes, finally she is. Something you never had to learn to do, I suspect." He grinned down at her. "You don't take direction well at all."

"You're complaining?"

"No."

They passed the rhododendron tree and the stone house came

282

into view. Sloane led her inside and up to the room in which he was staying. It was nicely decorated with subtle floral-patterned wallpaper and matching drapes. The quilt on the double bed was also coordinated. The fixtures and furniture all looked new, and there was even a bathroom attached. And, Dale noticed, there was a radiator in the room.

"No cold nights here," Dale commented, gesturing toward the heating fixture.

"Nope. Not that we'll really need it," he said, drawing her against him.

She pretended not to notice his provocative manner. "How did you find this place? It's beautiful."

"I stayed here a couple of years ago. It had been recommended by a friend who travels a lot. I would have tried it last time we were in England, but it's so popular, I knew it would be booked up. We're here earlier this year and the tourist season hasn't started yet."

"Do they serve the same breakfasts here?" she asked, toying with one of his shirt buttons.

"A little more elaborate. No grits though. Thank heaven!"

"Sloane Avery!" she said, pretending to be miffed. She gave him a little shove.

"You're flirting with me," he said with a grin.

"I am not."

"Are too. You can't fool me. You want to make love again."

"You men have only one thing on your minds," she said.

"So do you women. Come on. Let's do it with our clothes off this time." His voice was low and masculine near her ear as he held her by the shoulders. "You want to, don't you?" he said in a cajoling whisper. "We've been apart too long."

His voice and warm grip were making tantalizing sensations curl within her. She let herself lean against him. "Yes, I want to," she whispered back.

Sloane took off his jacket and they undressed. She could see then how thin he had become. Not that she found him unattractive, but it concerned her. "You need some grits to fatten you up again," she said, trying to be light.

"Grits won't do it." He pulled her down onto the bed with him. "Don't worry, I won't have any trouble gaining back what I lost. Not now that I know you're mine again."

"I was always yours." She stroked his chest as she lay beside him, facing him. A thought entered her head. There was still one question Sloane had never answered. "You never told me what your favorite movie is. I think we know each other intimately enough now. Especially after what we just did in the woods."

"You seductress," he said, touching her cheek. His hand moved down to her breast.

"Don't change the subject. What's your favorite movie?"

He took a deep breath and slowly exhaled. He was stalling for time, she saw.

"Come on, come on," she chided him. "You know my favorite is *Gone With the Wind*. Are you too embarrassed to say what yours is?"

His mouth quirked slightly. "Maybe a little."

"You like old kung fu movies or something?"

He laughed heartily. "No!"

"Tell me," she said, digging her fingers playfully into his stomach.

"I don't want to." He grabbed her hand.

"That's not fair," she said. She pulled her fingers from his grip and began tickling him once more.

He stopped her again. "Life isn't fair," he said.

She sighed in exasperation. A new idea came to her. Gently she stroked his stomach now, then moved downward. When her fondling had its desired effect, she edged him down on his back, then straddled him, sitting just below his hips on his muscular thighs. There she stayed, continuing to caress him, leaning forward toward him so he had the benefit of gazing at the fullness of her breasts.

"Oh, Dale," he murmured, reaching up to stroke her nipple. "You're driving me mad. Come to me, darling."

284

She stayed where she was, continuing to caress him yet not giving him the comfort of her body. "Tell me first."

"What?"

"Your favorite movie."

"My . . . That's blackmail! Come on, Dale. Play fair!"

"Have you ever played fair?" she said, smiling smugly. She knew she had him at her mercy. "All the trickery you've used on me. I'm just giving you some of your own medicine."

"But this is below the belt, if you'll pardon the expression."

"I won't."

"Rhett Butler never had to put up with this," he said.

"Frankly, I don't give a darn what Rhett Butler put up with. Anyway, he married a southerner. Maybe he did!" she said, delighted with her answers.

"You little wanton! They must have written that song about the vamp of Savannah for you."

She laughed. "Don't complain. You know you love it!" She imitated the tone of voice he always used when he said those words.

"You bet I do. But show some mercy."

"Just tell me your favorite movie." She gave him another delicate caress.

"*Gone With the Wind*," he said, giving in.

She stopped and looked at him. "You like the same movie I do? We never agree on movies!"

"I know. It's humbling to realize our critical tastes may be on the same level after all."

Grinning down at him, she said, "You mean you like all that old-fashioned emotion? Why, you're a closet romantic!"

He sighed. "So now you know my darkest secret. Actually, I'm just intrigued with the South, especially since I met you."

"Don't hide behind excuses. Sloane Avery—the cold-hearted critic unveiled," she said, teasing him.

"How about keeping your part of this bargain, you southern witch. Come on, Dale. Give me your love now."

Her smile softened. "I should have guessed it long ago." She moved forward over him like a sleek kitten, stretching her body over the length of his. "You're just a pushover underneath your prickly shell," she said. She felt the muscles of his stomach come against hers, arousing her. "Kind, sweet, romantic. I'll love you," she assured him, gently kissing his chin. "You won't believe how much I'll love you. Now, and tomorrow, and forever. You captured me. But I've got you in my power now. And you'll never escape."

"Never?" he said. He looked up into her eyes as he ran his hands down her smooth back to her derriere. Then with a movement of his body he made them one.

"Never," she said, the word laden with gathering passion. And then, as she'd promised, she loved him.